My frien___
enjoy the___ ___ ___ ___
from our Lord !
Signed in Jerusalem,
City of Gold.

Mandy Jarvis

the ORDER of HEAVEN

Published in San Diego, California, by Wakeful Dreams Publishing

Scripture quotations in the body of the book are from the New American Standard Version of the Bible.

This novel is a work of fiction. Names, characters, places, and incidents either are the product of the author's imagination, or are used ficticiously, with the exception of Corrie ten Boom. The story that was related about Ms. Ten Boom is purely fictitious, save the quotation from her sister, Betsy. Before she died, Betsy told Corrie, 'There is no pit so deep that God's love is not deeper still'. Any other resemblance to actual events, locales, organizations, or persons living or dead is entirely coincidental and beyond the intent of either the author or the publisher.

Library of Congress Cataloging-in-Publishing Data Txu 1-760-836
Jarvis, Amanda, date.
        The Order of Heaven
        ISBN-13: 978-0615507835

ISBN-10: 0615507832

Printed in the United States of America

By Amanda Jarvis

Wakeful Dreams Publishing

NAMES OF CHARACTERS TO REMEMBER:

Boston

Helen – Volkenburg's Housekeeper
Eddie Callahan – Joel's friend
Martha – Eddie's Nanny
Henry Worthing – Joel's best friend and neighbor

Sullivan Family:

John - Father	**Conor** – Age 17
Maggie – Mother	**Sean** – Age 14
John Jr. – Age 24	**Patrick** – Age 12
Petie – Age 21	**Mikey** – Age 7

Dan Moretti – Private Investigator from Boston
Beth – Dan's assistant
Ruth – Woman Hessa met on the plane – Lives in Connecticut

Israel

Bishara Family and Employees (Meanings of Names):
Husaam – 'Sword'
Muna – 'Desire; wish'
Hessa – 'Destiny'
Imaad – 'Support, pillar' – Hessa's brother
Safiya – 'Serene, pure' – Imaad's wife
Basem – 'Smiling' – Imaad and Safiya's son
Qasim (kah seem') – 'Divider' – Hessa's fiancé
Mahmoud – 'Praiseworthy' – Qasim's father
Mustafa – 'Chosen' (name for Mohammed). Man assigned to guard Hessa
Iyad (ee' yad) – 'Pigeon' – Mustafa's partner

Fatik Nidal (fah teek' nah dahl') – Joel's kidnapper – Large man employed by Husaam Bishara

Jad Said (jahd sah' eed) – 'Curly; frizzled' – Joel's other kidnapper – Small man employed by Husaam Bishara

Anna's Sister and Family:

Klara Milgrom – Anna's sister

Yuri Milgrom – Klara's deceased husband

Benjamin Milgrom – Klara's son

Giovanna - Benjamin's wife

Others in Jerusalem:

David Appel (ah pel') – Jewish Pastor in Jerusalem

Miriam Appel – His wife

Joseph Schur – Concierge at the Tikvah Hotel

Tikvah – Hotel – Means Hope

Abigail – Waitress at the Little Jerusalem

Omri Segen – Former IDF, friend of Dan's

Levi Hirschfeld – Reporter from Channel 1 in Jerusalem

England

Douglas McLaughlin – Officer from Scotland Yard

Mary Flynn –Petie's love interest in England

Bridget – Mary's friend

Egypt

Eshe (Ee'-shay) – Means 'life'; Egyptian woman who helped Joel and Muna

Jabari – 'Brave' - Eshe's brother

Ahit (ah heet') – 'Assistant' - Jabari's wife

Tripoli, Libya

Ngozi (n go' zee) – 'A blessing' - Truck driver
Aman– 'Security, peace, safety' – Ngozi's wife
Ali – 'Noble' - Drove Ngozi, Joel and Muna from An Nawfaliyah to Tripoli
Yo'el – Pronunciation for Joel in Hebrew

Tunis, Tunisia

Nadeem – Ngozi's friend – Name means 'friend'
Rashid – Ngozi and Nadeem's friend – 'Rightly guided, having the true faith'
Clotilde – Nadeem's wife – Means 'Famous in Battle'

Rome, Italy

Ferdinando and Gisella Biaggio– Owners of Villa Incantato
Anders Lokken – Guest at Villa Incantato

South Carolina

Craig – Ruth's son
Linda – Craig's Wife
Seelah and Charis – Craig and Linda's daughters
Susannah Margate – Owner of the Manley Plantation
John – Horse guide at the Plantation

D.C.

Robert Williams – Plain clothes officer in D.C.

CHAPTER 1

Joel Volkenburg walked across Harvard Yard with a spring in his step. It was his senior year at Harvard, and he was heading down the home stretch. His goal of achieving Summa Cum Laude was in sight. He had dreamed of earning that high honor since his freshman year in high school, and now here he was—beginning his last fall semester as an undergraduate that seemed to have swept him up in a whirlwind. He couldn't believe he was entering into what promised to be a glorious conclusion to his first four years at this fine institution.

On this warm day in early September, the sun shone brilliantly as Joel hurried across Harvard Yard to get to his first class. As he was turning the corner of Austin Hall a flurry of students, looking lost and anxious, caught his eye.

He stopped in his tracks and let out an audible gasp. The most beautiful creature he had ever seen crossed his path. She was of average height, very slender, wearing a crisp white blouse and jeans. Her shiny black hair was pulled back severely into a very long ponytail.

As she looked up from a piece of paper in her hands she glanced at him, and Joel felt drawn into her large black luminous eyes, exotically turned up at the corners. Suddenly she turned and hurried away and out of sight. For a moment Joel forgot what he was supposed to be doing.

He stood stupefied for a few moments then snapped to, realizing he was about to be late for his first class. He hurried into the building, but when he sat down in the classroom amid the excited chatter of students, his mind was jumbled and he had to shake himself back into the present.

What's happening? he thought. He hadn't had the time or inclination to think much about girls as he pursued his dream. He had of course had dates, but many of the girls at Harvard were aggressive and forward, and he didn't like that.

What Joel didn't realize was that he was a handsome young man. His features were very fine, from his Dutch roots. His dark, wavy hair was swept back away from his face, and his slim, muscular runner's frame towered over the rest of his family.

Many people had commented to his parents on Joel's looks. They didn't pass this information on to their son, however. They felt it would make him vain, so they impressed upon him his intellectual capabilities more than those of his physical attributes. Joel remained quite unaware of his appearance.

The professor droned on and Joel's attention went back to the subject at hand. *Get back in the ballgame,* he told himself. *Keep your eye on the prize. It's within your grasp.*

He did just that. Typical of Joel's routine in school, he typed notes into his laptop, and then put a reminder in his phone to get with his friends to organize their study group schedule. Class ended and Joel walked outside quickly, head down, typing away into his phone.

He looked up when he heard his nickname: "Burgermeister! Can you believe we got stuck with Clifton for Business Law? Man, what a witch!" It was his friend Eddie Callahan, who was in the same class with Joel.

"Hey Eddie. I didn't see you. Yeah, Clifton is a piece of work. I don't' know how we're gonna handle her for a whole semester."

What happened to Grayson? I specifically chose him for this class 'cause I knew he'd be an easy 'A'."

"I heard Mr. Grayson is sick, and announced his retirement right before school started. He's such a great guy. Isn't that just the way life goes? Someone as great as Grayson gets sick and old Clifton lives on to torment everyone in her path."

2

They laughed and pulled out their phones to start scheduling their study groups. They parted company and each went off to his next class. The day flew by, and Joel started to walk to his car to go home. He'd gotten his first semester study groups pretty much firmed up, since he had about half a dozen buddies on the pre-law track alongside him. When he was just about at his car, his friend Henry Worthing spied him.

"Burgermeister! Where've you been all day? I've been trying to track you down! Why haven't you answered your texts?"

Truth be told, Joel had been caught up in other thoughts…the mysterious beauty he had glimpsed earlier that morning had jarred him pretty well emotionally. He wasn't about to get into that discussion with his friend, however.

"Sorry. You know me. I need to get organized or I go crazy. Eye on the prize, bro', eye on the prize."

"Yeah, I know," Henry said. "You'd think I'd remember that by now. You've been like that since kindergarten. Come on, let's go to Noch's. I'm hungry."

Joel got a hesitant look on his face and looked down at his phone, as if it had the answer.

"Listen", Henry said, "before you get into your typical 'Joel process', just hear me out. We need to make this the best year ever. We both know that law school is gonna kick us to the curb. Let's just have some fun."

"Okay, "Joel replied.

"Yeah! Petie's over there right now holding a table. Let's go," and the two friends took off at a dead run, laughing like two little boys as they raced across Harvard Yard.

They walked into Noch's and their friend Petie Sullivan motioned Joel and Henry over to the table. Eddie had gotten there just a few minutes before them, and had already ordered a pitcher of beer.

Joel, Eddie and Henry had grown up going to the same schools from childhood. Joel and Henry had been friends since kindergarten, and

Eddie had moved to Boston from Providence, Rhode Island, when he was in second grade. They'd been inseparable from that time on.

The three of them had been sent to Deerfield Academy in Western Massachusetts for prep school in ninth grade, where they met Petie. He hailed from Vermont, and stepped right into the group as if he'd always been a part of it.

Petie was quite different from his three friends. While Joel, Henry and Eddie had been raised in homes with money, prestige, and meticulous attention to social appearance, Petie had been raised in a very large, warm, boisterous family.

≈≈≈≈

"Hello boys, how goes academia?" Petie said, loud enough for the whole place to hear, his smile wide and mischievous, as usual. The four friends ordered a large Sicilian pizza.

"I don't know what I was thinking when I put my class schedule together," Eddie said. "You'd think by now I'd figure out how to plan better. I'm running from one end of the campus to the other all day. I'm gonna be dead by the end of the semester."

"Why do you do that?" Henry asked. "Every year you do the same thing. If you *are* dead by the end of the semester, I'm not going to your funeral."

Petie took his opportunity to provoke Eddie. "Boys, you see before you the master of the collegiate universe. Oh yeah, you heard me. I'm coasting this year and lovin' it." Petie loved to get a rise out of Eddie.

He continued, "Hey Eddie, if you would've followed the master and stuck to academics, you wouldn't be in the mess you're in. Why'd you get involved with Hasty Pudding, rowing, *and* ski team? No wonder you're dyin' on your feet."

Eddie wasn't about to be drawn in by Petie's taunts. It never worked out. Petie always got Eddie riled up, and Eddie would somehow end up feeling stupid.

He replied sarcastically, "It's to get experience. My resume's gonna be a lot more interesting than yours."

Henry interrupted: "Okay guys, calm down and eat your pizza. I need to leave in a few minutes to meet Audra. She's freakin' out about her calculus class."

"You two are getting pretty friendly, huh?" Petie asked.

"I like her. She knows what she wants, and she'll do what it takes to get there. Plus, she doesn't tell me what to do. She's cool," Henry replied.

"Well, that's okay for you, but I want a girl who can cook like my mom! I don't think I'll find someone like that at Harvard though. Guess I'll just have to go back to the sticks in Vermont to find my gourmet wife," Petie said.

Henry noticed that Joel hadn't said a word the whole time.

"What's with you, man?" he asked Joel.

"What?" Joel replied. "Oh, yeah…"

"Yeah what?" asked Henry.

"Uh, I dunno—I'm thinking about things I've gotta get done."

"You need to lighten up, buddy. You *know* you already have your whole semester planned. You'll be okay," Henry said.

"Yeah, I guess. Guys, I need to take off. I'll see you in the morning," Joel said, and got up to leave.

"I think I'll come with you. I need to get over to the library to meet Audra," Henry replied.

As the two walked out, Henry asked again, "What *is* with you? Something's going on."

"Nothing. I just have a lot on my mind."

"I *will* get it out of you eventually," Henry said. "I've gotta get going. See ya tomorrow—relax!" Henry walked off into the night, leaving Joel with his thoughts.

Joel's mind was in a whirl. He was angry at his lack of discipline, and for letting the captivating girl he'd seen that morning creep into his thoughts. He'd started to work out in his mind when he needed to be back

5

at Austin Hall tomorrow morning in order to catch another glimpse of her, and what he could say to her if he did see her.

What am I doing? he scolded himself. He shook his head as if to physically rid his brain of any more thoughts of her. He got to his car, climbed in, and turned the key. He had never felt this way before.

He thought to himself how uncanny it was to be going along in life, perfectly happy with the way things were, and how a complete stranger could suddenly appear out of nowhere and turn his whole world upside down. He drove off into the night, feeling alone and confused.

CHAPTER 2

The next morning after his business law class, Joel walked over to his father's lecture hall to get some clarification on an issue that had come up in class. Eli Volkenburg was a Harvard alumnus and esteemed professor at Harvard Law, as well as a senior partner at one of Boston's largest law firms. Hoping to follow in his father's footsteps, Joel planned to go on to Harvard Law.

He greeted his father as he was putting a stack of papers in his briefcase.

"Hey, Dad, I have a question on intellectual property."

"Joel, I have to be in court at one o'clock. Why aren't you going to your business law professor with questions?"

"He had a ton of people around him after class, so I thought I'd just ask you."

"I'm not going to be able to address any of your questions until the weekend. By the way, David is coming to dinner on Saturday," his father said, snapping his briefcase shut. "I'd like you to be there."

Fighting his disappointment, Joel responded, "Okay. See you Saturday."

He walked out of the building feeling dejected. Eli Volkenburg had never seemed to have time for him or his brother. He was rigidly focused on his life of academics and law, and they'd rarely seen him deviate from his stern and serious demeanor.

Joel's brother, David, was more than five years older than him. They had never been close. David left for prep school when Joel was only eight years old. Joel fought his loneliness by learning to get himself invited to dinner at Henry or Eddie's houses, where the dinner hours were less rigid. Henry, Eddie and Petie had been more like brothers to Joel than his own flesh and blood.

After prep school David went to Harvard, and astounded everyone by graduating at the age of 20. He went on to medical school and became a research scientist specializing in nanomedicine. Being a scientist was right up his alley, since he was more of a thinker and an introvert. His position allowed him to avoid direct dealings with people on a day-to-day basis.

Contrary to his brother's example, Joel occasionally wandered off the academic path his parents had set for him. Whenever he came up with his own ideas, they would firmly direct him back to their strict plan for him.

Growing up in a Jewish household with parents who had first-hand knowledge of the atrocities of the Holocaust, the thought of going without an education was unacceptable to them. Joel could feel their heavy hand continuously redirecting his efforts to achieve their goals.

"You're very fortunate to have a brilliant mind," his father would say to Joel. "Don't waste it on things that don't matter." David, on the other hand, seemed to have been born 30 years old, never really needing the stern parenting Joel was assigned to bear.

As Joel wandered into the library, he thought about the chances his dad would set aside time for him that weekend. *Probably better off doing the research myself,* he thought. His father would likely get caught up in class preparation or court prep work and dismiss his questions as unimportant.

❊

Fall flew by, and as September passed into October, the trees all over Boston took on a myriad of colors. Joel usually loved the fall, playing touch football with his friends and many weekends taking road trips to the Sullivans' house in Vermont.

He opted out of extracurricular activities as his routine ground along, and he pored over his studies, staying singularly-minded on school. He had actually gotten ahead in work for several of his classes, and had spent hours in the library completing papers that wouldn't be due until the end of the semester.

He did, however, keep to his traditional morning run. Crisp fall days were his favorite time of year for this treasured activity, which cleared his mind with every breath of cold, damp air he gulped into his lungs.

November rushed in, and before he knew it the famous Harvard-Yale football game had finally arrived. Joel temporarily threw aside his focus for one of the school's most anticipated events. This year it would be held at Harvard, and the four friends made their way to the famous Volkenburg tailgate party before the game. Joel's father had his annual 'tent party', complete with catered hors d'oeuvres and full bar.

The boys would make their obligatory visit to Joel's parents' tent, and proceed to stuff themselves with an array of gourmet food. They eventually moved on to tailgate with a large group of friends who had a much less sophisticated fare of hotdogs and hamburgers.

The four friends shared a house about a mile away from school, and carpooled to campus the day of the game, since parking was at a premium. They found a space and walked over to the Volkenburgs' tent. The boys exchanged greetings with Joel's father, who looked each of them up and down.

"Boys, where's your school spirit? I don't see much 'crimson' on you," Eli said.

"Don't worry, Dad," Joel replied. "We have crimson blood running through our veins!"

His father half acknowledged him and turned back to his cronies, asking who needed their drinks freshened. Joel and his friends gathered up all the food they could pile onto their plates, grabbed beers, and walked outside to do some people-watching.

"Man, I love being your friend, Burgermeister," Henry said. "Your mom and dad throw the best tailgate parties on campus!" Henry's parents hadn't shown up yet, but were always on the guest list at the Volkenburg tent.

As the four friends stood arguing about Harvard's chances to win this year's game, Joel spotted the girl he'd seen the first day of school. She happened to walk right by them with a group of girls. Their eyes met once more, and Joel, meaning to say 'hello', choked on the drink of beer he had just taken.

He started to cough and Petie, always ready to pounce with a sarcastic remark, said to Joel, "Burgermeister, you okay? Those things you just saw? Those are called 'girls'. Can you say 'girls', Burgermeister?"

Joel immediately turned the color of his football team's jerseys, and wiped his mouth with his hand.

"Shut up, Petie," Joel said as his eyes followed the girl, who once again disappeared from sight.

He looked around at Henry, who was a little more observant than the others. Joel noticed Henry was eyeing him with a suspicious look on his face. He knew Henry wasn't going to let this rest. He would be after Joel for more information, which Joel wasn't ready to give.

The four friends walked back into the tent, and true to form, Henry's parents hadn't shown up for the party yet, so they went over to Joel's parents, thanked them for the food, and departed for the next gathering.

They headed over to a large group of students who had set up several tables and chairs around a barbecue grill. Another table was filled with plates, utensils, and all the fixings, along with a huge keg of beer. Henry indicated to Joel to hang back so he could talk to him.

"Joel," Henry said. "You looked at that girl back there as though you had seen her before. Do you know her?"

"No."

"I've never seen you so rattled, man. You're kind of acting like you were on the first day of school. Does that girl have anything to do with your being so weird that day?"

"No, uh, no."

"You know, it's okay to like girls, even if you're in law school," Henry joked.

10

Joel got very quiet, and was again angry with himself for having such a strong reaction to someone he'd never met. After a few moments of silence he turned to Henry and said, "I'm not gonna give up my hard work for anyone right now. I don't have time to waste on relationships."

"Wow, that's deep," Henry replied. "Has anyone ever told you that you should get a part-time job as a romance writer?"

Joel lightened up a bit. "Very funny. I don't exactly see you as Don Juan. Your relationship with Audra is like a business deal."

"Let me tell you something, old man," Henry replied. "Audra is a smart girl who's not bad to look at, and her dad can hook me up with an awesome job right out of law school. How much better can I do?"

"Yeah, I guess you're right."

Somehow the words Joel spoke were covering how he really felt inside. Was following in his father's footsteps all he wanted out of life? Was he destined to marry someone because of her social and financial connections?

All of a sudden a strange emptiness crept in. What was wrong with him? Why did he feel this way? He thought once again, *how could seeing someone I don't even know make me feel this way?* He physically shook himself free from his conflicting thoughts as he had when he first saw the mystery girl, and punched Henry on the arm.

"I'm thirsty! Race you to the keg!" and their conversation about girls quickly turned to throwing out bets as to who could down a glass of beer faster—their buddy Jimmy, or Jimmy's friend Sean. Eddie collected the money for the bets, and Petie filled the cups of beer to the rim.

Sean grabbed his beer, yelling, "Jimmy, you're going down, man!"

"That's what you think, pal. Choke on it!" Jimmy shot back.

Eddie counted down, "Three, two, one, GO!"

Jimmy seemed to have opened his throat and dumped his beer down without swallowing until the whole cup was empty. As Sean tried desperately to keep up, the crowd shouted encouraging chants: 'Drink! Drink! Drink'! The whole party erupted at the same time in cheers and

11

boos as Jimmy crushed his cup in his hand, having gulped his beer down several seconds before Sean.

"Okay losers, move aside while I divvy up the winnings," Eddie said as he distributed the cash, waving it in the air. He did his best to make sure they felt their loss, taunting them mercilessly.

The game was about to start, so they all pitched in as they packed up their barbecue belongings and hauled the grills, coolers, and miscellaneous items back to their cars. The group then made their way into the stadium, arguing excitedly about which team's chance for winning was better. Once again Eddie had elected himself as bookie, this time for bets on the game.

They all climbed the steps to their seats to get positioned for the kickoff. The game got underway, and the group of friends yelled themselves hoarse, being encouraged when the Harvard defense picked off a pass after only a few plays, resulting in an early touchdown for Harvard. Their seats were positioned close enough to be within earshot of some of the Yalees, and they tormented their arch enemies with glee.

The game proved to be a barn-burner from beginning to end, and the whole stadium seemed to forget they had seats. Both sides stood stubbornly on their feet, as if the outcome of the game depended on it.

For the first quarter Harvard, buoyed by the initial touchdown, controlled the ball. Once the clock ticked down and was re-started for the second quarter, Yale began to fight back with screen passes and short runs, having possession of the ball for the lion's share of the 15-minute period. They were unable to get into the end zone, but made a couple of field goals, bringing them to within one point of their nemesis Harvard.

The second half was not dominated by either team. Both came out of the tunnel after halftime with strong plans to march the ball down the field. The defensive units for each team played fiercely and both quarterbacks were hurled mercilessly into the turf as they were sacked again and again.

They played a clean game with very few penalties, and as the minutes ticked down to seconds, Harvard squeaked out a win with a long touchdown pass from the forty-five yard line. The whole stadium broke out into a deafening roar. A home game win—nothing could be better! Yale had a slight edge over Harvard on total wins throughout their long rivalry, so this victory was particularly sweet. What a day.

The group of friends walked out of the stadium, slapping each other on the back and yelling, "Crimson rules!" They would become especially raucous when they saw the blue and white Yale colors, and yell even louder, "Crimson rules!" Eddie was in his element as he passed out the winnings, shouting and waving a fistful of money in the air toward those who had bet against Harvard.

As the four friends made their way over to Noch's to celebrate their victory, they ran into their friend Tim Sumner, whom they had also known from childhood. Tim had opted for Yale over Harvard, so they had lost track of him over the last three years.

Eddie was the first to spot Tim. "Hey, Tim! I don't see you hanging your head low enough in shame!"

Tim turned toward them at the comment. "Hey, long time no see. Congratulations on the win."

"Aren't you being a little too noble?" Eddie asked. "Well, okay, more bowing and scraping, please."

Joel interrupted Eddie's sarcasm. "Tim, come with us to Noch's. I don't think it would be too dangerous for you to show up, even if you *are* a Bulldog."

"I've gotta meet some friends later, but I'll come for a little while," Tim replied. He told the group he was with that he was going to Noch's, and a couple of them tagged along.

Noch's was packed body-to-body with students yelling and shouting excitedly about the day's momentous win. The group of friends who had tailgated before the game had gotten themselves a table, and pulled enough chairs around for the whole group to pack together. Tim sat next to Joel. They shouted over the roar in the small restaurant.

"Did you end up majoring in business like you planned?" Joel asked Tim.

"Yeah, but I'm not going to Spain."

"What are you gonna do?"

"I know this sounds crazy, but I'm moving to California next year to go to Bible school."

"What? I don't think I heard you right—it's so loud in here. I thought you said something about Bible school," Joel said.

"No, you heard right," Tim replied. "I'm actually going to a small Bible college in southern California."

Joel was stunned. Tim had been an excellent student all through school. He hadn't gone to Deerfield Academy, but they'd kept in touch by hanging out together on Christmas and summer breaks until they reached college.

Back in high school Tim had said he was going into international business, and had planned on going abroad for post-graduate school to get his MBA in Spain. Now he was throwing it all away for Bible school? Wow, they really *had* lost touch.

"I don't get it. What happened to you getting your MBA in Madrid?"

"I didn't really plan on this, Joel. I became friends with a guy from southern California when I started Yale. At first I thought he was the weirdest guy I'd ever met. After I got to know him though, he told me about his faith. It's just not something we talk about in New England."

Tim continued, "He challenged me to read a book about a guy who'd been an atheist and set out to disprove the Bible. He came to faith as a Christian just by reading the Bible to try and find errors and inconsistencies. He gave me the book to read, and I started really poring over the Bible. I found the same things he found, and became a believer myself. Now I want to learn more about the Bible, and to figure out what I'm supposed to do with my life."

"I don't know what to say," Joel muttered.

"It's okay, Joel. I can't expect you to understand", Tim replied. "I'm still trying to figure it out myself—it's all new to me."

14

Joel became quiet again. *What's happening to the world around me? One moment I have everything in control, and everything is right with the world. Then I see a girl I can't stop thinking about, and my friend becomes a religious nut.*

Suddenly the noise and the heat from so many bodies pressing together in a small space got to Joel, and he said, "I think I've had enough fun for today. I'm gonna try to convince my designated driver it's time to go home. See you later, Tim. Good luck with the God thing."

Joel got up, not waiting for Tim to say goodbye, and edged himself over to Henry, who had driven them to the game.

"Hey, let's take off," Joel said.

"What's going on, bro?" Henry asked.

"Nothing, I'm just done for the day. This place is crazy loud and hot, and I just wanna get outta here."

"Ok, I guess I'm over yelling at the top of my lungs. I've never seen it so packed here."

Henry told Eddie and Petie they were leaving. Eddie said he was going to stay and catch a ride later, and Petie decided to leave with Henry and Joel.

As the boys walked out, Joel spoke up about his conversation with Tim. "You guys wanna know something? Tim got religion. He's going to California with all the religious freaks to go to Bible school."

"That's funny," Petie laughed.

"No, I'm serious," Joel shot back. "He just told me. He's leaving in the fall of next year."

"Wow," Henry said, "you've had a rough day with lots of information overload, haven't you, buddy?"

"What do you mean?" asked Petie.

"I think our man Joel's world is changing. He's found he can't control it, and he's losing his mind!" Henry said.

"What else happened today, Burgermeister?" Petie asked.

15

"Nothing. Henry's exaggerating," Joel said. Henry didn't say anything else about Joel's second encounter with the mystery girl, for which Joel was grateful.

Joel, Henry, and Petie got to the car, and had the grueling task of sitting in traffic, inching along to get off the campus and head home. Henry pulled up to their house in Cambridge and dropped Petie off, then he and Joel continued on to Wellesley, where their parents' homes were just a couple of blocks apart. Often on the weekends the two would drive home to do laundry and have a few home-cooked meals.

The day was wearing on them and their conversation dropped off as Henry drove the few miles to their homes. Joel drifted back into thoughts of what Tim had told him earlier that evening at Noch's. *The guy is clearly delusional...but he sure spoke with a lot of conviction.*

Then he thought about the girl who had captivated him. He had seen her again. How could he get to talk to her? How could he find out about her when he didn't even know her name? *There you go again, Joel*, he said to himself. *Shake it off...shake it off...shake it off,* he said to himself, like a mantra.

Henry pulled up to the front of Joel's house, and they congratulated each other once more on Harvard's big win. Joel got out of the car and walked around to the door in the back of his parents' house. He climbed the stairs to his room and sat down on his bed in the dark.

He didn't know how much time had elapsed. He just sat deep in thought until he heard the front door close downstairs, and his parents' voices as they each went off to their respective bedrooms.

He didn't even take off his clothes to go to bed. He lay down, eyes staring at the ceiling in the dark, and after what seemed like hours he finally drifted off to a fitful sleep.

CHAPTER 3

December hit with a heavy snow. Boston was ablaze in twinkling lights for the holidays. Winter break was a week away, and Joel was trying to finish up as much as he could at school so he could enjoy the vacation.

Joel's parents weren't religious, so they didn't celebrate the traditional Hanukah holiday. Joel's mother loved decorations, however, so their home was a contrast in garlands draping the front stairway and fireplaces, and menorahs gracing the front hall and throughout the house for tradition's sake.

Joel loved winter. During the break, he and his friends always planned a ski trip to Killington, Vermont. They'd all grown up on skis, but it was Eddie who shined. He had dreamed of being on the Olympic ski team, but his parents had discouraged that when he was young.

Eddie's father had told his son that there was no way he would allow him to put all his efforts into a few races just so he can win a medal. His father wanted him to be well-rounded, so Eddie was shipped off to tennis camp in the summer and ski camp in the winter when he was only seven years old, and when he began attending Deerfield, he joined the crew team.

The four friends always drove from Boston to Bennington, where Petie's family lived. As usual, Mrs. Sully would be waving at the doorway when they drove up. They would drop off their things and load the car with a cooler Mrs. Sully had packed, filled with goodies for lunch and snacks. Then they would be off to Killington for a week of skiing.

Joel walked to the library at the end of the day to study for one of his last finals. The snow was cascading down heavily. He loved the quiet of snowfall. It seemed to muffle the voices in Harvard Yard. Footsteps couldn't be heard, just the 'crunch, crunch, crunch' of boots on the snow. He entered the library, set his books on a table, and took his coat off, shaking the snow that had matted to the wool. He placed it on the back of the chair, and proceded to walk over and look for a book his professor had talked about in class for research.

As he turned the corner, there she was. His breath caught in his throat, and he stopped as if paralyzed. She turned and looked at him with those magnificent exotic eyes.

He finally found his voice: "Hello," he said simply.

"Hello," she replied, looking back down at her book.

Joel fought for words to say…any words. "Um, I've seen you a couple of times on campus. Uh, I'm Joel."

"My name is Hessa," she replied. He noticed she had an accent, but he couldn't make out where it might be from.

His mind was jumbled and he began to shake, struggling madly to say something—anything. He couldn't let her get away again. As she closed the book she was looking at and started to walk away, he blurted out the first thought that came to his mind.

"That's a pretty name, where are you from?" He turned several shades of red, thinking how nervous he sounded, and what he thought was a completely stupid remark. It was all he could think of to get a conversation started.

"Jerusalem," she said simply, and looked down at her book.

Joel was intrigued. He wanted to know everything about her. "How did you get to Harvard?"

She smiled and answered, "By working very, very hard, and by begging my father for two years."

"Why wouldn't he want you to go to Harvard?" Joel asked, starting to calm down a bit.

"He is very old-fashioned," she replied. "He does not think girls should be so far from home."

The thought ran through his mind that his mother and father might be very happy if he brought home a nice Jewish girl, even though they didn't follow the faith. Joel probed further for information.

"How did you convince your old-fashioned father that you could handle coming to America for college?"

She drew a deep breath, and replied, "I finally convinced him that the only thing I wanted to do was study, and that I was not planning on staying here. I promised I would go back home when I graduated."

"What are you working on that brings you to the library?" Joel asked.

"I am studying for my philosophy final," she said.

"Well fancy that," Joel said, "so am I."

Hessa looked at Joel with a quizzical look on her face and smiled slightly. She turned to walk over and put her things down on a table. Joel went to the table where he had laid his books and picked them up. He turned around and walked over to her table and sat down across from her.

"Mind if I join you?" he asked.

"Yes…certainly," she replied shyly, with her head tilted down over her book.

Desperate to get to know her, Joel asked Hessa about her philosophy class, and told her what he'd been studying as a senior. He felt as though he was rambling on just so he could look at her.

"Have you seen any sights in Boston yet?"

"Not many. I saw a few places when I first arrived, but I have been so busy with my studies, I really have not had much time to do anything else. What I have seen is very beautiful, though. I love Boston. It is so very different from my home," she said smiling, her eyes twinkling.

As she talked Joel noticed she had a sheer joy of life, like a little child with her first glimpse of Disneyland. She was more than he had expected. He was completely captivated.

19

They finally cracked open their books and notes, studying for their respective finals. Joel had a tough time concentrating, but felt confident he knew the material for the next day's test. The two sat in silence as Hessa read her textbook and wrote down notes, and Joel typed into his laptop.

Time slipped away and before he knew it, it was after 10:00. He didn't want to say anything...he was afraid if they parted she would slip away and disappear, maybe this time for good.

Hessa spoke up first. "I cannot concentrate anymore today. I will have to hope this is enough studying for my final."

"I agree. This is tiring stuff," Joel replied.

They gathered up their books and walked out together. Hessa's room was close by at Thayer Hall, so Joel walked her to her dorm. As they got to the front door, he turned to her.

"It was nice having a study partner this afternoon, Hessa. Very nice meeting you."

"I enjoyed meeting you as well, Joel. Well, I guess the nicest thing about being a freshman is the locality of the dorms. Thank you for walking me home."

"Do you have any finals on Friday?" he blurted out.

"Yes, just one, and then I will be finished."

"Will you be coming back to the library tomorrow to study for any finals you have on Friday?"

"Yes, I am," she smiled slightly, her eyes cast down. "I had better go inside, Joel. Thank you again."

"Maybe I'll see you then," Joel said with a smile. "Goodnight!" he said louder than he meant.

"Goodnight, Joel." Hessa said as she turned and walked into her dorm.

Joel walked off and found his car by sheer instinct. When he got there he opened the door and got in, turning on the engine. He drove home lost in thought about the beautiful girl with whom he had spent the evening.

Hessa, he said to himself…*Hessa.* When he got home he parked his car and walked inside. He ran up the stairs to his room and sat down on the bed. He didn't even know how he'd gotten there he was in such a daze.

"Uh, oh," he finally said to himself out loud. "I'm in big trouble."

He got out of his clothes, hopped into bed, and stared at the ceiling. His resolve was melting away. *Snap out of it,* he thought. He felt as though he had fallen off a cliff and was helplessly plummeting through the air, with no branch to grab and save himself.

He then realized that somehow he didn't care. All he cared about was seeing her again. He drifted off to sleep, contented and happier than he'd been since childhood.

The next day Joel got up very early, feeling as though he could conquer the world. He would do his best to see Hessa again today and try to get to know her better.

Tomorrow was also the last day of school, and then a nice long break. He and his pals would be off to Killington the day after Christmas the following Tuesday. His three friends celebrated Christmas, so he would have to wait until their festivities were over.

Joel's classes dragged on that day. He was so anxious to see Hessa he squirmed in his seat in each class, willing himself to get through his finals. All day he had dodged his friends, not wanting to have to explain anything about where he'd been last night, and why he hadn't answered his calls or texts all evening.

Henry was especially intuitive, so Joel really wanted to avoid him today. He always saw through Joel, since they'd been best friends from kindergarten. Their families had even spent several vacations together. No, now was not the time to run into Henry.

Right before 3 p.m. Joel was hurrying across Harvard Yard to get to the library.

"Burgermeister!" It was Henry. "Where are you going? I need to go over to Ski Market to pick up my new skis. Wanna come?"

"No, I have a final to study for. I'm on my way to the library."

21

"Suit yourself. What are you doing tomorrow night? You wanna get together with the guys for pool?" Henry asked.

"No, I can't. I have to get ready for the trip."

"Joel, you're not a girl. You don't need five days to pack," Henry said sarcastically. "What's going on?"

"Henry, I have things to do, okay?"

"Okay, okay. Sorry to pry into your life. Let me know when you're ready to talk about the girl," Henry teased.

"Very funny," Joel retorted, and turned to walk away with a backward wave.

He opened the door to the library and walked to a table by the window, close to where he and Hessa had sat the day before. He decided to stake it out for them, spreading his books across the table, and sat down to pull out his notes. He fiddled with his notebook and scratched doodles on the front of a book cover, unable to concentrate.

A few minutes later Hessa walked in, and Joel turned to see her walking toward a table across the room. His heart raced and he could feel his face get hot. *What's more embarrassing than a grown man blushing?* he thought to himself.

He jumped up, almost knocking his chair over. Before it could make a loud crash on the floor, he grabbed it and set it upright. He hurried over to her as she set her books down.

"Hello again, Hessa," he said with a broad grin across his face, making him look like a little boy.

"Hello, Joel." Hessa began removing books from her backpack, keeping her eyes focused on her task.

"I have a table by the window. Would you like to join me?"

"So you have reserved a place for us?" she smiled, speaking her very formal English with her soft accent.

"Well, I thought I'd better grab one of the coveted window tables. I…just thought you might want to uh, share it with me," he stammered. He was completely flustered. Would he always act this way around her?

22

She smiled at him and put her books back into her pack. He hurried over to her and quickly scooped the pack up as he led her back to his table. They talked about their finals for a few minutes, and then got down to the business of studying.

Joel had a more difficult time concentrating today than he'd had the day before. He kept looking up, pretending he was deep in thought, but he actually just wanted to catch as many glimpses of her as possible. Her head was down, with long lashes resting against her cheek as she moved her lips in silent memorization of the material she was studying.

If I don't get back to work, I'm gonna flunk this test, Joel thought. *Eye on the prize, eye on the prize.* His idea of keeping his eye on the prize was beginning to change, however. The hours flew by, and Joel was finally able to get his mind on his work. He started to feel more confident that he would ace tomorrow's final.

It was getting close to 10 o'clock again. Hessa glanced down at her watch. "I need to get back to the dorm. My class is early tomorrow morning, and I am so nervous for this final, I hope I can sleep."

"You'll be fine. You've studied all the material, right? Just remember, it's all right up there," Joel said, tapping on his head. "All you have to do is relax and you'll remember."

"Thank you, Joel. I never thought about it that way. I feel better already," she said, smiling at him.

His head reeled at her intoxicating smile. As they packed up all their belongings and headed out the door, Joel struggled to find a way to see her again.

"Will you be going home for the winter break?" Joel asked abruptly.

"Yes, but I cannot leave until Monday. I did not make my flight reservations early enough, so I will have to stay the weekend."

"Where're you staying? Freshmen aren't allowed to stay in the dorms over holidays."

"This is something my father is very upset about. I am trying so hard to prove to him that I am responsible, so this does not look very good

23

for me. I have made reservations at the Charles Hotel, and have hired a car to take me to the airport on Monday morning."

"So you're staying at the Charles Hotel all weekend by yourself?" Joel asked.

"Yes. I have no choice. I was not thinking...I was too caught up in studying for finals," she replied.

"You can't stay in Boston alone all weekend. There's so much to do here, and you need a tour guide! Why don't I take you to dinner, and maybe a play or movie or something on Friday night?"

"But Joel, I cannot accept your invitation. That is very kind of you...I...simply cannot."

"I'm sorry, am I being too forward? I know you're not from here...am I out of line?" Joel asked holding his breath.

"You are a perfect gentleman to want to show me around Boston. I really should not, I...I," Hessa stammered, trying to find the appropriate words...why couldn't she just tell him the truth?

"I understand if you feel uncomfortable, Hessa. I didn't mean to make you feel that way. In America, we just like to make people feel at home. I'd feel bad knowing you're stuck in a hotel all weekend with nothing to do."

"You are right. My roommates will be leaving to go home to their families. None of them actually live in Boston, so I was planning to spend the weekend reading."

"You see? You *have* to go with me now! You don't want to be holed up at the Charles all weekend when you could be eating great food and seeing an American movie!"

"Thank you, Joel. That would be lovely," Hessa replied. "I must admit that I have been looking at the postings in the library of activities around town. There is something I would love to do. I...know men are not generally fond of the ballet, but do you think you could endure one? I have never seen 'The Nutcracker', but I have heard it talked about and read that the Boston Ballet has one of the best adaptations. I will understand if it is something you prefer not to see."

24

Joel would have sat through anything with her. "Of course! I guess that's one thing everyone should do if they're in Boston at Christmastime. I'll see if there's a way to get tickets. My parents have season tickets to the Boston Opera House so I'll check with my mom.

"Do you want to meet back here at the library tomorrow after our finals? That way we can talk about when I'll be back to pick you up, and to confirm our plans."

"Thank you, Joel. I will be at the library tomorrow at 3:00 p.m."

"I'll see you then," Joel said with a smile. "Well, Hessa, I guess I'll say goodbye for tonight. I look forward to seeing you tomorrow."

The next day Joel got to the library in plenty of time, and fiddled with his phone nervously as he waited for Hessa. Just after 3 p.m. she entered the library, her eyes sparkling when she spotted Joel.

He hurried over to her as he waved, smiling broadly. "Hi! How did your finals go today?"

"I think I did quite well. I remembered what you told me, Joel…to relax. It helped me immensely, and I am grateful." She couldn't help the smile that stretched across her lovely face.

Joel stood staring at her momentarily with a blank look on his face, his heart racing at her smile. "Yeah, uh, glad to be of service! Um, by the way, I have great news! I talked to my mom this morning and she gave me the tickets. She said they're really good seats. The ballet starts at 8:00, so I'll pick you up for dinner by 5:30. I made dinner reservations right around the corner. Do you like Italian food?"

"It is one of my favorites." She smiled again at him as she turned to head out of the library and back to her dorm. Joel followed her, taking her backpack and hefting it over his shoulder. As they reached the dorm, he handed the pack to her as she took it and hugged it to herself, thanking him.

"I will look forward to tomorrow night, Joel," she said as she turned and walked through the front door of Thayer Hall. Joel watched until she disappeared, then turned and slowly ambled toward his car, whistling to himself.

CHAPTER 4

Friday was an easy day, and Joel was done with school by noon. He was glad he had an easy escap, because his ego was keeping him from telling his friends about Hessa. He avoided them all day and still didn't answer texts or calls.

The last thing I'm gonna do is get harassed by everyone, Joel thought to himself. He'd always prided himself in keeping his focus on school, and this definitely didn't include relationships. He would see how long he could hold off his prying friends.

He spent the afternoon doing errands to get ready for his ski trip. When he got to his parents' house he went in, and his mother was in the kitchen as he entered.

"Hi, Joel. So you're finished for a while?"

"Yeah. It's good to get finals over with. Now I can relax for a few weeks."

"Well," his mother continued, "I was thinking that if your friend from school doesn't have plans tomorrow night, maybe we should have her to dinner. It's not right that she stay at a hotel by herself all weekend."

"Thanks, Mom. I'll ask her tonight, and let you know tomorrow."

Joel got ready for his date with Hessa, and was about to walk out the door when his mother saw him and told him to go back upstairs and put on a blazer.

"What are you thinking, Joel? You can't go out looking like you're going to a hockey game. You have orchestra seats at the opera house. Several of our friends have seats in the same area. I want you to represent the Volkenburgs with a little more dignity."

"Ok," he said resentfully, and ran back upstairs. He quickly tore off his shirt, put on a dress shirt, pullover sweater, and a blazer. He then ran back downstairs, and before his mother could say anything else he was out the door.

Joel got to the Charles Hotel and left his car running while he ran into the lobby. He spotted Hessa walking toward him. She came up to Joel, greeting him cheerfully. She was dressed in a long cream-colored cashmere coat, and wore long black boots.

If I spent the rest of my life with her, he told himself, *I would never get used to how beautiful she is.*

"Hello, Hessa. Ready for some sights and sounds of Boston?"

"I am very excited about the ballet!" she exclaimed.

They headed out the door and into his car. When they got to the restaurant, she had him order for them both, and he selected lobster salad for both of them, the Mafalde with Duck Confit for her and Sea Scallops with Potato Pancetta Risotto for himself. They ended up sharing their entrées.

The opera house was only a few blocks away, so they decided to walk their dinners off as they chatted about their families. She told him what it was like growing up in Jerusalem.

"I was actually born in Gaza," Hessa told Joel. "We moved to Jerusalem when I was five. My father did not feel Gaza was a good place to raise his family. Being Palestinian, Jerusalem is not always the best place either, however."

"You're...Palestinian?" Joel asked. "I guess I just assumed..." he trailed off.

"I was Jewish?" Hessa finished the sentence for him. "No, I am Palestinian, which, as I said, is not always the easiest thing to be in Israel. But I still love my home, and will someday return when I complete my degree."

28

"You don't wear any type of veils I've seen Muslim women wear. I guess that's why I was so surprised."

Joel felt as though someone had punched him in the stomach. The Palestinians and Jews didn't have good relations, and he knew if she was from a strict family, her father would most likely never approve of him. He tried not to let her know how this statement had affected him.

"I often wear a scarf called a 'hijab', or pashmina shawls over my shoulders, but I know it does not look very traditional. When I am at home, I wear the scarves in a more traditional manner."

"What does the name 'Hessa' mean?" Joel asked. "And I just realized I don't even know your last name."

"My name means 'Destiny,'" she replied. "My last name is Bishara."

Destiny. Well, that's ironic, Joel thought.

"Do you think you could ever be happy making America your home?" Joel asked, trying to probe about how rigid her family was in giving her freedom of choice in her life.

"From what I have seen so far, this is a wonderful place. It is so very different from my home, and even different from the places I have travelled to around the world. But I love my home, and would not consider leaving to live anywhere else.

"My father is a very stern man, and would not want me to live in America. It is a miracle he even let me go to school here. He is not fond of America or the Americans, but realized they have some of the best schools in the world, so he consented for me to be here only to get my degree."

Joel's heart sank lower. He tried to change the subject. "Where have you been in your travels?" Joel asked, trying not to sound too disappointed.

"I have spent a lot of time with my family visiting in Europe and England. We also have a home in Ibiza, where we spend our summers."

"Ibiza! That sounds fantastic. I've been to Spain with my family, but I've never been to the surrounding islands. I did an exchange program in England when I was sixteen," Joel said. "It was only for a semester, but

I really liked it there. Kind of cold and rainy, but I still liked the country. It was nice to get back to America when the semester was over though."

They entered the Boston Opera House, and Hessa gasped at the opulence of the place. She wasn't expecting this. It looked like something right out of Europe.

"You didn't think Boston would have something this sophisticated, did you?" Joel asked.

"I am surprised. When my parents brought me to school, we took a tour of historic Boston, and found the architecture and furnishings much more simple compared to this!" Hessa replied.

They walked to the row where their seats were located, and as they were sliding along, excusing themselves to get to the center, Joel heard his name. He turned around and there, to his dismay, were Henry's parents.

"Hello, Mr. and Mrs. Worthing."

"Well, isn't this a surprise, Joel?" said Mrs. Worthing. "I haven't seen you in months. You boys snuck off in quite a hurry at 'the game'."

"We waited around for a while hoping to see you, but had another tailgate party to get to," Joel said, being respectful. Mr. and Mrs. Worthing were notoriously late for everything, and it had been no different at the Harvard/Yale game.

"By the way, this is my friend, Hessa, from school."

Mr. and Mrs. Worthing said hello to Hessa. "Well, nice to see you, Mr. and Mrs. Worthing. Have a great Christmas." Joel said.

The Nutcracker started soon after they sat down, and Hessa didn't make a sound through the entire ballet. Her eyes were as wide as saucers, and the smile didn't leave her face the whole time. Joel casually glanced her way throughout the production, and was content just to watch Hessa watching the ballet.

When the production concluded, Joel made a point to exit the row in the opposite direction of the Worthings. He didn't want to risk their asking any questions about Hessa. As they walked back to his car, Joel asked Hessa to join his family for dinner the following evening.

30

"You do not have to feel as though you need to entertain me all weekend, Joel," she said.

"I really enjoyed this evening, Hessa. I'd like to get together again before you leave to go home. My parents aren't too scary," he laughed.

"Well then, I would love to," she said, smiling.

As they strolled along they talked at length about their families. Joel gave a detailed explanation about Boston. His love for his hometown was apparent. He thought Boston was the greatest city in America, and he never wanted to leave. He told Hessa about his father's positions at Harvard and the law firm. Joel expressed bluntly that his father had always had expectations of him someday joining his practice.

"Is this something that you want to do, Joel?" Hessa asked.

"I guess I've never thought about it much. It's always been assumed that I would go into law, especially since my brother went into medicine. A Volkenburg needs to take over the family law practice, and my dad is expecting me to do that."

When Joel asked more about her family, Hessa explained that her father was well-known in the Middle East, but didn't offer any further information. She quickly changed the subject, and told Joel about her mother and older brother.

Her brother was three years older than she, and married. Her sister-in-law was about to have their first child, due in January, so Hessa was anxious to be home for the event. She went on to explain how interesting the city of Jerusalem was. She was very knowledgeable about the history of the city, and the different cultures all living in a very small area.

As they got in the car and started to drive, Joel told Hessa when he would be by for her the next evening.

Hessa then turned to Joel and said, "We have spent the whole evening together, and I do not even know your last name. You know mine, but what is yours?"

"It's Volkenburg," Joel replied.

"Is that German?" she asked.

31

"It's Dutch. My father's family is from Haarlem, which is about fifteen minutes from Amsterdam. My parents have taken my brother and me there to visit, but my grandparents came to America before my father was born."

"Is your mother's family from there as well?" Hessa wanted to know.

"No, she's of Russian descent. Her mother and father were both born in America, but her grandparents emigrated from Russia. Her parents grew up in the same neighborhood in Boston, and married very young."

Joel neglected to mention he was Jewish—he was afraid he might scare Hessa away.

They pulled up to the hotel, and Joel got out and ran around to open the door for Hessa. He walked her into the lobby and stopped, turning toward her. He stood wordless, head down, scuffing his shoes against the tile floor. He finally looked up and noticed Hessa looking at him with a slight smile on her face.

"What's that look on your face?" he asked.

"Sometimes you seem so sure of yourself and at other times you look like a timid little boy." She smiled again and looked at him pensively.

Joel smiled back at her, getting lost in those black, twinkling eyes. He felt self-conscious at her scrutiny of him, but she suddenly looked toward the elevator and broke the silence.

"Joel, I had a wonderful time. You have been a very good host this evening," she said.

"I didn't realize I was being a host. I kind of thought of this as more of a date," Joel replied, relieved she'd finally said something.

"I thank you for the wonderful time all the same, though I must tell you Joel, I cannot date you," Hessa said.

"Why not?"

"It is still very common for marriages to be arranged in my culture," she replied. "My family has already chosen someone for me."

Joel felt as though his heart had dropped to his feet. "Have you met him?" he asked.

32

"Yes, I have," she replied, "several times, in fact."

"Do you like him? More importantly, do you love him?"

"It is not a question of love. It is my responsibility to my family. Our fathers know each other very well, and it has been planned since we were quite young."

"I'm sorry Hessa, but I just don't get it. You and I live worlds apart—not only physically, but culturally," Joel said. "Your father is living in the dark ages. Don't you want to make your own decisions for your life? Don't you want to choose whom you marry and where you live?"

"Please, Joel. I cannot talk about this. Maybe I should not come to your house tomorrow night. I feel as though you are judging me for what my family believes is best for my life. I think we should say goodnight," Hessa said.

"No! I'm sorry. I didn't mean to upset you. Please come tomorrow night as a friend. You don't want to disappoint my parents, do you? They'll think I chased you away, which I...guess I have. I didn't have any right to pry into your life."

"I understand how you can question arranged marriage," Hessa said. "I know it is not widely done any longer. I have never really thought about it. I guess compared to the West and most other parts of the world, we *are* strange.

She looked at Joel. His face was anxious and full of anticipation at the same time. Her eyes filled with a compassionate gaze. "I have never met a boy like you before. I feel so comfortable with you. You have been so thoughtful to make me feel at home, and wanting my approval of Boston. You have considered my feelings ever since we met. Thank you, Joel."

Joel's heart raced. "So you'll come tomorrow night?"

"Yes, I will be there," she answered, laughing slightly, thinking Joel certainly wasn't a man who hid his feelings. "I look forward to meeting your parents."

"Good. Then I'll pick you up here tomorrow night at six."

"I will be waiting," Hessa replied.

She smiled her lovely smile that made Joel's heart pound. She turned and walked to the elevator. He stood and watched her get in and press the button for her floor. The doors closed and when she disappeared, he stood thinking about their conversation.

Why had he questioned her culture and traditions? *What a big mouth*, he thought. He turned and walked out to his car, mulling over in his mind what he had said to her that evening. *Stupid, big mouth*, he thought to himself again.

He got in his car and drove off, condemning himself all the way home. He only hoped she would be waiting for him in the lobby tomorrow night.

CHAPTER 5

The next day Joel went for a run first thing in the morning, then showered and changed and went over to Ski Market to have the bindings on his skis checked, and to make sure he had everything for the trip. He restlessly kept himself busy all day, trying not to be too anxious for that evening. What would his parents think of Hessa? Would his father scare her away with his austere behavior?

Joel got ready for the evening and drove over to pick her up at the hotel. As he walked into the lobby, there across the large room was Hessa, sitting in a comfortable-looking chair. She was reading something that she seemed very engrossed in. He went over to her and looked down.

"Hi," he said simply.

She jumped in her seat. "Oh! Joel, I am so sorry! I was reading an article in this magazine I found on the table here. I got lost in it, and didn't realize you were standing there."

"Shall we go?" Joel held his arm out for her that she accepted, and they walked out together to his car. When they got situated and drove out of the hotel driveway, he asked, "What article were you reading?"

"It was something on the Middle East, and the strained relations. Certainly not something I am ignorant about, but the article was written in a much different point of view than I have ever heard."

"Hessa, I noticed the magazine you were reading. Don't believe anything you read in it. Those people have no idea what they're talking about," he said curtly.

"The article wasn't like anything that I have ever read, and didn't match my own beliefs, but don't you think it is interesting to see something from someone else's point of view sometimes?" she asked.

"If it has merit," he answered. "That magazine isn't worth my time reading, though."

"I think Americans are as passionate about their political beliefs as we are in the Middle East, but it is more restrained here," Hessa said thoughtfully. "Let's talk about something else."

"You're right," he smiled. "Something lighter, like the sights of Boston. You said when you first got here you went on a tour. What did you see?"

"My mother and father brought me to Boston, and before they left, we took a tour of Beacon Hill and Boston Common."

"You haven't seen anything yet! There's the Freedom Trail, Faneuil Hall, Plymouth Rock, the Museum of Fine Arts, the Aquarium...I could go on forever!"

Joel got excited at the prospect of taking Hessa to see more of Boston.

"When you go to elementary school in Boston, you go on field trips all over the city. I could be a tour guide for a living," he laughed.

"I must admit, I do not know much about Boston's history. I would really love to see more of the sights. This city is different from anything I have ever seen. It is like England in a way, but much simpler," she said.

"Well, you still have tomorrow here. Why don't I take you around? After my personal tour, I'll take you ice skating!"

"I have never been ice skating. I would love to have a tour of Boston, but I cannot try ice skating. It would be too embarrassing to have you see me falling all over the place," she said.

"I'll be there to help you. Don't worry, it'll be fun," Joel said, completely elated that he had been able to plan another day with Hessa before she left for home.

They pulled into the long driveway that led to Joel's house, and drove around back to the garage. The Volkenburg home was very fitting to the town of Wellesley. It was an enormous light grey colonial with black shutters and a large red front door. Joel parked and walked around to open the car door for Hessa.

As she stood up, she looked around at the yard in the back of the house. It was very large, and sloped downhill with terraced patios, verandas and plantings surrounded by stone walls. At the bottom of the hill was a small house in the same architectural design as the main house.

"Who lives in that house down the hill?"

"That's where our housekeeper lives. It used to be a guest house, but Helen's husband died, so she moved in there. She's almost like a part of the family she's been with us so long. My mother hates to cook, so Helen cooks dinner at night for us, too."

Joel and Hessa walked in the back door, and Joel greeted Helen as they passed by the kitchen. "There's my boy," she said. "Your mother's in the den, dear."

Joel introduced Helen to Hessa, and they continued on into a sitting room that seemed small for such a large home. The walls were brick red, with built-in bookcases at one end of the room. The furniture was elegant and fit right in to the look of the house. Joel's mother was sitting reading a magazine when they walked in. She stood up when they entered.

"Hi, Mom. This is my friend, Hessa," Joel said.

"Hello Hessa," his mother answered. "Welcome to our home. I'm glad you could join us for dinner."

"Thank you for inviting me, Mrs. Volkenburg. Your home is very lovely."

"Where's Dad?"

"He's in his office, doing some work. He'll join us for dinner in a few minutes. Hessa, would you like a tour of the place?" Mrs. Volkenburg asked.

Hessa and Joel walked out of the room with Joel's mother as she took Hessa through the house, and to her surprise the home was newer than she had expected. She explained that they had built the home just over fifteen years ago, when Joel was in kindergarten. They wanted to get away from being right in Boston. They had lived in Cambridge to be in close vicinity to Mr. Volkenburg's office and the campus, but decided it would be better for the boys to have more space as they grew up.

"One could get lost in this house, there are so many rooms," Hessa exclaimed.

"My parents did that so they wouldn't have to hear us boys making noise," Joel replied, trying to tease his mother.

She didn't look amused. "Joel, that's not true," she said. "We need to have plenty of room. Mr. Volkenburg and I do a lot of entertaining, and this is a good house for that."

Hessa looked back and forth between Joel and his mother and noticed there was some tension between them. He didn't kiss or hug his mother when he saw her. Their relationship seemed uneasy and distant. She felt bad for him, since she and her own mother had always been close.

Helen came around the corner and let Mrs. Volkenburg know dinner would be ready in five minutes. "Mr. Volkenburg will be in shortly," she said.

Joel's mother led them to the dining room, which had a very warm feel to it. It had a large, arched doorway, but was completely enclosed otherwise, giving a feeling of privacy. There was a long buffet against a wall with two antique lamps giving off a soft light.

Against the wall opposite the door was a cushioned bench. Above it was the only window in the room, which looked out to a wooded area beside the house. The room had a feeling of coziness to it, and had been built just for family meals. There was another, very large formal dining room on the other side of the kitchen meant for company.

"Hessa, why don't you sit here next to Joel," his mother said.

38

As they got themselves situated, Joel's father walked in. He had a commanding presence, even though he looked like he was a couple of inches shorter than his son. Joel looked at his dad when he came in, but instead of greeting him, he looked at his father with what seemed like fearful, uneasy respect. His father looked unsmilingly at Hessa, and glanced back at his son. He seemed to fill the room with his powerful air, which made Hessa very uncomfortable.

As he sat down he asked Joel, "Are you going to introduce me to your friend, Joel?"

"Dad, this is Hessa," Joel said simply.

"Hello young lady. I hope Joel has made you feel at home?"

"Yes, sir, thank you," Hessa answered.

She could see right away that the dynamics of the Volkenburg household were stiff and formal. She took her time putting her napkin in her lap, feeling very small but conspicuous. Joel's father seemed very much like her own—stern and unyielding. Her head started to pound.

Helen brought in soup for the first course. In honor of their guest she had prepared a Boston classic: clam chowder. She explained the history to their guest.

"Hessa, clam chowder has been around Boston for over 250 years. The first known printing of the recipe was in the Boston Evening Post in 1751. I try to keep it as close to the original recipe as I can, so hopefully this won't be a problem with your kosher needs. If it is, I can bring you something else."

"Oh, I am not Jewish, Helen, but thank you for being so thoughtful," Hessa replied.

"I was sure Joel had told us you were, Hessa. You're from Jerusalem, correct?" his mother asked.

"Yes, I am from Jerusalem, but I am Palestinian," she said hesitantly.

"Do you think your family would approve of your choice in a Jewish friend, Hessa?" Joel's father asked.

"I did not know Joel was Jewish, Mr. Volkenburg. We had not discussed that," she said, feeling ashamed and guilty, somehow.

"Well, I just hope we aren't getting you into any trouble," Mr. Volkenburg said.

Joel felt his face get hot, and the anger rising in him. *Good one, Dad. Always the perfect host*, he thought to himself. Growing up, Joel had very infrequently invited friends to his home. His father's cold, austere behavior kept his friends from wanting to be there. Joel's search for companionship took him anywhere but his own home to find a more casual, friendly atmosphere.

The tension in the air was almost palpable, so Joel tried to lighten things up.

"Tomorrow I'm taking Hessa to see some sights around Boston."

"That's nice of you, Joel," his mother said. "Don't forget to take her to the Museum of Fine Arts. That's not to be missed. By the way, Hessa, how did you enjoy the ballet last evening?"

"It was wonderful. Thank you so much for the tickets. I loved looking at the beautiful architecture and furnishings almost as much as the ballet," Hessa said.

Joel responded to his mother's suggestion: "The museum's actually a good idea. It's so cold out right now, you wouldn't enjoy walking the Freedom Trail. We can't spend the whole day outside tomorrow, but I'm taking Hessa ice skating at Frog Pond in Boston Common," Joel said.

"Just make sure you return her to her family in one piece, Joel," his mother said.

Joel's father barely said a word the rest of the meal. Helen served duck with a cherry sauce, over which Joel and Hessa exchanged glances, and smiled impishly at one another.

Joel's mother asked if there was a problem, and they explained they'd had duck last evening for dinner. She didn't share in their amusement. They ate the rest of their dinner in relative quiet.

Helen came in to clear away the dishes, and Joel's mother asked her to bring coffee and dessert into the living room.

As they got up and started to make their way to the living room, Joel's father said, "I'm going to need to excuse myself. I have a pile of work to do. It was nice meeting you, Hessa. Safe travels." Hessa thanked him for having her, and he disappeared into his office.

As they were settling into the living room, Joel attempted to cut the tension.

"How are things with David?" he asked finally, explaining to Hessa about his brother.

"He'll be in London next month for a conference. He's one of the presenters, so he's been hard at work preparing for it," his mother said.

Helen came in to let Mrs. Volkenburg know she had a phone call, so she excused herself as well. Joel and Hessa sat down, and Helen brought in a chocolate mousse with raspberry sauce and served them.

"Sorry about my father, Hessa. That's just the way he is. Mr. 'Life of the Party'."

"I understand, Joel. My father is very similar…not very talkative. He seems to only know how to give orders." They looked at each other knowingly and nodded at the same time. They both laughed, realizing they shared something that crosses any race or religious boundaries.

Joel's mother walked back into the room and apologized for having to take the call. She explained that she was chairing a New Year's Eve fund raising event, and had the horrible news that the orchestra they'd hired had to cancel.

"I'm just not sure what I'm going to do at this point. With New Year's a little over a week away, I have no idea where I'll be able to find

41

another orchestra. This is an absolute disaster. Well, I guess I know what I'll be doing for the next few days," Joel's mother said.

Joel and Hessa chatted for a while as his mother sipped her coffee thoughtfully. He finally stood up and thanked her for dinner, and told her he was going to take Hessa back to the hotel.

"Hessa, it was a pleasure meeting you. Thank you for coming. Have a good trip home," Mrs. Volkenburg said.

"Thank you, Mrs. Volkenburg. I enjoyed meeting you and Mr. Volkenburg, and seeing your beautiful home. Please thank Miss Helen for dinner."

Joel and Hessa put their coats and gloves on and walked to Joel's car in silence. The evening air was very cold and still. Hessa looked up at the sky, marveling at how clear it was, and how many stars she could see when they got outside of Boston.

Joel looked up at the sky as though he was trying to see what she was looking at, and seemed to read her thoughts.

"When I was a kid, I used to go out to the backyard at night and lie in the grass and look up at the stars. I used to stare at them for hours, trying to find the Big and Little Dippers, and wondering what else was out there in the universe."

"This must have been a wonderful place to spend your childhood," Hessa said.

"It was okay," Joel said, thinking about how lonely it had been in that big house with virtually no one to talk to during his younger years.

They finally walked to his car, and Joel opened the door for Hessa. As they drove back to the Charles Hotel, Joel told her about his friends, and how they'd grown up together. When they arrived at the hotel, Joel got out and opened Hessa's door for her, walking her into the lobby.

"Joel, thank you again for a wonderful evening," she said.

"I'm sorry for my parents, Hessa. They're a little stiff and starchy. That was their way of entertaining my friends. You can see why I spent a lot of my childhood at Henry and Eddie's houses," he said with an uncomfortable laugh.

42

"I understand, Joel. My father is the same way. My mother is very kind, though, and we are close, so I am thankful for that."

Joel told Hessa when he would be over to pick her up the next day for the museum. He walked her to the elevator and waited with her until the doors opened. She smiled at him and waved as the doors were closing.

He walked out of the hotel to his car, and went over in his mind how he would be able to get her to open up about her family life, to see what her true feelings were about this life of control and strict obedience in which she was subjected.

He drove off into the night thinking about her, trying to memorize in his mind every feature on her face, how she walked, the soft fragrance she wore, grasping for anything to hang on to as he faced the invevitability of her leaving for home. The thought stabbed at his heart, and he realized he was falling in love with a woman he barely knew—a woman who had been promised to someone else.

His emotions were mixed with sorrow and anger, motivated by the urge to fight for her, but he felt helpless. What could he do? He had always found a way to get what he wanted in life, but this...what was the answer? He knew he would have to find a way...somehow.

CHAPTER 6

The next morning Joel showed up at the hotel, and Hessa was waiting outside. His heart jumped at the sight of her.

"What are you doing outside?" Joel asked without saying hello.

"Look at this day!" Hessa exclaimed. It was cold and crisp, but sunny and clear. "I needed to be out in this beautiful sunshine!"

Her cheeks had turned bright pink, and she looked like a little girl who had been out playing in the snow.

Joel opened the car door for Hessa, and they drove to the museum. As they entered the drive that led up to the place, Hessa exclaimed, "This is magnificent! I had no idea..."

The place was enormous, and she looked wide-eyed at the majestic buildings that stood before her. They spent a good part of the day there, with Joel acting as tour guide. He was happy he'd remembered so much about the different exhibits so he could impress Hessa.

They began in the Chinese and Japanese art, and walked to the opposite wing to the Egyptian and Italian exhibits, continuing on to the Old Masters Paintings which led to the European exhibit. Hessa was especially fond of that exhibit, so they spent quite a while going from painting to painting as Joel happily showed her his favorites.

They stopped for lunch at a restaurant inside the museum, and chatted about everything they'd taken in so far. After lunch Joel took her into the museum gift shop, and when they got to the jewelry, she made a comment about a necklace in the case that she found very unusual.

She walked on and found a book that displayed many of the museum exhibits, which she picked up and paged through. While she did

45

that, Joel quickly bought the necklace. It really *was* beautiful, and even though his motives weren't totally pure, he didn't care. He wanted her to have something that would make her think of him when she wore it.

The necklace was white gold with exotic branches and leaves swirling and intertwining around each other. They met at a point in which a single pearl hung down.

Hessa walked over to the cash register to buy the book for her mother and father, and then turned to look for Joel. He was standing at the end of a counter, looking at her with a smile on his face. She walked over to him.

"What is on your mind, Joel? You look as though you have a secret."

"No," he simply answered, and took her hand to guide her out.

She gently pulled her hand away, pretending to look for something in her purse. They walked outside and as they approached Joel's car, he pulled something out of his pocket. It was a box. She looked at him quizzically, and he handed it to her.

"What is this?"

"Just something to remember your day at the museum," he answered. She opened the box, and there was the necklace she had commented on in the shop.

"Oh Joel, I cannot believe you did this!" She stared down at the necklace, glimmering in the bright December sunlight. "I cannot take this."

"Sure you can. Put it on!" he said excitedly. He took his gloves off and pulled the necklace out of the box. He fastened it around her neck.

She looked at him hesitantly and then, seeming resigned, she asked, "How does it look?"

"Beautiful," he said, looking down at her with a smile.

She turned away as she felt her cheeks get hot, embarrassed at her reaction to him.

They got into his car and drove to their next destination—Frog Pond. When they arrived, Hessa looked around and smiled.

"I recognize this place. This is in the same area where my parents and I took our tour when I first arrived."

"Yeah, this is Boston Common," Joel replied. "Come on, let's get you some skates!"

Joel got his own skates out of the trunk of his car, along with thick socks for himself, and socks he'd bought for Hessa when he was at the Ski Market the previous day. After they picked up Hessa's skates, the two sat down to lace up. Joel finished tying his skates first and noticed Hessa was having trouble getting hers tied tight enough.

"Here, I'll do it."

As he kneeled down to unlace her skates and start the job over, she looked down at him. *He is so handsome*, she thought to herself, *and he has a quiet confidence.* He seemed so concerned with how she felt and what she thought.

The tender way he looked at her, his easy smile, his laughter—all made her heart stir. He seemed big and powerful, yet had a sort of gentleness about him. Joel was so very different than any man she had ever known. She felt a sudden sadness, and realized she was developing feelings for this young American man.

"Oh, no," she softly said aloud.

"Is something wrong? Did I tie your skates too tight?" Joel asked.

"No…no, they feel fine. I…was just thinking about something I needed to do before I leave for home," she lied.

"Can it wait 'til you get home tonight?"

"Yes, I suppose…it will be all right." She said, trying to regain her composure.

Joel completed his skate lacing task and stood up, taking both of her hands in his. He pulled her up and her skates promptly slipped out from under her. He put his arms around her and pulled her back up, making sure she was standing securely on her two feet before letting go.

47

She stood for a moment, and again the skates seemed to have a mind of their own.

"You're not starting out very well," Joel teased.

"I do not know if this was such a good idea," Hessa replied, looking down at her skates, arms spread out wide.

Joel took one of her hands and put his other hand around her waist. "Let's start out slowly. It's just a matter of getting a good rhythm. Push off with your back foot, and glide, then with the other foot. Push, glide, push, glide. That's it! You're getting it!"

Hessa held on for dear life, asking Joel to stay with her and not let go. "Never," he said, looking down at her.

When she looked up at him, the warm reflection in his eyes made her heart leap once again. She was afraid the emotion in her own eyes might betray her, so she quickly looked away, and furiously tried to concentrate on her newly acquired ice skating technique.

As they continued skating around Frog Pond, Hessa gained confidence in her new experience. She finally let go of Joel, and playfully skated ahead of him. He skated past her, and turned around to skate backwards. She tried to gain on him, but he skated faster backwards than she did skating forward.

He continued building momentum as he wove blindly around the rink, and started to laugh at her efforts to catch up with him. All of a sudden he hit something with a thud, and before he could think, the person he had run into fell down and Joel tumbled backwards right over the top of him. Hessa didn't know how to stop her skates, so she followed him into the pile.

The older man on the bottom of the human mound was very large and heavyset, and was laughing so hard his face had turned red. Joel and Hessa, after realizing he wasn't hurt, started to laugh just as hard.

The three lay in the middle of the rink in such hysterics they were unable to get up. Every time they made an attempt they all fell into fits of laughter again and fell back down. Tears were running down their cheeks and they began losing strength from laughing.

When the hilarity finally did subside, Hessa looked at the jolly old man and exclaimed, "You look like Santa Claus!"

Joel turned to her and asked, "How do you know about Santa Claus?"

"Just because I'm from Israel doesn't mean I'm completely cut off from the rest of the world. I have seen pictures of him, and there are Christian sections of Jerusalem that decorate with Santa."

The 'Santa Claus' man spoke up. "Well, ho, ho, ho. Merry Christmas, kids. You made my day. I haven't laughed that hard in a long time." When the three finally made it back to their feet, 'Santa' waved and skated off.

"Would you like some hot chocolate?" Joel asked.

"After that I could use a break," Hessa said smiling and dabbing her eyes.

They skated over to the warming hut, walked in and took off their skates. Joel bent down to rub Hessa's feet as she drank her chocolate.

"Oh, my feet do hurt," she said. "That feels so good!"

"You know, I think that's enough skating for you today, young lady," Joel said. "Are you hungry? I have another historical monument for you to see, but we can eat there."

Hessa did admit she was tired and hungry, so Joel returned her skates while she put her boots back on. He pulled his own boots on and put both their pairs of socks inside his skates.

As they walked to his car, Hessa was tired but brimming with excitement. "That was the most fun I think I have ever had!" she exclaimed.

"Really? Skating?" he asked.

"Oh yes. I would like to do that again sometime," she replied.

Joel guessed she probably hadn't been exposed to a lot of sports with her family background.

49

"If you think that was fun, you should try skiing. It makes skating look boring."

"I could never ski," she admitted.

"That's what you said about skating! When you get back from winter break, I'll teach you how."

They got in Joel's car and started to drive. "You said we are going to eat at a monument?" Hessa asked.

"Well, not exactly. It's an historical landmark, though. It's called the Union Oyster House, and it's the oldest restaurant in Boston. It was built in 1714, and opened as a restaurant in 1826. It has an interesting history, including some of the people who lived there. One of the most interesting is Louis Philippe, King of France, who lived there in exile."

"Really? I cannot wait to see it," Hessa said.

"Well, don't get your hopes up. It's on a very narrow street, and it doesn't exactly jump out at you. It's not very fancy inside, but the food is great, and it's just fun to experience it."

They walked in and true to Joel's explanation the Union Oyster House was plain, dark, and smelled like heaven. They sat down and ordered, chatting about the day. Hessa teased Joel about the history of Boston going back less than 400 years. She told Joel about things in Jerusalem that dated back thousands of years.

"Well, in America, we like to tear old things down and build new things," he laughed, and reminded her that America itself wasn't actually that old.

<hr/>

After dinner, Hessa started to feel the activities of the day catch up with her. "I am sorry, Joel. All of a sudden I am so tired and achy. I had better go back to the hotel before I fall asleep sitting up."

They made their way out of the restaurant, taking along a box of tea from Union Oyster House, with an explanation plastered over it about the Boston Tea Party. She thought it would be fun to give to her brother and his wife.

As they drove back to the hotel, Hessa leaned back in her seat and closed her eyes. She was completely worn out. Joel looked over at her as she absent-mindedly rubbed one of her arms.

"I think I pushed you a little too hard today. I was so anxious for you to experience everything in Boston, I think I got caught up in the excitement and literally dragged you from one end of downtown to the other."

She opened her eyes and looked over at him. "I had a wonderful day, Joel. Even if I am tired and have a few bumps, it was worth it. Thank you so much for showing me your city."

"I'm sorry I didn't think about how sore you're going to be tomorrow. I guess I was just having too much fun."

"It is still early enough for me to get plenty of sleep. My flight doesn't leave until mid-morning tomorrow, so I will take a long hot bath before I go to bed."

"May I drive you to the airport?" Joel asked.

"I've hired a car…"

"Why don't you cancel it? I can take you."

"No, Joel, you do not need to drive all the way over here just to take me to the airport. That is such an inconvenience. I can take the car."

"It's no inconvenience. I'll pick you up tomorrow morning, and I won't take 'no' for an answer," he teased.

"All right—if you are sure it is not too much of an imposition," she replied.

As they arrived at the hotel, he pulled up in front of the entrance and ran around to open the car door. He helped her out, noticing she was already feeling the affects of their afternoon of ice skating. He took her arm and let her lean on him as they walked into the lobby and over to the elevator. She loosed the grip on his arm, but took his hand and quickly squeezed it

"I do not know when I have had so much fun, Joel. Thank you again for a wonderful day."

"I'll be waiting for you here tomorrow morning."

"I will look forward to seeing you," she said, her eyes sparkling.

She smiled at him as the elevator doors closed. Joel turned once again and walked out of the hotel, happy that he would see her one last time before she left to go back home.

As he got into his car, thoughts of her were turning over and over in his mind. Did he see something change in her today? He could swear he felt she was warming up to him. Was he imagining it, or did he sense she had feelings for him?

The thought crept in of her leaving and not being able to see her for another month. His stomach began to churn at the notion. He didn't want to think about that just now. He remembered the two of them lying on top of 'Santa' after the three of them had fallen, and he laughed out loud. What a great day. What an incredible girl. He was in love, and had to find a way to get her to fall in love with him.

Joel got up at the crack of dawn the next morning and stopped on his way to the hotel to pick up coffee for himself, and a mocha latte for Hessa. He'd had a difficult time falling asleep the night before, tossing and turning, trying to put thoughts of her out of his mind.

His thoughts turned into worry—worry about her father, and what he would do if he found out his daughter had been spending time with an American Jewish man. He pulled up to the hotel and walked into the lobby where Hessa was waiting with several large suitcases.

"It looks as though you're moving back to Israel," he teased.

She smiled, but her smile this morning was sad. Her eyes couldn't hide what she was feeling. She didn't want to leave Joel. She had been so excited to go home for the break to see her family and welcome her new little niece or nephew into the world. She'd spent the most wonderful weekend of her life with an incredible man, and now she felt as though her heart was being torn in two.

"You look like you're hurting from our ice skating excursion yesterday," Joel said.

"Yes, a little," she said with her eyes cast down.

The bellmen loaded her suitcases into Joel's car, and they started off for the airport. It was quiet for several long minutes. Finally Joel spoke.

"When will you be back from break?"

"Since the new semester doesn't start until January 25, I will not be back until the 20th," she replied.

"I'll miss you, Hessa."

"Joel, you mustn't say that. I had a wonderful time with you, but we need to remain friends only."

"I'm sorry Hessa. I can't believe you only have platonic feelings for me," Joel said quietly.

Hessa didn't answer. She felt so ashamed that she had betrayed her feelings, and he'd seen through her. She didn't have to admit it, however. Words failed her, and she could hear her heart pounding in her ears. Fear began to creep in…what if her father would suspect something? He knew her better than Joel. If Joel could see what was in her heart, wouldn't her father?

They drove along in silence. Joel knew he'd once again said something completely inappropriate. She came from a different world, and he didn't know how to handle himself with her. It was as if he was trying to corner a frightened young deer, and she was looking for a way to escape.

When they arrived at the airport, Joel pulled into the short-term parking lot and got out. He pulled her suitcases out of the trunk, and she picked up two of the smaller bags. He rolled the large one along, stacking another on top of it. They walked in silence for a while, and Joel finally turned to her.

"Hessa, I didn't mean to speak out of turn again. I seem to keep putting my foot in my mouth. I just like you so much." he smiled weakly.

"I like you too, Joel. Your kindness to me was something I will never forget. I like you too...." she repeated.

The two walked into the airport and up to the counter to check her bags. When she received her boarding pass Joel walked her to the security checkpoint entrance. He turned to face her, and she looked up at him. He impulsively bent down, and quickly brushed his lips against her cheek. Her eyes flew open, and she pulled away as she continued to look up at him, putting her hand to her cheek.

He straightened up, smiling hopefully at her. As she looked back at him, he wondered what was going on in her mind. His question was answered when a tear slowly made its way down her cheek. She bit her lip and looked up at him, but she said nothing. Another tear slid down her cheek.

"Don't cry, little Hessa," he said. "I was drawn to you the minute I saw you the first day of school."

"I remember you," she said, her eyes wide. "I saw you standing outside Austin Hall. Yes, that *was* you. Oh Joel, what have I done? Why did I ever agree to see you? I need to leave...I am going to miss my plane."

"Hessa, can I call you in Jerusalem?"

"No, please don't. If my father found out..." she turned and walked into the security gate without finishing her sentence. She moved forward in the line, her head down.

"Hessa, don't leave like this," Joel said as he inched along the outside of the security area. Just as she was about to go through the metal detector, she turned and waved to him, putting her hand to her lips. As she passed through security and picked up her things, she walked off without looking back and disappeared from sight.

CHAPTER 7

Hessa boarded the plane with her thoughts in turmoil. She hated leaving Joel looking forlorn and confused, but she had felt the same way. She found her seat by the window and looked out at nothing in particular.

She tried desperately to hold back the tears, but they couldn't be stopped. She put a book up to her face to hide the shameful display of emotion, but kept having to put it down to find a tissue in her purse to wipe her eyes.

The flight was packed, which was a disappointment to Hessa. She wanted to stew in her sadness without anyone looking over at her questioningly. The woman beside her was reading a book, and kept looking up to glance at her with sympathy.

The woman finally spoke. "I'm sorry dear, but I can't just sit here without asking you if there's something I can do for you."

"No," Hessa replied. "I'm sorry. I guess I am sad to leave America." It was the best excuse she could come up with.

"You must have had quite an experience here to be crying that hard over leaving," the woman said.

"Yes, I did," she said simply.

"Where are you from?" the woman asked Hessa.

"Jerusalem."

"What were you doing in Boston?"

"I am attending Harvard."

The woman looked at her quizzically. "Well then you must be on winter break. I imagine you'll be back soon. You *will* be back, won't you?"

"Yes, but I hadn't finished everything I needed to do before returning home," she said, trying to sound businesslike.

"Oh, a boy," the woman said, looking at Hessa like she was trying to read her mind. Hessa just sat looking straight ahead biting her lip, willing herself not to start crying again.

"What's your name, dear?" the woman asked.

"Hessa," she said sadly.

"My name is Ruth. Why don't you tell me about what's making you so sad? I'm a good listener, and we have a long flight to Tel Aviv. I wouldn't be able to live with myself knowing I'd sat with someone next to me for fourteen hours and didn't even try to do something to help. He must be someone very special."

"Oh, he is!" Hessa blurted out, at once ashamed for admitting the woman was right. Ruth smiled encouragingly at her, and she looked away for a minute, embarrassed she had said anything. Ruth patiently looked over at Hessa, waiting for her to continue.

Finally Hessa looked over at her and slowly began her story. She told Ruth how she and Joel had met, the things they had done together in the last few days, and the fear that her father might figure things out when she got home.

"I have never been treated this way. He is the kindest man I have ever met, but my father has already chosen someone else for me. I do not know what to do."

"Hessa, you need a miracle." Ruth said simply.

"I certainly do," Hessa replied.

"This is something you don't want to leave to chance, dear. You need a miracle, so it's time to get to work—on your knees in prayer," Ruth said.

"That's just the problem. I am Muslim and the boy I met is Jewish. This could never work. Even if my father hadn't chosen anyone for me, he would never approve of a Jewish boy. He is very strict and has beliefs that would never allow this to happen."

"Well, I believe in a God who can make anything happen. This could change the whole course of your life. Whether you believe what I'm saying or not, I'll pray for that miracle for you and ...what is his name?"

"Joel," she replied. "Joel Volkenburg."

"Volkenburg...do you know if he's related to Eli Volkenburg?" Ruth asked.

"Yes! That is his father. He is a professor of law at Harvard."

"Oh, my goodness! Eli Volkenburg—I haven't thought about that family in some time..." Ruth looked thoughtfully and seemed to drift away for a moment.

"Hessa, I actually know Eli, or know of him. Would you like to hear a story?" Hessa nodded.

Ruth was a bit older than Eli, but had a connection through his parents. She told of how she was originally from Haarlem, in the Netherlands. When Ruth was too young to remember, the Nazis invaded. Her family was Jewish, and the Jews were being taken to concentration camps.

Her mother and father had known a watch repairman by the name of Casper ten Boom. The ten Boom family started hiding Jews from the Nazis because of Casper's love and support for the Jewish people.

In early 1942, Ruth's parents took her and her two brothers to the ten Boom's house, where they had hidden in a secret room that had been built in the bedroom of their daughter, Corrie. They stayed there for several months until it was arranged for them to escape to America.

While Ruth's family was there, Eli's parents, Albert and Sarah Volkenburg, also came to stay. Albert's parents had been captured and taken to Auschwitz, but before his father was taken, he had told Albert of the ten Boom family. Eli's mother and father were newlyweds and very young. They were living with Sarah's parents.

One day when Albert and Sarah were away from the house, the Nazis came and took Sarah's sister and parents. They returned home to find the house empty. They knew they had to try to get to the ten Boom

57

home. The ten Booms were able to arrange for Albert and Sarah to escape to America, dressed as medical personnel.

When they arrived in Boston, Albert went to work as an apprentice in an investment house in Boston. He had no college education, but was a brilliant man, and worked his way up, eventually becoming president of the company.

"My parents and I miraculously survived the Holocaust. They kept in contact with the Volkenburgs for several years, but we moved to Connecticut when I was still very young, and they lost touch. I never met Eli. The most amazing thing about this story, Hessa, is that the ten Boom family wasn't Jewish. They risked their lives to save the Jews," Ruth concluded.

"I do not understand," Hessa said. "Why would they do that for people who didn't even believe as they? It has been my belief that people fight and die for their own religion, not for others'."

"It does seem that way at times. The ten Boom family was an incredible example of how people can look past their own differences to help others. Their whole family ended up in concentration camps. Casper died just ten days after he was captured. Corrie ten Boom survived, but her beloved sister, Betsy, died in the concentration camp. Before she died, Betsy told Corrie, 'There is no pit so deep that God's love is not deeper still.'"

"Whatever became of Sarah's family?" Hessa inquired.

"She never saw or heard anything of them again," Ruth replied.

Hessa was profoundly affected by the story. "What of Corrie ten Boom? What became of her?" she asked finally.

"In 1975, I heard Corrie speak. She'd written a book called 'The Hiding Place'. I'd heard she'd become a speaker and travelled all over the world for various speaking engagements. I wanted to meet her, since my family had stayed at the Ten Boom home during the war. When I read she was going to be in New York for an engagement, I drove down to where she was speaking. After hearing her, I went up to thank her for the incredible thing her family did for mine during the war.

"I was moved by her forgiveness of the Nazis. I'd read about how during a speaking engagement in Germany, the guard who had tormented and killed her sister Betsy approached Corrie. She recognized him as he walked toward her and when he put his hand out to shake hers, her hand stayed at her side. Angry, vengeful thoughts went through her. She then prayed silently to God that she couldn't forgive him, and that God would have to give her forgiveness."

Hessa sat spellbound as Ruth continued he story. "She said that as she took his hand the most incredible thing happened. Into her heart sprang a love for this stranger that almost overwhelmed her."

Ruth turned to Hessa and said, "How else could something like this happen without God?"

Hessa looked incredulously at Ruth and said, "I do not know what to say. I have never heard anything like this. Where I live, there is so much hatred between the different groups of people. I am amazed to hear such a story of love without conditions."

She thought about Mr. Volkenburg, and how cold he had been the night she'd spent at their house for dinner. She wondered if Joel knew anything about what had happened to his grandparents at the Ten Boom home.

Joel didn't appear to have a problem with her religion, however. He seemed as though he would love her no matter what. Her heart warmed at the thought of him and how he was so genuine in accepting her, even though she had told him about her strict father. She wondered if his love would last if Joel knew the full truth about him.

The plane finally touched down in Tel Aviv in what felt to Hessa record time. Her conversation with Ruth had been so captivating, the trip seemed to last just a couple of hours instead of fourteen. They rolled down the runway and up to the terminal. As everyone was preparing to leave the aircraft, Ruth turned to Hessa and gave her a business card.

"It was no coincidence we sat together. Make sure we keep in touch, Hessa. I want you to call me if you ever need to talk, and to keep me up on what happens with your Joel. Remember, I know where to find you!" she winked, and turned to get out of her seat.

As Hessa walked through the terminal to baggage claim, she got lost in the story Ruth had told her on the plane. *It is wonderful to know there are people like the ten Booms in the world. They certainly didn't need to help the Jews, but to risk their lives to help them was truly amazing*, Hessa thought.

Hessa turned the corner to baggage claim, and standing there waiting for her were her parents. She ran to them, hugging her mother then turning to her father she grasped his hands and kissed his cheek. Her father told them to wait there while he went over to get Hessa's bags.

She told her mother about school, and how difficult it was. Hessa then told her about how large her workload would be for winter semester. She was elated to find Hessa was adjusting and working hard at Harvard.

Her mother, Muna, had married Hessa's father when she was only eighteen, and was very close to Hessa and her brother. After Hessa's birth, her mother had complications that prevented her from having more children.

Her father had deeply resented Muna's inability to bear more children, but as yet hadn't divorced her or married a second wife to expand their family. Hessa's father, Husaam, ruled his wife and children with an iron fist. No one dared cross her father. What he said was law.

Hessa's father collected her suitcases and they walked out to the waiting car. The city of Jerusalem was so different from Boston, but the crowded feel to the city was very similar.

As they wound through the narrow streets, Hessa tried to get her thoughts straight—about how she would answer questions her father might pose to her. Her father asked her about her flight, and she told him how quickly it seemed to go, but didn't mention anything about the woman she had met on the plane.

Hessa and her mother got out when they pulled up to the apartment. Her father parked and got the luggage out. The Bishara family lived in the Old City of Jerusalem, just about a half mile from the Dome of the Rock at the Temple Mount. Hessa walked up to her small bedroom and stayed there unpacking until dinner.

When she was called to come down for the evening meal she took her time, trying to compose herself. She didn't want to say or do anything to make her father suspicious of her activities at Harvard. It had taken a lot of convincing for her to be allowed to go there in the first place.

As they were finishing dinner her father said, "Hessa, you are very quiet. You haven't told us much about school."

"I suppose I am just tired from the flight," she said. "School has been wonderful, but I am afraid I do not have time for much of anything more than my studies."

"Have you made any friends?" he asked.

"There are some girls in my dorm who have been very nice, but we are all so busy we haven't done very much together outside of school."

She changed the subject to her brother and the anticipation of the baby. Her mother was very excited to update Hessa on her sister-in-law's condition and their plans for a celebration after the baby was born.

Her father got up from the table and went to his office, closing the door. Hessa and her mother chatted about the differences between Israel and America, and how wonderful she thought American food was. She also told her about the football game she had attended with the girls in the dorm.

So far, so good, she thought to herself.

CHAPTER 8

Joel awakened on Christmas morning to the sun shining through his windows. He got up and looked outside. It had snowed overnight, and the sun glittered off the newly fallen mounds of white flakes in the backyard. He felt a stab in his heart when he remembered that Hessa would be in Israel by now.

He decided he'd better keep busy so he dressed and went outside for a long run. Christmas was such a lonely day for him. All his friends would be celebrating the holiday with their families, and it was just another day for him and his family.

For some reason this day had bothered him his whole life. When he was small he longed to be a Christian just so he could celebrate like his friends. He never mentioned it to his parents...they wouldn't have understood.

He ran by Henry's house, which was only two blocks away from his own home. It was all lit up, with several cars parked in the driveway. He had the urge to run up to the front door and ring the bell so Mrs. Worthing would invite him in to be a part of their day.

He shrugged his shoulders slightly and ran past their house, continuing to look into their windows, hoping to get a glimpse of life inside. He felt just as he had when he was a young boy--wanting to be a part of the Christmas celebration, but only being able to peer through the windows longingly.

He continued his run, and the further he went the better he felt. When he was finally exhausted, he returned home. He went inside and ran upstairs to shower and change. His mother came up to his door and knocked.

"Come on in."

"Joel, are you going anywhere today?" she asked.

"I just got back from a run, but I need to pack for tomorrow."

"When you're done packing, could you do me a favor and pick up dinner at White Horse? It'll be ready at five. Helen made enough dinners for the week since she'll be at her daughter's, but I'm in the mood for the White Horse fettuccini and baby vegetables."

"Sure, Mom," he replied.

Joel was actually glad she'd given him a task to keep his mind off Hessa. He put everything out that he would need for the week's ski trip and then packed it in his suitcase. He restlessly kept himself busy for the remainder of the day with little jobs, including shoveling snow off the back patio.

The last task was to run over to White Horse to pick up dinner. Frank, the owner, was waiting for him when he arrived. Business was slow, so he was sitting at a table reading the paper.

"Hello, Joel! How're things with the big Harvard man?" he asked.

"Great," Joel replied. "We're on break, so I'm leaving to go skiing tomorrow."

"Ah, to be young again," Frank said wistfully. "Make sure you ski a run for me, Joel. I used to be a great skier. Did I ever tell you that?"

"No, sir," Joel said respectfully.

"I was a ski jumper. Skied all over the United States and Canada when I was your age!" Frank exclaimed.

"You never told me that, Frank," Joel said.

"Yeah, I wanted to go to the Olympics. Then I met Gia, and my whole world changed."

"What happened?"

"She was visiting her aunt and uncle who'd moved to America. Her uncle loved to watch ski jumping, so they went to a competition in Lake Placid. I was there, and met her and her uncle. I wouldn't leave her alone! When she went back home to Greece, I followed her. She was from

64

a small island. Her father wasn't very happy at first, but I told him I was a successful American businessman. I lied," he laughed.

"It took some time for me to convince Gia to marry me and go back to America, but she finally realized she couldn't live without me," Frank said with a smile.

"That's not how I remember it!" It was Gia. "Don't believe a word of what this old man is telling you, Joel. He was so persistent I finally gave up and decided to put him out of his misery. We got married on the island where I lived, and I moved with him to America." She grinned at her husband. "It was hard leaving my family behind, but it was worth it."

Frank brought the fettuccini out and Joel could smell the parmesano reggiano and truffles. "Wow, that smells great Frank," he said, and took the bag of food.

"Enjoy your time skiing, Joel. Before you know it you'll find your own Gia, and go running off to convince her to marry you! It's called fate, my boy."

Joel said goodbye to Frank and Gia and got back in his car. As he was driving home, he thought about what Frank had said about 'fate'. The question darted through his mind about his encounters with Hessa. Harvard was a large school, and the chances of him running into her several times, he a senior, her a freshman, with different majors, was quite a coincidence—or was it?

He then reflected on how Frank had married a foreign woman who didn't want to leave her home. But he'd convinced her, and she was happy here in America. He felt encouraged by the story, and reached over to his stash of CD's and put one in, humming along to the music. He had no idea how he would convince Hessa, but Joel committed to himself that he would think of a way.

The day after Christmas Henry showed up in Joel's driveway before dawn. It was very dark and quiet, and the two were silent as they locked his skis on top of Henry's Range Rover and packed Joel's bags into the back of the vehicle. They drove the mile to Eddie's house, and the three started their journey to the Sullivan farm where Petie was staying for the holidays.

As they were leaving town, they stopped off to get some coffee and continued on their way. Henry and Eddie started to perk up a little from the caffeine and began talking about their Christmas activities. Joel felt a pang of jealousy as they laughed and exchanged stories about the different family members, and some of the things that had happened during each others' holidays.

Henry turned to Joel finally and said, "I've been trying to get in touch with you for days. Where were you all weekend?"

"I had a lot to do—things I was putting off till the break, and things my mom wanted me to do around the house."

"Yeah, I don't buy it, Joel. Your mom hires people to *water her plants!* What could she have wanted you to do?" Henry teased.

"Oh, you know, things with her computer, uh, shoveling the back patio." Joel stammered.

"You know, buddy, I won't think you're wimping out on school if you're dating some girl—that girl," Henry said, trying to find a way to open Joel up.

"What girl?" Eddie asked.

"There's no girl. Henry doesn't know what he's talking about."

"Remember when we were at Joel's parents' tent at 'the game'? A girl walked by, and Joel looked like he was gonna pass out. I know something's up, and I'm gonna drive you nuts 'til I get the answer," Henry said.

"Okay," Joel said finally. "I *did* meet someone. It was the girl you're talking about. I just took her out a couple times this weekend because her flight didn't leave for home till Monday, and she doesn't know anyone in Boston."

"You choked on your beer, man. I saw how you looked at that girl, and I gotta tell ya, she was hot!" Henry said.

"Shut up, Henry," Joel said defensively. "Don't talk about her that way. She's a good girl."

"Where's she from?" Eddie asked.

"Jerusalem."

"Wow, a girl from the 'old country'. That must have made your parents happy," Eddie said kiddingly.

"She's not Jewish. She's Palestinian," Joel said quickly.

"Whoa, Burgermeister! You better not tell your parents! I mean, could you have *picked* someone more controversial?" Henry asked.

"Henry, you're way out of line. We're not living in the dark ages. It's not like our families are going to start shooting at each other."

"Do you read newspapers or watch T.V., Joel? Where have you been? You'd better think long and hard about developing a relationship with this girl," Henry said.

"Let's change the subject," Joel said, and they finally moved on to other topics.

Joel's attention drifted back to their conversation. Would life be like this if he ended up with Hessa? Would people always assume they shouldn't be together because of their opposing backgrounds? Joel looked out the window, trying to keep Hessa's face clear in his mind. Then he leaned back and pretended to be asleep to avoid any more conversation about her.

The three friends turned into the Sullivan drive, and the wheels of the Range Rover silently crunched and squeaked on the newly-fallen snow. As always, Mrs. Sully was standing in the doorway, waving a greeting to the boys. When they got out she ran to meet them. She had dark strawberry blonde hair and a bit of extra padding on her small figure.

Joel loved being at the Sullivan's house. Every time they turned into the driveway, he felt like he was home. As they wove down the long drive, his mind drifted back to the first time the Boston friends visited the Sullivan farm.

67

The friends from Boston knew they were in for something different when they drove up to the gate for their first visit. Across the top of the gate was a large bronze pig holding a glass of ale. Underneath the sculpted pig were the words, 'Cheers from the Sullivans'.

Petie's father owned car dealerships all over New England, and was known simply as "Sully". He had hilarious ads on television, and was famous for the insane get-ups he wore in his commercials. His curly red hair, twinkly green eyes and portly frame gave him the look of a rather large leprechaun.

There was no false propriety in this home. The furniture was big, overstuffed, worn, and completely comfortable. The friends laughed, yelled at the dinner table, and had the occasional food fights along with Petie's five red-headed, freckle-faced brothers.

Petie brought the other three boys home with him often during their time at Deerfield. His home was in Bennington, Vermont, which was just over 50 miles away. The Sullivans lived on a 60-acre farm outside of town complete with horses, chickens, goats, pigs and dogs.

Joel had always been mesmerized at the affection Mr. Sully showed his wife. He marveled at the way Mr. and Mrs. Sully chatted with each other while their sons were shouting and wrestling, and his little displays of affection toward his wife.

Then there would be the sudden burst of a compliment; "Boys, isn't your mother the most beautiful woman in the world? I'm going to take her out to the barn for kisses after dinner."

The Sullivan boys would groan at their dad with feigned indigestion and retching noises, but Joel felt a strange sense of warmth when he witnessed those exhibitions of love. He had never even seen his father kiss his mother.

"Hello, my 'other sons'! I'm glad you made it safely. Come on in, Peter is just about ready. I have hot chocolate for you while you wait."

The friends walked in, took their boots off, and Eddie walked to the bottom of the staircase.

"Petie-Ann, Petie-Ann! Come on down, little girl! Do you have your makeup on yet?" Eddie wanted to get his taunts in before Petie had a chance.

He walked into the kitchen before Petie could answer. Joel and Henry were sitting at the kitchen table. Mrs. Sully's kitchen was always warm and inviting, and very colonial. The wood cabinets were dark and the floor was brick with a large braided rug covering it. Over the kitchen table hung a large wrought iron chandelier.

Mrs. Sully pulled a mug out of the cupboard for Eddie and poured hot chocolate for him. She put a handful of marshmallows into the cup and handed it to Eddie.

"Thanks, Mrs. Sully," Eddie said as he took the cup.

The younger Sullivan boys started to argue about how many marshmallows their mother had given the three guests.

"Boys, if you want more marshmallows, just ask."

She walked over to the cabinet, pulled out the bag, and poured the marshmallows into a bowl. The three younger Sullivan boys dove into it, grabbing as many as their fists could hold.

Petie came into the kitchen and immediately walked over to where Eddie was sitting. He wrapped his arm around Eddie's neck, pretending to strangle him.

"Does my makeup look okay?" Petie said in a girlish voice.

The younger Sullivan boys screamed with laughter as Eddie got up and punched Petie in the arm. Joel and Henry stood up and put their cups in the sink. Petie had already loaded his gear into the car, so they were ready to go.

"Okay boys. You be careful, and make sure you wear your helmets when skiing. Now, I'm expecting you all to be back on Saturday. You'll be staying the night here, right?" Mrs. Sully asked.

"Yes, Mommy," Petie said sarcastically. "We'll be back by about five o'clock."

"Good. That's plenty of time for dinner. Your dad and I have quite a surprise for you all after dinner. You won't want to miss it, so don't get too tired skiing all day!" his mother said.

Mrs. Sully walked the four friends to Henry's car and watched as they all piled in. As they pulled away Mrs. Sully, true to their family tradition, waved until the boys were out of sight.

They got to Killington, making good time because of the clear roads. The four quickly unloaded all their things into the rented condo located right at the bottom of the mountain. They proceeded to walk over to get passes for the week and carried their skis over by the quad chairlift, where they each stepped into their bindings and got in line.

They planned out their day while in line, where they would ski in the morning, and where to meet for lunch if they lost each other. As they sat down on the lift, Joel felt a surge of excitement as he was able to temporarily put thoughts of Hessa in the back of his mind and enjoy his favorite sport.

The week flew by and before they knew it, it was Saturday. They skied all Saturday morning and called it quits early in the afternoon, returning to the condo to get out of their ski clothes and pack the car.

Henry had pulled a muscle in his shoulder and asked Joel to drive back to the Sullivan farm. They all got in and chatted for a short time about their week before Henry, Eddie, and Petie all fell asleep, leaving Joel with his thoughts.

He'd been thankful for this getaway. It had kept him busy enough so he didn't have the pictures in his mind and memories of Hessa tormenting him constantly. But now he was alone with his reflections, and the things Henry had said just a few days earlier.

He didn't know what to do with all the conflicting emotions he had about the woman he'd fallen in love with. He turned things she'd said over and over in his mind, and things he had said to her he wished he could have taken back.

70

He drove on in silence as his friends slept, wondering how he would be able to get answers to all the questions floating in his mind. After an eternity of driving in silence he pulled into the Sullivan farm and there was Mrs. Sully again, standing at the door waving.

How does she do that? How does she know when we'll be here? She must have the boys on the lookout, Joel thought. He admitted to himself that he liked having her out there waiting for them. He felt closer to her than he felt to his own mother, and a stab of guilt shot through him.

"We're here, guys," Joel said.

The three stirred and stretched, commenting on how quickly they'd gotten back to the farm.

"That's because you guys slept the whole way. It wasn't so quick for me," Joel said sarcastically, and parked the car.

The four friends unloaded their bags and walked into the house.

CHAPTER 9

"**H**ere are my boys! How was skiing?" Mrs. Sully asked.

"It was great! Cold, but that made the snow better," Petie told his mother. "Wow, it smells great in here!"

"Well, come in and get your things put away. John Jr. has already gone back to Ohio. He's met a girl, and he went to spend part of the holidays with her family. One of you can take his room. Dinner won't be ready for an hour, so you can relax for a bit. I'm making the 'Harvard Special'!"

That was Mrs. Sullivan's way of telling them they were having steak and potatoes for dinner, with her famous creamed spinach—protein and brain food for hard-working students, she had told them. She turned and walked back into the kitchen.

After putting their things away upstairs, the four walked back down to the family room and flopped onto various over-stuffed chairs and sofas. They talked about where they should ski in the future, and made plans to take a trip to the Rockies on their next winter break. As Petie turned on the TV to channel surf, Joel got up and wandered into the kitchen to see if Mrs. Sully needed help.

"Joel, that's very sweet of you. I'll put you to work chopping vegetables for the salad."

"Ok, I'll give it a try," Joel replied.

As she instructed him on how to chop and dice the various vegetables, Joel asked, "How did you and Mr. Sully meet?"

Mrs. Sully explained to Joel how she was working at a restaurant in Maine during her 18th summer. Mr. Sully's family was vacationing in the seaside town and happened to stop in for a lobster dinner. She was their waitress.

"I couldn't get over how loud and excited the family was. Mr. Sully's father was making faces, and the six children were laughing hysterically. When they got their dinners he picked up his lobster and made it look like it was dancing across the table. The whole family was laughing so loud, the whole restaurant turned around to see what was happening. Then several tables nearby started laughing with them."

She smiled as she continued, "Mr. Sully's family seemed so happy. I had a younger sister, and growing up our family life was very bad. My father was an alcoholic, and we never knew what to expect when he came home at night. We lived in fear, so as soon as I had the chance I left and moved from Boston to Maine where I got a job as a waitress."

Mrs. Sully continued to explain that Mr. Sully was exactly as he is today—the life of the party. He was the oldest of four boys and two girls, and seemed to egg his father on the most to encourage his crazy behavior. When Mrs. Sully came to the table to ask for their order, Mr. Sully told her he had lost his appetite because he had just fallen in love. His father looked directly at his son and said right in front of her, "Then marry that girl!"

"I was swept up into the Sullivan family before I knew it. We married that fall, and have been married for 26 years. Mr. Sully was the best thing that ever happened to me, Joel. I believe God sent him to me to show me how wonderful life could really be."

"Well, I don't know if God had anything to do with it, but I'm sure glad you were able to have a better life with Mr. Sully," Joel said.

"Joel, that's a pretty cynical outlook for someone so young," Mrs. Sully replied.

"It's not cynical at all. Some people believe in a higher power, and others don't. My family has never believed. It just doesn't make logical sense. I was bar-mitzvah'd, and my brother before me, but it was just out of tradition and obligation to my grandparents. After my bar mitzvah I never heard anything about God again."

74

"That's too bad, Joel. But remember one thing—sometimes logic tells you one thing, but faith will tell you to believe in something that doesn't make sense. It's the substance of things hoped for, and the evidence of things not seen,'" Mrs. Sully said, but Joel had no idea she was quoting the Bible.

"I didn't know you were religious, Mrs. Sully. I've never heard you talk about a God."

"I've talked about God before, Joel. You just might not have been listening. It's actually more of a relationship than being religious. I always tried to be a good Catholic girl, going to mass and confession, but I felt empty inside because of my home life.

"When Mr. Sully and I first moved to Vermont, I met a woman who invited me to her home for a Bible study. I didn't know anyone, so I accepted the invitation. There were about a dozen women who met at her home, all from different backgrounds: Catholics, Protestants and one Jewish woman. They all shared a common belief though, and we've grown to be the best of friends," Mrs. Sully said.

Joel was confused, but strangely comforted. Maybe Hessa would be able to accept him as a Jew after all. Maybe they could come to some common ground where they wouldn't have to discuss religion or cultures and accept each other as they were. Mrs. Sully looked at Joel intently as he was digesting this information, and seemed to be reading his mind.

"What prompted you to ask about Mr. Sully and me?" she asked. "Have you met someone, Joel? Is she Christian and you're worried about the difference in your beliefs?"

"No..." he trailed off. He thought for a moment, and then decided, *Who could I trust more than Mrs. Sully?* He took a deep breath and shared the secret that was tormenting him.

"I met a girl. She's Palestinian, and evidently from a very strict Muslim family. I don't know if I have a future with her. I told Henry and Eddie on the way here and they got mad at me. They think I'm crazy," Joel said.

75

Mrs. Sully's face took on a painful look.

"Oh, honey, that *is* a tough one. I really don't know what to say. I know you don't want to hear this, but apart from a miracle, you might have one tough time on your hands with her family. Have you told your parents?"

"They met her. I brought her home for dinner a few days before she went back to Israel for the winter break."

"Well, this is good news," Mrs. Sully perked up. "Did your parents like her?"

"They didn't know she was Palestinian when my mother invited her to dinner."

Mrs. Sully looked at Joel with compassion in her eyes. "It didn't turn out too well, I assume?"

"Not really. My dad excused himself right after dinner and crawled back into his office. My mother barely said a word. It was really awkward. I finally made an excuse just so I could get Hessa out of there."

Mrs. Sully turned on the grill to heat it up for the steaks. "Hessa," she said, almost to herself. "What a beautiful name. I wonder what it means."

"Destiny," Joel said simply.

"Interesting," Mrs. Sully said with a smile. "Well, Joel honey, I know what my friends and I will be doing. You need to believe that a miracle could happen, so we'll pray for one."

"You don't need to do that, Mrs. Sully. I don't believe, so you'd be wasting your prayers."

"That's okay, Joel. God believes in you. He doesn't need you to believe in Him to work in your life."

Just then Patrick and Sean, along with little Mikey trailing behind, burst into the kitchen and yelled, "We're hungry! When's dinner?"

"I wonder if just once we could have you boys speak in a normal voice. You sound like I'm across the Grand Canyon," Mrs. Sully said shaking her head with a smile, and pulled the steaks out to place on the grill.

She got the orders of how everyone wanted their steaks prepared, and the boys set the table and put out the large bowl of salad that Joel had prepared. A few minutes later, Mrs. Sully told Sean to get everyone rounded up for dinner.

"Your dad's out in the barn, honey. Make sure you tell him, too. You can use the intercom," Mrs. Sully said.

Sean was happy for the job. The Sullivans' house was so large they had an intercom system throughout the house which the boys weren't allowed to use unless permitted. Previous abuses of the system had forced Mr. Sully to make it off limits. Sean ran over to the intercom and bellowed, "Dinner's on...HEY! EVERYONE! DINNER'S ON!!!"

"I don't think you needed the intercom, Sean," Mrs. Sully laughed.

Sean ran over to the side of the house to the 'mud room', got his boots and jacket on, and ran out the door to the barn, yelling for his father to come inside for dinner.

Everyone finally assembled into the dining room and all sat down, anxiously anticipating the steaks Mrs. Sully had prepared. The boys had helped her lay out all the side dishes on the buffet by the wall in the dining room. There were garlic mashed potatoes, the famous creamed spinach, salad, and hot rolls and butter.

Mrs. Sully came in with the large platter of steaks, which had little paper flags on top of each one with everyone's name so she could keep track of what each had ordered. On top of the steaks were sautéed mushrooms and onions. The Sullivan family and their friends dug into the feast with enthusiasm. Mr. Sully was the first to congratulate his wife on a job well done.

"I had Joel's help," she said.

"Oh, that's where you were!" Petie said. "We wondered where you went. Now we know. Joel wants to quit school so he can become a chef!"

They all laughed and teased each other for the rest of the meal, with the younger boys yelling to try and get a word in. Mrs. Sully finally got up and came back with two pies she had just taken out of the oven.

77

"Ok, boys, we have apple and cherry pie, and of course we need to support the locals, so we have about a dozen different kinds of Ben and Jerry's ice cream, if anyone's interested."

Everyone shouted at once, and through the chaos, Mrs. Sully was finally able to determine who wanted what. She had also brought out a plate of sharp Vermont cheddar cheese, primarily for Mr. Sully.

The group finished their pie, with Joel marveling once again at how Mrs. Sully had such patience with her large clan of boys. She didn't take any nonsense from them, but with her firm hand and Mr. Sully backing her every step of the way she was able to keep some semblance of order without raising her voice.

After the dishes were cleared away and put in the dishwasher by Sean and Petie, Mr. Sully had them return to the dining room to sit down.

"All right, men. Your mother told you before you left for your ski trip that we had a surprise for you. Ready to see what it is?"

The younger boys yelled, "Yeah! What is it?"

Mr. Sully stood up and said, "Everyone get their coats. We're going to the barn."

They all bundled up with Mrs. Sully holding Mikey back to give him his hat and gloves. The group filed out the door and made their way through the snow into the barn. Mr. Sully opened the double doors, and inside were four brand-new snowmobiles.

"Wow!" the younger boys yelled. "Cool!" They ran over to the snowmobiles and sat down on them, trying to figure out how to get them started.

Mr. Sully explained that a man who owned a snowmobile business had come in to see him about buying a couple of vans. They struck a bargain, and he had gotten a great deal on the snowmobiles.

"We're going to have to take turns, but why don't I take Mikey and Sean with me, and your mom can take Conor and Patrick. Petie, you and the guys can fight over who gets to drive the other two," Mr. Sully said.

Petie and Eddie got on one, and Henry jumped on the front of the last snowmobile. Joel obligingly climbed on behind Henry. After Mr. Sully gave instructions and warnings about the dangers of how easily snowmobiles tip over, they all started their engines and roared off.

The night was freezing and dark and clouds were covering the stars, preparing for snow to fall. The group made several stops to change drivers so everyone could get a chance to be at the helm. Mr. Sully finally gave Sean the okay to drive. He didn't have his driver's license yet, so this was a real treat for him.

Mr. Sully started to give his son some last-minute instructions when Sean took off like a shot. Mikey was holding on to his dad on the back end of the machine. He wasn't prepared for the jerk of the snowmobile, so tumbled off the back and into the snow. Mr. Sully yelled for Sean to stop, but he was so lost in the euphoria of his driving duties he wasn't paying attention. Mr. Sully finally leaned over and grabbed the brakes.

"Son, we lost your brother back there! Couldn't you hear me yelling to stop?"

"Sorry Dad," Sean said. "I wasn't paying attention."

The other three snowmobiles stopped, wondering what was going on. Mr. Sully shouted to his wife that they'd lost Mikey. She instructed Conor to let her drive, and the two went off in the direction where they had left Mikey. Joel was driving one of the snowmobiles now, and Eddie was driving the fourth. They both followed the Sullivans back to see about Mikey.

Mr. Sully was the first to reach Mikey, who was lying in the snow crying. He jumped off the snowmobile and ran over to him.

"Mikey, what hurts?" he said, trying to keep calm.

"My arm. I can't move my arm, Dad," he said tearfully.

Mr. Sully lifted Mikey and put him in front of him on the snowmobile. "It's okay, son. We'll get you over to the emergency room right away."

They raced off for the barn, with the rest of the family and friends close behind. When they parked, Mr. Sullivan carried Mikey over to their Suburban and placed him in the back seat. Mrs. Sullivan turned to the boys and assured them this wasn't the first time the local emergency room had seen a member of the Sullivan family.

She said goodbye and ran to get in the car with her husband and son, and they drove off down the driveway. The Sullivan boys and their friends walked back to the house, with Sean trailing, sullen and quiet.

"Sean, it wasn't your fault," Petie said. "Mikey just wasn't holding on tight enough."

"Yeah, I guess. I just feel bad because Mikey was really looking forward to going skiing for President's weekend. Dad was gonna take us to Mt. Snow," Sean said.

"He'll be able to go! Even if his arm's broken, he can ski with a cast on!" Petie said. The Sullivans had had several broken arms and legs among them. It just came with the territory when there were six boys in a household.

Several hours later Mr. and Mrs. Sullivan walked in with Mikey, who was in fact wearing a cast on his left arm. Patrick and Sean were in the family room asleep in front of the TV, and Petie was with his friends in the game room in back of the house, playing pool. They all heard the side door to the house open, so everyone went over to see what had happened to Mikey.

"It's okay, boys. Mikey broke his arm, but it wasn't bad—just a crack in the bone. He'll be good as new in a few weeks," Mr. Sully said.

Mikey looked tired from the trauma, along with the shot for pain he had been given at the hospital, so Mrs. Sullivan walked him upstairs to help him get ready for bed. The boys filed out of the mud room, with Patrick and Sean following their brother and mother upstairs to go to bed. Petie and his friends went back to finish their game of pool, and Mr. Sullivan went out to lock the barn. Within an hour the house was quiet. Everyone had given in to sleep from exhaustion.

CHAPTER 10

Hessa had been home for over a week. She spent a lot of her time reading a history book she had purchased at the Harvard bookstore. The book was meant for reading on the flight to Israel, but she had spent most of her time talking to Ruth. Delving into European history provided a temporary escape from the thoughts of Joel that kept creeping into her mind.

Very early one morning the phone rang. Hessa awakened with a start and heard muffled voices coming from her parents' bedroom. She got out of bed and went to see what was going on. Her sister-in-law, Safiya, had gone into labor. Her brother Imaad had called to let them know.

"Go back to bed, Hessa," her father said. "They will let us know when the baby is born."

"Could we go to the hospital to wait?"

"There is no need for that. There isn't anything we can do waiting for them at the hospital. We will see the baby when it is born."

Hessa turned and went back into her bedroom. She was very close to her brother, and had come to think of his wife as her own sister. She got into bed, but couldn't go back to sleep. She picked up her history book, but her thoughts kept going back to Joel and the kiss at the airport in Boston. She longed to be back at school. Never had she thought her life would turn out like this—falling in love with an American Jewish boy.

Yes, I have fallen in love with him, she thought to herself. What was she going to do? She had never given marriage a second thought. It had always been presumed she would marry Qasim, who came from a family very close to the Bisharas.

Now she could see why her father had been so opposed to her attending Harvard. She would be exposed to what life would really be like if she could make her own decisions. "I wish I had never gone to Boston," she said to herself sadly. She was confused, and her emotions were running away with her.

After tossing and turning while she attempted to go back to sleep, Hessa got out of bed and dressed, then walked downstairs to a still quiet and empty house. She made a pot of espresso, and put together a platter of cheese, cucumbers, figs and bread for the family. She sat alone in the kitchen, picking at the food and sipping her coffee when her mother walked in.

"Thank you for putting the meal together, *Hessa*. I sense you are nervous about Safiya. There is nothing to worry about. She's a very strong young lady. She will be fine, and the baby will be fine."

Hessa looked up at her mother and just nodded. She wished she could tell her mother what was really bothering her. Muna sat down at the table and looked at her daughter.

"You have been very quiet since you returned home. What is on your mind, Hessa? Are you really *not* happy at school? Do you think you made a mistake in choosing to go to Harvard?"

"No, I love going to school there. Sometimes I miss you so much Mother, but I know Harvard is the best place for me to be. I guess it is just different there, and I have had a difficult time adjusting to it." She was grateful that this seemed to be a good enough explanation for her mother.

The two sat and ate their meal as the sun started to shine in through the kitchen window. Hessa's father finally came in, dressed and ready for work. He picked up a cup from the table and poured espresso into it. His thoughts were clearly on other matters as he gulped down his coffee. The phone rang, and he went over to answer it. He went back over to the pot of espresso, refilled his cup, and left the room, immersed in his conversation.

"I have an idea. Why don't we go shopping for some items for the baby and Safiya? It will pass the time while we wait to hear of her progress," Hessa's mother suggested.

Hessa smiled at the idea and nodded happily. They got up from the table and put everything away. The two quickly cleaned up the kitchen, then went upstairs to get ready.

The sun shone brilliantly across a bright blue sky on that early January day. Hessa and her mother walked along the narrow winding streets of the Old City, finally stopping in a small shop. They had found a basket in the Jewish Quarter and brought it with them to a little shop that read outside, 'כ תינוקעבור ל', which in English meant 'All for Baby'.

Their basket quickly filled with everything from a baby monitor to bibs, books, mild soaps and lotions and a little stuffed camel with a big smile on its face. They finally left the shop and went down a few doors to their favorite bath shop. Everything was hand-made in different parts of Israel. They picked up lotion, soap and talc for Safiya, along with soft pink pajamas, a robe, and plush slippers.

They stopped for lunch at a little sidewalk café and as they were making their way to a table, Hessa heard someone calling her name. She looked up and there was Ruth, the woman whom she had met on the plane. She was sitting with a group of people at the café.

"What a surprise! It's so good to see you!" Ruth said to Hessa.

Hessa walked over to their table and introduced Ruth to her mother, and explained that they had sat next to each other on the flight to Tel Aviv.

"You have a lovely daughter, Mrs. Bishara," Ruth said. "Hessa told me about her plans to major in history, and how she wants to become a teacher. It's such an admirable profession—so needed. We had quite a discussion of world history on our plane ride. Your daughter is very knowledgeable."

"Hessa has always had a love for history. As she got older, she asked for history books as gifts, of all things," her mother said.

"Well, I hope we can keep in touch. I don't live far from Boston, so if you ever want a break from school and a home-cooked meal, make sure to call me. You have my card, Hessa. I know how homesick you must get, and sometimes it's nice to have a motherly-type to talk to, especially about boys! I want you to keep me informed of what happens with you-know-who." Ruth said goodbye to Hessa and her mother as they paid their bill and she got up to leave with her group.

Hessa and Muna sat down, and Hessa's mother looked across the table at her daughter thoughtfully. She finally asked, "What boy? What was she talking about?"

Hessa looked down at her hands folded in her lap, at a loss for words. Her mother continued to look at her, waiting for a response from her daughter. Hessa's face turned red, and her mother finally asked her again: "Hessa, did you meet a boy at school?"

"Yes, but it is not what it sounds like. He is a very nice boy I met who only wanted to show me around Boston. While I was staying at the Charles Hotel he took me to the ballet and to some sights around Boston—that is all. He felt badly that I was alone all weekend. There is nothing else to it. Please, mother, do not say anything to Father. It is nothing, I promise."

Her mother looked at her with a questioning look of suspicion, but her thoughts were interrupted when she received a call from her son. She answered her cell phone and her face lit up when she received the happy news.

"A boy! How wonderful, Imaad! Congratulations!" she exclaimed. "Yes, Hessa is with me. We will be over shortly with gifts for mother and baby!"

She called Hessa's father to inform him, and they quickly paid their bill and hurried to the car. As they were driving to the hospital, her mother brought up her concerns once more.

"I will not say anything for now, Hessa, but what you did was very inappropriate. You are meant for Qasim. You should not be running around Boston alone with some boy you met at college. Your father was right—you should not be alone in America. They have no moral values there. They are already trying to take advantage of you," she said.

Hessa tried to explain to her mother, but Muna wouldn't listen any longer. She finally told her daughter that she was worried her father would take measures to see that Hessa never returned to Harvard if he found out about what had happened.

"Just be very careful what you do in the future, and who you associate with," her mother said, indicating that the conversation was over.

By the time Hessa and her mother got to the hospital, Safiya had already been taken to her room. Hessa and her mother walked into the room to find Safiya holding the baby and Imaad standing next to her.

"He's perfectly healthy, Mother," Imaad said.

"Oh, look how sweet he is!" Muna said of her new grandson. "You are truly blessed."

"Thank you," Safiya replied. She looked exhausted, but happy.

"We brought some things for you and the baby," Muna said, and brought the basket over to Safiya to inspect.

"Thank you so much," she said, as her mother-in-law put the basket down on a table nearby.

Safiya told Hessa and her mother about her labor and birth experience, and let them know how long she would have to stay in the hospital. Muna could see her daughter-in-law was beginning to look sleepy, so she went over to Safiya and gave her a kiss on the forehead.

"Thank you for giving the family such a beautiful little gift. Now I think we had better let you get some sleep. I will call you tomorrow," she said.

Hessa said her goodbyes to her brother and family, and walked out with her mother to the car. They didn't say a word to one another until they were just about home.

Her mother finally asked, "Who *is* this boy you met, Hessa?"

"His name is Joel. His father is a professor at Harvard Law School."

"I see. Is he a Christian boy?" she asked suspiciously.

"No," Hessa said simply, her face turning hot and red. "Mother, can we change the subject? I really do not wish to talk about this anymore. There is nothing else to say."

"I think there is, Hessa," her mother said quietly. "This boy Joel—is he Muslim? Tell me, Hessa. What is his background?"

"He's…Jewish," she stammered.

"I cannot believe what I am hearing," her mother said. "Do you know what your father…" She didn't finish her sentence. "I am telling you, Hessa, never see this boy again. If your father ever found out…" she trailed off again.

"I won't, I won't!" Hessa replied, with tears welling up in her eyes. "I am sorry we ran into Ruth today. She ruined everything!"

"What do you mean, she ruined everything? I think it was very fortunate we ran into her today. Allah is looking out for you, my dear one," her mother said.

They parked the car and walked into the house. Hessa ran up to her room and threw herself on the bed, letting the tears fall. "Allah is looking out for me, hah!" she said to herself. She felt physical pain just at the thought of never seeing Joel again.

Finally she said out loud, "Oh Joel, Joel, why did you have to be who you are? If you could have only been Qasim! Why did my life have to turn upside down when I met you?"

She realized it was getting late and that her father would be home shortly. She quickly wiped her tears and went into the bathroom to wash her face. She went back into her bedroom to compose herself. She changed her clothes, pulled her hair back into a ponytail, and went downstairs to help her mother with dinner. *I just need to give it time,* she tried to convince herself. *I'll get over him in time.*

86

CHAPTER 11

On the seventh day after the baby's birth, Hessa and her mother scurried around trying to get everything organized for the Aqeeqah. They had prepared the slaughter of two sheep—some for charity, as was tradition, the rest for family in celebration of the new addition to their family. Hessa and her mother had gotten to her brother's house early that morning, along with Safiyah's mother and sisters, and were preparing a large feast.

This day would be for the naming of the baby, and for his circumcision. Family and friends filed into Imaad and Safiya's home, excited for the celebration. Everyone brought gifts, which were stacked against the wall of the baby's nursery. Hessa enjoyed the distraction of the party. All week she and her mother had been shopping and cooking in preparation. The day of the party she was up at the crack of dawn, loading things into the car to take to her brother's home.

At the beginning of the celebration, the ceremony of naming the baby took place. The baby was named Basem, which means 'Smiling'. The name seemed very fitting, since he appeared to be a happy baby thus far in his life.

After the ceremony everyone went into the kitchen to choose from an extensive buffet of favorites such as hwerneh, lentil salad, hummus and pita, musakhan, shakshoukeh, lamb kabobs, and for dessert, baklawa, halawa and kanafeh, along with bowls filled with candied figs and nuts.

Hessa stood at the food table serving guests when she looked up and saw Qasim standing in front of her. "Hello, Hessa," he said.

"Hello, Qasim," she replied, her face turning red from the guilt she felt, as if Qasim could read her thoughts about what had happened in Boston.

"I just got home from school a few days ago." Qasim was in his third year at the London School of Economics. "I knew I would see you today—that's why I didn't call."

"That is all right, Qasim. It has been quite a busy time."

"I was wondering if you would like to take a walk with me later," Qasim said.

"That would be nice. I will let you know when we get the place cleaned up, and then we can leave," Hessa said.

Qasim walked out of the kitchen, over to a group of men where his and Hessa's fathers were in a heated discussion. Hessa felt a sense of relief when Qasim disappeared from sight, and made mental notes of what she could talk to him about when they went for their walk.

The day drew to a close as the sun lowered in the sky. It had been a wonderful celebration, and no one seemed to want to leave. By early evening, everyone started to make their way to the door. They complimented the women on the wonderful feast as Hessa, her mother, Safiya and her family stood at the door saying goodbye. As Hessa and her mother were just about finished washing the dishes and putting the food away, Qasim came into the kitchen.

"Hello Qasim. Did you enjoy the celebration?" Hessa's mother asked.

"Very nice. The food was exceptional." Qasim answered. "Hessa, are you ready to go?"

Hessa was looking for things to do to stall the inevitable. Spending time with Qasim was not on her list of things to do while she was home. She liked him enough, but he was a very serious person. She wondered if he'd ever had fun in his life.

Her mother spoke up. "Hessa, you go ahead with Qasim. We can finish the rest."

88

Hessa walked to the front hallway and pulled her jacket from a pile of coats on a bench. Qasim came up behind her, and nodded his head to his father, indicating he and Hessa were leaving.

"Should we walk to 'La Quisine' for espresso?" Qasim asked. Mr. Bishara was in conversation with Qasim's father and motioned to Mustafa, a man employed by Bishara, to accompany them on their walk. They made their way out the door and down the front steps.

"I was so busy today I did not eat very much, and I am tired. A cup of espresso and a cookie would be good," Hessa said.

They walked out into the cold night air, Mustafa trailing a short distance behind them, smoking a cigarette. Hessa was surprised that such a warm day could drop so suddenly to a temperature near freezing. She shivered and hugged herself from the cold, but Qasim didn't notice as he walked a few steps ahead of her.

Qasim's features were very dark, and he looked unshaven, no matter what the time of day. He was of average height, but very slim-- Hessa believed it was because of his high-strung nature. She felt awkward and quiet with Qasim. As they walked along, they exchanged information about their schools, with Qasim doing most of the talking.

When that conversation ended, they walked along in silence until they reached the coffee shop. They entered the little cafe and sat down, ordering espressos and a cookie for Hessa. She shifted in her seat, looking around nervously.

"What is on your mind, Hessa? You seem to be distracted," Qasim said.

"No, no. I have been hurrying around so much for the last few days, I think I'm having difficulty relaxing," Hessa said, trying to sound convincing.

The two sat in silence, sipping their espressos, and Hessa realized Qasim might say something to her parents about how anti-social she had been. She thought she'd better act more interested, so she asked Qasim about London, and what he had done outside of school. He told her his time was spent mostly in study, but he'd been to some rugby matches,

89

which he enjoyed. He also told her about the large Muslim population in London, and how at home he felt there.

"Some day I would like us to live there, after we're married," Qasim said.

"You would not miss your family here?" Hessa asked.

"I think living in London would far outweigh my missing family and friends. Besides, the family has many connections there.

"London has so much to see and do. I would like to experience the things I haven't been able to yet because of my studies. Whenever I *have* been able to go somewhere with friends, there is always something that intrigues me, and it makes me think it would be a good place to stay," Qasim replied.

Hessa had a sinking feeling, which turned into a sudden deep sadness. The realization further sank in that her life would be decided for her, and she wouldn't have any say in where they lived or what she wanted.

She thought it was funny how Joel was so concerned about how she felt and what she thought, and Qasim never asked her about herself or what she wanted out of life. She suddenly longed to see Joel's smile and his deep brown eyes looking down at her. She wanted to experience again his hand taking hers, making her feel safe and cared for.

"Hessa, are you listening to me?" It was Qasim.

"I'm sorry—did you say something?"

"Where are you? You look like you were a thousand miles away," Qasim said sternly.

"I am so sorry, Qasim. I guess I was thinking about the classes I have next semester, and some things I need to do when I get back to Boston," she lied.

"Living in America has changed you. It is as though you're a visitor here, and you cannot wait to leave." Qasim replied. "I was watching you today at the celebration. You didn't seem to want to be there, even with your own family."

"That is not true. I am very happy to be home, and was glad to be able to be here for little Basem's birth."

"Well, you could be a little more interested in me, and what has been happening in my life," he said resentfully.

"We should be going, Qasim. I have been working since dawn, and I am very tired."

The two walked out of the little coffee shop and back to Imaad's house. Hessa made an excuse of needing to go in to make sure there wasn't anything left to do, and told him she would be riding home with her mother. Qasim resentfully nodded to her, said a curt 'good night', and left abruptly.

Hessa walked into the house and found her mother finishing in the kitchen with Safiya's mother. The two were standing with dish towels in their hands, talking. When they saw Hessa, her mother asked, "Where is Qasim?"

"He needed to go home," she stammered.

"Is everything all right?" her mother asked.

"Of course," she said, as she felt the heat rise in her face.

Her mother looked at her suspiciously, and turned back to Safiya's mother. "I think we have everything in order here."

She thanked Safiya's mother for her help and walked to the living room with Hessa, where Imaad was talking with his father-in-law. Mr. Bishara had come in a separate car, and since he was preoccupied with Imaad, Hessa and her mother said goodbye and walked out to the car.

As they were driving home, Hessa's mother asked once again, "Are you sure there isn't something you would like to tell me about tonight with Qasim?"

"No, I am sure. We just walked down to 'La Quisine' to get coffee. It was very nice."

"Hessa, you are a different girl than before you left for America. You seem to be changing. I feel as though I am losing you. It disturbs me," her mother said.

91

"Mother, you just feel that way because I am growing up, and have been living away from home. I would imagine this is very normal when children go off to college," Hessa said, proud of herself that she sounded so knowledgeable.

Her mother became very quiet. The rest of the ride home was spent in silence. Hessa felt fear sweep over her as thoughts of her conversation with her mother crept in. Would her mother tell her father about running into Ruth? Would she give her daughter away and tell him about Joel?

"I just want to warn you, Hessa," her mother said. "It is very dangerous for you to be moving off the path that was set for you by your family. The consequences of your actions could be very serious. Please do not make any decisions that could ruin your life and embarrass your family. Your father will never have that."

Hessa looked at her mother with sadness in her eyes, and Muna wanted to be able to comfort her daughter, but she didn't want to ignore the serious nature of such a grave situation. She ached seeing the pain in her daughter's eyes, but what could she do? She was aware of what could happen to her daughter for such disobedience. Better to stay strong in the words she shared with Hessa so that she wouldn't lose this child she loved.

They drove up to the apartment and parked. Hessa dragged herself up the stairs and into the front door. She said good night to her mother and walked up to her room.

She sat down on the bed and whispered aloud, "What am I going to do? I cannot marry Qasim. What miracle can happen to change the course of my life?"

She sat staring into the darkness of her room, imagining how she could escape marrying Qasim. She thought of how lonely her life would be living in London without seeing much of her family ever again, including her new little nephew.

She got ready for bed, and as exhausted as she was, she laid in bed staring at the ceiling. *What to do, what to do?* She was thinking. She realized that apart from the miraculous, she would end up marrying a man just like her father, and would live a life of loneliness and isolation just like her mother.

Why not take a chance? she thought to herself. *Do I really want to have a life like my mother? Her only happiness is her children, and now that we are gone she has nothing. The family gatherings are the only thing she has to look forward to for the rest of her life.*

Hessa continued to think of what could possibly happen to change her situation, and she came up with nothing. Then she thought of Joel— sweet Joel. He seemed to have been raised in a home without much love, just the pressure of expectations.

He did however seem to be completely trusting and much braver than Hessa. He appeared to want to take a chance on her, not caring about the consequences. Oh, how she longed to be that way. She smiled when she pictured his face as he was falling when he bumped into 'Santa Claus'. She smiled and laughed softly to herself.

She couldn't let go of the experiences that had meant more to her than anything in her life. She couldn't let go of a man who had shown more love to her in just a few days than any member of her family ever had. She whispered a prayer into the air, "Make it happen. Change my life. Let me be with Joel. I cannot live without him, and the kind of life that promises love and happiness."

The silent decision she made to herself in her bedroom made her feel at peace somehow. She finally drifted off to sleep, forcing out any thoughts of what the outcome might eventually be as a result of her life choices.

CHAPTER 12

$\mathbf{H}$essa spent as much time visiting her brother as she could before she was to return to Boston. She enjoyed being at his house, holding little Basem. Looking down at this little person as she held him made her want a child of her own.

She cooked meals for her brother and sister-in-law, did laundry, and helped with their shopping needs. Keeping busy with chores helped pass the time quickly, and before she knew it there were only a few days left before her holiday was over.

The thoughts from the night of the celebration dogged her, and she couldn't get over the nagging feeling that there must be an answer to her dilemma out there somewhere. She needed to know if the situation was out of her hands, and if she was to be relegated to a life of feigned servitude to a husband she didn't love.

Early one morning Hessa was in the mood for a little excursion, and felt drawn to drive to the center of Jerusalem. She didn't want to run into anyone she knew on her private search for direction in her life. Bookstores were one of her favorite places, and there were many in Jerusalem, so she drove to the heart of the city and got out to walk.

The morning was clear and the sun was shining. There was a wonderful feel to this part of the city, and she enjoyed being on her own, away from questions and the suspicious glances of her father.

She found a quaint little book shop that carried both new and second-hand books. There was a coffee bar with various types of pastries, bagels and cookies. Large, comfortable-looking chairs lined the perimeter of the store, inviting people to stop and relax while they investigated the books.

Hessa hadn't been able to forget the things she and Ruth had talked about on the plane, and was drawn to do a little research of her own. She wondered about this God of whom Ruth had spoken.

She thought about the story of Corrie ten Boom, and how her family had risked their lives for complete strangers who didn't even share the same faith. She especially couldn't stop thinking about how Corrie had forgiven the very man who had murdered her sister.

She wandered around the store not actually knowing what she was looking for, or what to read. Finally a woman not much older than herself approached Hessa.

"Good morning. Is there something I can help you find?" she asked.

"I am not sure," Hessa answered. She didn't know how to ask for something she felt would be like contraband in her parents' home.

The young woman smiled and said, "Well, you're standing in the devotional aisle. Were you looking for a particular devotional?"

"What is a devotional?" Hessa asked.

"Oh, well, it's a book that has inspirational writings, things to comfort and uplift you in whatever situation you might be. Typically a devotional will also have Bible verses that pertain to the situation the author is writing about," the woman said, realizing Hessa wasn't a Christian by the hijab draped around her head and shoulders.

"What would you suggest," Hessa asked. "I mean, if you are going through particularly difficult things?"

"Why don't you get *Streams in the Desert*? She replied. "It's been around for many years, and has topics that are relevant to just about everything that happens in life."

"That sounds exactly like something I would like to read." Hessa then turned to face the young woman directly. "Do you have Bibles?" she asked very quietly.

"Yes, they're back here, against the wall. I'll help you select one that's translated to your native language, and will be the easiest for you to understand."

Hessa walked up to the counter and paid for the two books. She also bought a cup of coffee, and sat down in one of the chairs by a window to look at her purchases. She picked up *Streams in the Desert* and opened it. She noticed that each entry was for a day of the year. She flipped through the pages to the current date and read:

> '*Is anything too hard for the Lord? Not when we believe in Him enough to go forward and do His will, and let Him do the impossible for us....*
>
> '*...The only thing too hard for God is deliberate, continued disbelief in His love and power, and our final rejection of His plans for us. Nothing is too hard for God to do for them that trust Him.*'

"Oh my goodness," Hessa said softly to herself. She stared down at the page, and read the entry over and over to herself. The top of the page gave a reference to the book of Genesis, chapter 18, verse 14. She opened the Bible and read the scripture reference to herself. She was so intrigued she went to the beginning of Genesis and read all fifty chapters. When she was finished, she stared down at the Bible like she had found buried treasure.

She suddenly realized she had been gone for a long time, and that she should be getting home. She put her new books back in the bag, picked up her purse and walked out, filled with new hope. She got into the car and drove off toward Jerusalem, unaware of the person watching her in the car parked across the street from the bookstore. It was Qasim.

Qasim quickly got out of the car and walked into the bookstore. He walked over to the young woman he had seen Hessa speaking with.

"Excuse me. The young woman you were just helping a few minutes ago. What did she buy?" Qasim asked.

The young woman happily obliged, thinking he was looking for the same material to buy as Hessa.

"Oh, yes. Let me get them for you," she said. She walked over to the devotional area and picked up *Streams in the Desert*, and then walked back to the wall of Bibles and picked out the one she had chosen for Hessa. "Is there anything else you need? We have some wonderful commentaries…"

Qasim turned and hurried out of the store. He tore down the street and headed back to Jerusalem. When he got into town, he drove over to Hessa's house. He walked up to the door and knocked loudly. Hessa's mother came to the door, and when she opened it, she was alarmed at seeing the look on Qasim's face.

Without saying hello, she asked, "What is the matter, Qasim? You look as though something terrible has happened."

"I would like to see Hessa if she's at home."

"Your timing is perfect. She just got home. Come in and I will get her."

Hessa came down a few moments later, and fear suddenly gripped her when she saw the look on Qasim's face. His anger was apparent—she slowed down and walked calmly over to him, trying to gain her composure.

"Hello Qasim. What brings you to my house today?"

"Can a man not come for a visit to see the woman he will someday marry?" he said curtly. "Hessa, will you walk with me to La Quisine for coffee?"

"I just got home and…" she said but he interrupted.

"We need to talk—right now." He said, and the look in his eyes told her he wasn't going to accept excuses.

"Of course, but what about a chaperone?" she said, trying to mask the fear building in her.

"Tell your mother to accompany us," he said.

She went into the kitchen to let her mother know Qasim was there, and asked if she would be able to walk with them to La Quisine.

Mrs. Bishara wiped her hands and followed Hessa to the door. The three walked down the street in silence, with Hessa's mother trailing at a distance. When they had almost reached their destination, Hessa finally turned to him.

"What is the matter, Qasim? You seem very angry about something. Is there anything I have done?" she asked.

"I would like you to tell me what you were doing in the city this morning," he said angrily.

"Jerusalem? Oh…well…I was…just looking at books. There is a wonderful little bookstore in the middle of town…" her voice trailed off as he interrupted once again.

"Hessa, I went into that bookstore after you left. The girl told me you had purchased a Bible and another Christian book. What are you doing? What are you *thinking*?" he said, trying to keep his composure.

"I am taking a class on world religion next semester, and wanted to get some books to familiarize myself," she said quickly.

"Then why didn't you get any books on other religions?"

"Oh…I will, but I wanted to read these first," she lied.

Qasim looked at Hessa, trying to read what was behind her eyes. He could see she looked fearful, but was trying to act calm by sitting up stick-straight and clasping her hands together. She was hiding something.

"I do not believe you," he spat out.

"You need to realize, Qasim, that part of my history major includes world religions. I intend to do well at Harvard, and if it includes having to read about other religions, then that is what I will do," she said, proud of how calm she sounded. "Why did you follow me into the city, anyway?"

"You have been acting very strangely since you returned home. Your mother and father have noticed it as well. Maybe Harvard isn't the

99

best place for you to be, Hessa. Perhaps you should be in London with me, where you won't be getting yourself into trouble."

"I am not a child, Qasim. It has been my dream to go to Harvard. Please let me have that dream. We will be together soon enough," she said waveringly.

⁂

They wordlessly continued drinking their coffee. Hessa looked out the window, pretending to be interested in what was going on out in the street. Qasim sat in petulant silence, staring straight ahead, deep in thought.

Finally he spoke. "I hope you are telling me the truth, Hessa. You know that I could tell your father, and the marriage would be off. I do not think he would act favorably if this happened."

"Please do not say anything to my father. I truly bought those books for study purposes only. You need to believe me. You have travelled to other parts of the world, Qasim. You know that things are much different in other cultures. It is not a bad thing to be aware of what other customs and beliefs are out there. I think it gives us a better idea of how to handle relations internationally," she said pleadingly.

"You do not need to study them to know what is right, and I think you have taken this too far. Your father would agree with me. Besides, what do you need to have a degree for? I will take care of you financially, and I do not want you working when we have children."

Hessa realized trying to reason with Qasim was useless. The sadness she felt about her future crept in again, and panic began to overtake her. She looked over at Qasim. His face was rigid, his mouth in a tight line. She knew that once they were married she would have to do her best never to cross him. She decided once again that she would try to find a way to escape this cruel situation.

Qasim abruptly stood up and told Hessa he needed to get home. They walked the short distance back to Hessa's house, and once they

100

reached the front door, he left her standing there and turned to walk back to his car. He got in and roared off without a backward glance.

Hessa's mother then walked up, and they stood together watching after him, her heart fearful of what her parents would say about the growing rift between her and Qasim. In a very short time, her whole way of thinking had been changed by a couple of Americans: Joel, in his kindness and love, and Ruth in her story of faith and forgiveness.

She walked into the house and hurried to her room to avoid having to explain the conversation to her mother. She kept herself busy by packing some clothes she wouldn't need for the remainder of her stay at home. She walked over to the bag she had placed in her suitcase and pulled out the Bible. She looked at it, feeling a strong urge to open the pages and continue reading what she had begun that morning.

The thought of Joel being Jewish popped into her mind. She wondered if that would eventually cause a rift between them. *Why does religion have to separate people?* Hessa wondered. She opened the Bible and thumbed through it, finally settling on the Psalms. She went from one Psalm to the next, and was more drawn in with each page she turned.

She was jarred to reality when she heard footsteps on the stairs. She quickly put the Bible back in the bag and slipped it under some clothes on the bottom of her suitcase. There was a knock at the door, and it was her mother once again asking if everything was all right with Qasim.

"Everything is fine, Mother."

Her mother stepped into her room. "I know it is not always easy, Hessa. You will find a way to get along with Qasim. He is intense, just like your father. I learned long ago that it is best to let him vent his anger and to keep silent. It passes quickly enough, and life goes on. He will be a good provider, and you will have me close by to help with your future family."

"Qasim wants to stay in London. He does not want to return to Israel," Hessa said with her head down.

Hessa noticed what looked to be a stab of pain that shot across her mother's face, but she saw her mother covered it quickly. "This is the first

101

I have heard of this. Well, London is only a plane ride away—we will visit. I will miss you, Hessa, but we should not think of that right now. We still have two whole days until you leave. Let us enjoy the rest of your stay."

Suddenly her mother looked very tired and careworn. She gave Hessa a hug and said goodnight. As she turned to leave the room, she looked back at her daughter with a sad smile on her face. Hessa understood that her mother couldn't do anything to help her daughter, so she would do what she had always done in these situations. Hessa knew her mother would resign herself to the fact that her only daughter would be moving several thousand miles away.

A rush of sympathy flowed through Hessa for her mother. Since she and her brother Imaad had left, her mother must have been very lonely. Hessa's grandparents on her mother's side had both passed away, and her father spent a lot of time out of town. Her grandparents on her father's side were in agreement with their son that Muna had brought shame to the family for not being able to bear more than two children, so they had shunned her. She felt completely helpless to do anything for her mother.

She wondered if her mother would ever consider visiting her in Boston. They could have a fabulous time together seeing the sights. Her mother had commented on how she had enjoyed her time visiting when she and Hessa's father had taken her to school.

Hessa decided to ask her mother the next morning if Muna would like to return with her to Boston. She felt a surge of encouragement at this idea and hoped her mother would have the fortitude to go on an adventure with her daughter. She also hoped that her father would agree to this unusual request. Hessa got ready for bed that night, and brightened up at the thought of what she had planned for the next day.

CHAPTER 13

Hessa awoke early the next morning. She put on her robe and slippers and padded downstairs to open the curtains. The sun was coming up, shining off the Dome of the Rock, which they could see from their living room window. It was going to be a glorious day. She only hoped her father would listen to her request to have her mother accompany her back to Boston.

She went into the kitchen to start breakfast. Her mother had been to the market the previous day and picked up fresh eggs, along with several types of cheeses and vegetables, so she decided to make a large omelet for everyone to split.

She went into the refrigerator to pull out everything she would need, and set it all on the counter. She made coffee, which seemed to wake her parents and draw them down to the kitchen.

"Good morning," her father said as he walked into the kitchen. "What gets you up so early this morning?"

"I went to sleep early last night and woke up very hungry," she replied. "Would you like some omelet, Father?"

"No, but I will have some of that coffee you are making, and slice me a piece of bread, if you don't mind."

She poured the coffee into a large cup, and put two slices of bread onto a plate. She set out various spreads for her father to choose from. "So, you leave for Boston in a couple of days, eh?" her father asked, taking a bite of bread.

"Yes," she answered.

"I hope you enjoyed being back at home after being in an exciting new place. Before you leave you and your mother should make sure you have everything to last you the rest of the school year."

"I have been making note of the things I need to pick up before I go back to Boston. Thank you, Father. There is one thing I would like to ask you, however."

He looked up at her, waiting for the question.

"I would like to ask you if Mother could accompany me back to Boston. It would be nice to have her with me to help with all the things I am taking back. Plus, school will not be starting for another five days after I return. We could spend some time together."

"That actually sounds like a good idea, Hessa. Maybe she should stay in Boston for a week. That way she could get an idea of what your day is like, and possibly meet some of your friends. Yes, I think this is a very good idea."

Hessa was elated. She couldn't wait to tell her mother, who didn't know yet about what her daughter had thought up. She finished chopping the vegetables for the omelet, and began adding them to the egg mixture she had just poured into the pan. Pita bread was heating in the oven, and she had put a bowl of dates out to nibble on.

Her mother walked in, dressed and ready for the day. "Good morning, Hessa. It smells delicious in here. What is in the omelet?"

"I chopped some of the onion, eggplant and herbs you picked up at the market yesterday. The eggs looked so good I decided we should have them for breakfast. Would you like some coffee? The omelet is just about done."

"Thank you, I will get it myself. We do not want the omelet to burn," her mother said as she poured her coffee. She walked over to pull the pita bread out of the oven, and placed it on the table. Hessa cut pieces of omelet and put them on plates for the two of them, and they sat down.

Her father was sitting at the table already, reading the paper as he drank his coffee. "Well Hessa, why don't you tell your mother about your idea?"

104

Hessa's eyes sparkled. "Yes, thank you Father! Mother, would you like to return to Boston with me and stay for a week? I have some time before school starts again, and I could show you around. Please say yes!"

Her mother looked at her for a moment and then looked at her father, surprised that he would allow her to go so far away for such a long time.

"This was your idea, Hessa?"

Her daughter nodded excitedly. Muna looked at her husband, and asked, "This is all right with you, Husaam?" He nodded, and turned back to his paper.

"Well, what can I say then? Of course I will go back with you. Since Imaad and Safiya are settled in with little Basem, I think it is fine to take the trip with you."

"Good! Now we just need to make a list of everything you and I will need before we go, and you need to make arrangements for the flight! While you do that, I will make reservations for you at the Charles Hotel, where I stayed before I came home. It was a wonderful place to stay," Hessa said, beaming that she would have her mother with her for a while longer.

They finished their breakfast, and Hessa told her mother she would clean up so Muna could start preparing for their trip back to Boston. There was a lot to do, and her mother would need every minute in the next two days, since their flight would leave at 5:30 in the morning.

Her father finished his coffee and put the newspaper down on the table. "Hessa, make some reservations for you and your mother at a hotel in Tel Aviv. I think you should leave tomorrow night and stay near the airport so you do not miss your flight the next day."

"Thank you, Father. That is a good idea. We would not have been able to sleep much if we left from here on Wednesday morning. I will get right to it."

Her father got up and walked over to his daughter, patting her between the shoulder blades. "I will take you to Tel Aviv myself," he said, and walked out of the room.

Hessa finished the dishes and put everything away. She then made preparations for the trip back to Boston. She and her mother ran errands all afternoon, making sure Hessa would have everything she needed for the remainder of her stay at school.

At the end of the day, they made it back home with the car trunk full of bags of every size. They giggled like little girls as they carried their packages from the car to the house.

"You would think we are going to live in a tent in the middle of the Sahara Desert!" her mother said laughing.

They spent the following day finishing everything they needed to do to get to Tel Aviv that evening. Her mother had things scheduled that needed to be cancelled, and people to call to let them know of her plans, including Imaad, who was quite surprised that his mother was going to be travelling without her husband.

Late that afternoon, Hessa's father came home with Mustafa and started to pack the car with the suitcases and carry-on bags his wife and daughter had stacked at the front door. He then went upstairs to his bedroom and closed the door. Muna was putting on her coat, and had started to leave the room to go downstairs.

"I want you to take note of everything Hessa does while you are in Boston. She acted very strangely while she was here. I believe she is up to something, and I intend to find out what it is," Husaam said.

"So that is why you want me to go with her? I am to spy on my daughter?" her mother said, trying to hold back her anger.

Husaam lifted his eyebrows and scowled at his wife. "If you want to look at it that way, then yes. I have every right to know what my daughter is doing. You are her mother. You should be concerned about her welfare also."

"I am, but I feel badly that she thinks you allowed me to go to Boston just to enjoy spending time with her."

"Think what you want. This is for her own good. Just be happy you can go to spend time with your daughter, but I want to make sure she is safe from things that might lead her astray. Mahmoud mentioned that

106

Qasim has also been acting strangely since Hessa came home. We both have our worries."

"I will enjoy my time with Hessa, and if there is anything unusual, I will certainly take note of it. It would only be right to report anything back to you that she might be doing that causes concern," her mother replied, not wanting to escalate their conversation to a fight. Nothing was worth that.

They finally got the luggage packed tightly into the trunk. Hessa's father commented about women's foolish need to have just about their whole house with them on any trip. The traffic was terrible. It was rush hour, and for the first time since Hessa had been home, it started to rain.

The three sat in silence for much of the trip. Hessa felt tension between her parents, and wondered what they had been talking about in the bedroom before they had left the house. Her mother seemed agitated, and had kept silent except to ask Hessa questions about their plans once they arrived in Boston.

After the unusually lengthy trip from Jerusalem to Tel Aviv, they arrived at the David Intercontinental Hotel. Hessa got out of the car and walked over to her father. She grasped his hands and kissed him on both cheeks.

"Thank you for everything, Father. Thank you for letting Mother come with me, and thank you so much for letting me attend Harvard. It has been a wonderful experience. We will call as soon as we reach Boston."

"Make sure not to lose one another at the airport," he said. The bell staff at the hotel had already loaded their things onto a cart, awaiting their guests. "Look after each other," he said as he nodded his head to Hessa's mother and turned to get into his car.

The two women followed the bell staff inside as they led their guests to the check-in counter. When they got to their room, their luggage was piled up against the wall inside the door. Hessa and her mother looked at each other, thinking the same thing.

"Father was right! What were we thinking, packing all of this?" Hessa said.

They both burst into laughter. Hessa took off her coat and flung it over a chair, kicked off her shoes, and sank into the large, inviting bed.

Hessa's mother went over to open the curtains. She looked down at a large pool below, and out to the Mediterranean Sea.

"I think we should stay here for a few days!" she laughed.

The hotel *was* beautiful. Hessa could see that her mother was starting to relax and enjoy herself. They unpacked a few things they would need for their stay, and laid out the clothes they would be wearing for the next day's flight.

After preparing for what would be a very early next morning, they went down to the hotel restaurant for dinner. Hessa ordered a veal chop with truffle mash potatoes, and her mother ordered lamb chop on polenta. The two ate off each other's plates, chatting away like little girls.

Hessa was amazed at how her mother was opening up more by the hour. She gave the impression she had been set free, like a wild animal escaping its cage at the zoo. As her mother talked about trips to Tel Aviv she had taken with her parents as a little girl, she seemed to grow younger and more animated.

There could not have been a better idea than taking Mother back to Boston. She has absolutely come alive, Hessa thought to herself.

They finished dinner, and realized they needed to get to bed if they were going to get to the airport in time for their 5:30 a.m. flight. The two quickly got ready for bed, arranged for a wake-up call and snuggled under the covers, still chatting for several minutes before they drifted off to sleep.

CHAPTER 14

Hessa didn't get much sleep that night. She was excited to get back to Boston, even though she knew she wouldn't be able to see Joel right away. It was comforting to know her mother would be with her for a short time. Hessa tossed and turned in bed as her mother slept. She wanted to wake her mother to talk, but didn't have the heart to disturb her.

The wake-up call came at three a.m.. Hessa was already awake, looking at the clock. Her mother stirred, and they both arose to prepare for the trip to the airport. They moved about the room, packing their belongings without conversation.

They called a bellman to take their things to the front of the hotel where a car awaited them. It was quiet at the hotel. Very few people were leaving for the airport at that hour.

Time sped by quickly as mother and daughter boarded the plane and took their seats in first class. Hessa's father had flown over a million miles on this airline, so there was no shortage of free tickets and upgrades. Hessa fidgeted in her seat, trying to get comfortable as the plane prepared for takeoff.

"Hessa, I have never known you to be nervous flying. Why are you squirming so much?" her mother said.

"I do not know. I guess I have gone so long without sleep, now I cannot relax," she said, knowing full well that she was just anxious to get back to Boston.

"You did not sleep well last night?" her mother asked.

"Hardly at all. I hope I am able to sleep on the plane, or I will have to sleep for a whole day once we are in Boston," she replied.

Hessa's mother did something very much out of her character. She ordered a glass of champagne for her daughter.

"Mother! It is 5:00 in the morning! What are you thinking?" Hessa asked.

"You need to relax and go to sleep. Since you do not drink alcohol, this should help you get some sleep. I do not have any medication that would make you drowsy, and the only thing I could think of was champagne," her mother replied.

The flight attendant brought the champagne, and Hessa took a sip. She made a face. "This is very fowl tasting," she said, puckering her lips.

Her mother laughed. "Well at least I know you will never have a problem with alcohol."

Hessa forced as much of the bitter stuff down as she could. It did in fact help her. She felt extremely drowsy and light-headed, and looked at her mother, giggling because of the way everything seemed to start rocking back and forth.

"I think I will go to sleep now," she slurred as she put her head back on her seat and closed her eyes.

Muna smiled at her daughter, who looked like a little child as she drifted off. Hessa smiled in her sleep as one without a care in the world. The plane backed away from the gate, and Muna pulled a book out of her purse to read as her child slept.

Hessa awoke as the plane touched down in Boston. She had slept nearly the whole way from Tel Aviv. She looked out the window of the plane, and was surprised the pilots were able to land. Snow was coming down in giant flakes, and there were gusts of wind causing the snow on the ground to swirl across the tarmac.

As they pulled up to the gate, Hessa and her mother gathered their things and made their way out of the plane. They spotted their driver in the

110

baggage claim area, and began what would be a very slow commute to the Charles Hotel. Hessa planned to stay at the hotel with her mother until the Sunday before school started.

They finally pulled in to the hotel and dragged themselves up to their room. Hessa had slept practically the whole way to Boston, but still felt exhausted. It was mid-afternoon, but their bodies told them it was 10:00 at night.

Hessa's mother suggested they go downstairs for a bite to eat, since they had picked at their food on the plane, and both were now very hungry. They headed into one of the hotel's restaurants, where Hessa had eaten several times while staying at the Charles Hotel before she left on winter break. The food was fabulous, and after they finished their meal, they decided to bundle up and take a walk before it got dark.

Hessa walked with her mother to Harvard Yard as the sun started to set. The school was eerily quiet, and the trees were heavily laden with newly fallen snow. The few lights that shined in the Yard caused the snow to sparkle, and they felt as though they were the only two people on earth. Mother and daughter didn't speak. They both seemed content to just take in the clear, cold night, and the wonderful feeling of being able to get out and stretch their legs.

As Hessa and her mother walked past the library where she had first met Joel, her heart leapt within her when she pictured him walking up to introduce himself to her. Suddenly she had an overwhelming desire to see him, but quickly forced the thought out of her mind. She stopped abruptly and turned around, heading back in the direction of the hotel. She told her mother they needed to get back before it got too dark.

They walked briskly toward the hotel, the temperature seeming to drop by the minute as the sun disappeared. Hessa felt a strong sense of peace being back in the town where Joel lived. Just the thought of being within a few miles of where he was made her more content. The cold evening walk had revived them, but as soon as the two were back in their room, they realized how exhausting the day had been, and settled in to bed.

111

Hessa and her mother slept late the next morning, and ordered room service so they could get started on their day more quickly. Once they were ready to go, they decided to walk to one of the art museums on campus on the other side of Harvard Yard from the Charles Hotel. It was less than a mile to the museum, and the snow had stopped falling. They enjoyed their day, spending several hours wandering from room to room.

On their way back at the end of the day, Hessa took her mother to the local hangout in Harvard Square for pizza.

"It's called Noch's, and I have been there a couple of times with some of the girls in my dorm. The pizza is wonderful," she explained.

Her mother agreed to go, and since they had started with a late breakfast, they hadn't eaten anything that afternoon. Both of them were famished, so when they arrived at Noch's, they ordered a Sicilian pizza with the works and an antipasto salad. As they waited for their dinner they talked about their favorite exhibits at the museum, and Hessa told her mother about her interest in taking an art history class.

As they were chatting, Hessa looked up as she heard the door to the restaurant open, and her heart stopped…in walked Joel with two friends. She felt her cheeks turn hot as her heart pounded, and she lost her breath. He was talking and laughing with one of his friends as he came through the door. He turned to look for an open table, and as he scanned the room, their eyes met.

Joel's breath caught in his throat. She was even more beautiful than he had remembered. She had a camel-colored wool coat on with a light purple scarf around her neck. Her cheeks were blazing pink, and her eyes seemed to sparkle when she smiled at him.

"Hessa!" he breathed the word more than spoke. He walked over to her as if in a trance, and his two friends followed behind. "You're back. It's good to see you….Hello," he said to her mother. "I'm Joel."

112

The woman with Hessa seemed to have a physical reaction to his name. Had she mentioned him to this woman dressed in Middle Eastern clothes?

"Hello Joel. I am Mrs. Bishara—Hessa's mother."

"It's nice to meet you. I see the resemblance now, Mrs. Bishara. Oh, these are my friends, Henry and Eddie," he pointed them out to the two women. "Hessa, I don't think you've met my friends yet either."

"No, it is nice to meet you both," she said.

"How was your trip to Israel? Did you have a good time with your family?" Joel asked.

"It was very enjoyable. Very busy, but enjoyable, just the same." she replied.

"When did you get back to Boston?"

"Just yesterday. I took my mother to the museum today. It was wonderful. We spent nearly the whole day there!"

Joel stood smiling at Hessa as Henry said, "Well, it was nice meeting you both. Joel, there's a table right over here." Henry turned and started to walk to a table nearby, Eddie close behind.

Joel looked down at Hessa and asked, "Would you mind if we join you?" Hessa happily nodded as her mother looked over at her incredulously, but her daughter avoided eye contact with her.

"Okay!" Joel said as he waved his friends back over to their table.

Joel sat down next to Hessa, and Eddie sat next to Mrs. Bishara. Henry grabbed a chair from another table and pulled it over.

Joel and his friends ordered their food, and then told Hessa and Mrs. Bishara about how they had all met and grown up together. They chatted about their experiences at Harvard, and Joel explained how he and Hessa had met.

Hessa told her mother about the hospitality of Joel's parents, and how she had gone to his house for dinner, explaining in detail the beautiful place where Joel had grown up. She also told her mother about how they had seen the Nutcracker Ballet, and gone skating as well. They both laughed as they told the story about literally running into 'Santa Claus'.

113

Hessa's mother looked back and forth at Joel and Hessa as they spoke so animatedly about their adventures together.

Eddie and Henry told Hessa and her mother stories about Joel as he grew up, and the things he used to do to get invitations to their homes. Joel had always thought he was so savvy about the way he had finagled invitations, but obviously everyone knew what he had been up to, including their parents.

Before they knew it they were finished eating and had been talking for over two hours. The dinner crowd started streaming in to Noch's, and Mrs. Bishara told her daughter it was time to get back to the hotel.

Hessa looked over at her mother, who seemed quite taken with the boys. All three of them had been completely charming and entertaining. Hessa knew it had been quite a while since her mother had had a carefree and happy time with friends, much less virtual strangers. Finally Hessa reluctantly agreed that it was time to leave.

"What do you have planned for this weekend?" Joel asked.

"We have a list of things we want to see, so we have hired a car to take us around for the rest of the weekend. My mother leaves next Thursday, so we are going to try to take in as much as we can for the next few days. With school starting Monday, I won't be able to be with her as much as I would like during the week."

"Why don't you come to Vermont with us tomorrow? We have a friend who lives on a farm outside a little town called Bennington. You can see Boston any time, but Vermont is where you get to see what small town American life is like."

"Thank you Joel, but we could not possibly. Your friends do not even know us, and we could not impose," Mrs. Bishara said.

"They'd love to have you," Joel answered. "They're the greatest people in the world. Mrs. Sullivan is like my second mother. Eddie, Henry and I practically lived at their house during prep school. I'll call her right now—she'd be really happy to have you. They have a great big house with plenty of room. They always have guests visiting from somewhere."

114

Hessa looked at her mother hopefully. "We could always see the Boston sights when you come back in the spring," Hessa said.

"Oh, so I am coming back in the spring?" Hessa's mother asked, smiling at her daughter.

"Of course, Mother! I will need you to help me take everything back home for the summer!"

"Just let me make the call to Mrs. Sullivan. She'll be happy to have guests besides just Henry, Eddie and me. It'll be good for her to have women in the house for a change," Joel said with his disarming grin.

Mrs. Bishara gave Joel a look of resignation, and smiled at Joel as if to give him the go-ahead to make the call. Joel quickly dialed the Sullivan's number and got up from the table to walk outside so he could hear Mrs. Sully on the other end of the phone. After a couple of minutes he walked back in and asked Mrs. Bishara to come outside with him. Hessa looked at Joel with a quizzical look on her face.

"Mrs. Sully wants to give you a personal invitation," Joel said to Mrs. Bishara.

Mrs. Bishara took the phone and greeted Mrs. Sully. She listened for a moment, and started to laugh. After listening for a few more moments, she laughed again, and said, "Of course. Oh yes, yes. I will leave the details up to the boys. Thank you so much for the kind invitation. I look forward to meeting you in person also. Goodbye."

She handed the phone back to Joel, who thanked Mrs. Sully for having them all for the weekend, and hung up the phone. "Well, that's that. We can't avoid the invitation now, can we? Are you staying at the Charles Hotel?"

"Yes," she replied.

"We were planning on leaving town tomorrow morning at about eight a.m., if that's not too early for you," Joel said.

"No, eight a.m. is perfect. I must say, Joel, I do not think I have ever gone to stay at the home of someone whom I have never met."

"Well, there's a first time for everything, right?" Joel replied.

"I guess that must be true in America!" she said with a laugh.

115

They walked back in to Noch's and sat down at the table. Joel told everyone that it was all set, and they would be leaving tomorrow morning. Joel said he would drive his car so he could take Hessa and her mother with him. Eddie volunteered to take his car with Henry, since Henry was typically the one who was stuck with driving duties.

Joel then offered to take Hessa and Mrs. Bishara back to the hotel, since it was getting late and was dark outside. Henry had driven that night, so they all squeezed in, and dropped the two women off at their hotel.

Joel got out and walked them to the lobby, and told them he would meet them in the same spot the next morning. He turned and walked back out to the car, beaming with a large grin over this chance meeting.

"Man, you look like a complete idiot," Eddie said to Joel. "That girl has messed you up!"

"Yeah, and I don't care," Joel said, smiling like a fool.

After saying goodbye to Joel and watching him leave, Hessa and her mother turned and walked toward the elevator. Mrs. Bishara noticed Hessa glowing with a dazzling smile. She couldn't help but smile at how happy her daughter looked. It warmed Muna's heart to see such happiness in Hessa's face when she thought she had raised a quiet and sometimes very sad little girl.

She only wished Hessa wouldn't have to walk away from this relationship that had obviously changed her life. A stab of sadness shot through her, but she didn't want to think about that just now. She herself felt happy, free and young again, just being able to have this experience.

They got onto the elevator and Mrs. Bishara turned to her daughter. "I do not know what just happened, but I suppose I do not really *want* to know at present. Let us just enjoy ourselves, and we will figure out what to do later."

Hessa nodded happily and smiled. Nothing mattered right now except that she would be with Joel again in just a few short hours.

116

CHAPTER 15

The next morning Joel was at the hotel bright and early, and had coffee waiting in the car for Hessa and her mother. Henry and Eddie had gone on before them and would meet them at the Sullivans'. Joel waited in the lobby, anxiously pacing back and forth.

Shortly after eight a.m., Hessa and her mother got off the elevator and walked over to greet Joel. "Good morning, Joel! It is a beautiful day, and perfect for traveling!" Hessa said brightly.

"I'll say," Joel answered, taking in every detail about Hessa. "It's good to see you again, Mrs. Bishara."

They walked out to Joel's waiting car, and he opened the door for Hessa and her mother. After getting them settled in he put their suitcases in the trunk, and they were off.

Mrs. Bishara sat in the back seat and listened as Joel and Hessa talked animatedly about how they had spent their winter breaks and about their course load for the next semester. Joel finally looked in his rear view mirror at Mrs. Bishara and asked how she was doing in the back seat.

"The scenery is absolutely beautiful. I would love to see the countryside in summer. I imagine it is very green and lush," she replied.

"It's like a postcard. You'll have to come back at the end of May when school is out, and I'll take you to western Massachusetts," Joel replied. "Hopefully Mr. Bishara can accompany you at the end of the school year."

"He is very busy. I do not think his schedule would ever allow much time away," Mrs. Bishara said, not wanting to have to explain for her husband.

117

Joel realized by Mrs. Bishara's tone that this was a subject he shouldn't touch. He redirected the conversation and asked Mrs. Bishara about her new grandson. She was happy to be able to talk about little Basem, and told Joel she would show him pictures later.

Joel felt the need to describe the Sullivan family to Hessa and her mother. He told them about how large the family was and to be prepared for loud, wild behavior.

"Let me just apologize for them ahead of time," he laughed. "I don't want to scare you; I mean, they're not animals, they just act a little crazy sometimes. Believe me, you'll love the whole family once you meet them."

Hessa's mother laughed at Joel's description of them. This would be a very unusual experience for both her and her daughter. Hessa was anxious to meet them. She hadn't yet met Petie, but Joel had spoken of him several times before.

They finally turned into the Sullivan driveway, and Hessa asked Joel, "What is that sign on the gate? What does it mean?"

"That's just a little taste of what you're going to experience at the Sully home. The family is Irish, and the pig represents them. There's an old saying that says 'As Irish as Paddy's pig'. Paddy is a word for the Irish, and the pig represents farming. The mug of ale he's holding represents their celebration of life." Mrs. Bishara looked at the sign in amazement, but kept her thoughts to herself.

Joel parked and opened the car doors for Hessa and her mother. He went to the trunk to get their things out and true to form, there was Mrs. Sully standing in the doorway grinning from ear to ear, eagerly awaiting her guests. She ran out to greet everyone, and Joel introduced them.

"Welcome, I'm so happy you're here!" She hugged Hessa and Mrs. Bishara, who was very surprised at her open friendliness and affection to complete strangers.

"Come in, come in! It's so cold outside! I have tea ready, and a little late-morning snack for you. Joel, did you feed your guests?"

"They ate breakfast at the hotel, so we didn't stop on the way. We just had coffee in the car."

They walked into the house, and Petie hurried around the corner to the front entryway, along with Henry and Eddie.

"Burgermeister! What took you so long? We've been here for hours!" Eddie said tauntingly.

"Yeah, I believe you," Joel said as he rolled his eyes. Joel introduced Petie to the Bisharas and said, "You remember Henry and Eddie", as he pointed out each one.

Mrs. Sully asked Petie to take the ladies' things up to the guest room she had prepared for them, and told Joel to usher them into the living room.

"We're going to have a fancy tea, since I actually get to entertain women!" she said.

She came back from the kitchen a few moments later with a tray full of goodies. She had taken out her sterling silver tea service and set it down, along with her fine china. She had made scones, muffins and puff pastries filled with warm raspberry compote, and told them to help themselves as she poured the tea.

Petie finally came back downstairs and blurted out, "So Joel, is this the girl you've been hiding from us? Man, you're good Henry! You had this figured out back last fall!"

As he looked over at Hessa, he realized he had embarrassed her. She put her head down, her face blazing red. He looked over at Joel, who looked like he wanted to punch his friend in the mouth. There was an awkward pause and Petie tried to smooth over the mess he'd just made.

"Woops. Sorry, Hessa. I didn't mean to embarrass you. Mrs. Bishara, my apologies. I have a very large mouth in which I'm able to fit my entire foot!"

Mrs. Bishara started to laugh unexpectedly. She had never heard this saying, and it struck her funny. Hessa and Joel looked at each other and smiled awkwardly, embarrassed that their relationship had been the subject of conversation.

119

Mrs. Sully changed the subject and asked Mrs. Bishara about her home and family in Israel. "Please call me Muna," she said, and Mrs. Sully asked her to call her 'Maggie'.

She explained that her name was actually Mary Margaret, but there were so many 'Mary's' when she started school, the teacher began calling her by Maggie just to keep her students' names straight. The name had stuck.

While they were all chatting and sipping tea, Patrick and Mikey came in the door at the side of the house with several friends, all talking at the same time, laughing and shouting.

The door slammed, and the group in the living room could hear the loud thud of snow boots coming off and being dropped on the floor. The boys came into the living room, and taking in this dignified scene, started in on the older boys in the room.

"Tea time! Oh, may I have a crumpet?" Patrick said in a girlish voice.

"One lump or two?" Patrick's friend Brady chimed in, pretending to sip tea with his pinky finger raised.

The pack of friends laughed and pointed at the older boys with tea cups in their hands.

Mrs. Sully spoke up. "Okay boys, that's enough. Go back to the family room, and please keep it down. Otherwise, Brady, Regan and Finn will have to go home."

"I apologize for my band of hoodlums, Muna. This is what I get for having all boys!"

"I love all the energy and activity! It seems you have non-stop liveliness in your home," Muna said, her eyes lit up. She seemed fascinated by the rambunctious dynamic of this household.

"That's so true. Later I'll have to introduce the two boys in that group who were mine. The other three are neighbors. So Muna and Hessa, how would you like to do something away from all of these male hormones? Why don't we go into town? There are wonderful shops, galleries and a book store. The boys will hold down the fort, won't you, Peter?"

"Oh sure. If anyone gets out of line, they'll get a flogging." Petie said sarcastically.

Mrs. Bishara's eyes widened and she looked over at Mrs. Sully.

"Don't pay any attention to Peter—he's only joking. He has a flair for the dramatic. All right boys, I'm taking our guests on a tour of our little village, and we'll be gone for the afternoon. I have a big pot of vegetable beef soup in the kitchen, with sandwiches in the refrigerator. Peter, I expect you to be the host."

"At your service, Mother," Petie said smiling as he wiggled his eyebrows teasingly at his mother.

Hessa hesitated, and then turned to her mother. "Would you mind if I stayed here to rest? I didn't sleep much on the plane, and I have been having a hard time catching up on sleep."

"Well, I am not sure that is such a good idea, Hessa. You have no chaperone..." her mother said with a worried look in her eyes.

"Grandma and Grandpa Sullivan have been visiting for the holidays, and they're just upstairs in their room packing. They'll be here for the rest of the day, but they'll be leaving after dinner tonight to go home. They can be Hessa's chaperones."

"I suppose that would be all right," Muna said hesitantly.

"I'll just go upstairs to tell them to keep an eye on your daughter, Muna."

The senior Mrs. Sully came downstairs with her daughter-in-law to introduce herself, assuring Muna that she and her husband would keep their band of rambunctious boys in line.

As the two mothers left, Petie and his three friends piled the dirty dishes on a tray and removed them to the kitchen. Hessa was straightening up in the living room when Joel came around the corner. He smiled at Hessa and walked over to her.

"The guys said they would clean up, and we probably won't eat for a couple of hours. Do you wanna go for a snowmobile ride?" he asked.

"I am not sure what a snowmobile is, but whatever it is, I would love to—especially since I don't have to have skates on my feet!" she laughed slightly at the memory of skating at Frog Pond.

Petie told Joel where they had put Hessa and her mother's bags, so he led her upstairs to show her their room. Hessa went in to change into warmer clothes, and Joel walked down the hall to his room to grab his jacket, hat, and gloves. On his way to the stairs, he knocked on Grandma and Grandpa Sullys' door.

"Hessa and I are going for a snowmobile ride, Grandma."

"You be careful with that young lady, Joel! I hope it's all right for her to be with you alone. I suppose since you're outside…"

"It's fine, Grandma. I'll be a gentleman, don't worry."

"I have no doubt about that, Joel! Have a good time."

Joel and Hessa met downstairs a few moments later, walked through the mud room and out the side door to the barn. As Joel opened the barn door, Hessa gasped. The snowmobiles were much larger than she had imagined, and very powerful-looking.

Joel went over to the wall where the helmets hung. He put on his own helmet as he walked back over to Hessa, and put a smaller helmet on her, fastening it under her chin.

He got on the front of the machine and told her to hold on to him. Joel started it up and revved the motor. Off they went, with Hessa squealing and laughing. She held Joel tightly as they travelled in blissful silence. They were content just to be together. Joel's heart raced at the feeling of Hessa's arms around him. She seemed so small and slight; he felt very protective of her.

Joel finally slowed down as they neared a pond on the property. To the far end of the pond was a deer. It was visible in the clearing of some woods, and watched the two humans with guarded curiosity. Joel stopped the snowmobile and turned to Hessa, whispering that he had spotted the beautiful creature, and pointed in its direction. They watched in silence, and suddenly it bolted and darted from sight.

Joel turned back to Hessa. "Do you wanna drive?"

122

"Oh, no! You are taking your life in your hands with me driving. You go ahead. I feel safer with you steering this thing."

"You know you want to," Joel said, smiling as he winked at her. "Don't worry Hessa. I'll be right behind you, guiding you if you need it."

"Ok, but I do not want to be held responsible for what might happen," Hessa laughed.

She sat behind the handle bars and Joel started up the motor, jumping on the seat behind her. He gave her some basic instructions, and off they went. Hessa screamed with delight, giggling like a little girl. It didn't take her long to gain confidence in her new skill as she sped off across the open field, and drove through a wooded area.

As they came out the other side of the woods to a clearing, she headed up a hill. The snow was quite deep, and it became more difficult to maneuver. Hessa tried turning the snowmobile to go back down the hill, but she swerved too sharply and they fell over sideways into a snow drift.

Luckily the snow was deep enough to cushion their fall, but Hessa had tumbled head first into a snow bank. Joel jumped up and moved quickly to her, picking her up out of the snow and dusting her off.

She turned to him, snow still on her face, eyes twinkling as she fell into a fit of giggles. Her laughter was infectious and Joel, feeling relieved that she wasn't hurt, joined in. He pulled her onto his lap and they fell back in the snow, laughing until they ran out of breath.

As they settled down Joel looked over at Hessa, overwhelmed with his explosive feelings for her. He pulled her on top of him and lifted his head up to kiss her. He caught her face between his hands and pulled her down to him, kissing her passionately. She didn't pull away, but instead surprised him with her response.

Suddenly she pulled free and sat up. "I am so sorry. I should not have done that. We should go back to the house." Her mind was in a whirl, and she felt just as she had when her mother gave her the glass of champagne on the plane.

"It's my fault, Hessa. I got carried away. I'm in love with you. I would do anything to be able to be with you."

"Well, I admit…I have been struggling with trying to get thoughts of you out of my mind. When I think about you, I feel so content, like this is the way life should be," Hessa replied.

"So you love me too, little Hessa?" Joel asked.

She turned and looked at him intently, not knowing what to say. Then she looked away, pulling herself up, and walked back to the snowmobile. "We really should get back to the house," she said awkwardly.

He got up and walked after her to pull the snowmobile back upright. "You know, Hessa, the month that you were gone was the worst month of my life. I can't go through that again. I know I can convince your father—I know I can."

"You will never be able to convince my father, Joel. Any love you have for me would eventually fade with the tensions between our families."

"You know that isn't true, and I'm pretty sure you have feelings for me too. There has to be a way for us to be together."

She looked up at him. He was such a strong man, but had such humility and openness. "You have been so wonderful. Never in my life has a man been so kind to me. It has been like a gift, but it's wrong of me to tell you. It would take a miracle…" her jumbled thoughts drifted back to the conversation with Ruth on the plane.

Joel smiled at her hopefully as they got on the snowmobile and headed back slowly toward the house. He wanted this time alone with Hessa to last as long as it could. She wrapped her arms tightly around him, laying her head against his back. "Oh, I do love you," she said softly, the roar of the motor drowning her out. "I love you so much it hurts…"

124

CHAPTER 16

Hessa's mother was fascinated by the little shops in the village of Bennington. She and Mrs. Sully spent hours wandering through each shop and chatting with the owners. Mrs. Sully knew just about everyone by name, and she was excited to tell everyone about her new friend and where she was from.

Each person they spoke to seemed interested in hearing about Muna's impression of their little village. One of the country stores they visited had several varieties of Vermont-made foods. The owner was anxious to have Muna taste just about everything. The cheeses were rich, the fudge melted in her mouth, and the maple syrup was like nothing she had ever tasted.

She bought some cheddar cheese, and chose a selection of fudge to take home as gifts. She also picked up several bottles of maple syrup, along with a cookbook the owner told her had myriads of recipes using maple syrup.

The two women had lunch at a little inn at the end of town. The place was very quaint, with a large fireplace on each end of the dining room. There were colorful Persian rugs throughout the place, and they were fortunate enough to get a table at the far end of the dining room in front of a fireplace.

Mrs. Sully made sure Muna ordered something typical of New England, and after sampling bites of Mrs. Sully's food, asked if this inn had a cookbook as well. Mrs. Sully laughed at Muna's enthusiasm, and the two talked at length about the many differences in their cultures.

After they finished lunch and Mrs. Sully paid the bill, she said to Muna, "I'd love to have a typical Middle Eastern meal, Muna. I might have to put you to work in the kitchen this weekend!"

"I would be happy to cook for your family. We would have many spices to buy, however!" Muna looked over at Mrs. Sully and smiled, thoroughly enjoying the company of this very unusual woman.

The two got back into the car and Mrs. Sully drove Muna to several sights in the area, explaining their history.

Late in the afternoon, Mrs. Sully noticed she had completely lost track of time, and they looked at each other like two children who had discovered they were in trouble. Mrs. Sully turned the SUV around and hurried back home.

By the time they returned to the farm it was dark, and Mrs. Sully was prepared for the famished men in her house. Muna got out of the car and hurried upstairs with her packages and Mrs. Sully ran into the kitchen to start fixing dinner. Tonight it would be simple, as she would make spaghetti and meatballs. She always had a supply of homemade meatballs in the freezer for days like this.

As she started dinner, Muna came in and thanked her hostess for their day together. "I cannot remember when I have enjoyed myself so much," she said. "I have never known any Americans, and I think we make assumptions about people we do not know. I have never met anyone like you, Maggie. You have made me feel so at home, I think I will never want to leave!"

"You're welcome to stay as long as you like. Today was fun for me, too! I'm around men so much, it's nice to have a day with just the girls once in a while," Mrs. Sully said.

The two stood side by side in the kitchen as Muna helped Mrs. Sully prepare the meal. The boys were scattered in different parts of the house, and Petie had taken Hessa to the game room to teach her how to play pool.

Mrs. Sully heard a door close at the side of the house, and Mr. Sully yelled, "I'm home! Where is everybody?"

126

"Oh honey, come into the kitchen! You need to meet our guest. I'm sorry I wasn't at the door to greet you, but I have tomato sauce all over my hands," Mrs. Sully said.

Mr. Sully walked into the kitchen, and Muna gasped as Mrs. Sully burst into laughter. He was wearing a red wig in a pageboy haircut, thick black oversized glasses, freckles painted across his nose, and a set of very large buck teeth. He wore a giant yellow bow tie and red suspenders. He acted as though this was perfectly normal.

He walked over to Mrs. Sully and said, "Hello, dear. How was your day?" He leaned down and kissed her cheek, then turned to Muna. "How do you do, my name is John." Muna didn't know what to say. She just stared up at this crazy person wearing the most ridiculous get-up she had ever seen.

"What on earth are you wearing?" Mrs. Sully asked, laughing as she patted her husband's arm.

"Don't you remember the TV show in the 70's called 'Laugh-In'?" This was one of the characters they had on the show. We did a commercial today, and I had the whole staff dress up as the Farkle family. I think it'll be our best commercial yet."

"You forget that I'm several years younger than you, honey. I don't remember 'Laugh-In". So, why are you still wearing your costume?" Mrs. Sully asked.

"We finished shooting the commercial pretty late, so I just got in the car and drove home. I thought you could all use a laugh anyway."

Mrs. Sully couldn't stop laughing. "Those glasses are so big they make you look cross-eyed."

Mr. Sully looked intently at his wife through his huge glasses, eyes crossed, teeth protruding. With a solemn look on his face he replied, "Maggie, you need to take me seriously. This is going to be one of our best commercials. I really need your support on this."

She simply looked up at him and stood up on her toes to kiss him on the cheek. "You're quite a character, honey."

Just as he was finishing what he was saying, Patrick and Mikey walked into the kitchen. As soon as they saw their father they broke into screams of laughter. Mikey jumped up and down as he was laughing, and Patrick ran out of the kitchen, yelling for everyone to come into the kitchen to see Dad.

Sean and Conor ran in and immediately burst into peals of laughter. The older boys and Hessa filed in behind them, and soon the whole house was in an uproar. Muna finally realized that this must be normal behavior for Mr. Sully, and covered her mouth as she laughed hesitantly.

Mr. Sully told the family about his costume, and the commercial that was to be his masterpiece. The Sullivan boys dissolved into another wave of hysterics, obviously approving of the idea.

Mrs. Sully finally spoke up. "I'm so sorry, Muna and Hessa. There is no excuse for him. This is just what you get when you visit the Sullivans." She looked over at her husband and said, "Okay dear, why don't you get changed and boys, you need to wash your hands for dinner. Conor, please go to the chore list to see who's setting the table tonight."

"If you ladies will excuse me, I'll see you at dinner," Mr. Sullivan said, and walked out of the room.

Conor informed Sean that it was his turn to set the table, but Mrs. Sully asked Conor to help his brother. They added another leaf in the table and got out the linens Mrs. Sully had asked for. Patrick poured water in the glasses and Mrs. Sully filled a giant pasta bowl with the spaghetti. Muna had made the salad and set it on the large buffet in the dining room. Mrs. Sully also made fried ravioli stuffed with cheese, and put out her famous garlic cheese bread.

The house smelled fabulous with the mix of hot bread, cheese, garlic, and tomato sauce. A fire blazed in the fireplace at the far end of the dining room, and the pine logs that burned just added to the wonderful odors that seemed to infuse the home. They said a blessing over the food and everyone dug in.

128

Mr. Sully described what had happened that day while shooting the car dealership commercial. The group started laughing all over again. After the hilarity died down, he finally asked the two female visitors about themselves.

"I want to hear all about where you're from, your family, and how you got to Vermont!" Mr. Sully said, grinning.

Muna was the first to speak up, and gave a broad explanation of their homeland in Israel. She told them about her son and new grandbaby, and how Hessa had decided on attending Harvard.

"What does your husband do?" Mr. Sully asked.

"He is an attorney," she said.

"What type of law does he practice?" he asked.

"Human rights," she said simply and changed the subject to Hessa and her love of history, and plans to become a teacher.

They finished dinner and the boys all pitched in to clear the table. Mrs. Sully made coffee and brewed tea, putting it out on the buffet. For dessert she made fondue. There were three pots: one filled with chocolate, one with caramel, and one with strawberry sauce.

She put the pots in the middle of the table and brought out several plates of sweets to dip in the sauces. She had cut up and cubed pound cake and brownies, sliced strawberries, and made bite-sized chocolate chip cookies to dip in the sauces.

Hessa and her mother had devoured their food, and they both commented on how wonderful everything tasted. When dessert was over, Mr. Sully suggested they move into the family room for games.

Joel and Hessa sat next to each other, and her mother couldn't help but notice something developing between them. When they spoke to each other the attraction between them was almost palpable.

As he instructed her on the game he would smile and wink at her, squeezing her arm or nudging her. Mr. and Mrs. Sully exchanged glances as they observed the chemistry between Joel and Hessa. There was no denying it—Joel was more than just interested in this girl.

It started getting late, so Mrs. Sully told Patrick and Mikey to get ready for bed. Conor also excused himself to go to bed, since he was going to be up early to go snowboarding with friends the next morning. Mr. Sully asked Sean to go out to the barn with him to check on the animals.

Mrs. Sully asked Henry about his relationship with Audra, hoping at the same time to get some idea of what was happening between Joel and Hessa.

"Things are going okay," he said. She's been In Switzerland skiing with her family for the holidays, so I didn't see anything of her over Christmas. She's actually getting in tonight, but I'm not going to see her until school starts on Monday. I'm sure she'll be tired from her trip, so she'll probably just rest tomorrow."

"What about you, Eddie? Is there anyone special in your life?" Mrs. Sully asked.

"No, Mrs. Sully. You're already taken, so I'm going to wander the earth alone for the rest of my life," he said with a theatrical sigh.

Mrs. Sully laughed and leaned over to tousle his hair. "You're so adorable, Eddie. You just make sure you meet someone who deserves you."

"Stop, you're making me blush!" he said grinning.

"We just need to help Eddie find someone from his own species," Petie said, punching his friend in the shoulder.

"Watch it Petie. Just because you have your mommy here to protect you doesn't mean I won't give you a good thumping when you're asleep tonight," Eddie replied, smiling deviously.

Mrs. Sully ignored them as she turned to Joel and asked, "What about you, Joel? You never told me how you met Hessa."

Joel explained how they had met at the library. He told them that he had found out she would be all alone for the weekend before she returned to Israel for the winter break, so he spent the weekend showing her the sights of Boston.

Hessa's mother listened intently to Joel's story with conflicting thoughts and feelings. He was kind, thoughtful, handsome, brilliant.....and

130

Jewish. *Poor Hessa,* she thought. She wanted so much for her daughter to be happy, never having had a chance for happiness herself.

Every experience she'd had since arriving in America had been fabulous. The Sullivans were the most loving and warm family she had ever met...so very different from her world.

She was sure that she'd never had so much fun in her whole life than the one day she had spent with the Sullivans. Her walls and defenses had crumbled and she felt as though she was a part of this family in a very short time. She had gone a lifetime feeling alone and separated from her real family, married to a man she didn't love, and who didn't love her.

Could there be a way for Hessa to find this kind of happiness? Muna thought to herself as she watched her daughter looking adoringly at Joel. *Maybe a miracle...*

131

CHAPTER 17

The next morning Muna awoke feeling disoriented. There were no sounds of the city; the quiet of the farm had lulled her into a deep, dreamless sleep. It was still dark outside, so she looked at the clock on the bed stand. It was 5:30 a.m. She got out of bed and pulled on her robe, walking downstairs quietly so as not to disturb anyone.

On her way to the kitchen to make herself a cup of tea, she noticed the light on in the living room. She walked around the corner and found Mrs. Sully wrapped in a blanket, sitting in an over-stuffed chair, reading in front of a roaring fire in the fireplace. She looked up and greeted her guest. "Good morning, Muna. I hope I didn't wake you."

"No, I did not hear you get up. I slept so well that I woke up full of energy. I was going to make myself a cup of tea. Would you like some?" she asked.

"Let me get it—you're the guest!" Mrs. Sully answered, and started to get up.

"Please stay seated. You look so comfortable. I know where everything is," Muna replied, and walked into the kitchen. Maggie smiled to herself as Muna walked toward the kitchen to get the tea. Obviously her guest felt very much at home.

Muna came back shortly with a teapot and an assortment of teas. She set them down on the coffee table in front of Mrs. Sully, who put her book down and picked out a bag of her favorite English breakfast tea and put it in her cup, pouring the hot water over it. Muna found some jasmine tea to try.

"What are you reading?" Muna asked.

"The Bible—this is the only time of the day that I can read and pray without any interruptions."

"Yes, that is generally when I start my prayers, but I pray five times a day," Muna said.

Mrs. Sully smiled. "There's nothing more wonderful than to know the Lord is listening, don't you agree?"

"You really think He's listening when you pray?" Muna asked.

"Oh, absolutely! When I have this quiet time with Him in the morning, I sense His presence and experience great peace."

Muna was curiously interested. "I have read the Koran all my life and prayed several times each day, but have never felt a peace, and certainly have never felt the presence of Allah. I do not even know if he hears my prayers, because I am a woman."

"The Bible talks a lot about the peace God gives you. Not as the world gives, and not a peace that we can humanly understand. It's something that comes from a close relationship with Him, whether we are male *or* female."

Muna felt sadness creeping over her. She almost felt jealous of the personal way Maggie spoke about her God. She edged a little closer to opening up about her life.

"I admire you, Maggie, and I envy you with the joy and happiness of your home. I love being here."

"Do you miss your family and friends at home?" Mrs. Sully asked.

"I miss my son and grandson, of course, but my husband...." she trailed off.

"Tell me," Maggie urged gently.

"He is a very stern and harsh man. Our marriage was arranged. I did not meet him until our wedding day. I knew when I met him that my life would be very lonely. Hessa and her brother have been my only joy. Now Imaad is married with a family of his own, and Hessa is attending school here. My life no longer has much meaning." Muna looked down, embarrassed she had shared so much.

134

Mrs. Sully moved closer to Muna on the couch. She put her arm around Muna's shoulder and squeezed it. "You know, Muna, God says to call to Him, and He will answer and tell us great and mighty things that we do not know," Maggie said. "Ask Him to reveal Himself to you. Seek Him, and you'll find Him."

"You have been so kind to me, and Joel is like a part of your family. I thought Christians hated Muslims...and Jews for that matter. I have been wrong on both accounts. I wish I had what you had. There is such turmoil inside me, and sometimes my sadness is overwhelming." Muna fought to keep back the tears.

"You've definitely come to the right place. You're loved here, Muna. I wish I could have you here longer, but I wouldn't want to be disrespectful of your husband." Mrs. Sully said.

"He expects me back next Thursday, and I would never be able to change that. I dread returning. We have no life together. I do not know where he is travelling most of the time. My parents are no longer alive, and I cannot spend all my time at my son's house. He has his own life. It is such an empty feeling."

"You don't have to feel empty, Muna—even though the relationship you have with your husband is distant. You said you would like to have what I have. It's not just the loving family life you see in our home. It's also the relationship we have with God."

"I sense that. But I am a Muslim, and everything you believe is different from what I believe. I could never change the things I was raised to believe all my life. Besides, there are very serious consequences for Muslims who become Christians," Muna said, looking nervous.

"I understand," Mrs. Sully answered. "But tell me, if you're praying five times a day and hold to the teachings of your Koran, why do you feel empty?"

Muna looked at Mrs. Sully, confusion written on her face. "I have wondered about that many times," she answered.

"Let me challenge you. I'll give you a Bible. Read it and see what you discover. God will make a trail in your life so you can find Him. He

135

won't hide Himself from you. I won't say any more on this…the rest is up to you. But remember Muna, there are no coincidences. There was a reason you came to stay."

Mrs. Sully got up from the couch and left the room for a moment. When she came back, she had a small black Bible in her hand. "Please take this as a gift from me. If you feel uncomfortable having it with you when you get home, just leave it somewhere. I know this could get you in trouble at home, but maybe you could read some of it on your trip back to Israel."

"Oh thank you Maggie, this is very kind of you. I am intrigued by what you say. There is love in the words you speak, and that in itself makes it worth looking into," Muna said, and opened up the Bible.

The room felt a little chilly, so Maggie went over to a cabinet outside of the living room and brought back a quilt. She laid it in Muna's lap, and sat back on the couch, wrapping herself in her own blanket. The two sat side by side reading and sipping tea as Muna occasionally asked her a question.

❧❧❧

Shortly after seven a.m. Mikey padded into the living room and found his mother and Mrs. Bishara sitting on the couch talking. "Mom, are we having pancakes and sausage today?"

"Well of course we are, my little man!" Mrs. Sully said. "Will you go into the kitchen and take out everything we'll need to get breakfast started?"

"Sure, anything for pancakes!" Mikey yelled as he ran to the kitchen.

"Well, I guess our moment of solitude is over for today," Mrs. Sully said smiling. "Why don't you go upstairs and get dressed, and I'll go into the kitchen to see what kind of mischief my little one is getting himself into."

Muna smiled at Maggie and turned to make her way back up to her bedroom. She'd had a wonderful time this morning with her friend.

136

She loved everything about this house—the big comfortable furniture, the smells, the wonderful food…but most of all, the family that had embraced her and her daughter. Maybe there was something to what Mrs. Sully had said that morning. She aimed to find out one way or another.

The aromas of the coffee brewing and pancakes on the griddle drew the household downstairs one by one. Mikey was having a ball flipping pancakes with his mother supervising close by. She was busy making syrup from blueberries she had picked and frozen the summer before. Four enormous pieces of sausage simmered in a large skillet, looking like enough for an army.

Mr. Sully walked in, newspaper in hand, and kissed his wife good morning. He poured himself a large cup of coffee and walked into the family room to read his paper.

Conor came running into the kitchen, asking his mother if he could grab a couple of pancakes before his friends picked him up for snowboarding. She quickly piled a stack of pancakes on a plate, and set out two small pitchers of syrup—one blueberry and one maple for his choice. Then she cut off a piece of sausage and dropped it on his plate.

"Thanks Mom!" he said, wolfing down his breakfast as he walked to the kitchen table.

Sean and Patrick were in the family room watching TV. Petie, Henry, Eddie, and Joel all filed into the kitchen, set the table, and put everything out that would be needed for breakfast. Hessa and Muna walked into the kitchen just as the food was ready to be served.

Mr. Sully went over to the fireplace in the dining room and started a fire, then sat down and continued to read his newspaper, waiting for the kids to fill their plates before going over to the buffet himself. Conor finished his breakfast in the kitchen, grabbed his gear, yelled goodbye and off he ran out the door to the waiting car.

Mrs. Sully brought out the blueberry pancakes and syrup, and their staple—Vermont-made maple syrup. Everyone ate in relative quiet. The pancakes were delicious and the boys continued to pile more pancakes on their plates and stuff themselves.

137

Finally the whole group groaned about having eaten too much.

Mrs. Sully asked the older boys to clean up the kitchen while she and Mr. Sully, along with Muna and Hessa, finished drinking their coffee.

Mr. Sully spoke first. "Ladies, how has your stay been so far? Has our clan of boisterous young men gotten to you yet?"

"Oh no," Muna answered. "I love being a part of the activity. My home is so quiet, I wish I could put all the noise and laughter in a bottle and take it with me when I leave."

"I think that could be arranged. Maggie, which of our boys shall we send home with Muna?" Mr. Sully wiggled his eyebrows and gave them a mischievous grin.

"Don't pay any attention to him, Muna. I promise he's only kidding. John, you shouldn't tease like that. The Bisharas are likely to take you seriously," Mrs. Sully said.

"I will take Mikey, Sean and Patrick," Muna said, laughing. "I know the older boys have too many activities to be able to come home with me."

Hessa looked at her mother. Barely two days had passed since their arrival at the Sullivan home and Muna was a different person. She was relaxed and happy. Hessa had never heard her mother joke about anything. This family seemed to positively impact the life of anyone who met them.

"Now, Miss Hessa, you don't have to answer this question, but I'm curious. It looks as though you and Joel are something of an item. You both seem as though you're walking on air. Is this love?" Mr. Sully asked.

Hessa's face blazed red, and she looked at her mother nervously. "I um...Oh, no, Joel and I are friends. I am grateful to him for his hospitality to me and my mother. I am also grateful for being able to spend the weekend with your family," she said quickly, looking down at her hands folded in her lap.

"John, shame on you for prying," Mrs. Sully said. "Besides, I don't think Hessa's mother and father would appreciate our trying to be matchmakers."

"Hessa is promised to a man back in Israel," Muna replied. "It was arranged many years ago."

"Well now, that sure is disappointing!" Mr. Sully exclaimed. "Those two are clearly developing feelings for each other. I wouldn't be surprised if they were already in love."

"John! Oh, my goodness, I'm so sorry Muna and Hessa. Mr. Sullivan really shouldn't be allowed to talk. Honey, don't you need to go and feed the pigs or something?" Mrs. Sully asked.

"I know when I'm not wanted," Mr. Sully said, shrugging his shoulders. "I guess men just see things as they are. I'm very sorry if I've offended you, ladies. I believe that we should do anything we can to make the best of this life. I'm sure you would agree with that, honey." He looked over at his wife, smiling.

"I understand, Mr. Sullivan. I am not at all offended. Your ways are different from ours, and I am beginning to think that is not such a bad thing," Muna replied.

Hessa looked at her mother again. *What is happening with her?* Hessa thought to herself. *It is like we have crossed over into another universe, and there is a stranger talking who looks like my mother.*

"I'm going to excuse myself before I get into any more trouble," Mr. Sully said with a grin. "I actually do need to feed the animals and take care of some other things outside to stay out of mischief. Good morning to you, ladies."

Mrs. Sully watched her husband walk out of the dining room, and then turned around to look at Muna and Hessa. She shrugged her shoulders and said, "As I said before, there is just no excuse for him." The three women looked at each other and laughed.

Mrs. Sully went over to the buffet to get the pot of coffee and refilled everyone's cups. Muna looked at her daughter thoughtfully and asked, "What *is* happening between you and Joel?"

"Nothing, Mother," Hessa replied.

"Would you like to be alone to talk?" Mrs. Sullivan asked.

139

"No Maggie. I am comfortable with you here. I think you could be very helpful, since I am not familiar with American relationships," Muna answered.

Mrs. Sully described a typical American courtship to Muna. She told her about how parents didn't have much of a say in their children's relationships, and that young people chose their own spouses. She went on to explain that many times a young couple would make their marriage plans without very much feedback from the family at all.

"I'm sorry to be so hard on my country's casual ways on marriage, but there you have it," Mrs. Sully said.

"Won't you tell me anything, Hessa?" her mother asked.

"I will admit to you that Joel has been very kind to me. He has been a perfect gentleman, and would not compromise me. I have never known anyone who is more concerned about me than Joel. You must admit, Mother, this is very unusual for a man."

"I can understand why you are drawn to him, Hessa, but what can we do? You have been promised to Qasim. There is no way to change what has been decided," her mother said.

"Well, there is a way, but it won't be anything we can do on our own," Mrs. Sully said.

"What do you mean?" Hessa said, her mother nodding in agreement to the question.

"We can't force our hand in this—we need to pray for a miracle," Mrs. Sully said.

Hessa's eyes widened and her mouth dropped open slightly.

"What is it, Hessa?" Mrs. Sully asked.

"That is just what a woman on my flight to Israel said a few weeks ago."

Muna and Hessa smiled hopefully at one another, taking each other's hands. Mrs. Sully reached out and grasped the other two women's hands tightly. A bond knit them together by a silent vow they made to await the extraordinary.

140

CHAPTER 18

The rest of the weekend flew by and before they knew it Muna and Hessa were saying goodbye to the Sullivans. Muna walked slowly toward the door, looking sad and dejected. As Joel put their suitcases into the trunk of his car, Muna and Maggie chatted, and then embraced as Muna tried to hold back her tears.

"Thank you again, Maggie. This has been the most wonderful time I can ever remember. I will never forget you or the kindness you have shown to my daughter and me."

"This won't be the last time we see each other," Maggie promised. "I want you to keep me up on everything that happens with both of you."

Hessa hugged Mrs. Sully and thanked her for letting them stay. Mr. Sully and the boys came out to say goodbye, and the two women got into the car. Joel hugged Mrs. Sully and shook Mr. Sully's hand and got into the car. The boys ran inside, but Mr. and Mrs. Sully stayed at the door to wave until the car was out of sight, as always.

The three sat in relative silence for the first few minutes of the trip, each lost in their own thoughts. Muna finally spoke up. "Joel, I want to thank you for inviting us to the Sullivans' home. I had a wonderful time. I feel as if I have friendships that will last for the rest of my life."

"The Sullivans are the best. They've treated Henry, Eddie and me like family since we were in high school. Our families are very different from them. I have to admit, they're a lot more fun than my family."

"Why do you say that?" Muna asked.

"My father and I have never been very close. He's always supported my education but has high expectations for me. I never feel like I'm living up to his requirements, even though I've always done well in school."

"I know how you feel," Hessa said. "I am so afraid of upsetting my father. I never know when I am going to do something that displeases him. I try very hard to do the right thing but"…she trailed off, and looked back at her mother.

"I am sorry, Mama. I did not mean to speak badly of Father."

"I understand, Hessa. But your father is your elder, and you still need to respect him."

"Yes, Mama."

Muna looked back and forth between her daughter and Joel. Two brilliant, wonderful human beings sat in front of her, yet they both felt like they were failing somehow.

"It is difficult to hear you both feel as though you are inadequate in your parents' eyes. Hessa, I can tell you that your father is proud of what you have accomplished in being able to get into Harvard. I know he did not want you to go at first, but he has realized the high honor of being accepted by that school, so now he boasts about you."

Muna continued on, "Joel, I am sure your father feels the same way. How could he not be proud of you? It sounds as though your father is very much like Hessa's. They are just not very good at expressing how they feel. It does not mean he isn't pleased with your accomplishments."

"Thank you, Mrs. Bishara. I guess you're right. I know one thing—if I ever have a son, I'm gonna make sure he knows I'll be proud of him no matter what. I won't want him to think he has to do anything to earn my love or approval," Joel said.

"That is very admirable, Joel," Mrs. Bishara said. She changed the subject. "I do not mean to pry, Joel, but Mr. Sullivan said something this morning that caused me to wonder."

"What's that?" Joel asked.

"He seems to think there is something more than just friendship between you and Hessa. I believe I agree with him."

"Have you and Hessa talked about this?" Joel asked, looking over at Hessa, who quickly looked away.

142

"We have, but she has not come right out and admitted to anything other than having a deep regard for you," Mrs. Bishara said.

"Mama, please, can we change the subject?"

Muna didn't answer her daughter. "I want to tell you Joel, that Mrs. Sullivan and I had a conversation about the two of you this morning. Maggie implied that she would like my daughter to be able to decide for herself in marriage. Hessa has mentioned to you that she is intended for someone else, has she not?"

"Yes, she did mention it," Joel said quietly. He thought about how he could respond, but after a few moments, he blurted out: "Mrs. Bishara, I love your daughter. I want you to know that she hasn't told me she loves me. She's been true to the man she's intended for, but I can't help the way I feel about her."

Hessa turned back to Joel with a horrified expression on her face. She then looked over at her mother with what appeared to be a mixture of fear and anticipation written all over her.

"I admire your honesty. I must admit that I never went through anything like what you are experiencing. I married very young, and had no chance to think my life could be different than what was planned for me," Mrs. Bishara said.

Hessa listened to the conversation between Joel and her mother. She couldn't fathom the change in her mother over these few days. Her experience on this trip had profoundly affected her. She had completely opened up and expressed things Hessa had never heard from her. She seemed to want more for her daughter than what she had been forced to settle for.

"Mother, I think that we should do what Mrs. Sullivan told us this morning. We need to pray for a miracle, and just wait," Hessa said. She looked over at Joel, who reached over and squeezed her hand.

"If you think that'll work, then by all means do it," he said.

They changed the subject for the remainder of the drive back to Boston.

School started the next day with a flurry of activity. With the classes he had this semester, Joel realized he would have to knuckle down and concentrate. He immediately arranged his study groups and organized his schedule. The last few days had been amazing and he couldn't get thoughts of Hessa out of his mind.

He knew it was going to be difficult to stay on task at school, and he realized he would have to be disciplined about the time he and Hessa spent together. He would have to speak with her about limiting their time together; he knew he shouldn't interfere with her workload either.

After his last class Joel went by Thayer Hall where he knew Hessa would be stopping before going to meet her mother. He waited for twenty minutes before she showed up. She came around the corner, looking glorious in a dark blue jacket and white turtleneck, wearing a little navy and white cap with a matching scarf.

He smiled broadly and ran to her, lifting her up and hugging her tightly. He set her down and gazed at her as though he wanted to memorize everything about her.

"How was your first day back? Did you get through it okay, or were you thinking about me too much?" He asked with a mischievous look in his eye.

"Well yes, just barely," she said smiling up at him. "And you? How was your day?"

"It was really busy and hectic. There's something I want to talk to you about. When are you meeting your mother?" Joel asked.

"Not until 5:00. We're having dinner together. Mrs. Sully suggested a couple of places for her to visit today, so she's still away."

"Could we grab some coffee over at Crema?" Joel asked.

"I guess I can go for an hour or so. I have some things to do before I meet my mother," Hessa replied.

They walked hand in hand across Harvard Yard to Harvard Square and made their way to Crema Café. They placed their orders, and walked

144

upstairs where they found a small table. They sat sipping their coffee, gazing at one another, happy to be back in each other's presence.

Joel was the first to speak. "Last weekend was great. I don't think I've ever had so much fun at the Sully's, and I know it's because you were there. Just waking up each morning, knowing I was going to see you made me happy. You've become everything to me, Hessa."

He stopped and searched her face, wanting to know what she was thinking. She looked confused, so he continued, "When we got back and I dropped you and your mother off at the hotel, I felt empty inside. I just wanted to be with you again. I sat in the lobby for about an hour after you left, hoping you would come back down for some reason. Sounds stupid, huh?"

"No, it does not sound stupid, Joel. I felt the same way. When my mother and I went to our room, she kept asking me what was wrong, and why I was so quiet. I didn't tell her. I am afraid she will be worried about my feelings being too deep, and that I will get hurt. We both realize how useless it is to try to change things."

"Hessa, I had to meet with you to tell you that I need to concentrate on my studies, and that we shouldn't spend too much time together during the week." Joel looked at Hessa. She smiled, but her eyes looked sad.

He took her hand and continued, "What I need to tell you is that I don't know if I can make it without seeing you every day. I don't know what I'm gonna do. It's like you've become a part of me, and when you're not around, that part of me is missing. Do you understand?"

"Yes, I do Joel. I feel the same way, but I need to apply myself to my studies as well. If I do not maintain my good grades, my father won't let me return."

They sat for a while longer sipping their coffee and trying to work out a solution to their problem. Before long, Hessa needed to return to the dorm. They got up and started the walk back to Thayer Hall. Hessa wrapped her arm in Joel's and leaned her head against him as they walked.

Nothing had ever made her feel as safe and whole as being with him. They got to the door and stopped.

"Okay," Joel said. "We're gonna make this work somehow. We have each others' class and study group schedules. At least we can call and text each other between classes. Hearing your voice will definitely help. I might just graduate after all!" He laughed and leaned down to hug Hessa.

She turned to go into the dorm, and looked back to wave at him. "I love you, Hessa," he said and waved goodbye.

She couldn't bring herself to return the words. She was so afraid of giving her heart to this man she knew she would someday have to leave. She was hoping for a miracle and had been encouraged by Mrs. Sully's words, but in reality she knew she would eventually graduate from college and return home to marry Qasim.

As she began to walk into the dorm, she turned once more to watch Joel walking away. The thought of someday leaving him and marrying Qasim sickened her. If that was to be her fate, at least she could spend the remaining time she had here with Joel. She ran to catch up with him. He turned when he heard her steps, and she jumped up, threw her arms around his neck, and kissed him passionately.

When she finally pulled back she looked at him and said, "I love you too, Joel. I do love you!" As quickly as she had run to him she turned and ran back into the dorm, disappearing from sight.

Joel felt dizzy. His head was spinning from her kiss. He stood looking after her until the door closed behind her. His heart was pounding, but he felt strengthened somehow. He would find a way for them to be together. He knew Mrs. Sully would be their advocate and he felt better just knowing she wanted to help them.

What do they say? Love conquers all? Joel thought to himself and smiled. Hessa had become the most important part of his life. He wasn't going to give up on the best thing that had ever happened to him.

CHAPTER 19

Hessa got to her room and put her things down. She called her mother to let her know when she would arrive at the hotel. She quickly changed her clothes and ran out the door, across Harvard Yard, and down to the Charles Hotel. When she arrived at her mother's room she started to knock, and heard a deep voice from the other side of the door.

Before a thought could register in her mind, her father opened the door. Her heart stopped and she froze before him. "Hello Hessa. Aren't you going to welcome your father to Boston?"

"Of course, Father. How are you?" She took his hands, but he brushed her aside. She walked into the room, and he closed the door behind her.

"Not very well. I grew concerned when I didn't hear from your mother for several days. She tells me the two of you were in Vermont, visiting friends. I must say, Hessa, for someone who said she doesn't have much time for friends, you certainly had time to get to know someone well enough to be invited to stay in their home."

"Americans are like that, Father. I have found that they are very solicitous and hospitable. They...." Hessa said before her father cut her off.

"Enough!" Her father roared. "You and your mother will pack your things. You are coming back to Israel with me!"

"But, I..." Hessa stammered.

"Do not anger me any more than you already have! When your mother is finished packing we will go to your dormitory to get your

147

things," her father said, fury written on his face. He frightened her into silence.

Her father sat down in a chair, then got up and paced back and forth. He turned back to Hessa, and said in a quietly menacing voice, "Do you think that you could get away with what you have been doing?"

"I haven't done anything wrong," Hessa said in a small voice.

"When your mother didn't call, I decided to look into where you were. It didn't take much time to find out where the two of you had run off. These are *my* phones, Hessa. I can check phone records.

"I found calls made to a 'Sullivan' name, and calls you had received from a 'Volkenburg' name. Evidently you have been quite busy, my dear. I did some investigation, and found you have kept company with this 'Joel Volkenburg'.

"How did you..." Hessa tried to finish, but again her father interrupted.

"Do not ask me how I know! How do you think I got to where I am without having sources for all sorts of information? Do you think it would be difficult for me to track the activities of my own daughter? You should have thought about this foolishness before you started a relationship with this, this...person," her father said sneering at her menacingly.

Hessa's mother finished packing and put her suitcases by the door. Her father called for the bellman to pick up her things, then made a call for a car service to pick them up once they arrived in Tel Aviv.

When the bellman reached their room, he nervously hurried to get the luggage packed onto the cart as quickly as possible. They rode down the elevator in silence, and Mr. Bishara moved the women quickly across the lobby and out the door, pushing them into a waiting car.

"You have twenty minutes to pack your things, Hessa. I also expect you to put your hijab on before we go anywhere else. You disrespectful little..." her father trailed off, so caught up in his rage he'd forgotten the driver in the front seat. When they got to the dorm, Mrs. Bishara offered to help Hessa pack.

148

"You two have twenty minutes to get everything ready. Whatever you can't pack, I will arrange to be shipped back to Israel. Get going!" he shouted.

The two scurried up the walk and into the dorm. As soon as they were inside, Hessa burst into tears. She cried convulsively, taking in deep gulps of air. When they got into Hessa's room, her mother began to cry silently, trying to console her daughter.

"I cannot leave, Mother! I cannot! I will never see Joel again! I love it here, and I love..." she caught herself.

"You love Joel," her mother said with tears streaming down her face. "It was not difficult to tell. Love radiates from both of you for each other. I am so sorry, my dear one."

Suddenly the door opened and it was Hessa's roommate, Courtney. She smiled to greet them, but immediately realized something terrible had happened.

"What's wrong?" she asked, her smile turning to a look of concern.

"My father wants me to go home," Hessa said sniffling and taking in ragged breaths.

"Why? Did something happen?" Courtney asked, confused.

"No, he just doesn't feel Harvard is the right place for me. He has some concerns," Hessa answered, trying to pack as quickly as possible.

Hessa's mother had gotten all of her things out and put them on the bed to pack into the suitcases. "We only have ten minutes left, Hessa. We must go soon."

Courtney stood looking at them, confused. "I feel so bad we didn't get to know each other better, Hessa. I really like you, and you were the best roommate I could have asked for. I'll really miss you."

"I wish you all the very best things Courtney. This is such a wonderful school, you are so fortunate to be able to complete your education here," Hessa replied, and turned to concentrate on her task of packing.

Hessa's mother finally got the last bag packed and zipped it closed. There were a few items she wasn't able to fit, so she asked Courtney if she would be able to mail them to their home in Jerusalem.

Mrs. Bishara gave her the address and said, "Thank you so much for your kindness, Courtney. Hessa always spoke well of you. We must be going now. Goodbye, and do not feel you need to hurry to mail those items." She gave Courtney some cash to take care of the cost of the package.

Courtney ran over to Hessa and hugged her. "I'll write to you, Hessa. Maybe I can visit you someday. I'd love to see Israel," Courtney said.

"Thank you, Courtney. I would love it if you wrote to me. I have come to love you Americans." She smiled a weak smile as she and her mother turned and walked out the door, trying to juggle the suitcases.

Courtney picked up a couple of things that had fallen and followed them down to the waiting car. Hessa's father got out of the car along with the driver, and they fit everything but one smaller carry-on bag in the car.

Mr. Bishara turned to Courtney and requested she mail the suitcase to their home. "But my phone is in that one," Hessa said.

"Leave it!" Mr. Bishara shot back at her. "You won't need it." He turned and got into the car, and they drove off into the night.

Courtney stood looking after them, wondering what kind of trouble her friend might have gotten herself into. *Her father sure is a scary guy*, she thought to herself. *I hope she'll be okay.* She shivered, mostly from the fear Hessa's father had planted in her, then she turned and walked back into the dorm, sadly mourning the loss of her roommate.

Hessa's father barely said a word on the flight to Israel. He wouldn't look at her, and only said one- or two-word sentences to her mother. Otherwise, he was deeply involved in typing into his laptop, and reading papers he had brought with him to Boston.

150

Muna had been afraid before in her life, but this time it was different. She didn't know what would happen when they got back to Jerusalem, and she feared for her daughter as well as for herself. If her husband knew Hessa had developed a relationship with Joel, he could take drastic measures of discipline for both of them.

She tried to sleep, but couldn't even close her eyes. She looked over at Hessa, who seemed to be having the same trouble. Now and then they would exchange glances, but they both silently knew it was best to remain quiet.

Hessa finally fell into a fitful sleep. Her dreams were strange, and kept awakening her. She would have glimpses of Joel in her dream, and suddenly Ruth, the woman from her flight back to Israel, entered into her subconscious telling her everything was going to work out for the good.

Then Mrs. Sully popped into her vision, saying beautiful things that sounded poetic: *Your unfailing love will last forever. Your faithfulness is as enduring as the heavens.* Then, *those who know Your name trust in You, for You, O Lord, have never abandoned anyone who searches for You.*

Her eyes flew open and she sat up. Hessa realized she had been crying in her sleep. She touched her face, and quickly wiped away the tears before her father noticed. She looked over at her mother, who sat reading a magazine. Her heart went out to her mother, who had never experienced the love of a man in her life—had never experienced companionship and friendship.

Hessa ached deeply for her mother, not knowing how she could ever help her. She felt lost and desperate, and wanted to fall back to sleep so she could hear Mrs. Sully saying those beautiful things in her dreams again.

Her thoughts went to Joel, wondering what he would say or do when he found out she was gone. She hoped he would realize that going back to Israel wasn't her idea—that she had no choice. She choked back tears that felt about to burst out of her once more, overwhelmed at the thought of never being able to see him again.

151

God, oh God, are you listening? If the words I read about you are real, then please show Yourself to me. Are you loving like that book says? Help me, help me. Please help me! She sat staring at nothing, hoping to see or feel something, or Someone. It was a couple of hours before she was able to fall back to sleep, and finally she slipped into dreamless peace.

CHAPTER 20

Hessa woke to the feel of the plane descending. The flight back to Israel seemed an eternity, and she wasn't happy to be here this time. She dreaded what her father would do when he got them back home. Hessa's mother had been a very submissive wife, so there hadn't been much reason for her father's anger to be released on her.

This time was much different, however. Her mother had taken a step of independence, and her father had experienced a much different wife. Hessa feared for her mother more than for herself.

As the plane landed, Hessa peered over at her mother. She had a very strange look on her face—a mixture of relief and fear. She couldn't quite figure out what might be going on in her mother's thoughts. They pulled up to the gate, and Hessa's father immediately got out of his seat and pulled their carry-on luggage down. He forcefully motioned for his wife and daughter to get out of their seats and to start moving.

After they collected their bags from baggage claim, Hessa and her mother walked quickly after her father, trying to keep up with him as they reached the car waiting to take them home. There was more silence in the car; the only noise they heard was her father making or receiving calls.

He became aggravated at someone on the other end of the phone. After a few moments, he told the person on the phone he would take care of the problem after he got home, and hung up abruptly. The call only seemed to enrage him further.

When they arrived home Hessa and her mother worked quickly to get their luggage out of the car and went up to their rooms. After they had brought everything into the house, Hessa ran upstairs and shut the door to her room. A short time later her mother knocked on her door and without waiting for an answer, entered her room. She sat down on the bed and looked at her daughter, despair written on her face. Finally she spoke.

"I do not know what will become of us. I do not know what his plans are. We must stay together, Hessa. We must support one another. Do you understand?"

"I do not know, Mother. This is all very confusing. I do not know how Father could have known there was anything going on between Joel and me. When we talked on the phone, it was just to make plans."

"That is all he had to hear, Hessa. Keep in mind he could have had someone watching you as well," her mother said, her voice shaking.

"I tell you, my dear Hessa, I would not change anything about our visit to America. It was the most wonderful thing that ever happened to me. I will never forget it. It was worth whatever the consequence may be."

"Why do you think something is going to happen? He just wanted me to come home, didn't he?" Hessa asked hopefully.

"Let us hope it is only that," her mother answered.

Hessa's father barged into the room without knocking. "What are you two talking about? Could it be about America? Well ladies, you will never set a foot in that country again, I can assure you."

Hessa and her mother looked at her father, afraid to say anything. Muna closed her eyes as if she was trying to block out the furious look on her husband's face. She bent her head down and clasped her hands together as if to will herself to keep calm.

Finally Husaam spoke again. "Hessa, I have made arrangements for you. I have enrolled you at King's College in London. It will fit into our plans much better than Harvard—you can get your degree there. You will be approximately 45 minutes from where Qasim attends London School of Economics, so you will be able to see him more often. I believe you should be spending more time with the man who you will marry rather than some American Jew."

Hessa stared at her father, too afraid to say anything or to question him. It was useless to plead with him to stay home or to promise she would

154

focus on her studies and nothing else if he would just allow her to stay in Jerusalem. She choked back tears and simply nodded at her father.

Mr. Bishara acknowledged her and simply said, "Don't bother unpacking. You will be leaving early Friday morning. School starts on Monday." He turned without another word and left the room.

Terror filled Hessa's heart as she realized her fate had been decided for her once again, and there was nothing she would be able to do about it. She would never see America again, never again see Joel. She knew in her heart that her father would make it so she wouldn't see much of Israel again either.

She would go to London and be forced to live far from home with a man she didn't even like, much less love. She sank into despair and sat down on the bed next to her mother, who had been silent through her husband's tirade. She put her head down and the tears fell freely, as though her heart had been torn open.

How could such a wonderful holiday end this way? Hessa thought to herself.

Muna took her daughter into her arms and choking back tears, she finally whispered: "Hessa, I think we need to pray. Maggie told me about the God of the Bible, and in fact..." she got up from the bed and went to get her purse. She brought it back to Hessa's room, and pulled out a small black Bible.

"She gave me this," Muna said, and showed Hessa the little Bible. "I have been reading it whenever I have had the chance. It is like nothing I have ever read!"

Hessa gasped, and immediately got up and walked over to one of her suitcases. She opened it up, and from a side pocket she pulled out her own Bible.

"Mother, do you remember the day I drove into the city? I went to a bookstore and bought this and another book. I have been reading them almost every day." She held up her Bible and the *Streams in the Desert* devotional she had purchased.

Her mother looked at her incredulously. How could this have happened to both of them at about the same time, but in utterly different circumstances? Hessa continued, "Mother, do you remember the day Basem was born? You and I went shopping, and when we were at lunch we met a woman named Ruth."

"Yes, I remember her; the woman from the plane. She was the one who mentioned Joel," her mother replied.

"Well, if you remember, she did not actually mention him by name, but I had talked to her about Joel. The point is that she told me about her God. The strange thing was that she was Jewish, but she believes Jesus is the Messiah, like the Christians. She told me to pray for a miracle, and that it wasn't a coincidence we had met," Hessa whispered.

"Yes, you mentioned that to Maggie the last day we were at their home. Earlier that morning Maggie said the very same thing to me!" Muna said much too loudly.

She looked at her daughter intensely and took her hands, holding them tightly. "We are going to ask for a miracle, Hessa. We are going to believe what these two women from two completely different places told us. This truly could not have been a coincidence!"

Mother and daughter hugged one another, sealing the pact they had made to pray and expect a miracle. They had both been profoundly affected by the two women they had met, and realized they shared something very powerful. Hessa's heart lightened, knowing that her life could change by believing God thought enough of her to make a way of escape for her and her mother.

Muna got up from the bed and said softly to her daughter, "I think I have spent more time talking than I should. I had better leave before your father comes in again. Good night, my precious child. I am so glad that we have each other." She walked to the door, quickly brushing the tears from her eyes, and turned back to Hessa, mouthing the words, *I love you* to her, and left the room.

Hessa opened the suitcase and put the Bible securely back into its place. She then took out her pajamas and things she would need to get

156

ready for bed. She felt strangely optimistic about her life. The circumstances hadn't changed—she was still going to London, but she felt confident that even if she *did* go to London, maybe she and Joel could somehow find a way back to each other. The only thing to do now was to pray for a miracle—just as Ruth had said.

Hessa snuggled under the covers and thought about the vastness of the universe, and this God she had always thought of as austere and distant. She was beginning to see Him so differently—as a Father who was somehow holding her hand, leading her onward.

"When I think about how large this world is, and the whole universe for that matter, who am I that You would think about me?" she whispered, "Yet somehow I know that You do", and she drifted off to sleep, feeling as though she was wrapped in a blanket of peace and profound love that was beyond her understanding.

CHAPTER 21

Joel woke up feeling like he could conquer the world. Hessa had returned his declaration of love, and it made him feel as though they would be able to get through anything together.

It was still dark when he got out of bed and pulled on his sweats to go for a run before school. Being out in the cold air invigorated him. Breathing in the crisp air as he picked up speed hurt his lungs, but made him feel even more alive.

He returned to his house and took a shower, hurriedly getting ready for school so he could stop by the dorm to see Hessa before class started. He had left her a message, but hadn't heard back from her yet. He stopped to get coffee on his way to the dorm, picking up Hessa's favorite latte along with black coffee for himself.

He tried to get in touch with her a couple more times without success, and assumed she was in the shower. As he approached Thayer Hall he called again—still no answer. He waited outside the dorm and after a few minutes a young woman in a jean jacket, pigtails, and black horn rimmed glasses opened the door. He approached her as she was still walking through the door.

"Excuse me—hi, could you tell me if you know someone named Hessa who lives here?"

"How do you know her?" The girl asked.

"She and I...we're very good friends. I've been trying to call her, and she's not answering. I'm kind of concerned," Joel replied

"Uh...I think you'd better wait here. I'll get her roommate," the girl said and ran back into the dorm.

Joel waited impatiently, and finally a girl who was about the same height as Hessa, with blond hair, striking green eyes and freckles walked up to him.

"Are you Joel?" she asked.

"Yes, I am," he replied, his heart starting to beat wildly with apprehension.

"I'm Courtney, Hessa's roommate. She told me about you. I'm sorry to tell you this, but she left last night," Courtney said.

"What do you mean, she *left*?" Joel asked, feeling as though the wind had been knocked out of him.

"Her father came to get her. He seemed really angry. Hessa and her mother were in our room packing when I came in. They didn't say much...just that Hessa was going back to Israel. Her father evidently told her Harvard wasn't the right place for her. They packed her things so fast I didn't get much of a chance to talk to her."

"Did she say she was going back to Israel for sure?" Joel asked breathlessly.

"Not exactly, but I told her I wanted to visit her there someday. I just assumed..." Courtney trailed off.

"What do you mean you 'assumed'?" Joel said louder than he'd meant to.

"Joel, don't get worked up. I don't know what was going on. It just looked like Hessa was really upset. She and her mother both looked pretty scared. I guess I'd be scared too if I had a dad like hers. Man, he looked like every bad guy you've ever seen in a movie."

"What, what..." he said, searching for words. "Did she tell you where she lived or anything?"

"Yeah, I have her address. I have to mail some of her things back to her. They couldn't fit it all in the car. Let me run upstairs to get it."

Courtney disappeared as Joel stood looking at her in disbelief. He paced back and forth, trying to make sense of what he'd just heard. His thoughts went to their last conversation. There wasn't any indication that she had worries about her father. Come to think of it, she hadn't mentioned

160

much about her father, but anything she ever did say seemed to have an edge of fear.

He stopped pacing for a moment and said out loud, "I need to find her. I need to leave right now!" The pacing began again, only the back and forth got shorter and shorter.

Courtney came back out with a piece of paper in her hand. "Here you go. I wouldn't do anything rash. Hessa's dad looked like a pretty scary guy. You'd better not mess with him. These people live in a part of the world where bombs routinely go off in the streets. You're not prepared for that kind of thing, Joel. I know you're from Boston, and I know who your dad is. Judging by that alone I don't think you're qualified to deal with this."

"Don't you think you're being a little melodramatic, Courtney? I'm not going to just put my hands in my pockets and walk away. People don't just pack their bags and leave in the middle of the night like they have something to hide."

"They didn't leave in the middle of the night..." Courtney said when Joel interrupted.

"You know what I mean! It's just strange. I'm gonna find out what's going on. I'm going to Israel, that's for sure. Thanks for the information, Courtney," and before she could say anything else he headed back to his car at a dead run.

Joel got back to his house in record time, making phone calls on the way home to arrange a flight to Israel as soon as possible. He parked in front of his house in Cambridge and ran up the front steps. He opened the door and slammed it behind him with a loud 'bang' and ran upstairs.

Henry was in the kitchen making coffee and walked out to see what was going on. He saw Joel disappear upstairs, taking the steps two at a time. Henry followed his normally laid-back friend to see what he was up to. He walked into Joel's bedroom to find him pacing back and forth, looking confused and anxious.

"What's wrong, man? Did you set your pants on fire and come home to change?" he said smiling.

161

"Not now, Henry. I need to leave."

"What do you mean, you need to leave? You're a little late for class, bro."

"I'm not going to class. I need to pack," he said as he pulled things out of his closet and bureau, piling them on the bed.

"Pack for what? Where are you going—field trip?" Henry teased.

"Henry, you need to get out of here...really."

"I'm not going anywhere till you tell me what's going on," Henry said, becoming serious.

"Hessa's gone. Her dad came last night and took her back to Israel," Joel said, suddenly stopping in the middle of his room and turning to his friend.

"What? Are you kidding? Why?"

"I don't know. My best guess is that maybe he found out about Hessa and me." Joel said, trying to piece things together as he spoke. "I'm going there to get her."

"Hey, slow down, buddy. You can't do that!" Henry said. "You don't know what you're getting yourself into. Didn't you say she's Palestinian? I mean, you're asking for trouble just showing up over there by yourself. Come on, think man! This is crazy!" Henry said, his voice steadily getting louder.

"Henry, I'm telling you; stay out of this. I don't care what you say. I love this girl—I'm not gonna just let her go."

"This is the flipping Montagues and Capulets, Joel, and you know how Romeo and Juliet ended up. You can't do this! You're my best friend and I'm not gonna let you do something that you'll regret for the rest of your life," Henry pleaded.

"I'll regret it for the rest of my life if I *don't* do something. I'm going to my parents' house—I need a larger suitcase. Don't say anything about this to them. I swear Henry, if you *do*..."

"All right, I won't. Listen Joel, you need to keep in contact with me the whole time you're there, though. How are you going to find her

162

anyway? Are you just gonna wander the streets of Jerusalem showing them pictures of her from your camera phone?" Henry asked sarcastically.

Joel rolled his eyes. "No! I have her address. Her roommate gave it to me."

"Well, that's a start. What can I do, since I can't talk you out of this craziness?"

"Nothing. Just don't tell anyone. I really don't want my parents to worry. They'll never know I'm gone. I'll be back as soon as possible."

After piling his clothes and shaving kit on the bed, Joel ran back downstairs and out to his car, Henry trailing him.

"You take care of yourself. If I don't hear from you at least twice a day I'm coming after you. Are you listening to me Joel? I'm serious!" Henry shouted.

"Yeah, I hear ya. I'll keep in contact and call you as much as possible. Thanks for understanding, Henry. You really are a decent guy. I love you, man," he quickly hugged his buddy, slapping him on the back.

Joel got into his car and roared off to his parents' house. On the way he started to think about what he would say to Hessa's father when he got to their home. He thought of the reasons they should be together and how he would be able to take care of her financially. He even decided to tell Mr. Bishara he would move to Jerusalem so Hessa could be near her parents.

"That'll work," he said to himself, unable to make himself feel any better.

He pulled up to the family home and screeched to a stop. He jumped out of the car and ran in the back door. Helen was in the kitchen baking.

"There's my boy!" Helen said in her usual greeting. "Why are you home in the middle of the day? Are you playing hooky?"

"No, I just need to get something. I'm on a short break and then I'm heading back to school," Joel said as he walked quickly over to kiss her cheek. He ran out of the kitchen and through the house to the stairs.

Just as he mounted the steps two at a time his mother turned the corner, making her way down the stairs.

"Joel, what are you doing here? What's the big hurry?" she asked as pulled on her gloves.

"I just...need to get something," he stammered and continued up the steps.

"Well, I'm late for a meeting. Why don't you come to dinner this Saturday?"

"Ok, sure," he said, not even hearing what she had asked.

As Joel walked into a spare bedroom upstairs, he thought how fortunate he was that his mother was in a hurry. *No questions, no explanations,* he thought to himself. He went into the closet and pulled out a large suitcase. "This should do," he said aloud.

Grabbing the handle he picked it up and hurried downstairs. As he ran back through the kitchen, Helen turned around. "What are you doing with that suitcase?"

"Oh, just going on a trip with the guys," he said with a nervous laugh. "See you later, Helen." Joel ran out the door before she could ask any more questions.

As he got to the car he opened the trunk, threw the suitcase in, and slammed it shut. He got into his car and sat down, scrolling through available flights on the internet through his phone.

Unable to find anything he began calling every airline that had flights to Israel. He backed out of his driveway, madly calling one airline after another, only to be told the same thing. No flights available for two days.

"What's going on?" he shouted to no one. "Is everyone in the world going to Israel this week?" He hung up his phone and threw it on the seat next to him.

"What am I gonna do?" he said aloud, getting more agitated. He was frantic. He couldn't get his thoughts together. "I've gotta get a hold of myself. I've gotta calm down. This isn't gonna help me."

164

He did his best to settle himself, taking deep breaths. He drove along in silence for a while, willing himself to composure. He thought of happier times with Hessa—their first date at the ballet, taking her ice skating, that incredible weekend at the Sully's house. *The Sully's*, he thought to himself.

"I need to see Mrs. Sully. If I'm gonna be stuck here for two days, I'm going somewhere where I don't have to be grilled with questions," he said out loud.

On the drive back to his house in Cambridge, Joel called Mrs. Sully and explained what had happened to Hessa. She became very quiet, and he thought they'd gotten cut off.

"Mrs. Sully, are you there?"

"Yes," she said quietly. Joel asked her if he could come to stay for a couple of days.

"Of course you can, Joel. I'll be waiting."

Joel got to his house and parked out front; he pulled the suitcase out and carried it up to his room. He threw everything in that he'd piled on his bed, going over in his mind what he thought he would need for Israel, and then packed a smaller bag for his trip to the Sully farm. He loaded up his car and sped off for the Sully's. He felt very fortunate that he didn't have to explain anything to anyone else. Henry would tell Eddie and Petie.

On his way to Vermont Joel was finally able to book an evening flight out of Boston for Tel Aviv in two days. He was able to settle down and concentrate on his plans for his arrival in Jerusalem. The next order of business would be to map out directions to Hessa's house and prepare to speak to her father.

Things are starting to look up, he thought...

CHAPTER 22

Joel got to the Sully farm by late afternoon. The moment he entered the driveway he breathed a sigh of relief. He knew Mrs. Sully would be able to help him figure things out. She stood at the doorway waving, just the way she always had when he came to visit. He looked at this woman who had loved him like a son, and it saddened him that he would be the cause for her to worry.

He parked the car and jumped out, not bothering to get his things out of the trunk. He walked quickly to Mrs. Sully and hugged her, thanking her for letting him come on such short notice.

"Joel, you know you're my 'seventh son', she said and smiled warmly at him. "Come on in. You look as though you've been through the mill."

She called out to Conor, who was in the family room playing pool with a friend. "Conor honey, go out to Joel's car and get his things for him. He's leaving his keys by the door for you."

"Did Joel's arms fall off or something?" Conor called from the family room.

"I did *not* hear that, Conor. Joel and I are going into the kitchen to talk. Go get his things and take them upstairs."

Conor didn't reply but grudgingly went out to get Joel's suitcase and took it upstairs to the 'Joel and Henry room'. He ran back downstairs and into the family room, yelling as he went, "Done, Mom!"

Joel and Mrs. Sully had already gone into the kitchen and she asked Joel to sit down while she continued to prepare dinner. Joel had a hard time relaxing so he jumped back up and went over to see what he could do to help.

"We're having beef stew tonight. Could you peel those carrots for me, honey?" and then she asked Joel to explain in detail what had happened.

Joel was happy to have a task while he recounted the story. As he was peeling the carrots, he gave her as much detail of the last 24 hours as he was able. When he finished his account he stopped and looked at Mrs. Sully.

"I'm going over there in two days. I can't just sit here on my hands, hoping for her to come back. That'll never happen," he said.

"Joel, I'm not sure that's such a good idea."

"I knew you'd say that, but just listen to me. I think if I go over and tell Mr. Bishara about my intentions and that Hessa and I love each other, he might understand. I'm willing to live in Jerusalem so that Hessa won't be far from her family. Maybe he just doesn't like the thought of Hessa marrying an American and living here. If I tell him I'm willing to move there, and even become a Muslim, maybe he'll change his mind."

"I don't think you've given this enough thought. You're saying that you're willing to leave your family and friends and move to the other side of the world to marry into a Muslim family, not even knowing who they are or what they're about. I don't mean to sound blunt, but I'm not too sure Hessa's father would care whether you offered to convert to Islam or not. You're Jewish, honey. That's the material fact. You can't change that."

"Yeah, but I don't believe in God. My family doesn't even go to temple. I can't help that I'm Jewish by nationality," Joel argued.

"Joel, you can argue all you want, but one fact remains: there has been strife between Muslims and Jews from time immemorial. You aren't thinking logically if you believe you can just go over there and that Mr. Bishara will welcome you into his home. You're thinking like an American Jew, not one who has lived in an ancient, strife-ridden land.

168

Remember, she's already intended for someone else, and I would imagine their families are close."

Joel became quiet, looking dejected. "What am I gonna do? I've never loved anyone. I've never felt this way; I can't just stop loving her." He looked down at the floor, embarrassed over the words he'd just spoken. He swallowed hard, trying to gulp back his emotions.

Mrs. Sully looked compassionately at Joel with tears in her eyes. "You're breaking my heart, honey. I've never seen you like this before. You've always been so cool and restrained. I've always felt you loved being here and enjoyed our family, but you've never completely entered in emotionally. Since you met Hessa I've witnessed a completely different side of you. It's wonderful to see you open up."

"It doesn't help. In fact, my whole world turned upside down when I first saw her. I couldn't get her out of my mind, even when I hadn't met her yet. When I *did* meet her, I fell in love with her on our first date. You know, Mrs. Sully, I don't think many people really experience finding their soulmate. I mean, Henry's dating Audra because of her dad's connections."

"Well, you know that I found *my* soulmate," Mrs. Sully said. "My case was much simpler than yours, though. Mr. Sully is the most important person in my life. I really had little life before him. But I need to tell you something, Joel. I don't rely on Mr. Sully to be my happiness or fulfillment. He's a wonderful by-product of a blessing, but there's something much more important in my life."

"What?"

"My relationship with God," she said simply.

"You know, Mrs. Sully, I don't think I can hear that right now."

"All right, I'll drop the subject. But before I do I'll tell you a secret."

"A secret? Is this your way of tricking me into listening to some God thing?" he asked with a smirk on his face.

"No, Joel—but I must say, your cynicism is disturbing. When Hessa and her mother were here visiting, I spent time with Muna. I

169

actually gave her a Bible and she immediately began reading it. She said she'd never heard anything like what I'd talked about with her. I have a feeling she and Hessa talked about it."

"Hessa never mentioned it to me. I *would* like to know one thing, though," Joel said.

"What is it?"

"If there's a God, why is there so much strife in the world? I mean, it seems that whenever there's a problem in the world it has to do with religion. You know what else? Have you ever noticed that Israel is always in the news? There's always something going on with Israel, and everyone seems to be against them. Why does a country the size of New Jersey always seem to be in the center of all the world's problems?"

"You certainly asked a mouthful of questions. First of all, God didn't make up religion, man did. God created us to have a relationship with Him, and we complicated the whole thing. He didn't want us making up our own rules, as most religions have done. We have the Bible to guide us and to deepen our knowledge and understanding of God, but man came up with a whole bunch of other things outside of the Bible that just confused the issue."

Mrs. Sully continued, "As for Israel always being in the news— great question. Why *is* such a small, seemingly inconsequential country always in the news? Are they a major producer of oil? No. Do they have other things the world is clamoring for? Not really. Joel, the Middle East is where time on earth began, and it's where it will end *as we now know it.*

"The fascinating thing is that the history of Israel is in the Bible, and things that were prophesied thousands of years ago have come true, and continue to come true. If you studied it for yourself, I think you would be surprised at how accurately everything has come to pass."

Joel looked at Mrs. Sully thoughtfully as she continued: "There *is* no logical explanation apart from God. Just think about the order of things on earth. Think about our DNA. You've studied biology, Joel. How on earth could anyone look at the amount of information in one single strand of DNA and not believe there's a Creator?

170

There are things in this life you just have to take by faith, and God is one of them. You'll need to figure this one out for yourself. No amount of talking on my part is going to convince you."

Mrs. Sully got up and left the room for a moment, and then returned to the kitchen.

"Here." she said, and handed Joel a Bible. "Read for yourself. Prove to yourself that there isn't a God, or that the Bible has inconsistencies. As a scholar Joel, you know that you should do your own research before coming to conclusions. Don't you think that's fair?"

"Yeah, I guess so," Joel replied. "It's funny, I have a friend who told me the same thing. He said he read the Bible to disprove it, but in doing that He found God."

"All right, Joel. Read it yourself. The rest will fall into place. Now, promise me you won't go running off to Israel. Nothing good can come of it. I really fear what could happen if you go looking for her."

"I'll think about it," Joel said, not wanting to get into an argument about why he should or shouldn't go to Israel. "Mrs. Sully, do you have any wine in the house? This has been a stressful day and I think a glass of wine would calm my nerves."

"I can't help thinking of you boys as still being 14 years old," Mrs. Sully said smiling. She went off to the large pantry at the far end of the kitchen, and came back with a bottle.

"Do you like red wine?"

"That's the *only* kind I like!" Joel said, and Mrs. Sully poured him a glass and a small one for herself.

Mrs. Sully raised her glass in the air for a toast; "To the truth."

Joel clinked glasses with her. "To the truth," he echoed, and took a sip.

Dinner was relatively quiet that evening. Mr. Sully was out of town on business, Mikey and Patrick had hockey practice, and their coach had taken the team out for pizza. Sean was at a friend's house for dinner, and Conor's friend joined the Sully's for dinner, so much of mealtime was spent arguing over whether or not the Bruins would make the playoffs.

171

Mrs. Sully left the boys to their heated conversation and cleared the table. She was in the kitchen loading the dishwasher when Joel walked in. He'd finished clearing the table and helped Mrs. Sully clean up the kitchen. They worked together in silence until Joel finally mustered up the courage to tell Mrs. Sully what was on his mind.

"Thanks for talking to me today, Mrs. Sully. I don't think I've ever told you, but you're like my other mom. As a matter of fact, I feel guilty about saying this, but I think I'm closer to you than I am to my own mother. I would never talk to my mother the way I talk to you. I love you, Mrs. Sully. Your family has been the best thing that ever happened to me, besides Hessa."

"That means a lot to me," Mrs. Sully smiled, walking over to Joel to hug him. "It breaks my heart to think you're not close to your mother. Maybe if you tried to talk to her you might be surprised at how she responds. Do you think you could ever tell her how you feel?"

"I don't think she'd know what to do with the information," Joel said sadly. "I feel like Petie, Eddie, and Henry are my brothers. I'm closer to them than I am to my own brother David. I'm just glad I have all of you, and when Hessa came into my life, I realized how much I wanted to have someone to love. I didn't know how much I could love someone."

"There's nothing like it, Joel. You never know, miracles do happen, and I'm a praying woman. Stranger things have happened, honey. Your Hessa could turn up someday—who knows?"

Joel just nodded and smiled at Mrs. Sully. She didn't know that Joel was planning to make that miracle happen himself, and that he would begin his journey to the land of miracles in two days. He took the Bible Mrs. Sully had given him, and saying good night he hugged her and walked up to his bedroom.

172

CHAPTER 23

Joel didn't get much sleep that night. He tossed and turned, got up and paced back and forth in his room, then got back into bed again only to start the whole process over. He kept going over in his mind what he would say to Hessa's father, and what might happen if he didn't agree with Joel's explanation. He played back in his mind the last night he saw Hessa, and what might have gone through her head when she was abruptly taken back to Jerusalem.

Just before dawn Joel finally fell into a deep sleep out of sheer exhaustion. When he awoke, there were cracks of sunlight in the openings of the curtains. He looked at the clock: it was past 10 a.m.

Well, at least I got a few hours of sleep, he thought. He got up and went over to open the curtains. The sun shone brilliantly and there wasn't a cloud in the sky. He smelled coffee and something baking. He pulled on his sweats and walked downstairs to the kitchen.

Joel loved the Sullivan's kitchen. It was warm and homey, and always filled with wonderful smells. Mrs. Sully heard his footsteps as he entered the kitchen and walked over to kiss his cheek.

"Good morning, sleepy head. I thought you were going to laze in bed all day."

"I actually didn't get much sleep. I finally fell asleep at about six this morning", Joel replied.

"Well then, you need some good strong coffee. I baked some blueberry muffins and they're still hot. Sit down and I'll serve you."

"I think I'll go for a run first. Is that okay?" Joel asked.

"Sure. I still have some batter, so I'll wait till you get back and bake some more so your muffins will be hot," Mrs. Sully replied.

Joel turned and walked out the door into the cold sunshine. He looked around the farm appreciatively. It was so peaceful here. The boys were all at school, and the only sounds he heard were the animals.

He ran for quite a while before returning to the farm, exhausted. Joel went upstairs and took a shower, then walked back down to the kitchen and sat down at the table. Mrs. Sully poured him a cup of coffee and sat down with her own cup.

"Feel better?" Mrs. Sully asked, putting her hand over his.

"Yeah. Running really helps make my mind slow down. I feel like I'm going crazy and I'm really anxious, like I'm out of control."

"Be anxious for nothing Joel, but in everything by prayer and supplication with thanksgiving let your requests be made known to God. And you will have the peace of God, which surpasses all comprehension."

"You really have a way with words, Mrs. Sully. I could use a little peace right now."

"Those aren't my words. They're from the Bible."

Joel looked at her and then looked down at his coffee cup. "You know what? When I couldn't sleep last night, I opened the Bible you gave me. I started reading, thinking it would help me go to sleep faster. I thought it would bore me out of my mind, but it was pretty interesting. I read through the whole book of Genesis. It was fascinating, actually. I had a hard time believing some of those things really happened, though."

"Honey, those are actual historical events, not just stories. The Bible gives incredible insights to not only the Middle East, but the rest of the world and why things are the way they are," Mrs. Sully replied.

"I'm desperate. I need to find out what my purpose is. Right now I know it isn't in finishing school. At least, not for now."

"Joel, you're just months away from graduation. Don't throw that away. Hessa will still be there in June. Why don't you wait and go to Israel as sort of a graduation present to yourself?" Mrs. Sully asked.

"I don't know why, but I feel like I need to go right away. I can't wait. I may already be too late. I can't let her marry that guy. She loves me, Mrs. Sully. She told me. I'm not gonna let her go, and nothing you say will stop me."

"I won't try to stop you. You've already made up your mind, but I do need to tell you how I feel," Mrs. Sully said. "I love you so much. It worries me that you'll be travelling to a place you know little about. You'll be with people you don't know. One more thing—have you told your parents?"

"No..." Joel trailed off.

"If you don't tell them, I will," she said.

"If you do, they'll try to stop me. I would never forgive you if they screw up my plans to go over there."

"I'm a mother, Joel. If a parent knew one of my boys was going to do something like that and didn't tell me, I'd be furious. Don't you understand that?"

"I guess so, but I can't believe you're gonna tell my parents. The only thing they care about is my education and following in my father's footsteps. They don't care about me. They'll just be mad that I left and missed some school. My dad'll just be embarrassed that his kid messed up the last semester."

"I'm sure you're wrong, honey. They love you. Some people just don't know how to express their feelings very well," Mrs. Sully said. "I'm sorry, Joel, I can't be silent about this."

"I have to go," Joel said, and got up from the table. "Thanks for everything, Mrs. Sully, and thanks for the Bible. I appreciate everything you've done for me. I really love you!"

He turned and ran up the stairs into his bedroom. He took his clothes hanging in the closet and stuffed them quickly into his bag and grabbed his shaving kit out of the bathroom. Mrs. Sully was waiting for him by the front door when he came down.

175

"Joel, you don't know what you're doing. Please don't leave. Peter just called and he, Eddie, and Henry are on their way here. They're concerned about you, too. Don't do this!" She said as she raised her voice.

Joel ignored her pleas. "Thanks for everything, Mrs. Sully—see you soon."

Joel kissed Mrs. Sully on the cheek and put his free arm around her to squeeze her shoulder. He opened the door and ran out, throwing his suitcase in the trunk.

He started up his car with a roar and sped down the driveway at breakneck speed. Before he got to the end of the driveway he looked out his rearview mirror, and there was Mrs. Sully waving as always. This time, however, she didn't have a smile on her face. She was crying.

Mrs. Sullivan ran back into the house and got on the phone to call Petie. "He just left," she said simply when he answered.

"What? He left? Mom, why didn't you stop him?" Petie yelled.

"He's a little bigger than me, Peter. I did everything I could to try and stop him. I told him that he needed to tell his parents that he was going to Israel. He got upset and left. I'm going to call his mother to fill her in. There's no need for you boys to come here. Turn around and go to the airport. Try to intercept him there," Mrs. Sully said and hung up.

Petie hung up and turned to Henry, who was sitting next to him. "Joel just left my mom's house. It sounds like he's going to the airport, so we should head there."

He explained to Henry and Eddie what had happened between Joel and Mrs. Sully, and that Joel had left when she said she was going to tell his parents.

"I don't know what's happened to him," Eddie said. "This girl has made him a complete loon."

"You met her, Eddie," Henry replied. "She's an amazing girl. I guess I can't blame Joel for falling in love with her."

176

"What are you talking about Henry?" Petie asked. "You who're dating a girl because her dad's a famous sports agent and you're hoping to get a job with his company after law school? Come on!"

"Shut up, Petie! This isn't about me anyway! Our man Joel has changed into another person since he met her. I'm gonna support him in anything he does. Do you really think we're gonna stop him from getting on an airplane? Good luck," Henry said.

"Don't you care that he's going over to a place where he could be in danger? Geez, Henry, think about what you're saying. Joel is planning on just walking up to some Palestinian guy's house and telling him he's in love with his daughter. You don't see a slight problem here?" Petie asked.

"Well, now that you put it that way..." Henry said.

"Guys, let's just go to the airport and try to catch him before he leaves. I'll buy a ticket if I have to just to get past the gate. There must be some way to talk some sense into him," Eddie said.

"All we have to do is to wait by the security check point. We'll get there before Joel. He just left Vermont, and we're only an hour from the airport," Henry said.

The four agreed this would be the best plan. Mrs. Sully would call the Volkenburgs to alert them about their son and the three friends would intercept Joel when he got to the airport. They were certain they would be able to talk their friend out of this foolish idea. They settled down and decided to change the subject to calm their nerves. Everything would turn out okay...

***

Joel drove into Pittsfield and pulled in to a small coffee shop off the highway. He sat at a table so he could call for flights leaving airports other than Boston. A waitress walked up and greeted him, and he ordered a large coffee to go.

He knew his friends would be at Boston Logan to stop him, and he was sure Mrs. Sully would tell his parents of his plans, so they would most likely be waiting for him there as well.

A flight leaving Bradley Airport in Hartford came up on his phone and he said aloud, "Hartford!" Several people sitting nearby turned and looked at him.

"Sorry," he said, and looked down at the phone. He called the airline that had a 3:30 flight to Tel Aviv and booked it while cancelling the Boston flight. *Why didn't I think of Hartford before?*

The waitress set his coffee down and he grabbed it, throwing some cash on the table and ran to his car, gunning the engine out of the small parking lot and back onto the highway.

The airport in Hartford was an hour closer than Boston, so Joel arrived in plenty of time to get his luggage checked and past the security point to his gate. He even had time to grab a sandwich before boarding the plane. He began pacing back and forth, eating his sandwich quickly, not even tasting it.

The passengers began boarding the plane and Joel excitedly walked down the ramp and onto the plane, finally feeling like he was on the right track to finding Hessa, and that they would be able to begin their life together. He relaxed, feeling certain he would see her soon.

CHAPTER 24

The flight to Tel Aviv would be a circuitous one. Joel had a layover in Newark and then headed on to Zurich. That layover would be substantial, so he wouldn't arrive in Tel Aviv until Thursday late afternoon. He kept himself busy by reading magazines and working on crossword puzzles. His phone kept alerting him of text messages, but he wasn't ready for conversations about where he was. His family and friends would just have to trust that he was doing the right thing.

When he arrived in Zurich the next day it was eight a.m. *Almost two hours 'til my next flight,* he thought. He left the plane and walked to the next gate to check on his connecting flight. He looked at the monitor. The flight was delayed two hours. "Oh, man!" he said aloud.

Frustrated, he wandered through the terminal looking for a place to have coffee. He found a small café and ordered a large coffee with a rich-looking pastry. He sat down, and as he sipped his coffee he decided to text Henry. He sent a brief message informing his friend of his layover in Zurich, which wouldn't be leaving for several hours.

He unzipped the front pocket of his carry-on bag, looking like a child getting into mischief. Embarrassed, he looked around as he pulled out the little Bible Mrs. Sully had given him. He picked up where he'd left off and began to read the book of Exodus.

The text alert went off on Henry's phone. He opened the message to read that Joel was in Zurich, waiting for his connecting flight to Tel

Aviv. "He's in Zurich," he told the group of family and friends that had congregated at the Volkenburg home.

"What did he say?" Joel's mother asked anxiously.

"Not much. He said his flight has been delayed for a couple of hours, so he's stuck in Zurich waiting," Henry replied.

"Well, at least he answered *someone's* text. I've tried calling and texting him a dozen times, and nothing. I just don't know what we're supposed to do. Did you boys have any idea of what Joel was up to?" his mother asked.

"We knew he was head over heels for Hessa, but we just found out on Tuesday that her father had taken her back to Israel. We had no idea he was gonna try a stunt like this," Henry said.

"Yeah, my mom called me to let me know Joel had gone to stay at the farm, and when she told me about their conversation Henry, Eddie, and I got in the car and headed out there as fast as we could," Petie said.

"Before we knew it, Joel was gone. We just assumed he would take off from Logan Airport, so we headed back to Boston. He must have known we would try to stop him. We did some digging online and found he most likely flew out of Hartford."

"Well, you did your best. I finally got in touch with Mr. Volkenburg. He's been at a convention in California, of all places. He won't be able to get home until Saturday. I don't know what to do until then," she repeated.

"I should go to Israel," Henry said. "Joel's my best friend. We've known each other since kindergarten. I can't just stay here and hope he's gonna be okay."

"If you go, then I'm going with you," Eddie said.

"Me too!" Petie added.

"Wait a second, boys. You can't just traipse off to Israel. You don't even know where this girl lives," Mrs. Volkenburg said.

"I know where I can get her address," Henry said.

"Where?" Mrs. Volkenburg asked.

"Hessa's roommate has it. All I have to do is ask some girls over at Thayer Hall. I'll find out who her roommate was in no time."

"Henry, this is a very serious issue. I don't think your mothers would appreciate your going off on a lark to find Joel. You stay put. If we don't hear from him again soon, I'll hire a private investigator to find him. I'm going to call your mothers right now, and I promise that if any of you boys disappear in the next day, we'll call the police," Mrs. Volkenburg said, and walked out of the room to call their mothers.

"She's right you know," Henry said. "What are we gonna do when we get there—drag Joel home against his will? He's a big boy. Once Hessa's father tells him to get lost, he'll come home with his tail between his legs and we'll be here for him. We just have to be patient."

"I guess so," Eddie said. "It's kind of crazy though, you know? I mean, Joel following some girl all the way to Israel. What's he thinking? He's always the one to be focused on school, and the one we could count on to be responsible. Who's the designated driver almost every time we tie one on? Joel. Who's the one whose favorite saying is 'Eye on the prize?' The Burgermeister!"

Eddie thought another moment and continued, "Now he's left the country and the thing he loved most—his education. And for what? Some Palestinian girl whose father is going to tell him to hit the road. Then where will he be? He'll have wasted at least a week by the time he gets back and might have blown his chance for Summa Cum Laude. Man, I'm so ticked off at him right now."

"I don't know, you guys," Petie said. "I have a bad feeling about this. It's not just that he's missing school. He's going to a place where people are constantly at war, and he's not exactly going over to see people who love Americans. Jerusalem is split up into Muslim, Jewish, Armenian, and Christian quarters, did you know that? It's the heart of conflict in the world. The possibility of Joel missing out on an award is the least of our worries."

The three friends became very quiet. Petie's words unsettled them, and each became lost in his own thoughts. Several minutes later Mrs. Volkenburg walked back into the room.

"All right boys, I've called all your mothers. We're going to keep close tabs on you. We can't have anyone else running off to the other side of the world. I also left a message for a private investigator that your mother told me about, Eddie. It seems she saw something on a news program about this man; evidently he's the very best at what he does. I'll let you know what he says once he gets back to me."

The thought of Mrs. Volkenburg contacting a private investigator sank in and the three friends looked at each other helplessly. Henry was the first to speak.

"Mrs. Volkenburg, I think we'd better go home. There isn't anything else we can do here. Just promise that you'll call us if you hear anything at all, and we'll do the same for you."

"Thank you for telling me so quickly, boys. We'll keep in touch as we get more information," Mrs. Volkenburg said as she walked the three friends to the door.

"By the way, please don't mention this to anyone else. I don't want this getting all over campus. It wouldn't look good for Mr. Volkenburg. Good-bye, boys," and she closed the door behind them.

As they walked to Henry's car, he said, "She has a lot of nerve, telling us not to mention this to anyone. We wouldn't want to hurt old Eli's precious reputation—God forbid! She cares more about the family's social status than for her own son."

"Yeah, she probably called our mothers to cover herself so she wouldn't feel responsible for us if we did go to Israel," Eddie said.

"Guys, I think you're being pretty harsh on Mrs. V," Petie said. "She's just as worried as we are—probably more. None of the Volkenburgs show much emotion. That's just the way they are. Let's go home. It's after two a.m. and I'm ready to pass out. "

182

They got into the car and drove back to the house in silence. The three walked up to their rooms and closed the doors. They all slept late the next morning, and Henry was the first to get out of bed. When he was able to shake off the haze of sleep, he picked up his cell phone and saw that Joel had sent a text a half hour before. He was boarding the plane to Tel Aviv, and would contact him once he arrived.

Relieved, Henry got up and walked downstairs to make coffee. A few minutes later Petie walked into the kitchen. He went over to the pantry to get a box of cereal and grabbed the milk out of the refrigerator. Eddie entered the kitchen and pulled a coffee cup out of the cupboard.

"Joel's on his way to Tel Aviv. Everything's okay so far. He said he'll text me once he gets there," Henry said.

"I just hope he has a way to recharge his phone. Do you think he remembered that before he left?" Eddie asked.

"I'm sure he can contact the cell company once he gets there if he needs to. He'll be fine," Petie said.

The three friends didn't know that Joel's cell phone would be the least of his worries.

CHAPTER 25

The following day a town car pulled up to the Volkenburg home, and Eli Volkenburg got out. Having his conference cut short didn't sit well with him. The driver pulled his luggage out of the trunk; Eli wheeled his suitcase up the steps to the front door, and walked into the house. Helen came around the corner and greeted him.

"Welcome home, Mr. Volkenburg. How was your trip?" she asked her employer.

"It was going fine until I heard this nonsense about my son. Where's Mrs. Volkenburg?" he asked.

"She's at a meeting for the spring fundraiser. She said she would be home around seven p.m. Are you hungry?"

"I'm starving. Please bring my dinner to my office, Helen."

She took his luggage and walked off to deliver it to his bedroom. He threw his coat on a bench just inside the door, walked down the hall into his study, and closed the door.

Mrs. Volkenburg returned home just before seven o'clock and walked in the back door to the kitchen. "Hello Helen, is Mr. Volkenburg home yet?"

"Yes, he's in his office. I told him you wouldn't be home until now, and that you were having dinner with friends. He's already eaten," Helen replied.

"Thank you," she said and walked in the direction of the study.

Anna knocked on the door to her husband's study. "Come in," she heard from the other side of the door.

"How was your trip?" Anna asked her husband.

"Like I told Helen, it was fine until I heard about Joel. What on earth is he doing? Has he lost his mind?" Eli asked.

"Evidently so. It seems he's fallen in love with the girl he brought to dinner in December. Do you remember her?" Anna asked.

"The Palestinian girl? Again, has he lost his mind? So you're telling me that he got on a plane and went over to get her and bring her back to Boston? That's the craziest thing I've ever heard. Her father will never approve of him. This is a complete waste of time, and just a few short months to go before he graduates. When he gets home I'm going to give him a piece of my mind." He snatched up the newspaper that Helen had placed on his desk and angrily snapped it open.

"Aren't you the slightest bit worried about him? There are a lot of problems in that particular part of the world. I've...called a private investigator."

"You've what? What can an investigator do? We know where Joel is. You said he's contacted Henry. By the way, doesn't that boy have the decency to call his own mother? Why is he texting his friends?"

"I would assume he feels more comfortable talking to them. He knows what you and I would say," she replied. "Oh, and the investigator told me the same thing. As long as we know where Joel is and that he's making contact with friends and family, he can't help us. Joel is over 21. He can do what he wants."

"Well, we don't need to jump to conclusions. He's just a foolish kid doing something thoughtless. He'll come to his senses and come home. But when he does I'll be waiting to discuss this with him. No girl is worth jeopardizing his education," Eli said angrily.

Anna looked at her husband. She thought about their marriage, and how they had lived very separate lives—even had separate bedrooms. Suddenly she had a painful stab of sadness shoot through her.

"Maybe Joel thinks she's worth it," she said to her husband, and walked out, closing the door behind her.

Joel arrived in Tel Aviv after 7:30 p.m. on Thursday. The flight from Zurich had been delayed five hours instead of two due to weather conditions. He had sat transfixed at the airport in Zurich, reading the Bible. He had no idea he would find it so fascinating.

The time went by much faster than he'd anticipated, and when he boarded the plane for Tel Aviv he looked out the window and realized it had been snowing quite heavily. There were drifts all over the tarmac, and teams of airport personnel were madly dashing back and forth on the runway with snowplows, clearing off the piles of white stuff that had fallen in heavy flakes.

The weather in Tel Aviv was much different. When Joel walked from the plane into the airport it was cool, but not nearly as cold as it had been in Massachusetts. He felt a sense of relief and made his way quickly to the baggage claim where he paced back and forth for what seemed to him like hours. Finally, when almost everyone had gotten their bags, Joel found his own and scrambled outside to hail a taxi for Jerusalem.

When he got into the cab, he pulled out his phone…it was dead. "Oh no!" he said out loud.

"What is the problem, mister?" the taxi driver asked.

"My phone died. I thought I'd be able to look up a hotel to stay at in Jerusalem. I didn't make reservations,"

"What kind of rates you want?" the driver asked.

"I don't care. Hopefully something nice but reasonable. Say, do you know this address?" he asked, and passed the piece of paper with Hessa's address written on it.

The driver looked at the paper when he stopped at a red light. "Oh yes, it is in Old Jerusalem. You want to go there?"

"No, not tonight. By the time we get to Jerusalem it'll be late. Would you take me to a hotel close to that address?" Joel asked.

"Sure, no problem," the driver replied. "I do not mean to pry, but I noticed the name on the paper. Hessa Bishara?"

187

"Yes, I'm going to visit her," Joel replied.

"Is that Husaam Bishara's daughter?"

"I don't know. I met her at college in America, and am here to visit her," Joel replied. "She left suddenly a few days ago, so I came to see if she's okay."

"Mister, you better check before you visit your friend. Husaam Bishara is part of Hamas. I could tell by your accent you're American. He will not take kindly to you visiting his daughter."

Joel was stunned. He sat quietly for several moments, looking straight ahead.

"You okay, Mister?" the driver asked.

"I don't know...do you really think he won't talk to me because I'm an American? I came a long way to visit Hessa. I can't just turn around and go home. Mr. Bishara—is he well-known here in Jerusalem because of being in Hamas?

"Yes, he is quite well-known. You can't just walk up to their house and ask to talk to Mr. Bishara. I tell you, you need to go home. Go back to your family and marry an American girl, have American babies. Do not go to the Bishara's home. He is not a man who will listen to reason. You seem like a nice young man; just be safe and go home," the driver said anxiously.

"You can't be serious! Why can't I just sit down with him and discuss this reasonably?"

"He isn't going to want to reason with you. I tell you, you will regret it. He is very well-known for his connection to some of the things that have happened in Jerusalem. Don't your American newspapers report on the conflict between Palestine and Israel? Go home, boy," the driver said once again.

Joel shrugged his shoulders and looked out the window. No one was going to scare him into returning home without at least trying to see Hessa. He ignored the driver's questions for the remainder of the trip, answering only 'yes' or 'no' when absolutely necessary.

188

The driver pulled into a driveway and up to the entrance of a hotel in Old Jerusalem. "This place is very nice, and not too expensive, mister. I think you will be comfortable here. They serve a nice breakfast for free," he said.

"Thanks. You've been really helpful," Joel replied, and paid the man. He got out and ran to the trunk and pulled out Joel's luggage.

"Here you go, Mister. Have a nice stay It will be nicer if you avoid talking to Bishara," the driver said warily. "Good luck to you."

"Thanks," Joel said as he turned and walked into the hotel. He asked the front desk clerk where he would be able to get an adapter for his cell phone. They gave him instructions to the nearest wireless store, and told him when it would open the next day.

When he got to his room, he had no choice but to call from the room phone. *This oughta cost an arm and a leg*, he thought to himself. He dialed Henry first.

"Hey Henry, it's me. I'm in Jerusalem, staying at the Tikvah Hotel. It's pretty late, so I'll be going to Hessa's house tomorrow morning. I'm just relieved to be here."

"Hey man, your mom is pretty upset. Your dad was still out of town when we were at your house, but I imagine he's pretty ticked off too. Joel, are you sure you know what you're doing?"

"Of course I do. I'll let you know after I talk to Hessa and her dad tomorrow. Don't worry! I don't know why everyone is making such a big deal of this. Just tell my mom and dad that I'm okay and that I'll call everyone once I get this stuff with Hessa straightened out."

"Just watch yourself, okay?"

"Henry, what's wrong with all of you? You'd think I was going to stay here forever! I'll talk to you soon," Joel said. He hung up the phone and sat on the bed. He smiled at the thought that he would see Hessa in just a few short hours.

CHAPTER 26

Hessa woke up before dawn on Friday morning. Her suitcases were in the hallway by the door, and the only thing she had to do before leaving was to get herself ready. She heard movement downstairs, so quickly went down to see who else was awake. Her mother was in the kitchen making coffee.

"I thought you might want a cup before you left for the airport," her mother said. Her face was blotchy, like she had been crying.

"What is the matter, Mother?"

"We cannot talk, Hessa. Your father is very angry. I asked if I could accompany you to the airport, but he said that you will be going alone. He has assigned Mustafa to accompany you to London. I do not know when I will see you..." her mother said, and was cut off by her father.

"Muna, go upstairs. I will take care of Hessa."

Muna quickly went over to her daughter and hugged her, kissing her cheek. She ran out of the kitchen, crying openly.

Hessa's father walked over to stand in front of her, his large frame intimidating in a dark suit.

"I assume you are ready to leave, Hessa? Mustafa will be here in a few minutes to take you to London. He has instructions to get you to your apartment, and will be staying close by. This time you won't be able to get into mischief. Mustafa will be there to keep an eye on you, and Qasim will be spending more time with you. His father and I have seen to that."

Hessa looked at him silently as she began to prepare breakfast. He looked at her and snapped, "Don't bother to eat. You will have plenty of time when you get to the airport. I don't want you to miss your plane."

Hessa took a sip of coffee, remaining silent. Nothing she said would matter at this point. It would only anger her father. A knock came at the door, and Hessa's heart sank as she realized this was the last time she would call this place her home. She would move to London, marry Qasim, and live there for the rest of her life.

She walked slowly to the entryway and picked up a small carry-on bag. Mustafa took the rest of the bags to the car. As she walked out the door, her mother came to the top of the stairs.

"Good-bye, Hessa! I love you, my precious daughter!" Her father turned around quickly and looked up, glaring at his wife. She ran back to her bedroom.

Her father turned her by the shoulders toward the door and ushered her out to the car. "Study hard and behave yourself. I do not want to hear of any more trouble with you, Hessa. Mustafa will call to let us know when you get to London."

She got into the car, and as Mustafa pulled away from the curb, Hessa looked out the window at the only home she had ever known, and tears silently streamed down her cheeks the rest of the way to the airport.

Husaam closed the door and walked up to the bedroom he shared with his wife. He walked in the door and over to the bed where she lay crying.

"Get up," he said angrily. She obeyed her husband, and rose to stand before him.

"Well my wife, I have learned quite a lot about you and Hessa. You two were very busy in Boston, and it seems you were very much a part of the friendship between this Joel person and Hessa. That was not wise. You have gone against everything that we stand for as a family and as a people. You should not have done that, Muna."

His voice was frighteningly quiet, his anger contained. Muna feared this change in her husband's manner more than his explosive temper. She hadn't seen him this way before.

"I tried to talk her out of this relationship...I knew you wouldn't approve, but she wouldn't listen..."

As she was speaking, something went over the top of her head, and she was encased in darkness. A pair of very large arms wrapped around her and lifted her off the ground. Everything went black as she felt a sharp blow to the back of her head, and she lost consciousness.

⁕⁕⁕

Joel left the hotel and hailed a cab. When he got in he gave the address to the driver. This man wasn't as talkative as the driver he'd had from the airport. Joel silently went over in his mind what he would say when he got to Hessa's house.

He worried that she wouldn't be home when he got there, but then realized that it had only been a few days since she'd gotten back to Israel.

Her dad couldn't have gotten her enrolled in another school so quickly, Joel thought to himself.

When the driver pulled up in front of the Bishara's apartment, Joel got out and paid the driver. The cab pulled away and Joel looked up at the building. He took a deep breath and walked up to the door, rapping on it loudly. Mr. Bishara came to the door and said, "Yes?"

"Hello Mr. Bishara. My name is Joel Volkenburg. Your daughter and I went to school together at Harvard. She left suddenly this week, and I wanted to see if she was okay, or if I somehow caused problems in your family."

"Come in, Joel," Mr. Bishara said in a deep, quiet voice. "Hessa and her mother told me all about you," he lied. "Sit down. Would you like a cup of coffee?"

"That would be great, thanks," Joel replied.

Mr. Bishara left the room and came back a moment later with a cup of black coffee. He presented it to Joel, and sat down across from him with his own cup.

"Now tell me Joel, how did you and Hessa meet?" Mr. Bishara asked with feigned kindness.

Joel went into a detailed explanation of how they had met at the library, and that he'd asked her to dinner and the ballet because she would be alone in Boston all weekend. He explained that they had become good friends by spending that weekend doing things together, and when she came back to Boston from winter break, he invited her and her mother to the Sullivan farm.

"That was very hospitable of you, Joel. Thank you for showing my Hessa such a wonderful time. You do realize, however, that she is going to marry someone else? Someone that her mother and I have chosen for her?" he asked quietly.

"She told me that, Mr. Bishara. I've tried to understand, believe me, but Hessa and I had a connection. It isn't every day that two people find love like we have," Joel said, starting to feel Mr. Bishara was a reasonable man.

"So it is love is it?"

"It sure is. Is Hessa here?"

"No, I am afraid not. She will be back later. She and her mother are out for the time being. I am sorry you came all this way to miss her, but I will let her know you stopped by. Where are you staying? Perhaps you can come for dinner and we can thank you for your kindness to my daughter and wife while they were in America. But I must tell you, Joel; marriage between a devout Muslim family and a Jewish boy will never happen. I hope you understand."

"I wish I could understand, but when you fall in love you don't always think logically. You must remember how you felt when you first met Mrs. Bishara."

"Yes, well Joel, I need to be leaving. We will be in touch," Mr. Bishara said, and called a cab for him.

194

"I'm staying at the Tikvah Hotel. I'll wait for your call," Joel said.

Mr. Bishara's cell phone rang, and he answered it. "I am sorry Joel, I have to take this call," he said, and walked out of the room.

Joel was encouraged by the conversation, and felt as though in time he would be able to convince Mr. Bishara that he and Hessa were meant for each other. Over all, he thought the morning had gone very well.

The cab driver pulled up and honked the horn. Joel spoke up so Mr. Bishara could hear him from the other room: "Thank you for seeing me this morning, Mr. Bishara. My cab is here."

Mr. Bishara walked around the corner and said, "We will be in touch tomorrow, Joel," and he walked back around the corner and out of sight.

Joel got into the cab and asked the driver to take him to the heart of the old city in Jerusalem. It was still early in the morning, so he also asked where he could take a tour of the city. On their way, the driver suggested several things for Joel to see while in Jerusalem, and made a phone call to a friend. He drove to a small café in the Jewish quarter and let Joel out.

"I have called my friend, Benjamin. He is the best tour guide in Israel! Since the economy is slow, Benjamin has some time to show you around himself, as a personal favor to me. He will meet you here in about fifteen minutes. Shalom!"

Joel paid the driver and thanked him, then made his way into the café and sat down with a cup of coffee and a bagel. Exactly fifteen minutes later a slight man in his sixties walked into the café. He came over to Joel's table and introduced himself.

"You must be Joel. You look just as Guri described you. I am Benjamin, but you can call me Ben. Are you ready for the best day of your life?" he laughed.

"I sure could use a 'best day'!" Joel said smiling.

The two left the café and got into Ben's van. They drove to the City of David, and then walked to Hezzekiahs' Tunnel. Ben was extremely

195

knowledgeable about Israel's history. He explained how the history of the Bible correlated to different places in Jerusalem.

He then drove Joel back to the Jewish quarter, and showed him his favorite shops, suggesting Joel take a look around. *Most likely belong to family and friends,* Joel thought, smiling to himself. Joel picked up little knick-knacks for his mom and Mrs. Sully. They stopped at a little café for an early lunch, and Joel asked about what they would be seeing that afternoon.

"Well my friend, we have come to the end of our tour; after lunch I will have to be on my way. I have a large group from Houston, Texas, America, this afternoon."

"Well, thanks for taking me around this morning, Ben. I really learned a lot. I have a question though," Joel said, lowering his voice.

"Ask me anything," Ben said.

"Do you know anyone who knows anything about Christian sights here?" Joel asked.

"I thought you told me you were Jewish," Ben replied.

"I am, but I'm just curious..." Joel said, wondering why he felt uncomfortable requesting this.

Ben told Joel to wait while he made a phone call. He got up from the table and walked outside, talking and laughing animatedly. He came back a few moments later and said, "It is all set, Joel. I have a very close friend who is available this afternoon. His name is David, and he refers to himself as a Messianic Jew who is also a pastor. He has some funny ideas, but he won't push his Messiah on you, I promise. He is truly the best person I know."

The two sat in the café talking about Israel, eating shawarma on warm pita bread. Ben was a storehouse of knowledge, and Joel soaked it up like a sponge. About a half hour later a middle-aged man of medium build walked into the café.

"There he is!" Ben exclaimed. "There's my old friend, David Appel. Come over here and meet my new friend Joel!"

196

Joel stood up and shook hands with David, who looked up at him. "Just like King Saul in the Bible, you are head and shoulders taller than anyone else, and such a good-looking young man!" David said.

"Wow, is everyone in Israel as nice as you guys?" Joel laughed.

"My friend would like to see some of the Christian sights around Jerusalem, if you don't mind, David," Ben said. "He's a good Jewish boy, so don't go filling his head with your strange ideas."

"I promise I won't say anything that I shouldn't," David said, winking at Ben.

"Well, I will leave you two on your afternoon journey. I must get to my tour of Texas Americans!" Ben hugged his friend David and turned to shake Joel's hand. He walked out, tipping his hat on the way to his car.

David and Joel walked to his car, which was very compact. The two got in and David told Joel he would try to show him as much as he could with the time they had left that afternoon. They started at the Mount of Olives, and moved down to the Garden of Gethsemane.

Joel was strangely affected by David's explanation of what Christ went through the night he prayed in the garden, right before He was to be betrayed. He stood looking at the olive trees that had been planted in rows in the garden, and marveled at the twisted, knotty trunks.

They moved on to the Pool of Bethesda, and David explained how Jesus had healed a lame man. He explained some of the other miracles that Jesus had done while on earth. They ended the day at the Via Dolorosa, the road where it was believed Christ had walked with His cross to Golgatha, where He was crucified.

"How come you believe in Jesus as the Messiah? I've never heard of a Jew who believed that," Joel said.

"I kept running into Christians who I would debate with at length. I asked them many questions. Then a Christian friend gave me a Bible with the New Testament, and I read it. Every time I had a question he explained it in such a simple way, it made sense to me. After a while I no longer had excuses not to believe.

"The one thing that finally convinced me was that I didn't have to work for my salvation—it was a gift by God's grace. I had never felt as complete as the day I made that commitment to become a believer in Yeshua as Messiah," David said.

Joel stood looking at David, silently soaking in everything he had said. "I've never believed in God. No one in my family does. The only time He *is* mentioned is when someone swears."

David laughed, but Joel wasn't joking. "I am sorry, Joel. I did not mean to make light of your situation. The saddest thing in the world is not to have the hope of a Creator. How can parents teach their children there is no God when every one of God's prophecies in the Bible is coming true right before our eyes?"

"What prophecies?" Joel asked.

"From the book of Genesis to the book of Revelation, the Bible is prophetic. You should stay in Jerusalem for a while and come to my church, Joel. There is much to learn," David said. "As for today, we have run out of time. My wife will wonder where I am! Are you hungry?"

"Yes, as a matter of fact," Joel said.

"Well then, why don't you come to my house for dinner? My wife is always prepared for guests. It is our very favorite thing having friends dine at our house. You will come, Joel?" David asked.

"Thank you, I'd love to come," Joel said, relieved he wouldn't have to be alone with his thoughts that evening.

David made a quick call to his wife as they drove to the Appel house. They arrived and got out as David's wife came to the door, smiling from ear to ear.

"Hello, shalom! Come in! It is getting cold outside. Come in where it is warm! My name is Miriam, and you are Joel?"

"Yes, it's nice to meet you Miriam. Thank you for having me," Joel said.

They walked into the house, which was very small, but very neat and tidy. The aromas coming from the kitchen were extraordinary. "Wow! It smells incredible in here!" Joel exclaimed.

198

"My wife is the very best cook. You are in for a big treat!" David said.

David offered Joel a glass of spiced tea and they sat down in front of a small fireplace. Joel felt very comfortable with these two strangers who had welcomed him into their home. Miriam told Joel about several family members who lived in America, in Ohio.

"I have a friend who lives in Ohio," Joel said. "I don't see him much, though. His brother is one of my best friends."

Miriam set the table and brought out a platter of Cornish hens with rice stuffing. Then she brought out grilled vegetables on a skillet. Everything tasted wonderful to Joel, who realized he hadn't eaten much since he had left the States. He felt guilty when Miriam gave him a second helping.

"You are very thin, Joel. You need to eat to put some meat on those bones of yours!" Miriam said, and disappeared into the kitchen to take a chocolate cake out of the oven.

A few minutes later she brought the cake out and cut a large slice for Joel, then poured him a strong cup of espresso. "Now this is a dessert!" she said, and sat down with the men.

During the meal David explained to Joel about their children, who lived close by. They had a son and a daughter, both married. His son had two children, but his daughter had only recently gotten married. Joel told them about his family, and how he was in his senior year at Harvard, with plans to go to law school.

"What brought you to Israel, Joel?" Miriam asked.

"I'll give you the short version. I met a girl at Harvard who's from Jerusalem. She left suddenly to return home, so I've come to look for her," Joel said.

"That is very interesting. She must be very special for you to come such a long way," Miriam said. "Why did she come home? She did not like Harvard?"

"She really liked it, but I think her father found out about me, so he went to Boston and brought her back home."

199

"I assume this girl is not Jewish?" Miriam asked intuitively.

"No, she's Palestinian. Her name is Hessa Bishara. Her father is Husaam Bishara."

David and Miriam looked at each other as their mouths dropped open. Then they looked back at Joel. "Have you found her, Joel? Do you know how to get in touch with her?" David asked.

"I went to their house today and spoke with Mr. Bishara," Joel answered.

"You went to their house..." David trailed off, looking incredulous. "Do not go back there, Joel. Mr. Bishara is a dangerous man. He is connected to Hamas, and they hate the Jews. Promise me you will not go back there. Nothing good can come of this. God has someone for you, Joel, I promise. Trust Him, and go back to America. I am sure your parents are worried about you."

"You're the second person who has said that to me since I got here. The cab driver told me the same thing. This guy must be bad news if two people within twenty-four hours have warned me about him. I have to talk to Hessa before I go back to Boston, though. Mr. Bishara said he would contact me tomorrow. He invited me to dinner, so he can't be that bad, right?" Joel reasoned.

"I wouldn't accept the invitation, Joel. It could be a trap," David said.

"I'll be okay. Thanks for your concern, though. It's really late, and I think I've over-stayed my welcome. It's already past ten o'clock!" Joel said, standing up. He turned to Miriam and said, "Thank you dinner, Miriam, I really enjoyed it."

"You are very welcome, Joel. It has been a pleasure having you. May the God of all peace bless and protect you," Miriam replied, and hugged Joel.

David and Joel walked out and got into David's tiny car. They continued to discuss everything they had seen that day, and Joel rattled off question after question to David, who was happy to answer and explain as

200

much as he could. They pulled up to the hotel, and David patted his new friend on the shoulder.

"There are no coincidences, Joel. God meant for us to meet. I will not cease to pray for you. The Lord bless you and keep you, and make His face to shine upon you, and be gracious to you. The Lord lift up His countenance on you, and give you peace[ii]."

"Wow, that was beautiful. Is that from the Bible?" Joel asked.

"Yes, that is from the book of Numbers," David replied. "It was the Lord blessing Israel. It is also a blessing from God to you, Joel. Take care of yourself, and if you need anything, here is my number. Please do not hesitate to call me any time, day or night."

"Thank you, David. I'm really glad I met you," Joel said, and shook his hand. He got out of the car and walked into the hotel, feeling as though he had a strong advocate in David.

CHAPTER 27

The next morning Joel went for a run, and when he returned to the hotel he had a message waiting on the phone in his room. It was Mr. Bishara, asking him to dinner that evening. When Joel returned his call, Mr. Bishara answered.

"Hello Mr. Bishara. I got your message about dinner this evening. I'd love to come," Joel said.

"Very good. I will have someone come to the hotel to pick you up at seven p.m. so you don't have to get a cab," Mr. Bishara replied.

Joel hung up the phone and felt encouraged by the invitation. After he showered and got dressed, he went down to the lobby to get directions to the phone store the front desk clerk had told him about the previous day.

The concierge suggested he rent a phone during his stay. He explained this was the least expensive way to make calls internationally, and offered to help Joel order a phone.

He made a call and after asking Joel a few questions, he gave the phone company all the information they needed and hung up. "The phone will be here by tomorrow morning, and I will have it waiting for you at the front desk," the concierge said.

"Thanks, you've been a great help," Joel replied, and asked the concierge where he might have breakfast outside of the hotel.

"You will want to go to 'Little Jerusalem'. There isn't a better place in all the city for breakfast and it is only two blocks away." The concierge gave Joel directions, who thanked the man as he turned and walked out of the hotel.

He wandered out the door of the hotel, and to the right side of the building was a newspaper stand. He picked up a newspaper and walked down the street to the restaurant recommended by the concierge. It looked like an English garden right in the middle of Old Jerusalem. He entered through a black wrought iron gate and sat down at a small table against a fence with exotic flowers climbing in and out of the wooden slats.

The waitress gave Joel a menu, but suggested the Jerusalem breakfast which included labana, a soft white cheese, and shukshuka—spicy scrambled eggs with tomato. A few minutes later the waitress came out with freshly squeezed orange juice and hot bread right out of the oven. She also set down a small plate of feta cheese and olives.

"I sure won't need to eat until this evening," Joel said as he smiled at the waitress. "I think I'll have to go for another run after breakfast!"

"This is a meal you will not soon forget," the waitress replied, chuckling. "So you are a runner?"

"Yes, I try to go for a run every day," Joel replied.

"It is my favorite thing. I try to run five times a week myself," the waitress replied.

Joel cut into the delicious bread and realized he could have made a meal of it alone. The waitress came out a short time later with the shukshuka, and Joel was glad he'd ordered the eggs. He was much hungrier than he'd thought, and ate almost everything in sight.

The waitress chatted with Joel while he ate, spending more time than was necessary at his table, asking him questions about himself and America. He told her the concierge at the Tikvah had recommended this restaurant for breakfast, and about his being a student in Boston and how he had come to visit his girlfriend, who lived in Jerusalem.

"The concierge? My brother is a concierge at the Tikvah! His name is David Schur," she exclaimed.

"I think that's the person who told me about your restaurant. The concierge's name was David. Now I see what's happening. Your brother sends business to you, and you send him business, right?" Joel laughed.

The waitress laughed and replied, "Oh, now you know our secret!" They talked for a few more moments, and she excused herself to go back to her duties.

After relaxing with the newspaper and coffee he walked to the King David Museum and was welcomed by guides dressed in biblical clothing. He spent a good part of the day at the museum walking through the various displays, and talking with staff members about genealogy.

His next visit was to the Holocaust Museum, where he spent several hours. At the end of the day he walked back to the hotel to get ready for dinner at the Bishara's home.

Just as he was leaving his hotel room to go down to the lobby to meet the driver, he noticed the phone blinking with a message. He decided to return the call the next morning and walked out to the elevator, leaving the message unheard.

When he got to the lobby a very large, heavy-set man with a crooked nose and thick lips was waiting for Joel. Mr. Bishara had given him a description of the young American, so he recognized Joel immediately and approached him as he got off the elevator.

"You are Joel?" he asked.

"Yes, Joel Volkenburg," he answered.

"Let me take you to the car," the man said, and Joel followed him out.

The man opened the back door for Joel, and he got in. As he sat down, he realized there was a man sitting in the passenger side of the front seat.

"Hi, I'm Joel," he said, happily thinking he would be meeting other members of Hessa's family.

The man in the front seat just stared straight ahead and grunted something indecipherable. The large man got into the driver's seat and without saying a word, quickly pulled out into the street and wound through Old Jerusalem, up and down streets, making erratic turns. Joel started to lose his sense of direction, and after about fifteen minutes his curiosity got the better of him.

205

"I don't know Jerusalem very well, but isn't the Bishara's home much closer to the hotel than this?" he asked.

"Yes it is, but we will not be going there," the driver replied.

"Did they make plans to meet us somewhere else?" Joel asked.

"You might say that," the man answered.

They drove on in silence for a while longer. Joel was confused, and tried to make sense of what was happening, since the driver didn't seem willing to explain. He looked out the window and noticed the road was much less congested and figured they were going somewhere outside the city. After another fifteen minutes, Joel spoke up again.

"Where *are* the Bishara's anyway? Mr. Bishara didn't say anything about going out of town for dinner," he said, puzzled.

The driver suddenly pulled the car to the side of the road. The man in the passenger's seat got out of the car and opened Joel's door. He had a keffiyeh draped over his head and across his face. His eyes were large, round and protruding, but Joel couldn't see anything else. He reached in and pulled Joel out of the car and threw him on the ground. Joel tried to get up, but the man pushed him back down with his foot.

"What's going on?" he demanded, more frightened than angry.

The man didn't say anything. He just pulled out a black piece of material. He came at Joel once again and drew something out from inside his jacket. It was a sizeable semi-automatic weapon—Joel wasn't familiar with guns so couldn't guess what it might be. The man aimed the weapon at Joel, but the large man who had been driving walked over and pulled the man's hands down.

"You fool, he said not to kill him! Just hit him hard enough to put him out and we'll be on our way."

The man walked up to Joel, lifting the gun and before he was able to react, slammed it into the back of his head. He put the black material over Joel's head, cinching it around his neck. He took some rope out of the trunk, leaving it open, and walked over to tie his hands behind his back and around his feet. He then lifted Joel up and threw him into the trunk,

206

slamming it shut. The two men got back into the car and quickly drove off into the night.

When Joel awoke, he had no idea where he was or how long he had been out. The back of his head felt as though it had been cracked in two, and he winced at the stabbing pain. The hood had been taken off his head, but his hands and feet were still tied.

He looked around him to take in his surroundings. He was in something that looked like a jail cell, but he didn't hear anyone around him. The ceiling didn't look very high, but at the top of the wall was a hole that looked like it was about six inches square. A small light shown through the little hole, but Joel realized it was still dark out. He must not have been unconscious for too long, he reasoned, since it was still night.

He tried to sit up, but the pain in his head made it impossible to move. He lay back down with the side of his face on the dirt floor. He had a funny taste in his mouth and wondered if they had drugged him, since he felt hazy and sick to his stomach.

He looked out into the dark and whispered aloud, "Is this what I get for loving someone? Is this what I get for reading the Bible? Am I being punished for something?"

He thought of his friends and family back home, and felt badly that he hadn't called anyone before he left the hotel that evening. *If only I had told someone where I was going, if only I had listened to everyone's warnings, if only...*

Then he thought of Hessa. *If this is what they've done to me, I wonder what they've done to Hessa?* As thoughts ran through his mind of her father and what he had done by kidnapping him, he wondered if something had been done to Hessa's mother as well. He struggled to get out of the ropes that bound him.

"This whole thing is my fault! If I'd listened to everyone to begin with I wouldn't have gotten Hessa and her mother into trouble, and I wouldn't be in this place where..." he didn't want to finish the sentence.

What if something happens to them? I'll be completely to blame. God, I don't know what I'll do if something happens to her! Joel felt tightness in his chest as tears began to gather in his eyes which he choked back, trying to keep from making any sound.

He rolled onto his back and felt an explosive pain shoot through his body. He immediately turned over to his side when he realized there was an open wound on the back of his head. Hot tears ran down his cheeks as he thought of how he hadn't even said goodbye to his family, and that he had brushed off Mrs. Sully's warnings. The tears traced themselves down his dirty face when he thought of how his best friends had frantically driven to the airport in search of him.

"I'll never see them again," he sadly whispered.

He thoughtfully mourned the loss of everyone and everything he had known in his short life. As he reflected over his twenty-one years on earth and the people who had been a part of it, memories of Hessa drifted in like an oasis in his desperate situation. He recalled the day he first saw her, and how he had first spoken to her in the library, their first date, the afternoon of ice skating, kissing her in the snow at the Sullivans', and when she told him she loved him.

He smiled slightly at the memory of her face when she'd spoken those words, and somehow it encouraged him to try to hang on and wait for a miracle to happen. *I do need a miracle. Is there someone somewhere who will listen to me and help me?* His head started to ache again, and as pain shot through him he finally passed out once more, exhausted.

CHAPTER 28

Anna Volkenburg sat at the dinner table, picking at her food. Joel hadn't called them since he'd left for Israel, and Henry had only received one message from the Zurich airport on Thursday, along with a quick call when he'd arrived in Jerusalem. It was now Saturday, and still no one had received any word. She hadn't slept much for two days, and her nerves were getting raw. She looked over at her husband, who remained silent about the issue.

"Eli, please say something. We can't just pretend everything is okay. Joel hasn't called anyone in days, and I'm beginning to think something is wrong," Anna said nervously.

"That boy hasn't even had the decency to call his own mother. His thoughtlessness is unacceptable, Anna. He won't be getting any help from his old man, that's for sure—he can fend for himself over there. If he's run out of money, he can wash dishes in a restaurant for all I care," Eli said angrily.

"You can't mean that. He's our son. Even if he's done something foolish, we still need to help him if he's in trouble."

"I came home a day early because of his irresponsibility, and for what? He sends a quick text message to his friend and completely ignores his own parents. I could easily have stayed at the convention and come home today. That boy has turned this household upside down with his selfish behavior," Eli said harshly.

"I have a very bad feeling about this. I wish you wouldn't talk like that; you're going to regret it if something *has* happened. Don't say anything out of anger that you don't mean," Anna replied. "By the way, I called the investigator again today."

"I think you're making a bigger deal out of this than you should."

"We need to take this situation seriously. Our child is in Israel and has gone there to bring his girlfriend back to America. Oh, and she just happens to be Palestinian. Don't you think this is cause to worry?"

"I think you're being a little dramatic," Eli said simply.

"Well, just to be safe I've asked the investigator to come here on Monday morning. You can be here for the meeting, or you can just go about your day as usual. I for one am going to be proactive about this situation," she said curtly.

"Go ahead. You're going to do it whether I agree or not. I think you'll find that you've blown this all out of proportion and you'll regret all the unnecessary worrying you've done," Eli said as he pushed his chair out and stood up.

"I have some work to do." He left the room without a backward glance and walked to the library, shutting the door.

Helen came into the dining room a short time later, and Anna was sitting alone, staring straight ahead looking forlorn.

"Mrs. Volkenburg, I'm so sorry about what's happening with Joel. I hope and pray he's all right...such a good boy," she said.

"Thank you, Helen. I hope so too," Anna replied, and walking over to the buffet she picked up a wine bottle and poured herself a glass.

***

Henry, Eddie, and Petie left school on Friday afternoon and drove to the Sullivan farm to try and make sense out of what had happened in the last few days. They sat with Mr. and Mrs. Sully until the early morning hours on Saturday going over what Joel had said, and comparing notes with one another of each communication they'd had with Joel before he left. Mrs. Sully had something tugging at her that she finally decided to get off her chest.

210

"Boys, I need to tell you something. Please don't get angry with me, and don't interrupt me," Mrs. Sully said.

"What is it, Mom?" Petie asked impatiently.

"When Hessa and Mrs. Bishara were visiting, I had a long conversation with Mrs. Bishara one morning," she said.

"What about?" Petie asked.

"I talked to her about God, and I gave her...a Bible. She told me some things that really concerned me about her husband and the life she led back in Israel. She seemed so lost and alone, I wanted to tell her that she didn't need to live that way," Mrs. Sully said, twisting the piping on a couch pillow in her fingers.

"Why do you think we'd be mad at you for that?" Petie asked, with Henry and Eddie nodding along.

"I know this might sound strange, but I think Mrs. Bishara and Hessa's visit has something to do with Joel's disappearance. I keep thinking that if she was that afraid to talk to me about her husband and her religion, what's keeping her husband from having people watch her while she was visiting?"

"Mom, it sounds like you've been reading too many spy novels. That doesn't happen in real life!" Petie exclaimed and let out a little laugh.

"Joel hasn't 'disappeared', Mrs. Sully. We just haven't heard from him since Thursday. He said he would call when he got this business with Hessa straightened out," Henry said, sounding like he was trying to convince himself as he spoke.

"I hope you're right, boys. I don't know why yet, but I feel something has happened. I can't explain it, but I've been up all night for the last two nights, praying. I can't help it. Maybe it's the mother in me, but I feel sick inside, and that our Joel is in trouble," she said, choking up and wiping her eyes.

"Your mom is pretty intuitive, Peter. I think we all need to pray that your friend makes it safely out of Israel and back home," Mr. Sully said quietly, which was very out of character for him. He leaned over and put his arm around his wife, hugging her closely to himself.

211

"I think I'll call the hotel later today to see if anyone has seen Joel. We need to keep in mind that it's seven hours later there. He could just be having phone problems. He's probably out sightseeing right now. Let's not jump to conclusions," Henry said.

�‑⚘‑⚘‑⚑

Hessa had arrived in London late Friday afternoon, exhausted. The last few days had taken an emotional toll on her, and she just wanted to get to her apartment to rest. She opened the door to her room, and what she found was less than impressive.

The room was tiny with one small window. Fortunately she was on the top floor and could see the River Thames. That was the only good thing about the place. The bed looked as though it needed a new mattress, the bedding looked questionable, and the carpet was worn and dirty.

She didn't even bother to unpack. She turned and hurried downstairs, pushing open the front door of the apartment, and seeing Mustafa, walked over to where he was leaning against a wall, smoking a cigarette.

"Mustafa, there are some things I need. Would you mind terribly if we went to the store?"

"MmmHmm," Mustafa said simply and threw his cigarette on the ground, stamping it out.

They turned and walked to the street, where Mustafa flagged down a cab. He got in the front seat and Hessa sat in the back. As Mustafa gave instructions to the cab driver, Hessa had an idea. She began to plan a way to make an excuse to get away from her guard so she could buy a phone card. Her father had strictly forbidden her to carry a cell phone in London, and had ordered Mustafa to keep close watch of Hessa's activities.

The cab driver pulled up to a large department store and Hessa got out along with Mustafa, who was close by her side. She got a basket and started to fill it with items she would need for her room. As they got in line at the cashier, Hessa pulled several items out of the basket and purposely dropped them on the floor.

212

As Mustafa bent over to pick them up, Hessa grabbed a phone card from the rack at the check stand. She apologized to Mustafa for being clumsy and smiled at him. He looked at her with a frown and put the items on the checkout stand.

"Forgive me Mustafa, but would you mind? I need to use the Ladies' Room," Hessa said, smiling sweetly at him.

Mustafa was visibly embarrassed, and told her he would pay for the items in her basket and meet her at the front door. She thanked him and walked toward a store clerk to ask directions to the restrooms. When he pointed out where she should go, she pulled out the phone card and asked if there was a cash register near the restroom.

"Of course. The jewelry department is in the back of the store. You can purchase it from them," the clerk said.

Hessa thanked the gentleman and ran quickly to the jewelry department. She pulled out most of the remaining cash in her purse and bought the phone card, stuffing it quickly into the bottom of her purse. She turned and walked to the front of the store where Mustafa was standing.

"I feel much better. Thank you for waiting, Mustafa," Hessa said, smiling again.

Mustafa looked down at her and frowned, turning to push the cart out the door and over to a waiting cab. They piled everything into the trunk and got into the car. Hessa felt encouraged as she thought of the phone card she had stashed away.

Before leaving Jerusalem for London, she made sure she had the card Ruth had given her on the airplane. She had also memorized the Sullivan's home number and Joel's cell phone number. She would find some way to contact them.

The cab pulled up to the apartment and Hessa got out. She and Mustafa walked around to the trunk and pulled out her bags. They trudged upstairs, and when they got to the room Mustafa dropped everything just inside the door, nodded his head to Hessa and left.

She closed the door and turned around, falling back against the door, breathing a sigh of relief. She had a phone card, but no phone. She would have to keep her eyes open and find one somehow.

CHAPTER 29

It was Monday morning, and Anna Volkenburg had been up since four a.m. The investigator would be at her house soon, and she kept herself busy by taking care of issues for the spring fundraiser she was chairing. She was in the upstairs office typing on her computer when she heard the doorbell ring.

Helen answered the door and ushered the private investigator into the den.

Anna hurried down to meet the man she hoped could help her. She walked to the small sitting room, and Helen was standing in the doorway with a tall, muscular man who looked formidable enough to take on just about anyone.

"Mrs. Volkenburg, I'm Dan Moretti," he said and extended his hand out to Anna.

"Thank you for coming, Mr. Moretti. Would you like some coffee?" Anna asked.

"I'd love some," he replied. Helen nodded and walked off to the kitchen.

"Please sit down," Anna said as she pointed to a wingback chair, and she sat down across from him.

"I read your biography online after my friend recommended you. I must say, it's very impressive. You're retired from the Office of Naval Intelligence?" Anna asked.

"Yes. I retired eight years ago and started my own business. Unfortunately there's a lot of need for what I do. When I retired I didn't have much of a break. Calls kept coming in from various places, asking for my help with one thing or another. That's when I realized I needed to do this for a living," Dan replied.

"Well, I appreciate your coming on such short notice, Mr. Moretti," Anna said.

"Let's get down to business then, Mrs. Volkenburg. When did you last hear from your son?" he asked.

"That's just the thing. We haven't heard from him at all. His friend received a text message from him at eight o'clock last Thursday morning Zurich time, but no one's heard from him since. We've called his hotel in Jerusalem and they said he's still registered, but no one has seen him coming or going.

They connected us with the concierge, who seems to be the last one who talked to him. Joel's cell phone wasn't working, so he helped him order a phone to rent while he was there. The phone arrived on Sunday, but he hasn't picked it up."

"When did the concierge say he last spoke with Joel?" Dan asked.

"At about nine o'clock in the morning on Saturday," Anna replied. "He said he saw Joel leave the hotel. He'd suggested a restaurant to Joel for breakfast, and that was the last time he saw him."

Dan sat with Anna for close to an hour and had her recount everything she could remember. She referred to carefully written notes she'd taken from what Joel's friends had told her. She'd even written down speculations the boys had made. She also told Dan about her conversations with Mrs. Sullivan. The two had spoken several times since Joel's disappearance. He had also been very helpful to Anna.

"I'm going to have to go to Israel. It's been close to a week since anyone has heard from him. Given the circumstances of Joel's visit, I would say there could be some cause for concern," Dan said flatly.

Anna's eyes welled up with tears. "I knew it…" she trailed off.

"Let's not jump to any conclusions. I'm not saying that your son is a victim of foul play, but the situation does merit closer investigation, considering the people he visited in Jerusalem. I'll be heading out as soon as possible, but there are a few things I need to wrap up here before I leave," Dan said.

"How quickly can you leave?" Anna asked.

"I'll catch the earliest available flight."

"What can I do to help? May I book the flight for you? I want to make sure you're able to get out tomorrow," Anna said nervously.

"Don't worry. My assistant will take care of that. Believe me, there's no one better at this than Beth. We can leave the travel arrangements to her. Let me assure you, Mrs. Volkenburg, I've done this for a long time, and have dealt with situations in the Middle East before.

I'm familiar with where things are and how people operate over there. I have connections that have been helpful to me in the past, and I'll be in contact with them immediately," Dan's voice resonated with confidence.

"I believe you *will* get my Joel home, Mr. Moretti," Anna said, then added, "I think you should call me Anna. My last name is quite a mouthful, and I have a feeling you and I will be communicating a lot."

"I will Anna, and please call me Dan. Now, try to relax. I'll let you know when I'm on my way, and when I expect to arrive in Jerusalem. You'll be hearing from me," Dan said as they walked toward the front door.

"Thank you, Dan. I can't tell you how much I appreciate your doing this for us," Anna replied. "I'll let Mr. Volkenburg know about our conversation this morning, and your plans."

The two walked to the front door and Dan let himself out. He looked back at the house and said to himself, "I wonder if his dad is aware of how serious this situation could be?' He turned toward his car as he unlocked it and got in.

<hr>

Dan's assistant, Beth, had a difficult time booking a flight to Tel Aviv. She looked at every airline and every route she could think of, and

217

the earliest she could find was in three days. She booked the trip and let Dan know he wouldn't be in Israel until Friday evening.

"Book it, Beth," he said. "Keep checking for any cancellations before then and let me know."

Dan called Henry, Eddie, and Petie to ask them about Joel, hoping to discover something that Anna might have left out. He also called Mrs. Sullivan, the last person to have spoken to Joel before his departure, and asked about her conversation with Joel.

He also contacted Hessa's former roommate Courtney, the person she had last spoken with before leaving the country. He asked to meet with her, and she was more than happy to help. Dan arrived at Harvard, found Thayer Hall, and spotted Courtney standing outside the entrance.

"Hello, you must be Courtney," Dan said.

"You are correct," she replied with a smile.

Dan spent close to a half-hour with Courtney, who gave him some new insight into the situation with Hessa. She was the only one who had seen Mr. Bishara, and described the situation in detail.

"He was a scary-looking guy," Courtney said. "Hessa and her mother seemed to be terrified of him. Hessa had always been kind of quiet around me, but very nice. When her father came, she seemed afraid to talk to me. Her mother hardly said a word, and seemed really agitated."

"I have the Bishara's address you gave to Henry Worthing, but do you happen to have her cell phone number?" Dan asked.

"Yes, but I've tried to call her several times and there hasn't been an answer. I'll give it to you, but I don't think you'll have much luck," Courtney replied. She dug around in her purse for her cell phone and gave Hessa's number to Dan.

"Thanks for seeing me on such short notice, Courtney. You've been very helpful," Dan said.

"Do you think something has happened to Hessa?" Courtney asked nervously.

218

"Don't worry about anything, Courtney. Joel Volkenburg's parents just haven't heard anything from him, so we're trying to get a hold of him, that's all," Dan replied.

"This is kind of creepy, Mr. Moretti. Am I in danger because I saw Mr. Bishara?" Courtney asked.

"You were Hessa's roommate—that's all. I wouldn't try to call her cell phone any more though, and don't talk to anyone about this for now," Dan said, and thanked Courtney again. Dan turned and walked to his car, leaving Courtney standing in front of the dorm, shivering from what may have been more from fear than the cold.

Dan spent the next couple of days organizing the notes he'd gathered, and mapping out Jerusalem and the surrounding area. He suspected that Joel was no longer in that city, but he would have to trace Joel's steps from his arrival and each day thereafter as best he could to be led to his current location. He wondered if Hessa or her mother would still be in the city, or if Husaam Bishara had relocated them in order to keep them quiet.

Dan realized this was going to be a difficult case, given the group of people he was up against. He researched any information he could find about Husaam Bishara and Hamas before he left, and knew he had his work cut out for him. After all, Hamas had been together since 1986. They had gotten very good at what they did.

CHAPTER 30

Dan arrived in Tel Aviv at 7:30 on Friday night. His assistant Beth had made arrangements for him to stay at a hotel across from the Tikvah, where Joel had stayed. By the time he got his luggage and arrived at the hotel it was after 9:30. He got to his room and ordered food to be sent up to him.

While he was waiting he phoned Anna to let her know he had arrived. Anna told him the concierge's name at the Tikvah Hotel was Joseph Schur, and would be on duty early tomorrow morning. He unpacked his things, ate his dinner and forced himself to try and sleep.

Early the next morning Dan got up and showered. After he dressed he went to his suitcase and pulled out a black wig with a ponytail and bushy eyebrows, along with a black leather jacket and boots. He would come back for those later.

He walked across the street to the Tikvah Hotel. When he entered, he went over to the concierge desk. There was a young man standing behind the desk, reading. He looked up as Dan walked toward him.

"Good morning, Sir! A beautiful day to be in Jerusalem!" he said.

"It sure is, and I'm starving. What's the best place for breakfast within walking distance?" Dan asked with a thick Southern drawl.

"It would be 'Little Jerusalem'. You will not find a better restaurant for breakfast in the whole city!" he replied.

"Thanks for the tip. I'll give it a try. So, is this where you send all Americans for an authentic Jewish breakfast?" he asked, smiling.

"Not only Americans, I send everyone there, and not just because my sister works there!" he said with a chuckle.

"Nothing wrong with a little nepotism," Dan replied with a smile. "What's your name, son? I'll let your sister know you sent me."

"It's Joseph Schur. My sister's name is Abigail. Be sure to ask for her!" he replied, and pointed Dan in the direction of the restaurant.

"Thanks for your help Joseph. It's been a pleasure," Dan said and walked out of the hotel.

He walked through the gate to the Little Jerusalem restaurant and was seated at a small table near the fence outside. As the hostess was handing Dan the menu he said, "I've just come from the Tikvah Hotel. The concierge highly recommended your restaurant and he said to ask for his sister Abigail, who works here."

"Oh yes, I will have Abigail serve you sir," the hostess said and walked away.

Moments later a slim girl with long, black, curly hair pulled back in a ponytail walked up to his table. "Hello, I am Abigail, and I will be serving you today. Would you like some coffee?" Dan nodded. "I understand you met my brother, Joseph," she said.

"I did. He was very helpful. He said to ask for you when I came," Dan replied. "Tell me, Abigail, what would you recommend?"

"Most definitely the Jerusalem breakfast," she said, and explained it to him.

"I'll take your recommendation," Dan replied.

Abigail walked off to place the order. After a few minutes she returned with a large plate. She set it down, and refilled his coffee cup.

"So do you get a lot of American tourists at your restaurant?" Dan asked smiling.

"We have not had many lately. This time of year is rather slow in Jerusalem. There have been very few Americans this week," she replied.

"Anyone from Oklahoma, like me?" Dan asked in his feigned drawl.

222

"No, not Oklahoma. There was a couple from California, and a young man who is a student from Boston. He was very handsome," she said, smiling.

"Really. A handsome college boy, huh? Well, you never know; maybe he'll show up for breakfast again and ask for a date!" Dan teased.

"He spoke of a girlfriend in Jerusalem he is visiting," she said smiling faintly and shrugging her shoulders. "Too bad. He told me he's a runner. I do not meet very many people who have the passion for running that I do."

She continued, "Besides, I do not know if he will be back. He was staying at the Tikvah Hotel, where my brother works. I asked my brother about him, and he said he hasn't been back to the hotel in a few days. His family and friends have been calling, but no one can locate him."

"Has anyone called the police?" Dan asked.

"I do not know. I hope he is all right," Abigail replied. As she was speaking, the hostess approached her to tell her a table had just been assigned to her.

"I had better be getting back to work," she said. "Besides, I have been talking so much, your food will get cold!" With that she smiled and turned to continue her duties.

Dan ate quickly, hardly tasting his food. He paid his bill and said goodbye to Abigail. As he walked to the hotel he called his old friend, Omri Segen, who had once been part of the Israeli Defense Force. They had been friends for over 20 years, and the two had quite a history together.

"Omri, my old friend, Dan Moretti here," Dan said.

"Dante! A voice that is always good to hear!" Omri replied. "To what do I owe the pleasure of a phone call from my American friend?"

"I'm in Jerusalem on business, but I'd like to get together. Could we meet for dinner this evening?" Dan asked.

"I have no set plans for this evening. I will call my wife to let her know I won't be home until later." Omri replied. "Have you been to the village of Ein Karem?"

223

"No, but I'll trust anywhere you suggest," Dan replied.

"There is a great little restaurant in the heart of the village. I will pick you up at your hotel at six p.m., if that's not too early," Omri said.

"Sounds good, Omri. I look forward to seeing you," Dan said, and they hung up.

When Dan returned to the hotel he asked to have a rental car dropped off for him. He ran up to his room and put on the wig, eyebrows and black leather jacket. As he walked out of his room he put a Red Sox cap on backwards.

A short while later he was ushered out to the front of the hotel where the car was parked. He got in the car and drove off to find the Bishara home. He had printed out the directions from his laptop and made his way the short distance to where Joel had been only days before him.

Dan slowly drove by the upscale apartment house, taking in as much as he could. The place looked very quiet. It was hard to believe anything bad could take place in this neighborhood. Dan turned around when he got a few blocks past the Bishara's apartment and drove back to park a couple of buildings away. He took out his phone and a newspaper and waited for any activity.

Late in the afternoon a black Mercedes pulled up in front of the apartment building and three men got out. One was definitely Husaam Bishara. Dan recognized him immediately from the search he had done. He picked up his phone and quickly took a couple of pictures of the group walking into the building, then put the phone to his ear, turning on the engine to leave.

As he drove past the building, the large man in the group turned around and looked directly at Dan, who appeared to be engaged in a phone conversation. He had the phone set on camera and clicked away as he drove by the apartment.

When he got back to the hotel he went up to his room and downloaded the photos to his computer. As he searched, he found the two men with Bishara also had ties to Hamas. The large man had been a

224

suspect in the bombing of a bank in Jerusalem, and Dan learned that his name was Fatik Nidal.

The small, wiry man with Bishara was Jad Said. There was a bit of information about him in connection with Hamas and Husaam Bishara, but he seemed to have been successful in escaping the spotlight. Dan saved the data in a folder on his computer and continued digging for more details.

⁂

Dan was waiting in the lobby when Omri Segen walked in shortly before five o'clock. Omri's wide grin showed a mouthful of large white teeth as he hurried over to shake his old friend's hand.

"Dante, good to see you!" Omri exclaimed.

"Good to see *you*, Omri," Dan replied.

The two walked out of the hotel and drove to Ein Karem. The ride to the little village was spent catching up on what had been happening in each of their lives over the last seven years since they had spoken.

When they arrived in Ein Karem, Omri parked the car outside the restaurant, and the two got a table in the patio section of the café. They ordered drinks and Omri looked at his friend, finally getting down to the point of the visit.

"So Dante, what is it that brings you to our fine city?" Omri asked.

"I was hired by a couple in Boston to look for their son who has been missing since last Saturday. He came over to Jerusalem looking for a girl he'd met at Harvard, where they were both attending school. They started dating, and she suddenly left a couple of weeks ago when her father showed up at Harvard and made her return to Israel with him. The girl was the daughter of Husaam Bishara," Dan said.

"That tells me quite a lot," Omri replied. "The American must not have had any idea of whose daughter he was dating."

"Well, things are a little different in America. Kids are pretty out of touch with what's going on in the rest of the world. The story gets worse, though, Omri. The kid's Jewish," Dan said.

225

"Of all the girls he could have decided to date, he chose a Muslim whose father is part of Hamas. What are the odds of that, I ask you?" Omri said.

"The kid's name is Joel Volkenburg. He's a great student, and has never given his parents a problem. That's what makes this so confusing. Evidently Joel didn't even date much because of how focused he was on school," Dan said.

"All it takes is one girl to make you fall in love. It can change your whole life—the way you think and react to things. Since Joel was so focused, that was probably worse than if he was a typical college kid going to parties and dating lots of girls. He was blind-sided. That's why he wasn't thinking when he ran off to Israel. He followed the Bishara girl all the way to Israel to rescue her, as though he was a knight in shining armor," Omri said.

"Good point, Omri. Well, now I need your help to figure out what Bishara would do with Joel, and how I can get to him."

"I can tell you that the boy is most likely not in Jerusalem. There are a number of places where he could be. Bishara and I go way back. He knows about me as much as I know of him. You and I will have to be seen with each other as little as possible."

Dan picked up his briefcase off the floor and opened it, pulling out his laptop. "I went by Bishara's house today. I was disguised, so I don't think there should be a problem yet, but a big guy who was with Bishara saw me. I took pictures, and wanted to see if you know anything about the men he was with." Dan pulled up the folder of pictures he had taken.

"The large one is Fatik Nidal. He has been with Hamas for years, and has worked very closely with Bishara for almost twenty years. Bishara uses him for his dirty work, and has taken care of Nidal and his family financially. He is very loyal to Bishara, and would do anything for him.

"The smaller man is Jad Said. He looks harmless, but can fit into any crowd, and is able to conceal himself because of his small stature. He is a sniper for Bishara. The Israeli Defense Force suspects he is responsible for many random shootings along the West Bank. It is believed

226

Bishara used him for his sharp-shooting skills during the Al-Aqsa Intifada. Many Israelis were killed, along with several foreign citizens who were caught in the cross-fire," Omri explained.

The two spent the rest of the evening discussing Husaam Bishara and the men Dan had seen that afternoon. Omri explained the technicalities that had kept Bishara and his Hamas group out of prison. He told Dan he would take care of getting footage of Joel from the hotel security videos. It would be helpful if they could see with whom Joel had been.

"When I find something, I'll give you a call. We need to keep you and your American accent as concealed as possible. Believe me, Bishara will figure out very quickly what you're up to," Omri said.

The two finished their meal and drove back to Dan's hotel. As Dan got out of the car and started to close the door Omri said, "I'll be in touch with you in the next couple of days. This isn't going to be easy, Dante. We need to be patient."

Dan nodded and thanked Omri for his help. He turned and walked into the hotel, his mind whirling with questions.

CHAPTER 31

Dan got to his room and turned on the television. The news was on, and he saw a picture of Joel Volkenburg on the screen. He turned the T.V. up and cringed when he heard what was being said:

"...American college student has disappeared. He had become friendly with Hessa Bishara, daughter of Husaam Bishara, a leader of Hamas. The two met while attending Harvard University in Boston, Massachusetts, in the United States. Mr. Bishara was seen recently on the Harvard campus with his wife and daughter. His wife was visiting their daughter in Boston, and Mr. Bishara arrived to take them both back to Israel.

It is believed Mr. Volkenburg travelled to Israel in search of Miss Bishara, whose enrollment at Harvard was withdrawn. His parents contacted international authorities when they repeatedly made calls to the Tikvah Hotel in Jerusalem where he was staying. They left numerous messages for Volkenburg but had no return calls. We approached Husaam Bishara as he was getting out of his car this evening:"

"Mr. Bishara, I am Levi Hirschfeld from Channel One. Your daughter was dating a young Jewish man from America who came to Jerusalem looking for her. That man has since disappeared. Do you know anything about this?"

"I know my daughter had a friend from college. He came to my house looking for her, but she is not in Jerusalem. I told him as much, and he left," Bishara replied.

"He has been missing for over a week. You know nothing of this?" Levi asked.

"I know you would like me to be involved in this, but do you think I would be so foolish as to do something to a boy from America who had been friendly with my daughter? I know that you would like me to be responsible, but you have chosen an easy target in me. Why don't you look for a better reason for him to be missing? Do not waste my time," Bishara replied, and walked into his house.

Levi turned from Mr. Bishara's retreating figure and said, "This is Levi Hirschfeld speaking to you from the home of Hasaam Bishara in Jerusalem. Back to the Channel One news room."

Dan turned off the television and called Omri. "Were you watching the news?"

"Yes, I saw it," Omri replied. "I believe he knows where Joel is. We need to keep close tabs on where he and his men are at all times. I promise you he won't be doing anything for a while. He knows he's going to be watched. We have to be patient."

⚜

Joel awakened with a start. He had been dreaming of skiing. It was very cold, and he felt a surge of happiness and freedom flying down the slopes. As he descended the air got warmer and warmer. It finally got so hot the snow was gone, and he was skiing on dirt and rocks. His skis came to a screeching halt, and he fell into a mound of rocks and hit his head.

His eyes flew open and he was breathing rapidly, his head pounding from the pain where he'd received the blow from the gun. He had lost track of time, since his drifting in and out of consciousness seemed like what had been ages.

Each morning someone would come by and pull open a latch in the bottom of the door, sliding a piece of bread or dried meat and cup of water through, then slamming it shut. Joel would lie on the ground, listening to the footsteps of the stranger. Every once in a while he would hear voices speaking in what he assumed was Arabic, but most of the time he felt as though he was the only person in the place.

230

This particular morning was different, however. He crawled over to get his piece of bread, and managed to sit up and lean against the wall. As he took a bite he heard what he thought was a woman's voice. It was very faint, but sounded close.

He stooped down and crawled over to the door, putting his ear against the small opening at the bottom. It was quiet for several minutes, and then he heard it again. The woman was crying softly. One of the men raised his voice to her, and there was silence.

Joel's heart raced. He couldn't make out the woman's voice. For a fleeting moment he thought it might be Hessa, but realized these people would never have the two of them in the same place.

Who could it be? The lack of food had made him weak, and the blow to his head had caused him to lose quite a bit of blood. He tried to concentrate and think, but it wasn't any use; he felt as though his strength was being drained from him a little more each day.

As he lay in the dirt Joel tried to remember what he had been reading in the Bible. He had gotten through several books of the Old Testament, and read the four gospels in the New Testament. He also thought over what Mrs. Sully had talked to him about before he left for Israel.

What did she say? To not be anxious, but to pray for everything, he thought to himself. *Okay God, I don't know about the anxious part—I can't help that. I just hope You can hear me. I don't know where I am, but if You're real, You do. Please show me if You are real and help me...and help that lady I heard crying. If there's ever been a time I needed You, it's now.* Joel said in his thoughts.

He sat up and moved over to where he could lean with his back against the wall for support. As he sat staring into the dark, dirty little room he suddenly heard almost audibly, "Call to Me and I will answer you, and I will tell you great and mighty things that you do not know."

"What?" he whispered out loud, incredulous.

"You will seek Me and find Me when you search for Me with all your heart."

231

Joel looked around him—no one was there.

Am I losing my mind? Joel thought to himself. The voice only became clearer.

"For God so loved the world that He gave His only begotten Son, that whoever believes in Him shall not perish, but have eternal life. For all have sinned and fallen short of the glory of God. But God demonstrates His own love for us in that while we were yet sinners, Christ died for us."

Is this from the Bible? I didn't read enough to recognize... Joel prayed in his mind, becoming silent from his injured head and the confusion it brought on. The voice very clearly spoke again:

"If we confess our sins, He is faithful and righteous to forgive us our sins and to cleanse us of all unrighteousness...I am the way, and the truth and the life; no one comes to the Father but through Me."

Joel looked around the room. He felt a Presence, and whispered aloud: "I know I've blown it, God. I went against the advice of my family and friends. I came here, and look what I have to show for it. I've lost everything, including the people I love most in the world—and Hessa.

"I never believed in You, but I never took the time to read the Bible, to give You the benefit of showing Yourself to me. I'm sorry...I'm sorry."

Joel lay on the ground, tears spilling out of his eyes onto the dirt, making small pools of mud. All of a sudden peace engulfed him, and the small cell he was trapped in became a place of light beaming all around him. He turned on his back, and suddenly realized the gash in the back of his head was gone.

He looked down at his hands—the ropes that had bound his hands and feet had fallen from him and lay on the dirt floor. He abruptly sat up and felt where the cut had been. No caked blood on his hair, no open wound, no pain.

He looked around the room, then said aloud, "You *are* real...You're who you said You are! It's You, it's You...You're here! You spoke to me...! Don't leave...don't leave me," he wept quietly, a strange mixture of deep remorse and joy filling him like he had never experienced.

Joel's life had been spent in wealth and comfort, having any material thing he could ever want, but he realized nothing could compare to what he had just found in this filthy little cell on the other side of the world from his home.

Joel sat whispering to God, tears falling intermittently over the next few hours. He knew that he would be able to get through anything now, even if it meant dying in this place.

Then he realized that he couldn't give up. His family and friends would be devastated if something happened to him—and he had an important story to tell. He would have to pray for a miracle. He prayed for God to get him out of this place somehow, and that he would be able to find Hessa. As he finished pleading before the Lord, he heard that still, small voice again:

"I know the plans I have for you, declares the Lord; plans for good and and not for calamity, to give you a future and a hope."

Joel knew at that moment that he would get out of this place. He knew God *did* have a plan for him. He wasn't sure yet what it was, but he was certain this was all happening for a reason.

"So I'm that stubborn, huh, Lord? You had to let me run off to Israel and allow me to get kidnapped just to get my attention…I mean that much to You, don't I?" Joel whispered, smiling to himself. "Wow…"

Just then he heard something again. This time it was on the other side of the back wall of his cell. A door had opened, and then he heard a thump. The door was shut with the sound of a bolt slamming against the wood. Joel moved over to the back wall and put his ear against it, straining to hear something—anything.

He sat as quietly as possible for several minutes, but heard nothing. He finally sat back down and stared at the wall as though it would reveal something. Then he prayed that if there was someone else being held in this place that he would be able to communicate with them somehow.

He had found a splinter of wood on the floor of his cell, and spent the rest of the day writing down the words he'd heard. He wrote in the dirt, tracing the words over and over again. He wanted to remember everything that had been spoken to him that day. He would memorize it all, and once he was free he would look everything up in the Bible.

Those beautiful words would be sustenance for him in his captivity, and he would never forget that God Himself had visited him that day and had spoken to him in answer to a simple prayer. Eternity was now etched in his heart.

CHAPTER 32

Dan called Anna Volkenburg and when she answered, he said abruptly, "I told you not to get in touch with the authorities over here until we could watch Bishara's activities. Why would you do that? You've increased the danger to your son by letting them know we're looking for him. Now there'll be no way he'll tip his hand; he won't go anywhere near Joel!"

Anna tried to explain, but realized she'd made a terrible mistake. "You must understand how terrified I am, and that I feel so helpless just sitting here doing nothing."

"You hired me to help you find Joel. Your job was to let me do *my* job. This interference has cost me a lot of ground. I can assure you that Bishara and anyone connected with him will intensify their efforts and won't allow anything to slip now," Dan said sharply.

Anna became quiet and Dan thought she'd hung up. "Are you still there?"

"Yes," she said shakily. "I'm so sorry Dan. My impatience has put my son in more danger than ever. You never realize how much you love someone until something like this happens. I would do anything to have Joel back."

"I'm trying to get him back for you; it'll just take more time now. Please Anna, leave this to me—that's why you hired me. You need to be patient. I'll be in touch with you," and he hung up.

Early the next morning Dan's cell phone rang; it was Omri. "I have some good news. I was able to get the video footage of the Tikvah's security cameras. I got the license plate number from a car Joel was getting out of. I traced it, and it belongs to a David Appel—he lives here in Jerusalem. I called him and he is anxious to be of help. I'll pick you up at ten a.m."

Dan was encouraged—they finally had a lead. He went down to the hotel restaurant and had breakfast. As he ate he e-mailed Anna to let her know of the meeting with David Appel. He then logged the information into his file on Joel, and did a search on the pastor.

David Appel had a fascinating background. Born into a religious Jewish family, David's father was a rabbi. He had been given a Bible by a friend and searched the scriptures for himself and had become a believer in the Christian Messiah. After attending Bible School in Austria, David returned to Jerusalem where he started teaching Bible studies and the little group grew into a sizeable church.

David's conversion had come at a high price. His family had had numerous death threats, but his church continued to grow and thrive. His father had disowned him, and even though David had tried numerous times to contact his father, the two hadn't spoken in several years. He remained separated from his parents and siblings, but his faith was immoveable.

"Hmm…interesting," Dan said aloud as he finished reading. This would be an intriguing meeting.

True to form, Omri showed up at the hotel precisely at ten a.m. The two got in his car and drove to the Appel's home. As they pulled up and parked, David opened the front door to the tiny home and waved at the two visitors.

"Welcome, my friends! Welcome to our home! Please come in," David said, motioning to them.

"Thank you for seeing us on such short notice, Mr. Appel," Omri said.

"Please call me David, and this is my wife, Miriam," David said.

236

"My name is Omri Segen, and this is my friend from America, Dante Moretti," Omri said.

"You can call me Dan," Dan added.

Miriam asked the men to sit down, and then left the room to start a pot of tea. David smiled at the two men and was the first to speak.

"Gentlemen, I understand you know my friend Joel Volkenburg".

"Yes. As you and I discussed, Joel has been missing for well over a week now. Unfortunately the news of him missing was leaked, so this is a bit of a setback. Whoever has him isn't going to make any moves for a while," Omri said. "David, could you tell us how you met Joel?"

"Yes, I saw the news, and was very grateful you were able to find me. Joel and I met through a friend of mine. I gave him a tour of Jerusalem, and then invited him to join us for dinner. He is a very bright, very nice boy," David said.

"Such a good boy," Miriam added as she entered the room with a pot of tea and plate of tahina, hummus, and pita bread. She set the tray down on a low table between their guests and poured tea for all of them.

David described the day he'd spent with Joel to his guests in detail. He told them Joel had seemed very intrigued about the Christian history of Jerusalem, so David had taken him to several spots he thought would be interesting to his young friend.

He explained further that Joel had told them about his relationship with Hessa over dinner. He had advised against Joel's going to the Bishara's home, but now knew that he'd gone anyway.

"I must tell you that I am very glad you are here. Until now I did not know what to do with the information I am about to tell you. I knew Joel would not take my advice about staying away from the Bishara's, so I asked a friend of mine to go to the Tikvah Hotel on the night Joel was invited to their house for dinner. He waited in the lobby until Joel came down, and when he saw who Joel left with, he followed them."

David took a sip of tea and continued, "The man who took Joel was Fatik Nidal, who works for Husaam Bishara. My friend walked out behind them and saw there was another man in the car. My friend did not

237

recognize him, but after a bit of research he found that his name was Jad Said, who is also part of Hamas."

David absent-mindedly blew on the hot tea and said, "My friend followed them until they were about 20 kilometers south of Hebron. They pulled over to the side of the road. He was afraid they suspected he was following them, so he drove on.

I would not like to speculate as to where they took him. They could have gone just about anywhere. My friend drove to Be'er Sheva and stopped at a restaurant parking lot just outside of town waiting to see if they would pass by, but he never saw them again."

"Those were the same men I saw at Bishara's home. Besides that, the only thing we know is that they drove south of Jerusalem somewhere, and then disappeared," Dan said.

"I am afraid you are correct," David replied.

The three continued talking and speculating about where they could have taken Joel based on Hamas' history of taking captives, and where they had held them in the past. None of them could come up with a thing.

"I must tell you, gentlemen, I will not cease to pray for my young friend. I will have the people in my church pray and fast for him. You will not have an easy time finding him. God will have to help us now," David said.

"I highly doubt sitting around praying will help the situation," Dan said.

"I disagree with you, my friend," David said. "It is the only solution at this point. You do it your way, and I will seek God. We will see the hand of the Lord."

The three men finished their business and Dan stood up with Omri following suit. The two walked out the front door, thanked David and Miriam, and walked to Omri's car.

"Please keep me informed of what happens with Joel, and I will keep you informed if anything is revealed to me. Is it a deal?" David asked.

238

"Absolutely. It might take some time, but I know something or someone will lead us to him eventually," Dan replied with a wry smile, disregarding the strange remarks David had made.

As they drove back to the hotel the two men conversed about the meeting with David. They both agreed that he was somewhat of an eccentric, but were glad they had visited him for the little bit of information he'd given.

As Omri pulled into the hotel, he told Dan he would continue soliciting help from his contacts, and that he would be in touch. Dan thanked his friend for his help, and assured Omri that between the two of them they would get Joel home.

CHAPTER 33

Hessa had been in London for a month, and making headway with Mustafa was slow. There had been times that she thought he was softening, but then out of nowhere he would turn on her angrily and become silent, alienating her.

A week into her stay, Mustafa had been joined by another man; Hessa assumed it was because her father wanted her watched 24 hours a day, and it was physically impossible for Mustafa to do so. The name of Mustafa's new partner was Iyad, and he was much different than his cohort. He was tall and slim, and a rather quiet man—not an imposing figure like Mustafa. His manner seemed to be shy and nervous rather than gruff and angry.

Hessa thought this might be an opportunity for her. The problem was that Iyad's watch was late at night. Mustafa would come to pick her up from school and stay with her until about ten o'clock at night. Iyad would show up to take Mustafa's place and stay close by all night, then take her to school in the morning. This didn't leave a lot of opportunity for her to get away to call anyone.

She had spent quite a bit of time at the library on campus and had gotten to know one of the librarians. The girl's name was Mary, and she was about two years older than Hessa. Mary had invited Hessa to several different events, but she had declined. Recently Hessa had opened up to Mary about her social limitations because of her culture and religion. Mary was empathetic about her situation, but their friendship grew in spite of Hessa's unwanted captivity.

Hessa was hard at work on a paper that was due in a few days, so she'd been spending even more time at the library than usual. One evening she told Mustafa she would be at the library until closing and asked him if Iyad could meet her at the library to take her home. Mustafa had agreed, and told her he would have Iyad meet them at the library at 9:45 p.m. Hessa had the phone card hidden inside her shirt, and finally mustered the courage to take a chance on calling her friends in America.

As she saw Iyad approach her study table, she greeted him happily and told him she would be right back, and that she needed to ask the librarian a few questions. He nodded, so she picked up a notebook and walked over to Mary.

"Hi Mary, I wanted to see if you could give me suggestions for a good reference book on the Inquisition," Hessa said.

"Oh, yes, come on over to the computer and I'll show you a couple of great books you can use. Let's make sure they're available," Mary replied.

Hessa walked over to the computer to join Mary, and as she turned to face the screen, she glanced quickly over at Iyad, who was reading a newspaper. She turned back to Mary with an anxious look on her face.

"Mary, do you have a telephone I can use? Please speak your answer softly, and do not look around," Hessa whispered.

Mary looked at Hessa quizzically, and then became concerned. "Is everything okay?" she asked.

"Yes, of course. I just need to make a couple of phone calls, and I never have the freedom to do so. I have a calling card, so it won't cost the library any money," she said.

"Hessa, I don't think we have the book at this location. Could you come back to the office with me? I can check further," Mary said aloud.

Hessa nodded, thankful that her friend had caught on. The two walked into the office, and Mary pointed to the phone.

"I'll keep watch," she said.

Hessa quickly dialed Joel's number. It rang once and went directly into voicemail. She tried the number again, only to get voicemail once more. She then dialed Mrs. Sully's number she only hoped Mrs. Sully wasn't out picking the boys up from school.

The phone rang three times. Hessa started to get discouraged when someone answered: "Sullivan residence, Maggie speaking," she said.

"Mrs. Sullivan! It is Hessa!" she said quietly.

"Hessa! How are you? *Where* are you? I tried to get in touch with your mother, but her phone's been disconnected. I haven't been able to reach anyone!"

"I am at King's College in London. My father sent me to school here to be closer to my fiancé. I cannot talk for long. I tried to call Joel, but it just went into voicemail. Is there any way you can get me in touch with him?" Hessa asked.

"Oh honey...Joel went to Israel looking for you, but he's been gone for over a month now, and no one can find him. His parents hired an investigator and they contacted the Jerusalem police, but they haven't heard anything. It's been on the news here several times, and the authorities are looking for him, but nothing has surfaced. It's like he...disappeared from the face of the earth..." Mrs. Sully said hesitantly.

"Father," she whispered.

"What, honey?" Mrs. Sully asked.

"I am sure he went to my house. My father has done something with him," she said anxiously.

"Oh Hessa, I don't think you should blame your father," Mrs. Sully said.

"You do not know him. He has to be behind this. He hates the Jews. He knew Joel was Jewish, and that is why he went to Boston to take me back home."

Mrs. Sully's words about Hessa's mother suddenly hit her. "What do you mean my mother's phone has been disconnected?"

"I called your mother a couple of weeks ago to say hello, and I got a recording saying the phone had been disconnected," Mrs. Sully said quietly.

"He's done something with my mother!" Hessa exclaimed.

"Hessa, you need to calm down. Haven't you called your parents since you've been in London? You need to call your father and talk to him before you accuse him of anything," Mrs. Sully said.

"My father took my phone away, and I have no way of getting in touch with anyone. I am at the library, using their phone. You need to understand, Mrs. Sully, my father is a leader of Hamas. If you knew about him you would understand that I have a reason to be concerned. I need to hang up now before Iyad sees that I am on the phone. Please pray for us, Mrs. Sully," Hessa said, as her voice cracked. "We need your help!"

Mary came into the office and said aloud, "Hessa, did you get that reference? The library is about to close"…and then whispered, "He's coming!"

"I must go," Hessa said, and hung up the phone.

Hessa breezed out of the office with a smile on her face. "Thank you so much for your help. I did find what I was looking for, but I am sure I will need your help again," Hessa said, and looked at her friend hopefully.

"Of course," Mary said with her eyebrows raised.

Hessa went back to her study table and picked up her things, stuffing her books into her book bag, and walked quickly to the door. She glanced at Iyad as he held the door open for her. He didn't seem to be suspicious of anything, so she breathed a sigh of relief that her first attempt had seemed successful.

When she got back to the privacy of her room, she put her things away and got into her pajamas. She sat on the bed, thinking over the quick conversation she'd had with Mrs. Sully. Her mind was in a whirl over what could have happened to her mother, and to Joel.

"Help me…help me," she said aloud as she covered her face with her hands. The tears began to flow as she felt completely alone and helpless, alienated from those she loved most in the world. Her thoughts turned to Imaad; she loved and trusted her brother. Surely he would tell her what had happened to their mother.

A wave of paranoia swept over her as she thought of how loyal he was to their father. Maybe it wasn't a good idea for her to contact him. If he told their father, she would be put under stricter supervision, or worse…

CHAPTER 34

Maggie stood in her kitchen staring at the phone. She didn't know what to make of the conversation that had just taken place, but as she gathered her thoughts, she picked up the phone and called Anna Volkenburg.

As she dialed the phone, she organized her thoughts and tried to calm herself.

"Hello?" Anna said.

"Hello Anna, it's Maggie Sullivan. I just had a very strange call from Hessa Bishara."

"Hessa called you? Where is she? Why hasn't she tried to contact us before? Does she know where Joel is?"

"She's been sent to school in London, and hasn't had a chance to call anyone. It seems her father took her phone away. It sounds as though she's being closely watched by someone named Iyad. I'm not sure if he's her fiancé or someone else. She tried to call Joel before she called me, but it just went to voicemail."

"You mean to say she hasn't even talked to her family since she's been in London? She knew nothing of what's happened? I can't believe this."

"I told her about how Joel has been missing for over a month, and that I'd tried to contact her mother. That made her more upset, because I mentioned her mother's phone had been disconnected...she thinks her father is involved with both Joel and her mother's disappearance."

"Oh my God..."

Anna thought for a moment as anger started to build in her. When she spoke again, her voice was louder than she'd intended.

"What kind of man would send his daughter away from home without a phone, and no way to contact her family...with a bodyguard, no less?

"There must be something to this if Hessa suspects her own father...I think it's time Eli and I get on a plane and go over there ourselves. I think we're going to have to take this matter into our own hands, and not just rely on Dan Moretti. I want some answers."

Anna's emotions got the better of her again as she blurted out, "What a mess Joel's gotten himself into! Of all the girls at Harvard he could have chosen, he gets involved with a girl whose father is part of Hamas."

"He had no idea, Anna, you know that. Poor Joel. He thought he was bringing home a Jewish girl, did he tell you that?" Maggie asked.

"No, he didn't. When Hessa came to dinner he mentioned that they hadn't discussed their backgrounds yet. He did tell us when he brought her for dinner that she was from Israel. I'm sure he thought she was Jewish. I'm sorry, Maggie. I'm just so spent from this whole ordeal. My nerves are pretty frayed."

"I understand. Believe me, I love that boy with all my heart. I've been stressed over this myself, and haven't stopped praying for him. I think we're going to need to tell the boys about my conversation with Hessa."

"You're right. I'll call Henry and ask the three of them to come over so I can tell them all at once. Then I think I'll make some plane reservations for Eli and me. We're going to Israel," Anna said.

"What are you going to do in Israel? I think you should leave this to the authorities. Making a trip to Israel yourself would be a waste of time at this point," Maggie said.

"I'd feel closer to him if I were there," Anna said quietly.

"Oh, I didn't think of that. Well, in that case, of course you'd want to be closer to where your son is."

"Did Hessa say she'd call you again?" Anna asked.

"It sounded as though someone was coming to look for her. She was at the library making a call from there. I don't know how she was able to do that—she didn't say.

"It seems she's in London to be closer to her fiancé, but she isn't able to contact anyone, for some reason. She just kept talking about her father, and said 'if I only knew him, I would understand why she was so upset about her mother and Joel'."

"This is so disturbing...I'm going to call Joel's friends and have them over to tell them. Then I'll make arrangements to go to Israel, with Eli or without him."

"My friends and I will continue to pray for his safe return and for your safety as well," Maggie said.

"If there's a God, I don't want to have anything to do with Him. How could a God that is supposed to know everything allow this to happen to my son?" Anna asked.

"Joel made his own decision to go to Israel, and God doesn't interfere when people want to do things on their own. I think it would be a good idea for us to continue to pray for Joel's safe return—He's the only one Who can help Joel at this point," Maggie said in a serious tone.

"You go ahead and pray, but I'll take my own steps to see if we can get some answers. I'll let you know when I have my arrangements made," Anna said.

The two hung up, and immediately Anna was on the phone to her husband. She explained the phone call from Hessa, and what she and Maggie had talked about.

"...and Eli, I think we should go to Israel. We can't just sit here waiting for bits of information every few days from Dan. Why don't you make some connections to try and get in touch with someone over there?"

"This *has* gone too far. I'll make some calls. We'll figure this out..." Eli trailed off as if lost in thought.

"I'll make arrangements for us to fly over as soon as you're able to get away," Anna said.

"I won't be able to leave until next Friday. I have to finish up a section, and next Monday is President's Day, so I'll be able to spend some time over there the next week. I'll make arrangements to have someone take over my class while I'm gone."

"That's a whole week away! You can stay here, but I need to make arrangements to go over there before you," Anna said.

"I think it would be best that you *do* go ahead of me…besides, I think you should contact your sister, since she's in Jerusalem," Eli said simply.

"Klara? I don't know…" Anna trailed off.

"You haven't spoken to her in fifteen years. I think it's time the two of you put your differences behind you. Besides, you should be glad you have someone in your family left," Eli said thoughtfully.

"She was the one who made a big stink out of such a small matter," Anna said.

"All she wanted was for you to stay at her home. You turned your nose up at her invitation and stayed at a hotel. She's your sister—your only family. Just call her, Anna."

"I guess you're right. But…what would I say to someone I haven't spoken to in fifteen years? I can't just pick up the phone and act as if nothing happened," Anna said.

"You'll think of something. I don't ask you to do much. You're able to live your life freely, without my interference. This is one thing I'm asking you to do. Our parents are all gone. I wish my brother was alive. When he died I lost my only true friend," Eli said quietly.

Anna was speechless at her husband's words. She had never heard her husband open up about anything. He'd been very private and introverted since the day they'd met. Between his professorship and the law firm, their conversation typically didn't venture far from those topics. Lately the two hadn't spoken of much at all to each other. She was thrown off-guard by this little glimpse of vulnerability in him.

"Eli, I've never heard you say anything like that. Well, if that's how you feel then yes, I'll go. I'll call Klara and try to make amends.

"You're right, after everything we've lost in life…and now our own son…." she trailed off, her emotions getting the better of her.

Eli hesitated and then said, "I know I've seemed indifferent to this situation with Joel. I was angry at first, and then I think I was a little afraid to face what could be too awful to imagine. We barely see David anymore—he hardly bothers to call. We can't lose Joel too. I need to take charge of this mess."

"Thank you. That means a lot to me," Anna replied.

"You get busy making our arrangements, and I'll start making phone calls. I'll be home at six, and we'll continue this discussion."

"I only hope Klara's still at the same address in Jerusalem," Anna replied, and said goodbye to her husband.

CHAPTER 35

Anna hung up and immediately called Henry. She asked if he could round up Peter and Eddie and meet at her house that afternoon. Henry told her to count on them being there by four o'clock.

Just after four p.m., Joel's three best friends knocked on the Volkenburg's front door. Anna ran to open the door and ushered them into her sitting room.

"Peter, your mother received a phone call from Hessa."

"What?" Petie asked, and the three of them started talking at once.

"Slow down, boys. Let me explain," Anna replied. She told them about the surprising phone call and what Hessa had said.

"Wow," Petie replied. "Why didn't my mom call me?"

"I just spoke with her about an hour ago. I had to call my husband to talk to him about it first, since we're going to make arrangements to fly to Israel as soon as possible," she said.

"I'm going to London," Henry said.

"Henry, I didn't tell you about this so you could run off to England," Anna replied.

"Mrs. Volkenburg, you didn't want us going to Israel, which we should have, so I'm going to London to see if I can get more information from Hessa. I can't sit here and do nothing. Joel's been gone for over a month now, and no one is doing anything. I can't wait any more. I'm going over there," Henry said.

"Me too!" Petie echoed.

"If you guys are going over there, I better stay put to keep track of any news coming back here," Eddie said. "I'll keep in touch with your mom and the Volkenburgs so you guys can stay in the loop."

"You boys need talk to your parents about this. With the two of you taking off and Joel being gone, I don't think they'll appreciate this. None of you will be graduating at this point," Anna said.

"Graduating, huh!" Henry exclaimed. "Mrs. V, I really don't care about that right now. My best friend is missing, and I feel so guilty that I didn't follow him to keep an eye on him while he played rescue warrior."

"I'm going to speak with your mother, Henry. It's only fair that she knows what you're up to, and that you'll be in some danger, even in London," Anna said.

"Say what you want, but I'm going over there. I'm almost 22 years old. What can my mother do?" Henry replied.

Henry, Petie, and Eddie got up and walked to the front door. As they turned to say goodbye, Henry reassured her.

"I'm not gonna do anything that'll put me in danger—don't worry. We need to make sure we're all in contact, though. Just keep in touch with Mrs. Sully, and we'll keep in touch with Eddie. Thanks again, Mrs. V," Henry said.

They walked out to Henry's car and drove to his house. His mother was home, and in the time it took the three to walk into the house, his mother was already speaking with Anna. She came around the corner as the three friends walked in.

She continued the conversation with her long-time neighbor and friend, all the while looking at her son with raised eyebrows and shrugging shoulders. When she hung up the phone she walked over to the boys, still standing in the front hall.

"What on earth are you thinking, Henry Charles Worthing?"

"Mom, Joel's been gone way too long. We found out his girlfriend is going to King's College in London, and Petie and I are going over there to see if we can get more information."

"Mrs. Volkenburg already told me all that. Why don't you just call his girlfriend? Don't phones work in England?" she asked sarcastically.

"Mom, Hessa's dad is part of Hamas. He sent her to college in England to get her away from Joel, and took her phone away. She even has body guards to make sure she doesn't escape or anything," Henry said.

"Aren't you being a little dramatic? Henry, that's just nonsense. Do you really believe a young girl who was going to Harvard is now being guarded so she won't escape? That's just silly," his mother replied.

"It's true, Mom, and I'm not gonna sit around waiting while my best friend's life could be in danger. Joel did a really stupid thing going over there alone. He should have had his friends with him, but we stayed here. I just hope it's not too late. You know things like this happen all the time internationally. Don't be so naïve!" Henry yelled at his mother.

"Henry, don't yell like that. Obviously you're very concerned about your friend. I know you only want to help him, but it doesn't make sense to go to London to try and find this girl. Leave this to the authorities."

"Mom, no matter what you say, I'm going to London. I have to help Joel. I need some answers!"

"Well then, I'm going to check on getting an investigator to go with you. He'll be better equipped to know what to do in this situation. I'll see if Anna can help with a reference. Maybe the man she hired knows someone," Henry's mother said.

"Okay, thanks. Now we're getting somewhere."

"I'd feel better having someone helping us who knows what they're doing," Petie said. "I'll call my mom on our drive back to Cambridge to let her know about our plans. Let's go, Henry, we've got a lot to do to get ready. Thanks, Mrs. Worthing."

"Okay, I'll let you know when I find someone who can go with you to London," Mrs. Worthing said.

The three friends ran out to Henry's car and drove as fast as they could to their house in Cambridge. The traffic was slow due to rush hour, but at least they were driving *into* Cambridge instead of out of it. As they drove, Petie called his mother to explain that he was going to London with Henry, and that they would have a private investigator with them.

253

"Oh honey, I know you want to help Joel, but this is just too dangerous," Mrs. Sully said anxiously.

"Mom, don't be like that! We're sick of waiting around. Henry and I are gonna get some answers so we can bring Joel home!" Petie exclaimed.

"I know how much you love your friend. I just don't know how much good you can do in a place you know nothing about."

"Mom, I'll keep in contact with you and Eddie. He's gonna stay here so he can keep in contact with everyone. He'll be getting notes from our classes for us, too."

"Let me know when you and Henry are leaving, and when you'll be getting into London. And don't forget to tell me who this investigator turns out to be that you're travelling with. I want his information also," Mrs. Sully said.

"I will, Mom. I love you and Dad, and tell the rest of the family that I love them too," Petie said.

"I love you too, honey—more than you'll ever know."

Mother and son said goodbye and Petie hung up, then immediately got on his phone to find flights to London. When Henry asked him what he was doing, he told him he was on a travel website.

"Don't you think we should wait 'til my mom finds an investigator to go with us?" Henry asked.

"Nope—he can meet us over there," Petie said simply, then: "Hey! Here's a last-minute fare to London from Boston tomorrow night! We have to stop over in Reykjavik, but the flight is only $500! If we apply for a credit card, we'll save another $100!

"Are you kidding me? You can't find anything better than that? Don't you think your dad will spring a few hundred bucks for a flight? He has more money than the Queen of England," Henry said.

"Hey, I was brought up knowing the value of a dollar, and this flight gets in only a half hour later than the flight going through Dublin, but that flight is $350 more!" Petie exclaimed.

"All right, Mr. Scrooge, book it," Henry said, smiling at his friend.

CHAPTER 36

Henry's mother called Anna back to ask her to get in touch with Dan Moretti for a referral of an investigator in London. She was able to get a hold of him, and he told her he would get in touch with Scotland Yard. He informed Anna he would call him and ask him to meet with the boys once they reached London.

When Henry and Petie got back to their house they immediately started preparing for their trip the next day. Eddie called to have pizza delivered. They were just about finished packing when Petie realized his passport was at his mother's house.

"What am I gonna do?" Petie wailed.

"Call your mom right now! You're gonna have to drive to your house to get it," Henry said.

Petie called his mother and asked her where his passport was. She told him she had it, and offered to drive out and meet him half way to get it to him.

"Can you meet me in Springfield, honey?" she asked her son.

"Yeah, absolutely! Thanks, Mom!" Petie replied.

They agreed on a place to meet, and she told him she would need to get the boys situated and call his father before she left, but would meet him at 8:30 p.m. Petie hung up and ran up to his room to print out his class schedule to give Eddie so he could collect notes for each class. A few minutes later the pizza delivery man came and the three sat down for a break.

"Audra and I broke up," Henry said as the three sat in the kitchen eating their pizza. "When I called to tell her I was going to London, she told me she'd had enough. She said I was too pre-occupied with this 'Joel stuff'."

"Can't blame her, can you?" Eddie said.

"I guess not, but I'm ticked off that my chances of working for her dad aren't good," Henry said.

"So that was your only reason for dating her?" Petie asked.

"Well, not the only reason…but probably had a lot to do with it," Henry replied, embarrassed. "How cool would it be to be a sports agent? Talk about the dream job! If you have to be a lawyer, you might as well do something you can have fun with."

"Aren't we a bunch of losers? The only one of us who has a girlfriend is Joel, and he can't even be with her!" Eddie said.

"You have a good excuse, Eddie. You've been involved with everything short of helping the janitors sweep the halls. For me, girls never take me seriously," Petie said.

"It's because you look like Elmo from Sesame Street," Eddie said sarcastically.

Eddie and Henry fell into gales of laughter. It felt good to break up the tension and stress they were feeling. Petie looked at his friends and chuckled at the remark.

"Thanks, man, you really know how to make a guy feel good," Petie retorted.

The three finished their pizza and Henry went up to his room to print out his class schedule for Eddie. Petie went to the hall closet and got his coat out.

"Okay, I'm off to meet my mom. I'll be home later. See ya," Petie said.

✦✦✦

Shortly after Petie left, Henry's phone rang. It was his mother, who called to let him know that Mrs. Volkenburg had gotten a hold of Dan in Israel. The bad news was that they hadn't gotten anywhere with turning up new leads, but the good news was that he had found a contact at Scotland Yard in London.

The man's name was Douglas McLaughlin. She passed his office number on to Henry's mother who called Mr. McLaughlin right away, even though it was still the middle of the night in London. She left a message in hopes he would call her before the boys left for England.

Petie got to Springfield in record time. His mother was already there, looking tiny as she waited in her giant Suburban. He pulled up next to her and got out, walking over to her car. She unlocked her door and stepped out just as Petie was walking up to greet his mother. The two hugged, then Mrs. Sully stepped back to look at him as if to study every inch of her son.

"Here's your passport. Now, you have to call me as soon as you arrive, and keep me informed of everything you're doing in London. Is that understood, Peter?" she asked.

"Yes Mommy, I understand," Petie retorted.

"I'm not kidding, honey. I don't want you to be flippant with me. You just remember your family, and how much we all love you. You don't want me going over there!" his mother exclaimed.

Petie couldn't help laughing at his mother. "I'm sorry Mom, but you look pretty funny trying to act tough. Seriously, I'll keep you in the loop at all times. Henry and I aren't gonna do anything stupid. We just wanna talk to Hessa. It'll help us feel like we're getting closer to finding Joel," Petie said, and hugged his mom.

"Do you have any idea when you'll return?" his mother asked.

"No, but I'll let you know. We're not coming back until we've talked to Hessa, and I'm not sure how long it'll take for us to find her. I was doing a search on King's College, and there are tons of dorms all over London where she could be staying, and I know they won't be giving out information on where she lives. The investigator is gonna have to help us with that," Petie said.

Mother and son stood outside for several minutes talking about everything that had happened, and marveling at how dramatically their

257

lives had changed in just a few months, all because of one girl. Mrs. Sully finally turned to open her car door, and hugged her son once more. She pulled him down so she could kiss his cheek. Even though Petie was of medium height, he towered over his petite mother.

"I need to get home. Your dad should be there by now, but I have to get Patrick to school early to help set up a project he's presenting. The morning comes soon!" Mrs. Sully said. "Will you be okay driving back to Boston? You look tired."

"I'll stop and get some coffee before I head back. Thanks for coming all this way tonight, Mom. I really appreciate it. We'll talk soon," Petie said, waiting until his mother was in her car and had turned on the engine before he walked back to his own car.

Before he got in he stood waving at his mother in the typical Sullivan fashion, until she was out of sight. He drove a short way to a shopping center where he saw a coffee shop. He ordered a large coffee and headed back to Cambridge, passport in hand.

Henry and Petie spent the next day preparing for their trip. Late the next afternoon the three friends walked out to Eddie's car and loaded everything in. They drove to the airport in relative silence. When Eddie pulled up to the curb in front of their airline, they got out and unloaded their luggage.

"Okay you two, don't do anything stupid while you're over there. Just because James Bond is from England, it doesn't make you spies!" Eddie teased.

"James Bond? He's got nothin' on us!" Petie laughed as Henry puffed his cheeks out and rolled his eyes. The three high-fived each other and grasped each others' hands, slapping each other on the back. Eddie said goodbye to his friends as he shut the trunk and got in his car.

Henry and Petie picked up their bags and walked into the airport as Eddie drove away. They got to the ticket counter and the agent asked for each of their I.D.'s. She found their reservations and said she had a surprise for them.

"Peter, your father upgraded both of your tickets to First Class. There's a message in my computer he wants passed along. He said not to drink too much free booze on the way to London," the agent said, smiling. Her face suddenly lit up and she asked, "Is your father 'Sully' from the car commercials? You look just like him."

"Yes, he is," Petie said, grinning.

"Is he as funny at home as he is in those ads? He's crazy!" the agent exclaimed.

"My dad is one of the funniest men I've ever known, and a great guy as you can see," Sully said, waving the boarding pass for First Class she had just given him.

The two friends thanked the agent and walked to the gate, boarding the plane a short while later. As they sat down the flight attendant asked if she could get them anything.

"Two beers!" they said at the same time, and laughed.

The flight attendant walked up and set down two glasses. She filled them up with the beer, leaving the bottles on their tray tables. As they sat silently drinking their beer, Henry's phone rang—it was his mother.

"Henry, Mr. McLaughlin finally got back to me, and I have his cell number for you. He said to call him tomorrow when you arrive in London." His mother told Henry about the conversation and gave him the investigator's phone number.

"Good luck, son. Make sure to keep in touch, and stay out of trouble! I love you," Mrs. Worthing said.

As the plane pulled away from the gate the two friends looked at each other, seeming to read the other's mind. Both breathed a sigh of relief at the thought of finding Hessa and possibly getting some answers.

CHAPTER 37

Henry spent most of the flight reading and typing into his laptop. Even the two beers he drank didn't do much to make him sleepy. He was annoyed that Audra had broken things off. He thought the plans he'd made for his life would pan out perfectly—he would marry Audra, get a job at her father's sports agency, and be set for life. His firm was one of the largest in America, located in New York City.

Henry loved everything about New York. There was always something going on in the Big Apple, and he wanted to be right in the middle of it. The thought that his dreams weren't panning out irritated him. He'd always been able to work things out to go his way.

I'll figure out how to get her back when I get home, he thought to himself.

The plane began its descent, waking Petie. "Are we here already?"

"You always were a light-weight," Henry smiled. "Do you know you've been asleep for almost five hours? It was just beer, Petie."

"Well, it knocked me out just fine," Petie replied.

The two straightened up their seats, and Henry put his laptop into his briefcase. As the plane flew over London the friends looked out the window, pointing to sights they could recognize.

They momentarily forgot the purpose of their trip to England. The captain reported that the weather was cold with intermittent rain. The boys were prepared, as they'd carried their rain jackets on board the plane.

They collected their luggage and walked outside to flag down a taxi. Before they left for England they found a hotel right near the King's College campus, which was less than a half hour from Heathrow Airport.

A short time later Henry and Petie pulled up in front of a rather ordinary-looking hotel. The inside was a different story, however. They'd

261

booked a single room due to the high price of the hotel, which was located in a very desirable area by the River Thames. The two friends opened the door to their room and were happily surprised when they saw the size and modern look of it. Petie walked over to the window and looked out.

"Wow, look at that view! Is that Big Ben? I think that's Trafalgar Square down that way! I wanna see everything!" he said.

"Just remember what we're here for, Petie. We won't be able to do a lot of sight-seeing. We need to find Hessa as soon as possible. Hey, that reminds me, could I use your phone? I didn't get mine set up for international calls before we left."

Petie went over to his suitcase and dug around for a few moments, finally locating the phone. He tossed it to Henry, who had pulled out Douglas McLaughlin's telephone number. Henry dialed the number, and thankfully Mr. McLaughlin answered.

"Douglas McLaughlin here," he said.

"Mr. McLaughlin, this is Henry Worthing. You spoke with my mother yesterday, and she said to call you when we arrived. We're here, staying at the Swissotel at Covent Garden."

"Henry, I'm glad you called. I've done a little searching and your friend is staying at the Kingsford Hall apartments on the Strand campus. I would try the Maughan Library to start. Go to the History section—that's what she's studying, so I'm sure she spends a good deal of time there."

Douglas excused himself to take another call and then came back. "I won't be joining you chaps. If I'm seen snooping around, things could get a little dicey. However, the two of you need to be discreet. Even if you see her, don't go running up to her. If you do, chances are you'll never see her again. Have I made myself quite clear?"

"Absolutely. My friend and I will go over there later this afternoon," Henry replied. "Thanks a lot, Mr. McLaughlin."

"You can call me Douglas. And Henry, ring me up as soon as you spot young Hessa. I want to make sure we don't have any international incidents here in London to match what's going on in Israel."

262

"I understand. Peter and I will get in touch with you as soon as we see her," Henry said, and the two hung up.

Henry told Petie about the conversation with Douglas, and where he'd suggested they start their search for Hessa. Douglas said he wanted to keep tabs on the boys, and that he wasn't about to let anything happen to them, but he also wanted to avoid any sort of conflict that could arouse suspicion.

Petie put his suitcase on a stand by the bed and looked over at Henry. "Are you hungry? I think I'll try to find a place where I could pick up a couple sandwiches."

"Sounds good. I'm just gonna lie down for a minute til you get back."

After Petie left, Henry's exhaustion from lack of sleep on the plane hit him. He took his shoes off and pulled down the covers, thinking he would just rest his eyes while Petie was gone.

When Petie finally did return Henry was fast asleep, so he decided not to disturb him, and went out to the balcony to eat his sandwich. Henry slept for well over an hour before a sound from the hallway abruptly woke him. Petie was sitting in a chair, reading.

"Why didn't you wake me up?" Henry asked. "It's one o'clock!"

"You needed to sleep. Besides, we don't need to go over to the library until later this afternoon. Want a sandwich?" Petie asked.

"Sure, I'm starving," Henry replied, grabbing the sandwich and wolfing it down.

The two friends made calls to their parents to let them know of their arrival, and unpacked their things. Then they walked to the library to make sure they would be there in plenty of time to find the history section and plant themselves in strategic locations.

They got to the library at about two o'clock and spent six hours walking up and down the rows of books, sitting at tables reading and chatting with the students. Eight o'clock came and went, and no Hessa. Discouraged and hungry, the two decided to go back to the hotel for a bite

263

to eat. After dinner they went back to their room. They still hadn't adjusted to the time change, so went to bed early and slept through the night.

The next few days were spent in the same way—in the morning they walked the campus in search of any sign of Hessa, and in the afternoons and evenings they would separate and hang out in different parts of the library, waiting and watching to see if she would arrive. Part of their search was during the weekend, so the campus became quiet, with very little activity.

One night as they arrived back at their hotel room tired and discouraged, Petie's cell phone rang. Douglas was calling to let them know about a lecture Hessa would be attending the next day.

"I've also acquired her class schedule and found out the typical days she goes to the library. Furthermore, I found that she spends much of the weekend in the company of her fiancé."

Petie thanked Douglas for the information and hung up.

"I think we finally have a break!" he exclaimed.

"What happened?" Henry asked.

"Douglas just gave me a schedule of all Hessa's classes, *and* the days she typically goes to the library. But best of all, she's going to a lecture tomorrow, and it's in a lecture room at the library! Woo hoo!"

"That's great! That means her guards won't be with her, right?" Henry asked.

"You've got it, my friend. The lecture is at four p.m. I think we should get there early and wait outside the classroom. Maybe we can sit in on the lecture and try to sit near her," Petie replied.

"We can call the school first thing tomorrow to see about auditing rules. Well, there's nothing else for us to do tonight, so what do you say we go to a pub?" Henry suggested.

The two walked down to ask the concierge for a recommendation. He proved to be very helpful, and wanted to know all about the two Americans. After they politely told him about Boston and Harvard, they asked again where they could get a glass of ale.

"Since the hour is getting late, I would suggest the Ship and Shovell over in Charing Cross. It's just a few minutes away by cab. Go outside and the cabbie will take you right over. You won't regret it, gentlemen--the Ship and Shovell is proud of their fine selection of ales. Drink one for me, mates!" the concierge said, and the two friends walked outside and climbed into a cab.

They arrived at the pub in about five minutes, and as they drove up they saw two buildings with the Ship and Shovell name on them.

"Which one is the pub?" Petie asked the driver.

"Both are pubs, but I suggest you go to the larger one. It's been around for 300 years and has more character," the driver said, and told them the fare.

The two friends walked into the pub and were transported back in time by dark paneled walls with mirrors throughout and red carpet. There was a fireplace with chairs and tables all around, but every inch was crowded with people trying to position themselves as close to the blaze as they could get.

Henry and Eddie walked up to the bar to order their drinks. The bartender greeted them with a strong Scottish accent. "What'll you boys have?"

"What's this stuff lining the bar?" Petie asked.

"Hops—appropriate thing to grow in a pub, don't you think? So, gentlemen?" the bartender asked.

"Do you have any suggestions for beer?" Petie asked.

"Depends—if you want a cold, rich brew, I'd suggest the Hofbrau Premium, but we're proud of the Blackthorn Cider and the Peroni. You might want to give the Hall and Woodhouse Tanglefoot a try as well," he replied, and explained each to them. They made their choices and went to sit at a small table in the back of the bar.

The table next to theirs had about six young women and three young men sitting around it, laughing and talking at the top of their lungs. Henry and Petie couldn't hear themselves think, so they sat in silence

265

smiling at the table of people next to them, content just to watch the behavior several ales had brought on.

One of the girls in the group glanced over at them as she was talking with a friend. She had twinkly eyes that were full of mischief and blazing pink cheeks. Her mouth turned up in such a way that she looked as though she was smiling even when she wasn't. For some reason she reminded Petie of Tinkerbell from Peter Pan.

She glanced over once again and asked Petie, "Do you lads go to King's College?"

"No, we're here visiting from America," Petie replied.

"America! Brilliant! Would you like to join us?" she asked.

Petie and Henry nodded and pulled their chairs over, squeezing in between the girl and her friend.

"My name is Mary, and this is my friend Bridget," the girl said.

"I'm Peter and this is Henry," he replied.

"Hey, everyone, this is Peter and Henry from America!" the girl yelled at the group of friends. They all called 'hellos' to Petie and Henry, who responded with waves.

"Where in America are you from?" Mary asked Petie.

"Boston," Petie replied.

"Are you students in Boston?" she asked.

"Yes, we both go to Harvard," Petie replied.

"Harvard—well, I suppose we have a couple of geniuses gracing our presence this evening," Mary said smiling.

Petie and Mary instantly fell into conversation. She told him that she'd lived in London all her life. Her father was in finance and her mother didn't work. She joked about her mother being a 'professional shopper', and that she could smell a sale from one end of London to the other.

Mary was in her last year at King's College majoring in history, and told Petie that she worked part time at night at the Maughan Library. Petie felt his stomach drop to his feet, but he tried to remain composed.

"Wow, that sounds kind of…boring!" he said, and they both laughed. He attempted to sound casual as he asked about the lecture taking

266

place the next day, explaining he was looking into summer classes at King's College.

"I checked out the website and thought it might be a good experience to spend the summer here in London. I asked my friend Henry here to come with me to look the school over. I saw that there's a lecture tomorrow on Medieval England. Do you think it would be okay for us to sit in?"

"I'm going to that lecture tomorrow. I know Dr. Hawthorne, so I'll ask him in the morning if you can attend. The lecture is called 'The Structure of English Landed Society in 1066', so I don't think people will be knocking the door down to get in!" They both laughed.

Mary and Petie continued to chat and laugh for the rest of the evening, seeming to forget everyone else around them. Mary's friend Bridget was shy and bookish, looking more the librarian than her pretty friend. She and Henry didn't have much to say to each other.

Henry finally excused himself and went to order another beer, purposely staying away from the awkward position he was in with Bridget. He stood by the television watching the soccer channel, sullen and completely uninterested. Almost two hours went by, and Mary's friends began to call it a night and make their way out the door when she looked at her watch.

"Oh blast, it's past midnight! I have class at eight a.m.! I'll have to be going, Peter, but if you give me your mobile number I'll ring you up to let you know about the lecture tomorrow afternoon," she said.

"Thanks Mary, I really appreciate it. I had fun tonight—it was great meeting you," Petie said smiling, and wrote his number down on the piece of paper Mary had given him. He stood up as he handed the paper back to her. She looked at him and smiled, making him blush profusely.

"Well, I gotta..." Petie began and then realized Henry was nowhere in sight. "Uh oh, I think I lost my friend."

"No you haven't, here he comes," Mary replied, and pointed over to Henry, who was walking back to their table.

"Are you ready to go?" Henry asked.

267

Petie and Mary said good night one more time, and Petie reminded her that he would be waiting for her call about the lecture. She smiled and assured him she wouldn't forget. He and Henry turned and started toward the door when Petie turned around and waved at Mary once more.

"Petie, stop acting like a doofus," Henry said as he ushered Petie out the door.

"What? Hey, I'm from a waving family. There's nothing wrong with that!" Petie said.

"Yeah, if you're waving bye-bye to your mommy, but you really need to grow up and be just a little cooler," Henry replied.

"Sorry we can't all be as sophisticated as you," Petie said dejectedly.

The two flagged down a cab and as they rode back to the hotel, Petie filled Henry in on the interesting news about Mary. The cab pulled up to the hotel, and as they got out and paid the driver, Petie turned to Henry, continuing to fill Henry in on the information he'd gotten.

"She works in the history section at Maughan Library! She also said she would try to get us into the lecture tomorrow afternoon. Pretty lucky we ran into her, huh?" Petie asked.

"Lucky for you. I was stuck with her friend, Bridget, who evidently doesn't know how to talk to guys. I ended up going over to the bar to watch television," Henry replied. "I have to admit that it was lucky you met her though."

Henry and Petie got to their room and closed the door, getting ready for bed as quickly as possible. By now Henry was completely exhausted; Petie was beginning to feel the effects of the long day, but his evening with Mary had given him a second wind.

He knew he would have to force himself to try and sleep, so he picked up a magazine sitting on a table nearby to try and settle down. As he began thumbing through the magazine he looked over at Henry, who was already asleep and snoring softly.

I guess I should try to sleep too, he thought to himself, and turned out the light.

CHAPTER 38

$\mathbf{P}$etie was the first to wake up the next morning, momentarily forgetting where he was. The activities of the previous evening eventually drifted into his mind and he smiled to himself. He hadn't had that much fun in quite a while.

He reached over and picked up his watch from the nightstand. It was nine a.m. He got out of bed and went into the shower, whistling and singing to himself. As he got out and dried himself off he walked into the room for his clothes.

Henry began to stir. "You sure are chipper this morning. Is it because of a certain librarian you met last night?"

"That could be part of it," Petie replied, smiling.

"So what do you say we grab a bite to eat and go over to Trafalgar Square? I wanna see the National Gallery," Henry said.

"Might as well take advantage of the time we have and see the sights," Petie replied.

Henry got out of bed and took a shower, trying to shake off the fatigue that had held on to him since arriving in London. After he got dressed he suggested they walk the mile and a half to the National Gallery.

The two friends made their way to the concierge desk and asked for the best way to the National Gallery. They'd both been a bit hungry when they left the hotel, but the walk and the wonderful smells wafting through the National Café inside the Museum made them ravenous for breakfast. Henry had a classic British breakfast, and Petie played it safe with something that looked very close to Eggs Benedict.

After breakfast they wandered through the Gallery asking questions and absorbing as much as they could with the time they had. Before they knew it the day had gotten away from them and they began their walk back to the hotel. They stopped along the way for a bite to eat, and after returning to the hotel to grab their laptops, they headed back to the Maughan Library.

While they were at the Gallery, Petie had a call from Mary to let him know that they were welcome to attend the lecture, and that she'd signed them up. She gave them directions to where it would be held and told him she would wait for them outside the lecture room. They arrived several minutes early and stood outside the door waiting for her. Just before the class began Mary walked up to the boys and greeted them.

"I'm so glad you could make it," she smiled. Henry and Petie followed her into the room. The three walked several rows back and sat down. In the daylight Petie was able to get a better look at Mary. Her hair was blond, and she was very fair. She had a smattering of freckles across her nose, much like all the Sullivan boys. Her eyes were bright green and twinkled when she smiled. Petie guessed she wasn't much taller than his mother.

Just as Dr. Hawthorne entered the room and took out his material for the class, Hessa appeared around the corner. Mary stood up and waved to her, indicating for her to come over and sit with them. Hessa smiled and walked toward them. Her eyes went from Mary to the two young men sitting next to her. She immediately recognized Petie and Henry and her eyes flew open.

Her jaw dropped as she slowed her pace toward them. Her heart began pounding so loudly she could hardly hear what was being said in the room. Mary saw Hessa's reaction and became concerned at the alarm written on her face, which had become flushed. She quickly stood up to steady her friend as she approached.

"Are you all right Hessa?" she asked without saying hello. "Do you know these lads?"

She looked past Mary and stared at the two young men who had stood up to greet her. "What are you doing here?" she asked, barely above a whisper. "Has something happened to…Joel?"

"Who's Joel?" Mary asked.

Hessa continued to look past her friend, unable to answer the question. She looked directly at Henry, waiting for his answer.

"Nothing has happened to Joel that we know of," Henry replied. "Petie's mom told us you called her, and we got on a plane right away. She was pretty alarmed and thought you might be in some sort of trouble. We wanted to see if you needed any help, and if *you* knew anything about Joel."

"I do not know anything about Joel except for what your mother told me, Petie. After my father came to Boston to take me home, I was only in Jerusalem for a few days before he sent me to London, and I have been here ever since. I have no mobile phone—he took it away from me. I used Mary's office phone to call your mother," Hessa said in a hushed tone.

"Who's Joel?" Mary asked again. "How do you know each other?"

Hessa finally looked at Mary. "Joel was someone I….knew at Harvard," Hessa replied. "Henry and Petie are Joel's best friends."

"Well I'll be snookered…" Mary replied.

"I think your relationship with Joel was more than that. Our friend is in love with Hessa. When she disappeared, he went to Israel to look for her, and no one has seen or heard from him in almost two months," Henry told Mary.

"I can't believe you two know each other! What are the chances?" Petie asked, looking back and forth between Mary and Hessa.

"How do you know Mary?" Hessa asked.

"We met her last night at a pub and told her we wanted to come to this lecture today. We wanted to attend, hoping we'd see you, but we

271

didn't know Mary was your friend. What are the chances?" Henry repeated.

"Are you okay, Hessa? My mom was really concerned about you. She said you sounded really scared, and that you had people watching you. Is that true?" Petie asked.

"It *is* true," Hessa said sadly. "I haven't heard from anyone in my family. My mother and I are very close, but she has not contacted me since I left Jerusalem. This is not normal behavior for her—I fear something has happened to her. Your mother said she has tried to contact her, but her mobile phone has been disconnected. I do not know what to do." Hessa put her head down and held back her tears.

"Excuse me, but the lecture has begun, and if you four would like to continue your conversation elsewhere I would most appreciate it," Dr. Hawthorne said in an irritated tone.

Mary looked up at him and mouthed 'sorry', pulling out a notebook. Petie and Henry had their laptops, so Petie passed his over to Hessa, who looked over at him, puzzled.

He reached over and grabbed Henry's laptop from him and opened it to a Word document. He had already done the same on the laptop he'd handed to Hessa. Typing notes on Word was the quickest and safest way for the two to communicate. They would be able to immediately and permanently erase everything.

He typed a question to Hessa asking her to explain exactly what had happened from the time she left Harvard to the time she'd come to London, and what she had been doing since. He turned the laptop toward Hessa, indicating he wanted her to read the question.

She turned to the laptop he'd given her and typed a detailed explanation of the whole ordeal. At the end she typed in large, bold letters: 'I NEED YOUR HELP. PLEASE TAKE ME BACK TO AMERICA WITH YOU!'

After reading what she'd typed he turned to her with an incredulous look on his face. He sat for a few moments thinking about what he should type back to her. He took a deep breath and gave his

272

answer. He explained that they would figure out a way to get her to America, but doing that right now could risk Joel's safety or even his life. He asked her to be patient and assured her that they would help her.

Hessa read the note and looked over at Petie with a look of gratitude and relief, mixed with anxiousness. Hessa noticed Mary reading the laptop notes as they were being passed between Hessa and Petie. The look of surprise and concerned confusion was written across Mary's face.

Hessa had been grateful for her friend, and knew that Mary had been anxious ever since the night Hessa had made the frantic call to America. Now the story was unfolding and Hessa felt she'd drawn Mary into the middle of it all, possibly putting her in danger. Mary *had* mentioned more than once that she wanted to help Hessa, whatever it took. Hessa now wondered if Mary still felt that way.

The lecture ended and Hessa looked over at Petie once more. "I need to leave now. My guard is waiting outside the classroom, and he can't see me speaking with you. Please do not forget about me!" Hessa stood up and hurried out the door.

Henry and Petie sat with Mary as Henry read the notes that had been typed into the two laptops. He finally looked up and glanced back and forth at Mary and Petie with a quizzical look on his face. Finally he spoke up.

"Well Mary, I'll bet you're glad you met up with us. It's just crazy that you know Hessa! What a coincidence. Crazy..." Henry repeated and leaned his face on his hand, obviously falling deep into thought.

"What are we going to do for poor Hessa?" Mary asked. "I'd really like to help her, so you can count on me for anything. I'll give you my hours at the library, and you have my mobile number. We can keep in touch that way. Hessa and I will figure out a way to communicate so the guards don't get suspicious."

The three picked up their belongings and walked out of the library. It was past six o'clock and they were getting hungry.

"Mary, could I take you to dinner as a thank-you for wanting to help us. Are you available tonight?" Petie asked.

273

"Yes, tonight is my night off. That's why I was able to go to the lecture this afternoon," she replied. "I'd love to go to dinner."

"Well, since you're the local authority, I'll let you choose any place in the city you want!" Petie said.

"If you don't mind, I think I'll sit this one out tonight. I'm going back to the hotel to make phone calls and get caught up on e-mail. Make sure to drink a glass of ale for me," Henry said. They said goodbye to Henry, who turned and walked in the direction of the hotel.

"I guess it's just us two. I'm at your service, Mary. Think of your favorite restaurant, or somewhere you've always wanted to go but haven't been able to yet." Petie said.

Mary thought for a moment and suddenly her face lit up. "There *is* a place I've never been to, but have always wanted to try. They say it's one of the top restaurants in London. Do you like French food?"

"I'm from a simple Irish family, so I haven't had much French food. I'd really like to try it though, so lead the way!" Petie said.

Mary flagged down a cab and gave the driver the address of the restaurant. As the cab pulled away from the curb Mary turned to Petie and asked, "So you're Irish? What's your last name?"

"Sullivan. What's yours?"

"Are you ready for this? It's Flynn! My father's Irish and my mother's British," she explained.

"Well, how do you like that? A Sullivan and a Flynn together in London!" Petie said with a grin.

The two chatted non-stop on the cab ride to the restaurant, and didn't stop talking for the rest of the evening, even while sharing bites of each other's food. Petie learned that Mary was also from a large family. She was the third of five children, with two older sisters and two younger brothers. She told Petie that her father had all but given up on having a son when her brother Conor was born.

"I have a brother named Conor, too!" Petie said, and explained how he was the second of six boys. He told Mary about his dad and the crazy car commercials for his dealerships, and described their farm in

274

Vermont. He told her more about Harvard and his plan to eventually move back to Vermont.

After they'd exhausted the conversation about their families, Petie told Mary about how Joel and Hessa had met, and that she and her mother had visited their farm in Vermont. He told her about Hessa's mother and how quickly she'd taken to their family, and didn't seem to want to leave.

He explained Hessa's sudden departure from Harvard, and how Joel had gone in search of her. He went on to tell Mary about how they had all tried to contact Joel, but hadn't heard a word from him in some time.

"….and that's how Henry and I got to London," he concluded.

"Simply fascinating story," Mary replied thoughtfully.

"Joel is the greatest guy I've ever met, and I'm not just saying that because he's missing. He's my best friend, and if I could trade places with him, I would. We just wanna get him back safe and sound," Petie said.

"Peter, I'll do anything I can to help you. I've always thought everything that happened in life was a coincidence, but somehow I can't imagine this has been a chance meeting," Mary said thoughtfully.

Petie and Mary finished their dinner and took a cab back to her dorm on campus where she was staying. He walked her to the entrance and she turned to him.

"I had a wonderful time, Peter, or would you prefer I call you Petie?" Mary asked.

"I really like it when you call me Peter," he replied. "You're the only person I've ever said that to." Petie looked down, embarrassed.

Mary tried to make eye contact with Petie. "Why Peter, I think you're blushing!" she laughed.

"I had the best time ever, Mary. Could I….kiss you good night?" he asked.

"Of course. Men typically don't ask…." And before she could complete her sentence, Petie leaned down and kissed her.

"Wow…" Petie said, smiling.

"I agree….wow," Mary echoed, as she stared up at Petie.

275

"Do you think I could see you tomorrow?" Petie asked.

"I have classes until two o'clock and then I head directly to the library. I don't get off work until ten o'clock, but you could come to the library. Hessa is usually there this time of the week.

"This would actually be a good thing. It would look like you're visiting me, and not Hessa," she paused and then added, "The man who comes to the library with her is quite scary-looking. We really need to help her, Peter." Mary said.

"I'll be there tomorrow night…and Mary?" Petie asked.

"Yes?"

"I'm not only going to see Hessa."

He leaned down and kissed Mary again, then turned to walk back to the waiting cab. Before he got in he looked over to see Mary had gone inside the double doors to the entrance of her building, and she began to wave at him. He returned the wave, and rolled down the window in order to wave good-bye to her until he was out of sight.

CHAPTER 39

Anna Volkenburg was wrapping up her preparations for her trip to Israel. It had taken her several days to delegate responsibilities to members of the committee for the spring fundraiser she was chairing. She made flight arrangements and a reservation at the Tikvah hotel where Joel had been staying when he disappeared. She only had one thing left to do—call her sister, Klara.

The afternoon before she was to leave for her trip, she finally summoned the courage to make the phone call. She didn't even know if her sister was still living in Jerusalem. She pulled out her address book and dialed the number. An older man answered the phone.

"Hello, I'm looking for Klara Milgrom," Anna said to the man, who answered in Hebrew.

Anna's small knowledge of the language did little to help her. She realized her sister no longer lived in the same place. She thanked the man on the other end in Hebrew and hung up.

She dialed Dan's number next. He answered and gave her an update on his meeting with David Appel, and told her about the research he and Omri were doing on possible places they could search for Joel. Anna was grateful for the information, and told Dan she would arrive in Jerusalem in a couple of days.

"By the way Dan, I wonder if you could ask your friend Omri to check something out for me," Anna said.

"Sure. What do you need?" Dan asked.

"My sister, Klara Milgrom, used to live in Jerusalem. I tried calling her to let her know I would be visiting, but someone else answered at the phone number I have for her. She must have moved, so I was wondering if you would track her down for me," Anna said.

"I'll call Omri to see if he can help you. When did you last speak to her?" Dan asked.

"Well…it's been about fifteen years," Anna said.

"Wow, that could make things a little tough, but I'll see what we can find. Can you tell me anything else about her?"

"She and her husband used to own a small bakery in Jerusalem, but I really don't know if they're still in business."

"Okay, I'll check into it and let you know."

The next morning Anna was up at the crack of dawn getting ready for the airport when she heard a knock on her bedroom door. She went over to open it and Eli was standing in the hallway.

"I didn't hear you come in last night," she said.

"I got home after ten. You must have been asleep already," he replied. "I just wanted to let you know I'll be in Jerusalem by Friday evening. I e-mailed you my itinerary."

"Thank you. I'll call you when I get there. I have a room at the Tikvah, but if you'd like a separate room, let me know and I'll take care of it for you when I arrive there."

"That'll be fine. We should be able to handle being in the same room for a few days, don't you think?" he asked with a wry smile.

Anna ignored the dig. "I think I hear the car pulling up. I e-mailed you my itinerary also. Make sure you get international phone service before you leave."

She put on her coat and slung her purse over her shoulder, picking up her small carry-on bag. Eli followed behind her with the larger suitcase. The doorbell rang and she opened the door for the driver. Eli handed the large suitcase to him and said goodbye to his wife as he closed the door.

Anna's flight arrived in London ahead of schedule. As she walked to the gate for her connecting flight she checked her voicemail. Dan said he had good news. He had found her sister quite easily. He'd left Klara's telephone number in the message, and told Anna to contact him when she arrived in Jerusalem.

Anna walked to the terminal for her connecting flight and went into a small restaurant near her departure gate. She ordered a glass of wine to calm her nerves, and dialed the number Dan had given her for her sister. A woman whose voice she didn't recognize answered the phone in Hebrew.

"Hello, may I speak with Klara Milgrom?" she asked.

"I'm Klara," the woman said in English.

"Hello, Klara.....it's Anna."

"Anna! Is that really you?" Klara asked.

"Yes, Klara. It's so good to hear your voice after all this time. I'm so sorry we've lost touch," Anna said.

"I can't believe it's you! What a surprise! You...seemed to want to be left to your life in America. I didn't feel you wanted a relationship with me any longer, so I haven't tried to get in touch with you."

"Oh Klara, I've been so stupid. I've been so caught up in my life and in keeping up appearances that I've forgotten the most important thing—my family. Now I'm on my way to Jerusalem, and I wanted to see if you could find it in your heart to forgive me. I'd love to see you and catch up on everything," Anna said.

"Of course I forgive you. You're my sister—my only family. I'd love to see you. It must be fifteen years since you were last in Israel. Things have changed quite a bit since you were here. My Yuri died two years ago, so I'm alone now.

"Benjamin lives in Italy. He met a woman while on vacation and moved there several years ago. They were married six months before Yuri died. Her name is Giovanna. He has a job in marketing and works out of his home in Napoli."

279

"My gosh, Klara, why didn't you call me to let me know Yuri had died? I feel terrible that I wasn't there for you. I'm so ashamed..." Anna said.

"I didn't mean to make you feel bad. These things happen in life, so what are you going to do? My life is very full, and I stay very busy. We'll have to have a long talk to catch up when you get here. When does your plane get in?" Klara asked.

"At about 5:45 a.m., but don't worry, I won't call you that early! I'll be staying at the Tikvah Hotel in Jerusalem, so I'll call you when I get settled. There's so much to tell you. I'll explain when we get together."

"Oh, I'm an early riser. By 5:45 I've already been up for an hour! By the way, I live in Tel Aviv now. Do you need to go to Jerusalem right away, or could you stay overnight at my house and go to Jerusalem the next day?" Klara asked.

"I'd love to stay with you, Klara. There isn't anything I need to be in Jerusalem for immediately. Anyone who needs to get in touch with me can call me on my cell," Anna replied.

Klara gave Anna her address and told her she would make arrangements to take the day off so they could be together. They chatted for a while longer until Anna's boarding call came over the loud speaker. She told her sister that she would call when she landed in Tel Aviv, and they hung up.

As Anna turned off her cell phone she wondered why she'd been so stubborn as to not call and apologize to her sister years ago for her poor behavior. Because of her snobbery she had robbed herself of a relationship with her only sister, and her one living immediate family member.

The plane arrived right on time, but Anna didn't locate her bags and get through customs until almost 6:30 a.m. She hauled her luggage out to the front of the airport as quickly as possible and flagged down a cab, handing the driver the piece of paper with her sister's address on it. She called Klara to let her know she was on her way.

The cab pulled up in front of a brand new building that seemed to be built mainly of glass. The building was right across the street from the Mediterranean Sea, and had palm trees and large pots of flowers everywhere.

"Beautiful!" Anna said to herself.

She got out of the car and the driver pulled her bags from the trunk. She made her way to the large glass doors at the entrance, her heart in her throat. Just as she was about to pull the front door open, her sister opened it for her.

"Anna!" Klara said with tears in her eyes, and embraced her sister.

Anna dropped all her luggage on the ground and put her arms around her sister. Tears streamed down Anna's cheeks as she held her sister. The two didn't say a word for several moments as they stood embracing in the doorway.

Finally Anna held her sister at arm's length to get a good look at her. She didn't look much different—a few more gray hairs, maybe, but she had a healthy glow. She looked happy and rested, which made Anna feel reassured.

When the plane left London for Tel Aviv she'd had plenty of time to think about the last fifteen years, and was worried that Klara had struggled financially—especially since her husband had died. She didn't know what she would face when she finally saw her sister.

"Klara, you look absolutely wonderful! You haven't aged a day since I saw you last!" Anna exclaimed.

"What are you saying? Look at *you*, Anna! You're stunning, but you always did have an eye for style. You look just beautiful! I think it's our strong Russian genes, don't you?" Klara joked.

"Let's go up to the apartment so you can rest. You must be exhausted from travelling. Are you hungry? I started breakfast, and made strong Turkish coffee."

They rode up the elevator chatting away like two school girls. They finally arrived on the 32nd floor, and Klara pulled Anna's large

281

suitcase along behind her down to the end of the hall. She opened the door and ushered her sister into the entryway.

Anna gasped as she took in the magnificent home. It was very modern, and beautifully decorated. As she walked into the living room she gasped again. The whole apartment seemed to be encased in glass. She looked out the window to a beautiful panorama of the Mediterranean Sea.

"I don't think I would ever want to leave this place if I lived here. It's absolutely beautiful, Klara!" Anna exclaimed.

"This is a brand new building. I moved in last year as soon as it was completed. I've always wanted to live on the Mediterranean Sea. Yuri was content to stay in Jerusalem, but after he died it was painful to continue living where we'd been for 35 years. I decided to start a new life for myself, so I moved here!" Klara said. "Here, let me take your things to your room."

Anna followed her sister down a hallway and into a very large, airy room. It was also decorated with light wood, but had a little more color than the front part of the house. The room was carpeted in a very light sandy shade, and the rest of the room was decorated in white and aqua, with light blue accents.

Klara explained that she loved to collect sea shells, so the room had some of her collection in beautiful glass jars. The paintings on the wall reflected the sea as well. It felt very restful and fitting for a home on the Mediterranean.

"Why don't you unpack later? I have a very French breakfast for us. The only thing I have left to do is whip up an omelet. I want you to tell me everything you've been up to since I saw you last," Klara said.

They walked into the kitchen, which was very roomy and well-equipped. Klara pulled a cup from the cupboard and poured the Turkish coffee for her sister. Anna sat down and looked at yet another beautiful view from Klara's kitchen window.

"Klara, this place....how," Anna faltered. "I mean, how is it you live here, in such a...you know. You and Yuri were struggling so much

282

financially with that little café in Jerusalem. Did you decide to get into some other kind of business?"

"Not another business. We just made changes to the existing café. We realized there were cafes all over Jerusalem with the same type of food we offered, so we asked ourselves, 'What type of food does Jerusalem really need?' We both agreed that a French pastry shop would do well. We closed the doors to the little café and completely changed it.

I went to baking school in Paris. We spent everything we had, and then some, to start our new restaurant. We named it Milgrom Patisserie. It was so popular we opened another one in a different section of the city, then another and another. Soon it became a large chain, with cafes from Jerusalem to Tel Aviv."

"Well, I'll be. Good ol' Jewish ingenuity. And I love the name! 'Pomegranate Pastries'. People probably don't know you combined your Russian name with the French word. Brilliant, Klara. I love it."

Klara asked Anna to fill her in on everything since they had last spoken, and why she was in Israel. Anna reminded her of Eli's professorship at Harvard and his law practice. She told her sister about David having graduated from Harvard early and having gone on to medical school. She explained what he was doing for a living, and that they didn't get to see much of him. This brought her to Joel, and she faltered when she brought up her younger son's name.

"Joel was attending Harvard until a couple of months ago. He met a Palestinian girl from Jerusalem, and when she left suddenly to move back home, he followed her here. We haven't heard from him in about two months. I've hired a private investigator, but he hasn't had much success in locating him. Joel was staying at the Tikvah Hotel, which is where I'll be staying. I just couldn't stand it any longer—I had to come to Jerusalem myself to see if anything could be done to find him."

"Oh Anna, this is terrible! I really don't know why I haven't seen anything about this on the news. Of course I would have realized it was Joel, but honestly, I don't watch the news or read the paper very often— it's just so depressing. Now I'm sorry I didn't know about Joel. I would

283

have gotten in contact with you right away. You see? This is why sisters need each other, Anna—to comfort one another in times like this."

"I regret cutting you out of my life, Klara. You'll never know how much. The good thing is that we have each other now, and you'll never be able to get rid of me, especially with this beautiful apartment!" and they both laughed.

Klara finished the omelets she'd been cooking on the stove, and served them with some pastries from her shop. She poured Anna another cup of coffee, and the two sisters spent the rest of the morning catching up on each other's lives and reminiscing about their childhood.

When it was close to noon Klara suggested they take a walk to one of her shops which was located just a couple blocks from her apartment. As they walked Klara explained the success of the business, which she attributed in large part to a team of very loyal employees. She told her sister that after Yuri died, her employees supported her in her grief just like family, and they had all grown closer from the loss.

When Anna and Klara walked into the little shop everyone greeted them cheerfully. The place was spotless and the smells were heavenly. Klara certainly had learned her stuff in Paris, and she had cleverly decided to close down by mid-afternoon each day, which gave her and her employees the rest of the day free.

After sampling some of the beautiful pastries, Anna and Klara walked back to her apartment and Klara started preparing dinner. They ate out on the balcony, which Klara had decorated like a combined outdoor dining room and living room. She explained to her sister that she practically lived out there in warmer weather.

They sat chatting until almost midnight when Anna started feeling the effects of the day. Suddenly she was exhausted. Klara told her to leave the dishes, and that she would wash them in the morning. Anna thanked her sister for their perfect day together and hugged her.

"Today has meant more to me than you'll know, Klara. Now I realize how much I've missed you over the years, and how much we missed of each other's lives. I wish I could turn back the time..."

284

"Let's not focus on the past, Anna. Let's put it behind us, and enjoy the future together."

Anna got up and hugged her sister again, then turned and walked toward her room to get ready for bed. When she pulled the covers over her she was asleep almost immediately, content to be reunited with her sister at last.

CHAPTER 40

Joel tried to keep track of how many days he'd been held in the makeshift prison, but he knew there were lapses in time because he'd drifted in and out of consciousness. Joel had marked off the days on the wall of his little cell from the time he'd had the encounter with God.

He also wrote on the ground of his cell the incredible words he'd heard, and would trace over the letters each day, making them deeper and more firmly embedded in the dirt. He hadn't heard much of anything in this place since the day the woman had been crying close by.

He wondered if she was on the other side of the wall from him, but then why was it so quiet over there? There had been the sound one day of a door sliding open and a thump on the ground, but after that he hadn't heard much more than the wind blowing and the birds outside.

There was one exception—every once in a while he thought he would hear that same door very quietly open and close on the other side of the wall. He would then dismiss it as wishful thinking because of how alone he felt.

Joel wondered what was happening over there, and where the crying woman had actually gone. Each day he would also play back in his mind the car ride to this place, trying to figure out in what direction they had taken him, and then pray that someone would find and rescue him.

On this particular day it was very windy and the air smelled like rain. After all the warm, sunny days in this place, today the temperature suddenly dropped and Joel was chilled to the bone. He crouched in the corner of the cell where he thought he'd heard sounds on the other side. It was a little more sheltered on this side of the cell, and he tried to keep as

287

far as he could away from any air that crept in through the cracks. The wind continually picked up throughout the rest of the day and by nightfall it seemed like a gale force outside.

Rain began to fall in torrents, and Joel noticed that the roof had some sizeable leaks. As the wind continued to howl through the cracks and the rain poured down, he got colder and wetter. The dirt floor became mud and puddles started to form.

The building suddenly shook as though it was about to tumble down, and then Joel heard a loud 'crack' and a couple of tiles shook loose from the roof and slid off, crashing to the ground. Two holes in the ceiling showed through where the tiles had been, exposing the cloud-covered night sky.

Through the wind and rain Joel heard a groan, and thought at first it was the wood starting to give way. Then he heard it again. He thought he might have begun to hallucinate from lack of food and water. *Was* there actually someone on the other side of the wall?

He moved over to where he'd heard the sound and put his ear up against the wood trying to listen more intently—there it was again. He heard a cough followed by another soft groan, and knew he wasn't imagining things. He waited to see if anyone would respond to the voice on the other side, making sure the guards didn't come to check on the noises being made. After what seemed to him an eternity, he mustered up the courage to say something.

He put his face up to a small crack in the wall between where he was and where he thought the other person might be. "Hello?" he whispered. "Is someone there?"

There was a long pause; then finally he heard "Yes." The voice responded so softy Joel could hardly hear.

"Are you okay?" he asked.

"I…do not know," the woman's voice replied. "Where am I?" She slurred groggily.

"I'm not sure," Joel replied. "What's your name?"

"Muna," she replied.

"Mrs. Bishara! It's Joel Volkenburg!" Joel whispered as loudly as he could.

"Joel...Joel. Oh *yes*...Joel! ...What...Why are you here, Joel? Are we in America?" she asked, confused.

"Mrs. Bishara, what's wrong? You sound strange, like you've been drugged," Joel said.

"Um...uhh..." she slurred again, then: "I...I think you are correct, Joel. They stick me with needles..."

"We need to get you out of here—we need to do something, but I have no idea where we are," Joel said.

He heard Muna groan again, and the wall between them creaked once more. Joel silently prayed for a miracle, and that he would be able to get Hessa's mother out of this place before they killed her with whatever drugs they were putting into her body. He prayed that the men would be unable to get to them so that he could find a way to help Muna escape.

"I need a major miracle here, Lord—please get us out of here," he prayed silently.

Joel started digging in the mud by the wall between himself and Muna. He started on a spot where the rain was running down the wall and had formed a puddle on the dirt floor. A surge of adrenalin ran through him as he felt hope that there may be a way to get out of this horrible place.

He wondered where the men were, and why they hadn't come to check on the prisoners. He continued to dig a hole big enough to be able to pull Muna through, and then he would figure out how to get the two of them out of there.

The wind picked up once again and suddenly Joel heard the sounds of footsteps splashing through the puddles as one of the guards ran toward their cells. There was a large crack of thunder, and the rain came in torrents.

The mud in Joel's cell became slick, and he couldn't keep his footing as he tried to tunnel under the wall to the outside world. The building started to creak and groan as though it was about to explode, and then the back wall of Joel's cell gave way.

The footsteps got closer and closer as Joel dug with every ounce of strength he could muster from his emaciated body. Muna slid down from the wall she had been leaning against. Lying on the ground with the side of her face in the mud, she was unable to shake herself free of the state she was in.

Another creak sounded on the back wall of Muna's cell and there was a deafening crash as the wall caved in, taking with it the building's sharp tin siding. Suddenly there was a loud shriek, and Joel heard the footsteps stop abruptly—then silence.

He momentarily stopped what he was doing and ran to the back of the building where Muna's cell had been. There in the mud lay Jad, one of the men who had kidnapped Joel—in a pool of his own blood.

The wall and tin siding had fallen on him, gashing the side of his face and head. Joel's mouth dropped open at the sight, but fearing the other man would appear at any moment, he hurried back. He picked Muna up and ran out the back of her cell over the rubble of the fallen wall.

Crying out to God as he ran, he hoped he would go in the right direction and that they wouldn't be seen. The rain continued to pour and Joel prayed the rain would stop so he could at least get an idea of where they were. He continued to trudge along in the freezing rain and wind for the remainder of the night, and would pause only to regain strength from carrying Muna.

Just before dawn Joel was overwhelmed with exhaustion and set Muna down on a large rock. He finally had a chance to have a good look at her—she was barely recognizable. She was skin and bones, and her face was so swollen she could barely open her eyes. It looked as though she had been beaten countless times, and Joel surmised she was most likely bruised all over her body.

The cold weather and rain slapping her in the head and face slowly began to bring Muna out of her drug-induced stupor. Still confused, Muna asked Joel once again if they had made it to America.

290

"Not yet, Mrs. Bishara. I'm trying to get us to Boston, but we have a ways to go," he said simply, knowing she would probably ask him again shortly.

He found a plant and picked one of the large leaves, pouring water into it from the other leaves that had collected little pools of droplets from the rain. When he had a decent amount he walked over to Muna and tilted her head back, pouring the water into her mouth. She was so thirsty she inhaled it quickly and began to cough.

"Slowly, slowly, Mrs. Bishara. I'll get you some more."

Joel walked back over to the tree. When he'd filled the leaf again he brought it back to her and asked her to drink slowly. This time she was able to get the whole thing down without choking.

He walked back again and filled the leaf with water for himself and drank. The sky seemed to be getting lighter, so Joel went over to Muna to pick her up again and asked her if she'd be able to climb on his back, explaining that it would be easier for him to carry her that way.

She looked up at him with a confused look on her face, and when he turned around, he pointed at his back to show her what he wanted her to do. She finally understood, and was able to stand and put a leg up for him to catch and heave her onto his back.

Joel walked on for hours, sitting intermittently to rest for short periods and then continue. He still had no idea where they were, and hoped they weren't walking into another country only to be arrested. After what Joel had calculated to be eight or nine hours of walking, the dawn began to break, and he was able to see a little of where they had come.

He still wasn't sure where they were, and knew it was useless to ask Muna. They walked along a dry riverbed with sand on either side. In the distance Joel could hear the ocean roar and he walked in that direction. As he trudged closer he saw a group of palm trees and hoped he would be able to find something—anything—for them to eat.

He entered the cluster of trees which also had shrubs surrounding the area. Joel helped Muna slide off his back and set her down against a palm tree. He paused to catch his breath and rub the ache out of his back as he straightened upright. He looked around and noticed there were date palms, and the wind had blown several clusters to the ground.

He went over and picked up a bunch that hadn't been destroyed by birds or bugs. They weren't very ripe, but good enough to eat. He broke off a few and handed them to Muna, who gobbled them down as quickly as possible. He took a few and popped them into his mouth, making a face at their surprising tartness.

Joel didn't want to rest for too long since they were exposed, being in such an open area. He was surprised that they hadn't seen anyone since they had left their confinement. The only things he'd seen since the sun had come up were sand dunes, fossil beaches in the distance, and flat granite-looking land, interrupted by the occasional sand and limestone hills.

Joel looked over at Muna, who looked pale and sickly. He worried that she'd become ill, and knew that he somehow needed to get help. "We've come this far. I know You won't forget us now," he said aloud.

He stood up and put his hands out for Muna, who didn't respond to his offer of help. He realized she didn't have the strength, so he bent down and put his arms under hers and lifted her up. He turned around to offer her his back once more, and she climbed on.

Joel's strength was slowly being drained, and he didn't know how much farther he would be able to go. He started in the direction of the ocean, which seemed close enough for him to reach, hoping to find someone who would help them.

Joel walked slowly for another hour, having to stop more often to put Muna down so he could rest. The beach was finally in sight. He picked Muna up once more and plodded along, concentrating on the pounding of the waves, which soothed his frazzled nerves. His pace slowed until he was completely out of strength. A short distance away he thought he saw a small building behind some palm trees, but he couldn't make it out.

"We'll just rest here for a few minutes, and then we'll see if we can get help," Joel said more to himself than to Muna. For the first time since he'd been in his cell he laid down on the ground, passing out from pure exhaustion. Muna lay in back of him blocking out the wind with Joel's body, and immediately fell asleep.

A couple of hours passed, and Joel was awakened with a start when he heard a thumping noise. A flash of the small cell where he'd been imprisoned went through his mind and his eyes flew open. He sat up, forgetting where they were.

He looked up and saw a woman gazing down at them. She was small and plump and looked to be about in her sixties. The cart she was pushing was filled with dates, pomegranates, peaches, almonds and apricots.

She spoke to Joel in Arabic, who replied, "I'm sorry, I don't understand."

"I speak little English," the woman said. "What is wrong? I help?"

"Yes, please help us! My friend has been hurt—you know...hurt?" he asked, pointing to Muna's cuts and bruises.

"You walk my house?" the woman asked.

"Yes, thank you!" Joel replied, and stood up, bending down to pick up Muna.

The little woman started walking in the direction of the small wooden building Joel had seen. He carried Muna the last few steps to the woman's house. She opened the door and pointed for him to go in.

The house was little more than a wooden hut. It had very low ceilings and one room with a bed, a large tattered rug in the middle of the room with two old but comfortable-looking chairs, and a small table with two small chairs in the area that looked like the kitchen.

"You hungry?" the woman asked.

"Yes, very hungry," Joel replied.

The woman had a small wood-burning stove that she stoked, and picked up a kettle which she filled with water from a container. She put it on top of the stove and hurried over to get a portion of bread out of a small cupboard. She brought the fruit and nuts she'd gathered into the house and cut up a peach and apricot, sprinkling almonds over the top of the fruit.

293

The water began to boil so she walked over to get two cups and filled them with loose tea, pouring the hot water over it to steep. She pulled out what looked like two old pie tins and filled each of them with the fruit and nut mixture, along with the sliced bread. She also pulled a small jar out of the cupboard with what looked to be some sort of jam or chutney.

Wordlessly she set everything on the small table, and motioned for the two of them to sit down. Joel had placed Muna in one of the chairs in the middle of the room, so he went over and picked her up. He helped her walk over to the table, half carrying her. She perked up when she saw the food, and grabbed the bread, stuffing it into her mouth. She picked up a spoon and began to eat the fruit mixture as fast as she possibly could.

Joel watched with fascination, wondering how on earth Muna was still alive. He was starving, but she looked as if they had fed her even less than he'd had. He ate appreciatively and quickly, keeping a close eye on Muna, making sure that she didn't choke on the food she was gobbling down. He hoped that the large amount of food she was consuming wouldn't cause her stomach to reject the nourishment after her lengthy forced starvation.

When they had finished the meal and were sipping their tea, the woman asked them if they wanted more. Joel realized that she had probably given them a few days' worth of her meals, so he touched her arm and shook his head 'no'. He thanked her for himself and Muna, whose face finally began to show a hint of color. She still looked exhausted, but Joel was encouraged that she might just survive this ordeal after all.

The woman told Joel her name was Eshe, and he introduced himself and Muna to her. The woman told Joel in broken English that Muna was ill, so she went over and indicated for Muna to lie down on the bed. She went into a makeshift wardrobe and pulled out a heavy-looking robe, indicating for Muna to put it on.

Joel turned his back to the women as Eshe helped Muna out of her wet clothes and into the robe. She then helped Muna lie down and covered her with a tattered and worn blanket. Muna thanked her and immediately fell asleep.

The woman walked over to Joel, who had picked up the dishes from the table and placed them over on the small counter. She waved her hands as if to tell him not to touch the dishes, and motioned for him to sit down on the larger chair in the middle of the room.

She walked back to the wardrobe and pulled out another old blanket, this one much smaller. When Joel sat in the chair she knelt down and pulled his wet shoes and socks off, and covered them with a scarf she'd also gotten from the wardrobe.

"Sleep", she said, and walked off to stoke the fire in the little stove. Moments later Joel had done what he was told and drifted off.

CHAPTER 41

Husaam Bishara paced back and forth angrily, puffing on a cigarette as Fatik, the guard who had taken Joel, sat watching him fearfully.

"Idiots! You are both idiots! How difficult can it be to guard two people who have no strength to put up a fight? Tell me why you were not there with Jad when the rains started?"

"I had gone into town to get food. The rain was not coming down so hard when I left. I could not see anything driving back, and the mud was coming down off the hill and onto the road. It made it very slippery, and my car slid into a ravine.

"I had to walk the rest of the way. When I finally made it back to the compound, Jad was lying on the ground. I thought he was dead at first, but when I found him still breathing, I called Burak to take him to hospital," Fatik explained.

"It will be your responsibility to find the American and Muna. With Jad in hospital, you will need to hunt them down yourself. Burak is involved in other things right now, and I cannot spare anyone else. Besides, Jad was always a useless fool.

"I tell you this Fatik, do not return until you have found both Joel and Muna and killed them. Enough time has passed. No one thinks they're alive any longer. It is time to get rid of them. They both must die. I do not want to hear from you until you have buried them. Now get out of my sight."

297

Fatik got up and hurried out of the Bishara's home and got into his car. He had already been investigating all around the compound where Joel and Muna had been, but there wasn't a single trace of them anywhere due to the heavy rains.

He had no idea where he would start since they had disappeared as if into thin air. He knew they wouldn't have been able to get across the border into Egypt without passports, so he decided to start heading north along the Mediterranean, thinking they might have tried to get on a boat to Europe. He drove back toward the compound to begin his search northward.

Eli had been in Jerusalem for several days. He and Anna had met with Dan and Omri, who hadn't been able to obtain any new information about Joel. Frustrated and exhausted from asking questions and following the footsteps of where Joel had been, they returned to their hotel room at the Tikvah.

Anna got in the shower to wash the city dirt off her weary and aching body. Eli sat down in a chair and turned on the television. He found a news channel and turned up the volume.

"...Rains this year have been particularly brutal all over Israel and into Egypt. During this past week as the rain continued to pour down on our city, seven injuries and two deaths have occurred. One person who was injured is Hamas member Jad Said. He was taken to the hospital with a serious head wound. The person who brought him to Emergency reported that he was struck in the head when a piece of siding from a building slipped off from heavy winds and rain, hitting him. Said is linked to Hamas leader Husaam Bishara...." the news reporter continued.

Eli stood up and ran into the bathroom where Anna was still showering. "Anna! I just heard that one of the men who worked for Bishara is in the hospital! I wonder if he had anything to do with Joel?"

298

Anna stepped out of the shower and grabbing a towel, she ran to the television. She stood in front of it to see if there was anything else on Bishara, but the weather report had begun.

"Nothing else," she sighed and walked back into the bathroom to towel off.

"Dan and Omri talked about a man by the name of David that Joel had spent time with right before he was kidnapped. Do you think we should go and talk to him? We've talked to just about everyone else," Eli said.

"I don't see why not. Omri seemed to think David was somewhat of a crackpot, but I'll talk to anyone who might lead us to anything about Joel."

Eli called Dan and asked for David's number. Dan tried to talk Eli out of calling David, saying it was a colossal waste of time. He explained that David was a Messianic Jewish pastor who had visions of grandeur about God.

"You'll just walk away disappointed," Dan said.

"Nevertheless, I'll take his number, if you don't mind," Eli said.

Dan hesitantly gave David's number to Eli, who hung up and immediately dialed David's home phone. A friendly voice answered.

"Shalom, David Appel," he said.

"Hello, Mr. Appel, this is Eli Volkenburg, Joel's father," Eli said.

"Mr. Volkenburg! I am so happy you have called," David replied.

"Mr. Appel, my wife and I are here in Jerusalem, and I'd like to see if we could take you and your wife to dinner. We understand that you spoke to Joel right before he disappeared, and we'd like to get any insight you might have on him," Eli said.

"We would be honored to have dinner with you. Your Joel is a fine young man. I have reason to believe that he is alive and well. There is much to talk about. When would you like to meet for dinner?" David asked.

"We have no previous plans, so we'll work around your schedule," Eli said.

299

"We are available tomorrow evening."

"Why don't we meet tomorrow at the Katif Restaurant at six p.m.?" Eli asked.

"We will look forward with great anticipation to meeting Joel's parents," David replied.

The two men hung up and Eli reported to Anna that they had a dinner date with David and his wife the next evening. Eli told Anna what David had said about thinking Joel was alive.

Anna was surprised at her husband's tone while explaining what David had said. Instead of her husband's usual negative cynicism, he sounded almost excited and hopeful. Somehow his optimistic attitude rubbed off on her, and she looked forward to meeting this man that Dan called 'a religious kook who thought he heard things'.

The next evening Eli and Anna prepared for their dinner engagement with eager anticipation. The Volkenburgs had already eaten at Katif when Klara had visited them a couple of nights before and treated them to what she called the most fabulous restaurant in all of Jerusalem.

They hadn't been disappointed and were happy to return. They hired a car provided by the hotel concierge and arrived at Katif right at six p.m.

As they walked through the front door to the restaurant, the Appels followed in immediately after them. Eli gave the hostess his name for the reservation. David overheard him and walked over to greet them, grasping Eli's hand and shaking it vigorously.

Eli immediately liked David. There were no pretenses about this man. He knew instinctively that he wouldn't have to put on airs, and that his position as professor and attorney wouldn't impress a man like David. He could feel himself physically relaxing as the two smiled and shook hands.

The two couples sat down at their table, and Eli asked for a wine list. The sommelier came to the table to make recommendations, and Eli chose a kosher red wine, made in Israel.

"You do not need to order wine on our account, Mr. Volkenburg. My wife and I do not drink, but feel free to enjoy some. I understand Israeli wine is quite delicious," David said.

"I don't want to offend you by drinking," Eli said. "I need to cancel that order." He waived the sommelier down, who immediately responded, having ordered an expensive bottle for the Volkenburg table.

"Please do not cancel your order! I would feel badly if you didn't enjoy a nice glass of wine on account of us," David said. "With all of the events happening in your life, a bit of wine will calm your nerves."

Eli waved off the sommelier, and the two couples made small talk as the server left and returned with the wine. They agreed they should be on a first-name basis as Eli asked David about his position as pastor.

"What made you convert to Christianity?" Eli asked.

"Very good question, Eli, but we refer to ourselves as Messianic Jews. We are still very much Jewish, but believe in Yeshua as Messiah," David replied, and told his story to the Volkenburgs with excitement and passion.

Eli and Anna were silent for a few moments, taking in what David had said about their lives in Israel as Messianic Jews. Throughout David's story of his conversion and life since then, they exchanged incredulous glances at the joy this man had displayed in the midst of so much adversity.

"I've never heard anything like that," Eli said when David finished his story. "You've been on quite an adventure, haven't you?"

"I would not trade it for anything. Yeshua has changed my life, and I am very thankful. Things will not always stay the same. I am very hopeful that someday my extended family and I will reunite," David said.

Eli took a sip of his wine thoughtfully and finally asked what he had been so anxiously waiting to inquire about.

"Not to change the subject, but you said something about believing Joel was alive. Could you explain?"

301

"I have tried to contact both Dan and Omri several times about this, but neither of them have returned my repeated attempts to tell them this very important information," David replied.

Anna's ears perked up when she heard David saying something about important information. She and David's wife, Miriam, had been deep in conversation, but they both became silent to let David have the floor. He looked back and forth at Eli and Anna and said, "My friends have tracked down where Joel was most likely held captive."

"What?" Eli and Anna said at the same time.

"I have some friends who have been trying to find the place where Joel was taken. Dan and Omri came to my home a while back to question me about Joel. I told them that my friend had followed the men who took Joel. The last he saw of the car Joel was in was when it pulled over to the side of the road south of Hebron.

"After my friend drove back to Jerusalem, he asked several more men in my church to begin a search for Joel. We started to lose hope when the heavy rains came, and then we got a break. A friend of mine was driving along the Gaza Strip one day, and as he drove further south the rain got worse.

"He got lost near a town called Khan Yunus. Right outside of town he noticed a car that had driven into a ditch on the side of the road. He was going to pull over to help, but he recognized the man as he got out of the car. He was one of the men who kidnapped your Joel," David explained.

Eli and Anna were speechless. They sat with their eyes glued on David, waiting for him to go on with his story.

"My friend continued to drive out of fear of being discovered and came upon a group of buildings at the end of a narrow road. He parked and got out of his car, and as he walked around the building he found Jad Said, who was the other man involved in the kidnapping. He was lying on the ground with a deep gash on his head.

"One of the buildings had caved in from the rain and evidently hit him. Joel was nowhere to be found, so my friend assumed he had escaped. He quickly got into his car and drove back to Jerusalem," David said.

"This is encouraging news, but we can't be sure yet if Joel is okay, although it does give us hope," Eli said. "One good thing is that Joel can't be tracked since the rain washed out any footprints. I just hope he didn't run into any other trouble along the way and that he'll surface somewhere, somehow."

"I promise you, Eli, your son is okay. The Lord is watching out for him. You need to trust that God is protecting your son. If you love him, you will pray for him," David said.

"I've never believed in God. It would be hypocritical of me to pray to something I don't believe in," Eli replied. "I can't believe there's a God who would allow millions of people to be murdered by a madman like Hitler."

"I do not understand why things like that happen, my friend, except that we live in a fallen world. Unfortunately there are evil people who deny God and seek power for themselves. They want to be their own god. It doesn't mean He doesn't exist. He allows people to make their own choices. When people choose to live separated from God, how can you expect them to do what is right?" David asked.

Eli thought for a moment about what David had said. "I get your point. I guess I never thought about it that way. I'll do anything to get my son back..." he said.

"A good start. And Anna, you need to pray also. You will get your son back, I promise. God is bigger than either of you. Although you may doubt Him, He can still answer your prayers. He is faithful even if you're not," David said with a smile as Anna's eyebrows rose at his last comment.

Eli and Anna spent the rest of the evening with David and Miriam, listening to David talk about this subject that they had both avoided their whole lives. It fascinated Eli that David was knowledgeable about so much—history, world events, politics, finance, and many other things.

303

There were things David talked about that Eli had never heard or read about. It just caused him to probe more deeply into David's deep storehouse of information on countless subjects, and how they all tied together.

At the end of the evening David hesitantly said that he and Miriam had to call it a night. They had to be up early the next morning for a conference where he would be speaking. The four walked out of the restaurant and the Volkenburgs thanked the Appels for a very illuminating evening. Eli and David grasped hands. Instead of shaking, David pulled Eli to him and hugged him.

"Thank you for treating us to this wonderful dinner, Eli. Do not forget to call me right away when Joel calls you to say he is on his way home. The Lord bless and keep you, my brother."

"Thank you, David. I appreciate everything you've done for our family. You can be sure that we'll keep you informed of any developments," Eli replied.

David turned to Anna and hugged her as well, and Miriam did the same. They walked the Volkenburgs to their car and watched as they drove out of sight and then made their way to their own car.

As Eli and Anna rode along the quiet streets of Jerusalem at the late hour, they agreed that there was something about this place that strangely drew them into believing the possibility that anything could happen—even miracles.

CHAPTER 42

The next morning Anna called Henry in London. She told him about their dinner with David and Miriam, and the hopeful news they had received about Joel's possible escape from Husaam Bishara's armed guards.

"We have no idea where he is, but evidently the men who took Joel had problems when one of them had a car accident and the other was injured in the storm. David was able to identify both of them as the men who took Joel from the hotel," Anna said.

"Why do you think he hasn't tried to contact anyone yet?" Henry asked.

"Maybe he's afraid of being located, or he could be unable to find a phone where he is," Anna speculated. "David felt very optimistic that Joel is still alive somewhere and we'll hear from him at some point."

"I sure hope so, because we found Hessa," Henry said.

"What? Did you say you found Hessa? How is she? Is everything all right with her? Is she okay?" Anna's questions tumbled out.

Henry explained everything that had happened since they'd been in London, and how they had met Mary, who helped them get to Hessa. He explained her situation with the men who guarded her day and night, and how careful he and Petie had been in getting to Hessa so they could speak with her.

"She asked us if we could take her back to America, Mrs. Volkenburg," Henry said.

"That poor girl…it must be much worse than we thought. Has she heard from her mother yet?" she asked.

"No. She's really worried about her mom, and says she's sure her father has done something with her, especially since she found out her mother's cell phone had been disconnected. Mrs. Bishara hasn't been in touch with Hessa at all," Henry said.

"We have to help her, there's no doubt about that," Anna said. "I wonder if Joel will try and find Hessa. I hope he has the sense to just get back to America."

"You know Mrs. V, that's a good point. Mr. Bishara will probably think Joel has escaped and is on his way to London to get Hessa. He's probably gonna beef up the security around her, or have her taken somewhere else. We need to act fast and get her out of here," Henry said.

"Henry, you're taking quite a risk in getting that girl out of the country," Anna replied. "You need to contact Mr. McLaughlin for help."

"That's a good idea. I'll call him as soon as we hang up," Henry said. "By the way, thanks for calling with the news about Joel. He'll be okay, Mrs. V. Our man Joel is tougher than we think."

"Mr. Volkenburg and I will be leaving for home tomorrow, so we'll start making contacts on our end. Don't worry Henry, Hessa will get to America, and we'll find a safe place for her to stay," Anna said.

Henry and Anna hung up, and as soon as he got off the phone, Henry told Petie about his conversation with Joel's mother. Petie immediately called Mary to let her know they would need to talk to Hessa and make plans to get her out of London as soon as possible.

Henry called Douglas McLaughlin and explained the dilemma with Hessa. He told Douglas about her background, her father's ties with Hamas, and that she was in London against her will. He asked about what they could do to take her to America with them.

"This is a sticky situation, Henry my boy," Douglas replied. "I'm going to have to do a little research before I ask anything specifically about your friend. I know someone at the Palestinian General Delegation here in the U.K. I'll start there, but this will take a bit of time. It's all a bit

306

dodgy, so let me get to work on it and I'll contact you directly when I have something to report."

Henry and Petie got to the library right at three p.m. and sat down with a stack of books, looking every bit the hard-working students. Their seats were close to Mary's station so they could pass information on to her more easily. They pulled out their laptops and started working on flight information as they waited for Hessa to appear.

Sure enough, Hessa walked into the library within the hour. She spotted Henry and Petie immediately, but tried to remain calm and act as normally as she could. She sat a couple of tables down from the two boys and pulled her books out of her back pack. Mustafa was with her, but after a short while he wandered outside to have a cigarette. Hessa got up and walked over to a row of books and Petie followed after her a few moments later.

"Hessa, I'm gonna talk fast before your guard comes back. We think Joel has escaped from where he was being held. It'll take too long to explain, but your father's men had accidents and it looks as though Joel might've been able to get away.

"He's not at the location where they think he was imprisoned. We're afraid your father is going to suspect that Joel will find out you're in London and come here to get you. We need to get you out of here as soon as possible," Petie said.

"Oh Petie, what are we going to do?" Hessa whispered, her eyes filled with fear.

"We have an idea. Henry and I are gonna get a disguise of some sort for you and smuggle you out of here. We'll make flight arrangements tonight. There's a flight tomorrow night at six p.m. with plenty of open seats.

"Meet us back here tomorrow afternoon after class and we'll bring the disguise for you. Mary will meet you in the bathroom with it. As soon as you change we'll be waiting for you outside at the north end of the building," Petie said.

Hessa looked at Petie with doubt and fear in her eyes. "I do not think we'll have time. You must understand that these men are trained in hunting people down. The first thing they will do is check the airports. Petie, I am so afraid," Hessa replied.

"You have to trust us, Hessa. You asked us to help you, and we're going to. I've already thought about the fact that they'll come after you. Tomorrow when you go into the bathroom to change, just tell the guard you're sick. That should hold him off for a while.

"Before you came we made some arrangements with Mary. She called a couple of her friends to help out with distracting Mustafa. They're gonna get his attention and do their best to keep him occupied for as long as possible," Petie explained.

"I do trust you, Petie, I do…" Hessa said.

"Good girl! Now, when you go back to your apartment tonight, think of all the things you'll absolutely need and put them in your purse. Don't worry about leaving the rest behind. We'll take care of everything you'll need once we reach America.

"There's only one more thing, Hessa. I have a feeling your dad knows that you stayed with my family, so we'll have to find another place with someone he isn't familiar with. Henry and I are still working on that."

Hessa's eyes lit up. "There may be someone, Petie. I met a woman on the plane who told me to call her any time. Her name is Ruth, and I have memorized her phone number. This woman was very special—I believe she would help me if I asked.

"When you call her, just remind her of the flight we took from Boston to Israel together, and the story she told me about Corrie ten Boom. I know she will remember me. Let me give you the number now." She had Petie write Ruth's name and number down.

Petie and Hessa discussed the rest of the details and went over the plans again. He urged her to try to be at the library the next day as close to three p.m. as possible. They were already cutting it very close as it was. Hessa promised to do her best to get there right at three o'clock.

The next day Hessa went through the motions attending each of her classes, trying to remain as calm as possible. She didn't want to give anything away to Mustafa, who stuck to her like glue. When she walked into the room of what was to be her final class, she sat right by the door so she could leave as soon as the lecture was over.

Just before three p.m. the instructor completed his lecture and reminded everyone of the paper that was due at the end of the week. Hessa had already put her things away, and as soon as class was dismissed, she jumped out of her seat like a shot. She hurried out of the room, and seeing Mustafa she told him quickly that she had to go to the library right away to finish the paper that was due Friday.

Hessa practically ran to the library as Mustafa wheezed along behind her, trying to keep up. He finally told her to slow down, and that he was running out of breath. She slowed slightly, but continued walking at a fast pace.

When they reached the library, Hessa headed for the History section, throwing her back pack down on a table close to the entrance. She pulled her things out and began a flurry of activity, trying to look busy.

Mary was behind the counter at her station eyeing Hessa, who looked as though she was about to explode with tension. Petie and Henry were at a table on the other side of the room, and didn't appear to have noticed Hessa. As they typed into their laptops, Mary walked out of the room. Hessa realized this was her cue to go to the bathroom.

"Mustafa, I am having women's troubles and do not feel well. I need to go to the ladies room. Please excuse me," she said, as Mustafa turned several shades darker, and mumbled something inaudible. As she hurried off to the ladies room, Mustafa walked outside for a cigarette.

When she opened the door to the bathroom Mary was waiting for her and handed her a tote bag. Hessa opened the bag and looked at the contents: a blond wig with a pageboy cut, light makeup, and an outfit Mary had brought for her to blend in as a typical British college student.

309

"I'm going back to my station to keep watch. I'll miss you excruciatingly, Hessa. Please don't forget me! I hope to go to Boston for a visit before long," Mary said.

"You have been a wonderful friend, Mary. I cannot tell you how much I appreciate your help. I will contact you when I can, but now I must hurry and change. Thank you again!" Hessa said, and the two friends hugged.

Hessa went into a stall to change, and Mary walked out of the bathroom toward her station. She noticed that Mustafa had disappeared, so she got on her cell phone and called her friends, who had been waiting outside for directions from her.

"He's coming. You need to do something right now!" Mary told her friends Bridget and Chloe.

Bridget let her know they had already spotted him. "We're on the job, Mary. I have to go. Chloe is over talking to him," she whispered.

Bridget hung up and walked over to where Chloe and Mustafa were standing, smoking cigarettes. Chloe had told Mustafa that she was having car problems, and that there was a strange sound coming from the engine. She asked if he knew anything about cars, and he told her he did.

"Do you think you could take a look?" she asked.

"Where is the car located?" he asked.

"It's over in the lot to the south of the library," Chloe replied.

Mustafa looked up to the second floor where Hessa was, as if he would be able to see her through the wall. He stood for a moment in thought, weighing whether he should go or stay. Finally he decided to take a quick look.

"I do not know if I will be able to find the problem, but show me to your car," he said simply, and the three of them walked off in the direction of the parking lot.

Hessa changed quickly and came out of the stall. She looked in the mirror and straightened out the wig, pulling a little beret on her head and pinning it to the wig. She walked out of the bathroom, deliberately slowing

310

down to calm her nerves. She looked over at Mary one last time, who gave Hessa a little wave before she left the building.

Petie and Henry were waiting at the north end of the library. They spotted Hessa as she walked out the double doors of the building. She ran to them and the three hurried over to a cab that Henry had waiting. They raced off to Heathrow Airport with Henry updating Hessa on everything that had happened in the last twenty-four hours.

He explained that Douglas McLaughlin had been an enormous help and had contacted people who would be able to assist them once they got to America. He also told her that Mr. Volkenburg was making arrangements for Hessa to come back into the country as a student once again.

"Oh, and I got a hold of Ruth," Petie said.

"You did! What did you tell her?"

"I explained your situation to her and she was really happy to hear from me. She was worried about you, Hessa. She told me she tried to call you about a month ago to see how you were doing, but the phone had been disconnected.

"She said that you're welcome to stay with her as long as you want. She also said to tell you 'It's what Corrie would do', whatever that meant," Petie said. Hessa looked at Petie and just smiled.

The cab ride to the airport seemed endless, but they finally pulled up in front of the airline entrance. They unloaded their things from the cab and ran to the ticket counter, checked their bags, and got their boarding passes. Fortunately for them the line through the security checkpoint was short, and they breezed through with several minutes to spare before boarding the plane.

"When was the last time you ate, Hessa?" Henry asked.

"I haven't been hungry all day—I have been too nervous. I do not think I could eat yet, Henry, but thank you for asking," Hessa replied.

"I think I'll pick up some sandwiches and snacks for us, just in case you start to get hungry," Henry said, and went off to a snack bar close by to load up on food for the trip.

311

Petie called his father to inform him that they were on their way to Boston, and let him know when their flight would arrive. Petie's father told him he would call the Worthings to give them Henry's arrival time. Mr. Sully told his son that he and his mother would be at Boston Logan to pick them up.

"Thanks, Dad. I'll see you soon," Petie said and hung up.

Petie made one last call to Mary, thanking her for all her help. "Don't forget, Mary, you promised to come to America for a visit this summer," Petie said.

"Oh I'll be there all right. Nothing could stop me, Peter. I had a wonderful time with you—at least until the end," she laughed.

"You and your friends were really brave, Mary. I told Douglas McLaughlin about what you did, so if you feel nervous about anything just give him a call," Petie said, and gave her Douglas' phone number.

Petie hung up and sat down, staring at his cell phone. He missed Mary already.

Before they knew it they were boarding the plane, and Hessa felt as though a thousand pounds had been lifted from her shoulders as they found their seats and sat down. She was on her way to America, and felt safer than she had in months as she sat between her two friends.

<hr/>

Mustafa attempted to start Chloe's car, but the engine refused to turn over. He lifted the hood and found a couple of missing spark plugs. He slammed the hood shut and turned to her.

"How did you even get this car here today with missing spark plugs?" Mustafa asked impatiently.

"What do you mean, missing spark plugs? It was working perfectly this morning. When I went to start it this afternoon, it hardly made a sound," Chloe said innocently.

"It sounds like someone stole your spark plugs," Mustafa said, narrowing his eyes suspiciously.

"What do I do now?" Chloe asked.

"There is a petrol service station close by. They have parts, so if you go and purchase the spark plugs I will put them in for you."

Chloe and Bridget thanked Mustafa for his help and walked in the direction of the service station, hoping they had held him off long enough for Hessa to get away.

Mustafa walked back into the library and up the stairs. He noticed Hessa still hadn't returned from the ladies room. Her book bag was still sitting on a nearby table, so he went over and picked up a newspaper and sat down near her bag. Almost twenty minutes passed and still there was no sign of Hessa. Mustafa stood up and walked over to Mary, who was standing behind the counter at her station.

"Have you seen a girl about this high with long black hair who was sitting over at that table?" Mustafa asked.

"I'm not sure. I could have seen someone, but haven't really been paying attention. Sorry, sir," Mary replied.

"She went into the bathroom about an hour ago, but hasn't come out yet. Would you go in and see if she is still in there?" Mustafa asked.

"Of course," Mary said, and slowly walked into the bathroom, waiting as long as possible before she returned. She walked back out and over to where Mustafa was standing.

"I'm sorry sir, but there wasn't anyone in there," Mary said.

Without a word Mustafa turned and ran out of the library, looking back and forth for any sign of Hessa. He called Iyad and told him what had happened, ordering him to get over to the library.

Moments later Iyad appeared. The two jumped into Mustafa's car and drove over to the apartment building where they were staying with Hessa. The two men ran up to her apartment and kicked the door in, looking around the tiny room. It looked as if nothing had been taken.

They tore all the drawers out of the dresser and opened the tiny closet—everything was there. Mustafa told Iyad that Hessa had been ill, but realized now that she must have been lying so she could get away.

"She may have found some way to leave the country. She's been gone for almost two hours, so we can't follow her now. If we go to the

313

airport, no one will give us any information," Mustafa said angrily, realizing he would need to contact Husaam Bishara and let him know that his daughter had disappeared.

CHAPTER 43

"**I** have surrounded myself with fools and halfwits! What is the matter with all of you? Has no one in my employ any sense?" Bishara yelled. I cannot send you two to America in search of her—everyone will know who you are by then. I want you and Iyad to get on the next plane back to Israel. You are of no use to me now," and slammed the phone down in Mustafa's ear.

Mustafa remained silent, afraid to say anything in his own defense. He put his phone in his breast pocket and walked next door to Iyad's room to let him know what Bishara had said to him, and told him to get packed as he made their flight arrangements. Mustafa walked back to his own room, fearful of what Bishara would do once he got back to Israel.

Husaam Bishara got back on the phone to arrange for another group of his men to fly to America immediately. He knew exactly where his daughter would be headed, and his men would be right behind her. He knew that he had been too lenient this time. When he brought her home, it would be the last time she would leave his sight until she was brought to justice for bringing him this disgrace.

Joel awakened to the sound of Muna's deep coughs. She had contracted pneumonia from the exposure to the cold and rain, and had nearly starved to death. Eshe had already jumped up to assist her and was trying to get her to swallow a homemade concoction to settle her cough. Joel sat up in his chair looking over at Muna with pity, feeling helpless as she hacked and wheezed, looking pale and weak.

He was beginning to feel better, but Muna hadn't been so fortunate. She seemed to get weaker and more ill as time passed. Joel had once again lost track of how long they had been staying with Eshe since he had slept on and off for several days out of sheer exhaustion. When Muna became ill, he and Eshe had focused all their efforts on nursing her back to health, but as the days wore on, she still fought for her fragile life.

Joel had developed a routine of going out each day to pick fruit from the nearby oasis. Eshe had a store of flour, and made fresh bread each morning as soon as she was awake. She also had a small garden on the side of her little house, and managed to grow a variety of vegetables such as artichokes, garlic, onion, tomatoes, lettuce, cucumbers, peppers, and fava beans.

She explained in very broken English and hand gestures that she had a brother in Cairo who would periodically bring supplies of flour, rice, and other things from the city for her. It seemed his visits were infrequent, but her eyes lit up when she spoke of the special treat of lamb from her brother, which was very rare. Her head nodded up and down and she smiled as she said the word 'kabob', and Joel smiled back and nodded in understanding.

Their days together were quiet and laid back, as Eshe taught Joel how to cook several dishes that were popular in Egypt. For her limited access to such a small variety of food, Eshe was a very creative little chef. She even taught him how to fish, which he had never done, and he found he enjoyed it immensely. She also had him memorize several words and everyday sayings in Arabic.

Many mornings Joel would be up even before Eshe. He would grab the little makeshift pole and tackle and run down to his favorite spot. He loved the sound of the sea and would sit on a large rock looking down at the beautiful variety of fish that made the Sinai Peninsula so famous with divers.

As the weather became warmer and sunnier, Muna's health slowly began to improve. Joel began taking her outside to sit on a blanket he would lay on the sand for her. She enjoyed looking out at the sea, but could only be outside for short periods of time before she felt weak and needed to be taken back to bed. Joel wondered if Muna would ever completely regain her strength.

316

Eshe did her best to feed Muna things that were full of vitamins, and herbs she knew would be healing to Muna's respiratory system. She also had teas that seemed to work wonders on Muna's cough. The pneumonia had taken a lot out of her, and the recovery time had been very slow, but she began to improve.

Muna had also been beaten quite badly, but Eshe had examined every part of her body and indicated to Joel that none of her bones were broken. The beatings had taken their toll on Muna, but the marks were almost gone, and the cuts had healed nicely with Eshe's homemade salve.

⚜

Late one afternoon Joel was out fishing when he saw a small truck pull up to Eshe's house. An elderly man stepped out and looked at Joel with a perplexed look on his face. He walked over to Joel and greeted him in Arabic.

Joel said hello in Arabic, but when the man continued to speak to him, Joel shrugged his shoulders and said, "Sorry, I can't speak much Arabic."

He responded, "An American?"

"Yes, I am."

"I speak pretty good English," the man said. "You are here with Eshe? It is her basket you have there." He pointed down at the fishing basket sitting at Joel's feet.

"Yes, my friend and I are staying with her. She has been very kind to us," Joel said.

"She is my sister. I am Jabari, from Cairo. I brought her some of her favorite foods, but I wish I had known you were here. I would have brought more," Jabari said with a smile.

"My name is Joel, and my friend is in the house with Eshe. Her name is Muna," Joel said.

"How long have you stayed with Eshe?" Jabari asked.

"For several months, I think," Joel said. "We were travelling and my friend became very ill. Eshe found us near her house and offered us

317

shelter. She's been a great blessing to us. I only hope I can repay her one day."

"She is a very kind woman. She needs nothing in return. Eshe has lived alone for many years, and will not move to Cairo with my family. The city frightens her so she stays here in the middle of nowhere," Jabari said.

"I didn't know we were in Egypt," Joel said, half to himself.

"Where did you come from?" Jabari asked, confused.

"Israel. It was raining very hard and I got lost. I guess I wandered right across the border!" Joel said, trying to sound casual.

"Mr. Joel, you could get in much trouble for coming across the border into Egypt without permission. Do you have your passport?" Jabari asked.

"No, we....left them," Joel said with his head down.

"Tell me boy, are you running from something or someone? If so, you could be putting my sister in danger by staying here," Jabari said.

"I'm sorry for putting Eshe in this situation. We had nowhere else to go. Please don't turn us in. We didn't know what to do," Joel said, angry at himself for blurting out so much information.

"Your secret is safe with me for now, but I need to bring the food inside. Help me with my packages. We will talk about this more," Jabari said.

The two men went to Jabari's truck and pulled out several parcels wrapped in brown paper. Jabari then reached into the cab of his truck for a small, battered suitcase and they walked into the little house.

Eshe was chopping vegetables for dinner, hoping that Joel had caught some fish. She turned when she heard the voices outside and ran to the door, hugging her brother. The two chatted happily in Arabic for a few minutes, and it looked as though she was explaining her guests to her brother.

Jabari and Joel went to the little kitchen and laid the parcels on the table. Eshe excitedly walked over to the table and ripped open the packages, revealing the treasure of food inside. Jabari had brought lamb, which made her squeal with delight. He had also brought Egyptian feta cheese, sesame candies and chewy bars of all sorts, along with Ghorayebah and El Menenas, Eshe's favorite cookies.

She turned to Joel and said, "Kabob!" holding up the lamb.

Joel laughed and nodded his head to show Eshe that he was happy about the meat also. Eshe got to work cutting the lamb into small pieces, then went to her garden to pick tomatoes, a pepper, and onion for the kabobs. She returned shortly, humming as she began to prepare the rice.

Muna was sitting in a chair in the middle of the room, and Joel introduced her to Jabari. He noticed that she seemed pale and sickly, and wondered what the poor woman had been through. As Eshe worked happily in the kitchen, Jabari asked Joel to sit down in the chair next to Muna, and he pulled one of the little chairs over from the kitchen and sat down.

"So Joel, you must tell me how you got from Israel to Egypt, and where you plan to go from here," Jabari said.

"I'll have to trust that our conversation will stay within the walls of this home," Joel said, and told Jabari the story of how he came to Israel. He explained that they had been imprisoned near what he could only assume was the Egyptian border. He told Jabari that they had travelled a long way through the rain and that he had no idea how far they had come, or where they were.

"Someone is looking out for you, Joel my boy," Jabari said simply. "I do not know how you were not spotted, but here you are, and my sister has taken good care of you. You could not be more fortunate than having her find you."

"I agree. The time we've spent here has been perfect for resting and healing. Mrs. Bishara has been very ill, but she's finally on the road to recovery. Jabari, we need to get out of Egypt and to try and find a way to get back to America. Is there any way you could help us? I don't want to put you in any danger, but we can't go back to Israel. We could be spotted there," Joel said.

"You say this woman's name is Bishara? So her husband is Husaam Bishara? Wait...now this all makes sense. He has been in the news lately. It seems he has been questioned on the whereabouts of his own wife and an American boy. You are the two he was questioned about," Jabari said, waving his hand back and forth between Joel and Muna.

"Now you can see why we can't go back to Jerusalem," Joel said. "We really need to get back to America. If we could just make it to an embassy in Cairo, we could get the help we need," Joel said.

"I will be happy to take you to Cairo," Jabari said.

Joel and Jabari continued to talk about what he'd been through to find Hessa. Jabari found the opportunity to ask Joel about America, and to see if all the things he had heard and seen on television were actually true.

Eshe finished the dinner preparations and everyone crowded around the little table in the makeshift kitchen. They ate the kabobs and rice until nothing was left. She made tea and served the cookies and bars for dessert as everyone chatted into the evening. Even Muna perked up for a short time, telling everyone about her home in Israel.

Joel and Jabari cleared all the dishes away after dinner as Eshe helped Muna back to bed. Everyone prepared to settle in to sleep as Eshe stoked the fire in the little stove one last time.

Jabari laid out a sleeping mat he'd brought along for his visit, and had brought extra blankets for his stay. He gave one to his sister, and lay on his mat fully clothed to stay warm in the desert climate, where the temperature dropped very quickly at night.

Joel looked over at Muna, who was already fast asleep. She had spoken more tonight than she had in all the time they had spent with Eshe. He smiled to himself, realizing that she was probably just as encouraged as he was at the possibility of finally being able to return to America.

CHAPTER 44

The summer passed as Hessa settled into her new home with Ruth. The two had become very close, and Ruth was a wonderful teacher of the Bible and mentor of Hessa's newfound faith. Mr. Volkenburg had been an integral part of getting Hessa enrolled at Yale University under another name for her protection. He had also helped Hessa apply to become a naturalized citizen.

Hessa loved living with Ruth, who was full of vitality for a woman her age. She never seemed to run out of energy. In the time Hessa had been with Ruth, the two had been all over Connecticut and had driven to New York to stay for several days. Ruth dragged her from one end of New York City to the other, treating her to a Broadway play as well as every major tourist attraction.

It was a week before the start of school and Hessa was preparing for her first day at Yale. She made a list of things she would need, and Ruth offered to take her shopping for supplies and clothes. She knocked on Hessa's door one morning, and Hessa called for her to come in. Ruth entered to see Hessa sitting on her bed, still in her pajamas.

"It's after eight o'clock, Hessa. It isn't like you to still be in your pajamas. Up and at 'em, as we say!" Ruth exclaimed.

"Yes, I suppose I need to get dressed now," Hessa said with a vacant look.

"What's the matter, honey? Are you tired of rushing all over the place with me? I suppose I *have* been dragging you around too much," Ruth said.

"No, I have enjoyed it very much. You have been wonderful to me, Ruth. I just miss my mother so much. Sometimes I am so sad that I think I cannot move. I miss Joel also," Hessa said looking up at Ruth, her eyes full of pain.

"We haven't talked about them much lately. I think I've tried to keep you busy so you wouldn't be left to your thoughts about them. I really should be more sensitive to what you're going through, Hessa."

"You have, Ruth. I do not know what I would have done without you. I also feel that I have been an imposition to you. I have no money, and did not even have many clothes when I came to live with you. I can only hope that when I graduate I will be able to pay you back every penny," Hessa said.

"Oh Hessa, that's not necessary. I know it looks like I don't have much, but when my husband died and my children moved away I sold our house and moved to a smaller home. I also inherited money from my parents. I'm very comfortable financially. You don't have any need to worry about my situation. I have plenty," Ruth said.

"You are truly a gift from God," Hessa said.

Getting up from her bed she went over to hug Ruth. "I only wish I could see Petie and Henry. I know they cannot contact me for safety reasons, but it would make me feel closer to Joel if I could at least talk to them on the phone every so often. I miss them."

"I know, honey. I wish I could arrange something so that you could see them, but I'm afraid that would put you in danger. One thing to look forward to is that you'll meet people at college and make some friends your own age. Won't that be wonderful?" Ruth said, trying to sound positive.

"You are right. I am just feeling sorry for myself. I'll get ready, and we will get everything taken care of for school."

"I don't want you ever to feel as though you can't talk to me about how sad you are, Hessa. We need to keep praying diligently for your mother and Joel. We still need to believe in miracles. Okay, I'm going downstairs to finish making breakfast. I'll see you in a few minutes."

Ruth turned and walked out, leaving Hessa to get ready for the day. She felt a little encouraged, and prayed that she could have the faith that her friend Ruth had.

The two spent the day at an office supply store and various clothing stores at the mall as Ruth encouraged Hessa to try on one outfit after another, along with at least ten different pairs of shoes. At the end of the day they returned home, exhausted. The two women brought their bags and boxes up to their rooms and unpacked everything they had bought.

Ruth went down to the kitchen to prepare dinner, and Hessa joined her a short time later. As Hessa set the table, Ruth put the food onto serving platters and set everything on the table. The two sat down, and when Hessa saw the food, she realized she was ravenously hungry.

"Mmm, this is good, Ruth. What is in the ravioli?" Hessa asked.

"Butternut squash. I got the recipe from a little restaurant outside of Hartford. Isn't it wonderful?" Ruth put down her fork and looked over at Hessa with a smile on her face.

"What are you smiling about? Do I have something on my face? I am eating too fast!" Hessa said smiling.

"There's nothing on your face. I just wanted to tell you about something I did this morning while you were getting ready," Ruth said.

Hessa looked over at Ruth with a puzzled look on her face, and before she could ask what it was that she had done, Ruth told her.

"My son lives in Myrtle Beach, South Carolina. He's a well-known chef down there. I gave him a call this morning and asked if he would like some company from his old mother and a friend. I haven't seen his family since last Christmas, right before I left for Israel," Ruth said.

"Do you think we have time? It is only about ten days before school begins," Hessa said.

"I know I'm dragging you off again, but we'll only be gone for a few days. You'll love it down there, and I think it would be nice for us to get away before you start school. You're going to be very busy once you have your homework assignments, and then you won't be able to go anywhere but the library!" Ruth said smiling.

323

"I would love to see South Carolina. I do not know anything about it," Hessa said, although she had mixed feelings over leaving Ruth's comfortable home where she felt so safe.

"Well then, why don't I make the arrangements? I'll book the flights and make reservations at my favorite bed and breakfast. There's a beautiful plantation outside of town. It's so quiet and peaceful there, you'll love it. All you have to do is put a few things in a suitcase, and we'll leave in a couple of days," Ruth said.

Then she added, "But Hessa, I want you to tell me if you feel uncomfortable about leaving on another trip."

"I agree with what you said, Ruth. Once I begin school, I won't be going anywhere for a while. I would love to go."

"Well, once we get there, you won't believe how quiet and relaxing it is. We'll stay at the plantation and just put our feet up," Ruth said, patting Hessa on the arm.

The next day Hessa got organized for school as best she could before packing for their trip to South Carolina. As the day wore on she happily anticipated an adventure to a new place. She was also eager to finally meet some of Ruth's family.

Ruth and Hessa arrived at the Hartford airport shortly after seven a.m. Lines were long, but they didn't have much luggage, so they were able to breeze through to their gate and relax. Before they knew it they were on the plane, heading to Myrtle Beach. Hessa hadn't slept well the night before, so it wasn't long before she drifted off to sleep as Ruth read and dozed off herself.

Their plane arrived shortly after noon, and Ruth's son, Craig, was waiting for them outside the security area. Ruth ran to her son and hugged him, then turned to introduce him to her young friend.

"Craig, this is Hessa—she's the young lady I was telling you about," Ruth said.

"Hello Hessa. Welcome to Myrtle Beach! I'm sure you're going to love it here. We have absolutely nothing planned for you to do during your visit!" Craig laughed.

Hessa liked Craig immediately. He looked just like his mother, which made her like him even more. On the drive to the Bed and Breakfast, Craig told Hessa all about how he'd moved to Myrtle Beach after attending the Culinary Institute of America. He was married and had two daughters who very were excited to see their grandmother.

Craig drove into the entrance of the Manley Plantation Bed and Breakfast. The road leading up to the house was very rustic, with weeping willows hanging over the road like a canopy. Hessa was amazed at the beauty of the old plantation. It was like stepping back into the 18th century. Craig pulled up to the house and helped his mother and Hessa get settled in.

"I'll be back for you at five p.m. I'm taking you and Mom to my restaurant for dinner, Hessa. My wife and children will be joining us, so be prepared for lots of chatter!" Craig said, and kissed his mother goodbye.

Ruth and Hessa walked up to the house they would be staying in. It was brick with lovely vines growing up the sides. Flowers bloomed all the way up the walk and along the front and sides of the house. Window boxes beneath each window spilled over with masses of colorful flowers.

"I hope you don't mind sharing a room. I wanted to make sure you're close by. This one has two beds, so I thought it would be best," Ruth said, still concerned for Hessa's safety.

"This is one of the most beautiful places I have ever seen!" Hessa exclaimed as she looked around the room at the four poster beds, the fireplace with two overstuffed chairs in front of it facing each other, and an enormous bathroom.

The two unpacked and went outside to walk the grounds that had originally been a rice plantation. They stood and watched as horses grazed in a field surrounded by pristine white fences.

They walked back toward the house along a canal lined with cypress trees. Hessa spotted a white heron and pointed it out to Ruth. She was fascinated by the Spanish moss growing on the oak trees that were scattered around the plantation.

Craig arrived shortly before five o'clock to collect his mother and Hessa, and drove them to his restaurant, which was called the Lighthouse. He led them to a beautiful window table that overlooked the ocean. Craig's two children ran to their grandmother, hugging her as she kissed the tops of their heads.

"My, you two are getting so tall! I don't have to bend down to kiss you anymore!" Ruth said. She introduced them to Hessa. The oldest daughter's name was Seelah, who was twelve, and the younger daughter was Charis, who was ten.

Ruth hugged her daughter-in-law, Linda, and introduced her to Hessa. They went to sit down, with Craig showing everyone to their assigned seats. The table was very large and had nine chairs around it. Craig had Hessa sit in a seat with empty chairs on either side of her, which confused her. Craig smiled and acted as if Hessa's sitting separated from his family was perfectly fine.

Ruth's granddaughters kept her busy talking about school and their many activities while Hessa politely listened. Craig ordered hors d'oeuvres for the table, and then excused himself, saying he needed to check on things in the kitchen. Moments later he returned with Henry, Petie and Eddie in tow. Hessa's eyes flew open as she jumped out of her seat and ran to her three friends.

"Oh my goodness, I am so happy to see you!" she exclaimed, and embraced all three boys, hugging each one of them, then going back and hugging them again. "I cannot believe you are here! I have missed you!"

"Ruth called us a couple of days ago and asked if we could meet you down here. She was nice enough to make reservations for us to stay at the Plantation, so we'll be able to visit for the next couple of days," Henry said.

"When did you get here? How did I not notice you were on the property?" Hessa asked.

"We haven't checked in yet. Craig picked us up at the airport and took us to his house. We're going back with you after dinner," Petie said.

326

The group talked nonstop over dinner, updating one another on what had been happening in each of their lives. They explained to Craig how they had all met, and the situation with Joel and Muna. They didn't get into details because of Craig's two young daughters, but his mother had already explained the situation to him when Hessa had first come to stay with her.

Craig's restaurant was wonderful. They served primarily seafood, which was fresh every day. Craig explained that his menu was based solely on the best catches of the day.

Each morning he got up at the crack of dawn and went down to the docks to meet with the fisherman, who shouted out what they had brought in from the sea. His home was on a large property, where he grew fresh organic vegetables for the dishes in his restaurant. In the winter he grew hothouse vegetables so that he didn't have to rely on questionable produce.

As the evening came to an end, Craig's wife and daughters hugged Ruth, said goodbye to everyone, and headed home. The rest of the group walked to Craig's SUV and got in, chatting and laughing. As they left the parking lot, a silver compact car followed them. No one noticed that they had been watched all evening and that this time there weren't only two men that had been sent for Hessa—there were four.

"We have found her, sir. We knew it was only a matter of time before the American boys led us to her," Fatik Nidal said.

The man who had kidnapped Joel was in America, this time looking for Hessa. He swore to his boss that this time they wouldn't fail to bring her back, and they wouldn't lose sight of her again.

"Very good. I will not congratulate you until I see you get off the plane with her in Tel Aviv," Husaam Bishara said, and hung up the phone.

CHAPTER 45

Jabari stayed at Eshe's home for several days, working and fixing things around the house and fishing with Joel. The two had become close in a short time, with Joel answering the countless questions Jabari asked about him, Muna, and America. He, in turn, told Joel about how he and Eshe were two of ten children, born in Cairo.

Eshe had married very young and moved with her husband to the Sinai Peninsula, where he had worked at a resort a few miles away. She was unable to have children, and her husband had died about ten years before. She'd lived alone ever since.

"Our whole family is in Cairo. Eshe is a very stubborn old woman. She has dozens of nieces and nephews, and they now have children of their own. She still will not come back to her home," Jabari told Joel.

Joel and Muna prepared to leave for Cairo with Jabari when he had completed all his tasks around Eshe's little house. She made one last dinner for the four of them, and seemed very sad that her house guests were about to leave. She told them in broken English that she would miss them very much.

"You family," she said sadly.

The next morning Joel and Muna said goodbye to Eshe, and the three stood hugging one another outside near Jabari's truck. Eshe began to cry, which made Muna choke up. The two had become like mother and daughter, and Muna expressed how grateful she was to Eshe for nursing her back to health.

Joel told Eshe that he would come back some day, and would repay her kindness. She didn't understand what he said, so Jabari interpreted for her in a hushed tone. She looked at Joel with confusion written on her face, but smiled and hugged him once more.

Joel and Muna slid into the truck and Jabari hugged his sister one last time. She handed him a small sack of fruit and nuts for the ride. He hopped into the truck and drove off down the little dirt road.

As they drove along Joel and Jabari chatted back and forth about the sights as they drove into the city of el Arish. It was a beautiful city—not large, but very modern, with luxurious hotels lined alongside the Mediterranean Sea.

Muna hardly said a word as they drove along, and Joel finally asked her if anything was wrong. She told him she was fine, but turned and looked out the window of the truck. About an hour later she asked if they could stop for a short break.

Jabari stopped when they got to Bi'r al Abd and the three got out at a small hotel with a café. Jabari excused himself as he answered a call on his cell phone, and after Muna returned from the restroom she approached Joel with an anxious look on her face.

"I heard what Jabari said to Eshe when he was interpreting for you. You told him to say that you will come back some day and repay her for her kindness. Instead he said to her something about how you and I are going back to Israel. We speak different dialects, but I understood enough," Muna said anxiously.

"Maybe you got it mixed up, Mrs. Bishara. Why would he tell her we're going back to Israel? They both know we're trying to get to America—that doesn't make sense," Joel replied.

"That is exactly what I am trying to tell you. I do not trust Jabari. There is something happening that I cannot quite figure out, but I am afraid to go to Cairo with him, Joel," Muna said. "Please believe me. I think he is going to turn us in. We need to find a way to get away from him," Muna said.

Joel studied the expression on Muna's face. She hadn't said much in the last few months, but now she spoke up distinctly and passionately about her distrust of Jabari. She was so sure of this feeling that he realized he'd better take her seriously.

She looked at him pleadingly and he was moved with compassion for this woman who had lived a life of fear and mistrust. Her instincts, he believed, were very good.

"Don't worry, Mrs. Bishara. I believe you. When we get to Cairo we'll make some sort of excuse so we can get away. I have no idea what we're going to do or where we'll go, but trust me—God will help us find a way of escape," Joel said.

Muna's face visibly relaxed and she hugged Joel, thanking him for trusting her. "By the way, Joel, since we have been together day and night for many months, I believe you should call me Muna," she said smiling at him.

"You're right—that *is* a little formal," he replied with a smile, and the two walked back out to the truck where they waited for Jabari to return.

⸎

Jabari walked around the corner from where Joel and Muna stood and answered his phone. It was a friend from Cairo who had finally gotten him the information he needed.

"It is about time, Rafik! What did you find out?" Jabari asked the person on the other end.

"These things take time, my friend. You need to be more patient. It is not every day that someone asks me to get the personal phone number of Husaam Bishara. However, you are in luck. I had to make many phone calls, but I have it for you," his friend said.

Jabari took the number down, quickly hung up, and dialed the number his friend had given him. A deep voice answered after several rings.

"Yes?" the person asked.

"Is this Husaam Bishara?" Jabari asked.

"This is Bishara," he replied.

331

"I have some information that might be very valuable to you," Jabari said.

"Who is this?" Bishara asked.

"Someone who knows where your wife and the American are," Jabari replied.

"Well, this is good news. Where are you?" Bishara asked.

"Mr. Bishara, I am not a fool. I know how much you would like to locate them. I am asking for payment directly to my bank account and I will keep them at my house until you come," Jabari said.

"Give me your bank information and directions to you home, and I will come directly," Bishara said. "If they are not at your home when I get there, the deal is off, and the money will be returned to me. Understood?"

Jabari agreed, fearful of being on the receiving end of Husaam Bishara's fury if he couldn't deliver on his promise. He told Bishara what time he would be at the bank to receive and confirm the deposit into his account. He would then give Bishara the information of where he could collect Muna and Joel. They hung up and Jabari walked back out to the truck, smiling at his companions.

"Ready to go?" he asked cheerfully.

Muna and Joel smiled back at him, trying not to give anything away. The three got into the truck and drove the last leg of their journey, arriving in Cairo several hours later. Jabari drove up to a building in the center of the city and told them that this was his home.

They parked in front of the apartment house. Many of his family members lived in the same building. Jabari had a fruit and vegetable stand in a large marketplace in Cairo where other family members had stands as well. He had relatives who sold herbs and nuts, flowers, meat and fish, and souvenirs. Joel and Muna got out of the truck and stretched their legs. Jabari led the way up to his small apartment where his wife met them at the door.

"Hello, greetings to you. Please come in. I am Ahit—please tell me your names."

Joel and Muna introduced themselves to Ahit. The apartment was dark and messy, but she seemed happy to have visitors. Jabari explained to her that they had been staying with Eshe and were trying to get to America. She welcomed them in and asked them to sit down while she prepared food.

"If you will excuse me Joel, I need to go to the bank before it closes. I hope you do not mind. Please sit and enjoy a small meal. When I return this evening we will make a true Egyptian feast for you!" Jabari said, and left.

As Ahit busily worked in the kitchen, Joel and Muna saw their opportunity for escape. They realized that they should have some food since it was uncertain when they would next have an opportunity to eat. She returned shortly with a large pot of tea and a platter made up of bread, cheese, melon, peaches, grapes and nuts.

"Please eat! You must be very hungry after your long journey today," Ahit said.

Joel and Muna stuffed themselves, and when she got up to take their dishes into the kitchen, they filled their pockets with as much of the food left on the platter as they could.

Joel stood up as Ahit returned from the kitchen, and pulling Muna to her feet he said, "There's an interesting souvenir shop we passed close by your building. I'd like to get out and stretch my legs. Muna, would you like to walk down there with me and take a look around?"

"A walk would be wonderful. I feel in need of some fresh air," Muna replied.

"That could very well be one of my family's shops. Let me go with you," Ahit said.

"We're just going down there for a quick look. We won't stay long since we've been travelling all day. I don't have much energy left, do you, Muna?" Muna just smiled at Ahit and shook her head.

"Then I will stay here and clean up. When you return you can rest until Jabari returns. Stay close to one another. You do not want to lose each other in this city," she said as Joel and Muna said goodbye and let themselves out.

They hurried down the steps to the outside. Joel and Muna stood momentarily in the street, wondering which way they should go. As they turned to head back in the direction from where they had come into town, they saw Jabari's truck rounding the corner.

They took off running in the opposite direction, catching Jabari's attention, and he accelerated his truck to intercept them. Joel saw a small alleyway to the left and directed Muna toward it as they ran down it to lose Jabari. He hid Muna in a doorway and poked his head out to see if he could spot Jabari, who drove past, looking anxious and angry.

Joel realized that Muna's instincts were correct as the two continued down the alley and through the back streets of Cairo, trying to stay as hidden as possible while struggling to find a way to safety.

After running for some time, Joel spotted a bridge that crossed the Nile River, and they ran toward the street that led up to the bridge. Just then, a very large truck passed by them. The driver looked over and pulled up next to them.

"Young man, you look lost. Are you searching for something in particular?" he asked in perfect English.

"No, no thank you," Joel answered, as he and Muna looked straight ahead, walking briskly.

"You are an American?" the man asked, and Joel nodded.

"I have a brother who went to school in America—the blessed land of freedom. He teaches at a college in Oklahoma."

Joel turned and looked over at the man questioningly. "Where are you headed, Sir? Maybe you could give my friend and I a ride," Joel said.

"But I am on my way to Tripoli. You are not going to Libya, are you?" he asked.

"We're trying to get out of Cairo. Would you take us with you?"

"Please get in then. I will take you out of Cairo, if you wish," the man said.

Joel and Muna hurried to climb up into the cab of the truck, and introduced themselves as they shut the door.

"My name is Ngozi. I sell textiles and handicrafts in Cairo. There are many people in and around Tripoli that I buy from and take their goods to Cairo where I can get a much better price. It is good for all of us," Ngozi said.

Ngozi explained to Joel and Muna how his brother had secretly converted to Christianity, and left his home to go to school in America. He decided to stay there after he graduated college, and rarely came back to Libya to visit.

"Because of my brother, almost all of my family has converted to Christianity. But there are very few Christians in Libya you see, so we must be careful who we tell about our faith."

"Huh...I'm beginning to think there are no coincidences when it comes to God," Joel said. "My friend and I are recent believers ourselves. I come from a Jewish background, and she's Muslim. Of all the people who could have picked us up..."

"What do you know about that? Thanks be to God! I do not often have the opportunity to speak with many people who share my beliefs!" Ngozi exclaimed.

The three talked nonstop as they drove along. The day wore on, and finally Ngozi told them that they were approaching the Libyan border. Joel had explained their situation, and told Ngozi that he needed to get to an embassy where he could contact his parents to replace his and Muna's passports so they could return to America. Ngozi agreed to help them, but as they got closer to the border crossing he knew he would have to do something to conceal his two companions.

"You need to get in the back of my truck and hide in the containers I have there. We need to pray that no one checks them as we cross the border," Ngozi told them.

He pulled over to the side of the road so Joel and Muna could climb into the back of the truck and get inside of the large containers he had for carrying his goods to Cairo. As he picked up the lids to place on

335

the containers he prayed that the guards at the border would overlook them and that God would keep his passengers safe. He put the lids over them and got back into his truck.

A short time later he pulled up to the boarder and was stopped. As the guard questioned Ngozi, he respectfully answered his questions, and then asked the guard if he could tell him a joke he'd heard that day. The man nodded, and Ngozi proceeded to repeat the joke he'd been told in Cairo. The guard burst into laughter, doubling over.

"Egyptians! They are the funniest people alive!" the guard said laughing, and waved Ngozi through. As he walked back to his post, he didn't know that he had missed a call about a report that had come through with the description of an American and a Palestinian who might be trying to get through the border. He sat down outside the little guard shack and lit a cigarette, chuckling over the joke he'd just heard.

CHAPTER 46

On the last day of Hessa's stay at the plantation she, Henry, Petie, and Eddie got up very early to go for a breakfast horseback ride. As they approached the stables, the hands were busy getting the horses saddled and packing everything into saddle bags for the breakfast they would cook during the ride.

Hessa had never ridden a horse, so she was a little concerned about getting on one of the large beasts. Her friends had all ridden before so they assured her there was nothing to it, and that she just needed to show the horse who was boss.

"I know who is boss, and it certainly isn't me," Hessa said with a worried look on her face.

The three boys laughed, but after looking at the fear on her face they realized she wasn't joking. They told her they would stay right with her and that the people leading the trail ride would be right there for her if she got nervous.

She finally decided she needed to be courageous and stop acting like a baby. She walked over to the horse that had been assigned to her, and one of the hands helped her up into the saddle. He spent several minutes giving her instructions on how to handle the horse.

The four were the only guests on the plantation who had signed up for the breakfast ride, and Hessa guessed it was because the mornings had become chilly, and they headed out at six a.m. The guide trotted over to the group and introduced himself as John.

Everyone started out slowly with the horses walking in a single line. Hessa began the ride in the middle of the pack of horses, but eventually trailed the others. When they had ridden for about an hour

Hessa asked if she could make a rest stop. Their guide brought them to a place where they could refill their water bottles and use the facilities.

Henry, Petie, and Eddie got off their horses and stood talking and laughing, teasing each other about their riding skills. Hessa wandered off to find the restroom the guide had pointed out, located beyond a grove of trees.

As she was walking out of the restroom she put her helmet back on, and was busy trying to get the straps clipped under her chin when she heard a noise to her right and looked over.

A large hand grabbed her from behind, and another hand covered her mouth.

"Do not make a sound or you die," a deep voice said.

A second person came up and gagged her as a third person tied her hands behind her back. The largest man threw her over his shoulder, and the group took off running as they made their way through the forest.

⚓

The boys got back on their horses and were waiting for Hessa and their guide to return when they saw John walking out of the trees toward them. He had a concerned look on his face as he walked past his own horse and stopped in front of the three.

"Have you seen Hessa? I was just in the restroom and I thought she was in the ladies room. I came back here, and when I saw she wasn't with you I walked back over there. I called her name a couple of times, but no one answered. After a couple of minutes I walked into the ladies room and called her name again, but no one was in there. Where do you think she went?" the leader said.

The three boys looked at each other, puzzled. They had been together the whole time and hadn't really paid attention when Hessa went to the restroom. She wasn't the type to go wandering off and not tell anyone.

They all went back over to the rest area and looked around for her, calling her name. Becoming increasingly concerned they started looking

338

around for any signs of distress. Then John found a shiny object on the ground—it was an earring.

"Does this look familiar to anyone?" he asked as he picked it up and passed it to the boys.

"Yeah, it's Hessa's. I noticed it this morning when we were at the barn, 'cause I teased her about wearing earrings for a horseback ride," Petie said. His eyes widened as a thought popped into his head. "Do you think Bishara's behind this?"

Henry and Eddie looked at each other and over to John. They quickly told John about Hessa's situation and that she could be in danger. He told them to spread out and look for her, explaining the lay of the land.

He gave each of them a direction to take, and he immediately galloped off in the direction of the only road out of the plantation, realizing that if someone had her, they were on foot and still had a ways to go to get to their car.

Henry had a sinking feeling and felt guilty for letting her wander off alone. "After what we went through in London, how could I think they would stop looking for her?" he said out loud, cursing himself for letting her out of his sight. He tore around on foot near the restroom, looking for any other sign that would help them.

Petie and Eddie had ridden off in different directions to look for Hessa—Petie in the direction of the main plantation house, and Eddie toward the canal. Henry had tied his horse up and continued walking around in the woods looking for a sign that would lead them to her.

John had gotten to the road quickly but was too late in catching up with a small silver car he saw winding around a curve at top speed. He wasn't able to get the license plate number, but noticed it wasn't a South Carolina license plate—it was a dark blue plate with orange writing.

"Delaware," he said to himself, and got back on his horse, taking off at full speed back to the plantation house.

John ran into the main house and over to the front desk. He asked Abigail, the clerk on duty, to get the police on the phone immediately, then went to the office and knocked on the door. The owner, Susannah

339

Margate, told him to come in. Petie was already in the office, and the two were busy making phone calls.

"I just told Abby to call the police," John said.

"Go back and tell her she doesn't need to, John. That was the first thing we did when Petie told me what happened. They're on their way," Susannah said. He told Susannah and Petie about the car he'd seen with the Delaware license plates.

"Okay, John, call the police back and tell them about the license plates. Those men will try and get Hessa out of the country as soon as possible. They need to intercept these guys," Petie said. John called the police once more and gave them the description of the silver compact car, which he guessed was a rental.

A short time later the police arrived and took down everything Petie and John described. The police let them know that they had already dispatched investigators to the car rental companies in the area, and they were keeping watch on the highways.

Petie had also called Anna Volkenburg to let her know what had happened, and asked for Dan Moretti's number, who had been back in America for some time now after Joel's father called him off the job of investigating in Israel. Petie got the number and quickly called Dan to ask what else they should be doing.

Dan told him the men who took Hessa would need to get a passport for her, so they would have to go to the embassy in Washington, D.C. for a copy, or back to Ruth's home to get the original. Dan let Petie know he would get in touch with authorities in Washington to keep an eye out for the men who'd taken Hessa. He would go to Ruth's house himself.

Henry and Eddie returned to the plantation house within a few minutes of one another, and Petie updated them on all they had done to try and intercept Hessa's abductors. Henry went over to a chair in the lobby and sat down, leaning forward with his head in his hands. Petie followed him out and asked him if he was okay.

"This is all my fault, you know. I should've known better than to let Hessa out of our sight. What was I thinking?" Henry said.

340

"What are you talking about? I'm just as much to blame. We should have taken precautions, but how many times have you and I been involved with kidnappings, Henry? Come on, we can't be too hard on ourselves. Don't worry, we'll get her back, Buddy," Petie said, trying to convince himself as well.

Susannah walked into the room several minutes later and told them that the police had found the company that had rented out the silver car they'd spotted.

"Well gentlemen, you were right. The man who rented the car is from Gaza. They're still checking on his background, along with the other men who were with him. The four of them were caught on security cameras getting into the car and driving off the lot," Susannah said. "Very good sleuthing, boys. Now I need to go and let Ruth know what's happened."

Susannah walked past the front desk and told Abby that she would be back shortly. She wasn't anxious to deliver the news to Ruth about her young friend. When she walked up to the guest house and knocked on the door, Ruth didn't answer. Susannah remembered that Ruth had rented a bike and gone to the nature preserve—she'd helped her make the arrangements.

Who knows when she'll be back? I just hope we don't have two missing people at the end of the day, she thought to herself, and walked back to the main house.

⚜

Dan Moretti was on the road out of Boston, headed toward Connecticut within a half-hour of receiving the call from Petie. While on the road he'd received more information on the men who'd abducted Hessa.

Police found the rental car abandoned in Florence, South Carolina. They guessed the men might go to Florence to catch a train going north. The train would arrive in Fayetteville shortly, so the police would be waiting at the station there.

As the train pulled in to Fayetteville, police were positioned around the station, and others searched the inside of the train, but there was no sign of the four men or Hessa on board. They also searched the car dealerships in the Florence area, and for anyone who had purchased a car with cash.

When Dan was just about to Ruth's house in Connecticut he received a call saying a car had in fact been purchased with cash at a dealership within five miles of where the rental car had been abandoned, but they hadn't finished the paperwork—they just got in the car and took off. The police got the description of the car and began a new search, putting out an A.P.B. along the border of South Carolina and into North Carolina.

⚓

As Ruth returned to the plantation she went into the main house to thank Susannah for making the arrangements for the bicycle tour of the preserve. She walked in the door and Abby intercepted her, asking her to wait while she called Susannah, who was somewhere on the other side of the property.

Susannah showed up a short time later, out of breath with a worried look on her face. She explained the situation to Ruth, who blamed herself for bringing Hessa and putting her in danger, just because she wanted Hessa to see her friends.

"Oh God, I'll never forgive myself if something happens to that girl," she said. "This is my fault! I'm to blame for this mess. Susannah, I'm so sorry I dragged you into this. I don't know what I was thinking."

"You all need to stop blaming yourselves for what's happened," Susannah said. "You had the best of intentions in trying to show Hessa a nice weekend. The boys feel just as miserable as you, so I say we just pray that these men will be found and that Hessa will be fine."

The two women walked into Ruth's office to stay close to the phone and to continue praying for Hessa's safe return.

342

CHAPTER 47

Hessa sat in silence as she and her father's four men made their way to Baltimore in the minivan they'd purchased in Florence, South Carolina. Fatik Nidal had made a phone call the previous day to the Palestinian Liberation Organization Mission, located in Washington, D.C.

He had told them about Husaam Bishara's daughter, who was visiting in America. He explained that she had lost her passport, and asked if he could have someone meet them at the Emirates Airline ticket counter in Baltimore the next day so they would be able to make their flight.

He spoke with the Communications Officer, who told Fatik that he would be able to have the passport ready the next day in plenty of time for their flight. Fatik assured the officer that he would take care of all expenses incurred.

Hessa's mind began to swim with ideas of how to escape. She would be in a very crowded area, so she doubted her captors would open fire in the middle of an airport. As the car raced down the highway, Hessa planned what she would do when she entered the security checkpoint.

She didn't utter a word the whole trip, and her father's men were tight-lipped about their plans for her. She assumed they would be taking her back to her father, who would discipline her severely, or worse.

She knew he would force her to marry Quasim immediately, if he hadn't already cancelled the wedding. If the wedding was in fact called off, she knew her fate would be unimaginable. She shuddered at the thought of being at the receiving end of her father's fury because of her rebellion.

As they crossed the North Carolina border into Virginia they stopped for gas, and one of the men brought snacks out for everyone. He tossed a soda and bag of potato chips to Hessa, who didn't touch them.

As they drove through Virginia, she finally nodded off for a short time out of exhaustion. Hessa awoke with a start when they entered the D.C. area and had to slow down for traffic.

It was after five o'clock when they finally arrived at the Baltimore Airport. They parked in a long-term lot and shuttled over to the entrance of the airline. The men surrounded Hessa as they walked. They were all so much larger than she, it was nearly impossible to see her in the middle of the group. As they walked toward the ticketing area, the agent from the PLO Mission approached them, recognizing the description Fatik had given him of their group.

Fatik took the passport from the agent and paid him for his expenses. He thanked the man for making the trip to the airport, and the agent turned to leave. As Fatik and his men headed to the ticket counter, he noticed a man approaching them, with three others behind him. As the man got closer Fatik spoke quickly to his men and the four of them turned and walked rapidly to the door, holding Hessa by her arms.

As they exited the front doors Fatik looked back. The man was still following him, and this time he was talking on the phone. Soon two other men approached them from another direction. They walked faster, and Hessa was nearly lifted off the ground as they hurried outside to a waiting taxi.

"Move, little fool! You will never escape alive—your father will see to that!" Fatik yelled at Hessa.

As they opened the door to the taxi Hessa dug her heels into the ground and quickly bent forward. She ripped her arms straight down and sat on the ground with a thud. She began to scream at the top of her lungs, and the group of men, looking around and realizing they were being closed in on, left her on the sidewalk as one of the men comandeered the taxi. He threw the taxi driver on the ground and tore off, crashing through the exit gate.

344

A tall man in a navy blazer and khaki pants hurried to her and helped her off the ground as four other plain clothes police officers and two uniformed officers jumped into squad cars and followed the taxi.

"Are you okay?" the man asked.

"I'm a little shaken, but not hurt," Hessa replied.

"You're a brave young lady, pulling off a stunt like that with four big men surrounding you. Kudos to you," he said.

"What is kudos?" Hessa asked.

The man laughed and led Hessa inside the terminal. He turned to her and said, "My name is Robert Williams. I'm with the Baltimore Police Department. Dan Moretti contacted me. He told me about your situation, so I went over to the PLO Mission. They let me know they'd had a phone call from someone asking to get a passport for you. We checked the airlines and found your reservation with Emirates."

"Thank you so much for helping me. I was beginning to feel safe here in America. I suppose I should have been more careful," Hessa said.

"Well, you're safe now. The police will round those men up, and they won't be bothering you again," Robert said. "Now I think we'd better make a phone call to the hotel down in South Carolina to let your friends know you're okay. You can use my phone, and then I'll call Mr. Moretti, who's at Ruth's house in Connecticut right now."

"My goodness, you certainly took care of all possibilities, didn't you?" Hessa asked, and took the phone Robert offered her. She dialed Ruth's cell phone, who answered immediately.

"Hello?" she answered.

"Ruth, it's Hessa! I'm all right," she said.

"Hessa! Oh, thank God you're safe! I'm so glad to hear your voice. Where *are* you?" Ruth asked.

"I'm in Baltimore. The men who took me work for my father. They were going to take me back to Israel," she replied.

"Oh honey, you must have been terrified. My heart has been in my throat all day! I should never have put you or your friends in danger like this.

"Ruth, you did something for me out of kindness. I was having a wonderful time until this morning," she laughed.

"I'm sure glad *you* can laugh about this," she said shakily.

"Remember what you often say to me, Ruth. Things always happen for a reason. Those men needed to be caught, and I think it would have been easier for them to get me out of the country if they had taken me from your home.

"Just think, your house is very close to an international airport, and my passport was in your home. Yes, I say our being in South Carolina was for a very good reason," Hessa said.

"I didn't think of that. Well, I'm just glad you're safe. I love you like a daughter, Hessa. I've enjoyed having you live with me," Ruth said, and then changed the subject. "By the way, where are you going to stay until I'm home tomorrow? All your things are down here with me."

"Let me put Mr. Williams on the phone. Maybe you should talk to him about arrangements."

She handed the phone to Robert, who told Ruth he would take Hessa to a nearby hotel, and would call the airline to get her flight changed.

Robert took Hessa to an airport hotel and got her checked in. He gave her his phone number in case she had any concerns. He also worked out her passport issues with the airline. After Hessa got the key to her room, Robert took her to get something to eat at the hotel restaurant. She was famished, and had a large bowl of pasta for dinner.

After dinner he walked her to her room and said, "Make sure to call if you need anything. I made arrangements for your shuttle to the airport tomorrow morning. I've told the hotel staff that you'll need assistance, so you just need to call, and they'll make sure you get there okay. Here you go." He handed her a piece of paper with the hotel manager and concierge's names and phone extensions.

She thanked Robert, said goodbye, and went into her room. She took a shower, feeling filthy from riding horses and sitting in between two big, sweaty men in the car for over eight hours. She got under the covers and breathed a sigh of relief, immediately falling asleep from exhaustion, thinking about how wonderful these people were who cared so much about her.

❈❈❈

The next morning Ruth said goodbye to Henry, Petie, and Eddie, whose flights would be later in the day. They had spent the previous evening together, and Ruth filled them in on everything Hessa had been through. As they parted company, Ruth promised to keep them all apprised of Hessa's situation, and would have Hessa communicate with them when she was able.

Ruth met Hessa in Baltimore, and the two flew home together from there. They got into the airport late in the afternoon, and when they arrived home Ruth ordered dinner to be delivered. The evening was cool, so Ruth made a fire in the fireplace and set the coffee table in the living room for dinner, and put pillows on the floor for the two to sit on.

When dinner was delivered the two went into the living room and dished up their Chinese food, chatting away nonstop, with Hessa going into more detail about her ordeal. It felt good to be back at Ruth's house. School would start shortly, and Hessa wanted desperately to try and get her life back to normal, and to focus on her studies.

Later that evening as she lay in bed, the reality of what had happened in the last couple of days struck her. She wondered if she would ever feel completely safe again, or if she would always be looking over her shoulder, suspicious of anyone who looked her way. She prayed for peace from the fear that had overtaken her.

Her thoughts drifted to Joel, and memories of him once again made their way into Hessa's heart. She wondered what had ever happened to him, and if he was still alive somewhere in the world. So many months had passed since she'd seen him. It felt like a lifetime since they had been together. Had it all just been a beautiful dream?

Apprehension for her mother creeped in once again, as it often did when she was alone at night with her thoughts. Her worries tormented her

347

about her mother, whom she feared had been killed for her disobedience and assumed betrayal to her husband.

She loved living with Ruth, but the deep ache in her heart for her beloved mother wouldn't go away. Tears streamed down her cheeks as she thought about what her mother's last moments on earth may have been like, and Hessa hoped she hadn't suffered too much before she died.

The pain of losing both Joel and her mother gnawed at her. It felt as though her heart had been torn from her, and the more she speculated about them, the more distraught she became, believing she had lost the two people she loved most in the world.

"There will never be another you, Joel," she tearfully whispered, then turned on her side and curled up into a fetal position. "Oh Mama, I miss you…I'm so scared…Mama," she said softly in jagged breaths, and cried herself to sleep.

CHAPTER 48

"Mr. Bishara sir, I am very sorry, but your wife and the American have gotten away. I went to the bank, leaving them at my apartment with my wife. When I returned I saw them running down the street, and they slipped down an alley and out of sight," Jabari said.

"You did not follow them?" Bishara replied angrily.

"Yes, I drove around for hours looking for them. I know the streets of Cairo like the back of my own hand. It is as if they disappeared into thin air," Jabari said.

"You need to get in contact with the authorities and let them know those two are in Egypt illegally," Bishara said. "Let the police track them down."

"That is a good idea, unless…" Jabari trailed off.

"What? Tell me at once!" Bishara demanded.

"They were able to get into Egypt with no problems. Perhaps they were able to get out as easily," Jabari said.

"How long has it been since you saw them?" Bishara asked.

"Four or five hours, I suppose," Jabari replied.

"They could still be in Egypt. Call the authorities—have them contact the border guards! Do not let them get out of the country!" Bishara shouted.

"I will be in Egypt as quickly as I can. I tell you, Jabari, you had better produce my wife and the American, or there will be trouble," and he hung up.

"What have I gotten myself into? My greed could get me killed," Jabari said nervously, and picked up the phone to call the police.

⚓

The rumbling of the truck lulled Joel and Muna to sleep. Muna leaned on Joel's shoulder, and Joel rested his head against Muna's. Ngozi had stopped several hours earlier to fill his tank and get them a bite to eat. The heat was almost unbearable, but Ngozi assured Joel and Muna that it would cool off as the sun set. Just as he'd said, the Libyan Desert cooled as the sun went down.

There wasn't much to see as they drove along the barren, dusty plains. The heat and lack of exercise had worn Joel and Muna out. Now that it was after midnight they slept on, bouncing as the old truck hit potholes and bumps in the road. At about three in the morning, Ngozi became so sleepy his eyes wouldn't stay open. He pulled to the side of the road for a short nap.

The sun peaked over the horizon several hours later, awakening Ngozi. He looked across the landscape and saw a troubling view—a dust storm had begun, and the wind was whipping the sand into a frenzied mass of dark swirling clouds.

Ngozi quickly started the engine and drove as fast as he could while he was still able to see the road. Before he knew it, the dust and sand had clouded his vision to the point where he couldn't see more than a few feet in front of him. Joel and Muna awoke and asked what had happened.

"This is what is called a 'Gibli'. It is a strong dust storm which is very common in Libya. Our country is mostly barren desert. The wind comes up from the south and creates the storm. It can last for several days. Let us hope that this one passes through quickly."

The three drove along at a snail's pace for several miles. Dust collected in the engine, which finally gave out. Ngozi pulled to the side of the road outside of a town called An Nawfaliyah. He looked over at his two passengers, who returned his glance with worry.

"I am sorry my friends, but the storm is so strong there isn't anything left to do but wait it out. I will go to the back of the truck for food and water. I believe I have a blanket back there as well. It will get very cold tonight if we have to spend the night in this place," Ngozi said, and got out of the truck.

As Ngozi searched the truck bed for supplies, Joel and Muna looked at each other with lost and confused expressions. They had been together for so long it was as if they could read each other's minds. They knew they would just have to trust that they would be delivered to safety eventually.

Ngozi returned with the supplies and passed dates, nuts and leka'ek to Joel and Muna. They shared a bottle of water, which he had gotten from an ice chest where all the ice had since melted, but the water was not yet hot. The three sat in silence eating their food slowly, trying to make each bite last.

After their meal, Ngozi pulled out a pack of cards and asked if they would like to play 'Romeeno'. He offered to teach them, and his passengers were more than happy to do something that would keep them occupied. As Ngozi explained the rules of the game, Joel's face lit up.

"This is just like Gin Rummy! We play this game in America," he said.

"Then I expect you to be a formidable contender of Romeeno, Joel," Ngozi said, and continued explaining the game to Muna.

The three played the game for several hours, laughing and talking as they played, with Muna winning most of the games, and Joel teasing her about having beginner's luck. The day wore on with no sign of the dust storm letting up.

As the next day turned into evening, Ngozi made the short trip to the back of his truck once more to see what food he could find. He came back coughing and wiping the sand off his face. He told Joel and Muna that they would be out of food by tomorrow.

"We need to pray this storm lets up. I only hope we can get the truck started once the weather calms down," Ngozi said, and passed a few

351

dates and Leka'ek to his friends. They shared a small amount of water and then settled down for the night.

The next morning the storm had cleared. Ngozi got out and lifted the hood of the truck. He tried to clear out the dust and sand from the engine as best he could, and asked Joel to try and start it. The engine didn't make a sound. He went back to work, tinkering with everything he could think of to get it to turn over, but the truck refused to start. He walked back and climbed into the cab.

"I have tried everything I know, but nothing is working. We will have to try and make it on foot to An Nawfaliyah...we are only about four miles from town," Ngozi said.

The three got out of the truck and started their journey into town as the sun began to beat down on them. Several hours later they walked into the outskirts of An Nawfaliyah, where they saw a small petrol station. A man was sitting outside a run-down building which was little more than a shack. Ngozi approached the man and spoke to him in Arabic, explaining their situation.

A few moments later he walked inside the little shack, indicating for Joel and Muna to follow him. He explained to them that the man had told him there wasn't an auto repair place close by. The man gave verbal directions to Ngozi of where a repair shop was located. They would have to walk another mile to the other side of town to get help.

Ngozi bought a few snacks for them and they continued on their way. Muna became weary when they had walked about a half mile across town, so Joel had her climb on his back, hoping his own strength would hold out. The three were becoming weak from the lack of food and water over the last couple of days, but the snacks Ngozi purchased helped them gain a little strength.

As their energy wore down, it took them almost an hour to walk the mile to the repair shop. When they finally arrived, Ngozi spotted a man inside the building, which looked as though it was ready to cave in. He explained their problem to the man, and pointed in the direction of where the truck had broken down. The man looked back and forth from Ngozi to Joel and Muna, and told them he would return shortly.

Ngozi peaked inside the small shop and saw that the man had a television set inside the building, and he was watching the news. When the man didn't return for several minutes, Ngozi became increasingly suspicious.

After almost ten minutes the man came back with a smile on his face and told them he would be happy to take them to the truck, and would fix it for them. As the three of them walked to the man's truck, Ngozi spotted another man peeking out from the side of the building. He quickly disappeared when he saw that Ngozi had spotted him.

"I do not feel good about this," Ngozi whispered to Joel as they followed the man to his truck. "For some reason I think he knows about you two. We need to leave right away."

Ngozi thanked the man for his time, and told him they were hungry and needed to get something to eat, and then they would return. The man waved his hands in protest at Ngozi and told him they needed to go right away because he wouldn't be able to fix the truck in the dark.

"We will take our chances, and if we get back too late, we will return tomorrow," Ngozi told the man.

The three turned and started to walk in the opposite direction, and the man shouted after them in Arabic, "You are going in the wrong direction! Come back this way, and I will show you to a restaurant!"

Ngozi waved as he continued walking, and told Joel and Muna to pick up the pace. The three walked away as quickly as possible from the man, who had gotten into his truck to come after them. Once again Joel and Muna found themselves running to get away.

The three ran down a tiny street which was too narrow for motor vehicles, and after running through several small passageways, they came to a marketplace full of vendors selling their wares. Ngozi pulled Joel and Muna aside and sat down against a building behind one of the vendors' tables.

"Joel, do not speak at all, do you understand?" Ngozi said, and Joel nodded.

The vendor noticed them and walked over, asking why they were sitting behind his stand. He was short and very heavy with a jovial face, dressed in a long white shirt with a black vest and cap.

"We came into a bit of trouble and are trying to find a way out of town. My truck broke down, you see," Ngozi said.

"You are in luck, my friend. I am on my way to Tripoli after we close down the market for today. If you are going that way, I will be leaving in about an hour. I only need to break down my stand," the man said.

"That is precisely where we were headed! Thank you, thank you!" Ngozi exclaimed. "My friends and I will be happy to help you take your stand down and load it into your vehicle."

The four proceeded to fold the table and take down the awning that the man had set up to keep the sun out. The stand was full of colorful vegetables and fruits, which the man offered to the three strangers. They gratefully accepted, and Ngozi offered him the last of his money, which he waved away. A short time later they climbed into the man's truck and the four drove off toward Tripoli.

"My name is Ali," the man said. "What are your names?"

"I am Ngozi from Tripoli, and these are my friends, Yo'el and uh, Du'a," Ngozi said.

Joel remained quiet with Ngozi answering for him, explaining that Joel was mute. Muna had little to say, only nodding or smiling when Ali asked her a question. Ngozi tried to get Ali's attention away from his friends by asking him about himself.

"My family is from An Nawfaliyah, but I have a sister who lives with her husband in Tripoli, where I occasionally go to visit. Tripoli can be frightening at times, but is a very exciting place, do you agree?" Ali asked.

"Oh yes, agreed," Ngozi replied. "It is my home, but I travel back and forth to Cairo on a regular basis. I think my truck may have taken its last trip to Egypt. I would like to enjoy taking some time off in Tripoli while I look for a truck to replace the old one," Ngozi said, smiling.

The two men continued talking into the night as they drove along at breakneck speed. Ali proved to be a very aggressive driver, and Ngozi found himself grabbing hold of the dashboard more than once. Joel and Muna slept from all the walking they had done, and being in the hot sun that had beaten down on them all day. Ali's erratic driving didn't seem to bother them a bit.

Shortly before midnight they approached Tripoli. Ali slowed down as they got closer to the city, and began looking in his rearview mirror every couple of minutes. Ngozi noticed his edgy behavior and asked what was wrong.

"I think we are being followed, my friend. Is there something you wish to tell me?" Ali asked.

"Only that we met a man acting very strangely in An Nawfaliyah. He seemed to want to do us harm, so we tried to get away from him," Ngozi said.

"That is why you were hiding behind my stand?" Ali asked.

"Yes, but I did not think he would follow us to Tripoli."

"Well, I guess we had better try to get rid of him. It is a good thing I know this city so well," Ali said, and took off like a shot.

Ali drove like mad around the outside of the city, trying to lose the car he believed was following them. Ngozi gave him instructions to where he lived, but Ali didn't feel it would be safe for them just yet. He wove in and out of traffic, up and down streets all through the city until he felt they had lost the car he'd seen following them for at least the last two hours.

He finally pulled up in front of Ngozi's apartment and came to a sharp halt. Joel and Muna had been awakened from Ali's crazy driving inside the city, and shot forward as Ali slammed on the brakes. Ngozi thanked Ali for taking them home and shook his hand, patting him on the shoulder.

Muna thanked Ali in Arabic, and Joel nodded his head and smiled. The four got out of the car and ran to the building as Ngozi pulled his keys

355

out of his pocket. As they entered the first-floor apartment, he slammed the door behind them.

"There is nothing more we can do today," Ngozi said to his friends as they all tried to catch their breath. "Tomorrow we will try to get you to the American Embassy, and see if we can get you safely home," Ngozi said.

His wife rushed out of the bedroom as she heard the door slam, and Ngozi quickly introduced her to the strangers he had brought home. He explained what they had been through and that they needed to help Joel and Muna get to America.

"It looks as though you all need a shower. I will show you to the bathroom, and if you do not mind, we have a small spare bedroom you can share for the night. Our sons are grown and no longer live at home. There are two beds you can use," Ngozi's wife said.

"Thank you very much," Joel said, as Ngozi led him down a small, narrow hallway to give him some of his own clothes to wear.

Ngozi's wife Aman led Muna to the bathroom and had her wait until she returned with a tunic and pants. She handed the colorful and beautifully embroidered clothes to Muna, who looked at the clothes she'd been handed, and then looked back at her hostess.

"I cannot take these beautiful things. They are far too valuable for me to wear," Muna said.

"Of course you can take them. Look at me! Do you think I could fit into this small tunic? I have kept it for many years just because it is beautiful, but I have not been able to wear it because I have become so fat!" Aman laughed.

"You are only saying that because you are being kind. I am sure you would fit into these clothes as easily as I," Muna said.

"Take them, Muna, I insist," Aman said, and walked out of the bathroom, closing the door behind her.

Muna hopped into the shower and stood under the hot stream, smiling as the water ran down her body. The heat loosened her tense muscles. All the aches she had from sleeping in a sitting position and

356

walking for miles in the intense heat seemed to melt away. She finally turned off the water and got out of the shower. Aman had placed a sleeping tunic on the counter of the small bathroom with some clean underclothes.

As she entered the tiny bedroom she would be occupying for the night, Aman was turning down the covers and airing out the room. All the windows were open, and a ceiling fan was quickly moving the air around, freshening up the small room that had been used primarily for storage.

Joel had gone in to shower, but before he went in Ngozi told him not to shave his beard. He warned that Joel needed to fit in as much as possible, and having heavy stubble helped him to blend in. He handed Joel a long white shirt and black pants. Ngozi was a bit shorter than him, but he was grateful he would finally have something clean to put on.

When he finished his shower and got dressed he walked into the bedroom where Muna was already fast asleep. He made up his mind that he wasn't going to worry about their next step. He was overjoyed that he would actually be sleeping in a bed for the first time in months. He climbed under the covers and instantly fell asleep.

CHAPTER 49

The sound of a car's engine being turned off in the street woke Joel very early the next morning. He got out of bed and tip-toed over to the window, peering out of a crack in the curtains. Two men had gotten out of the car, and were walking toward Ngozi's apartment building. There wasn't yet enough light for him to be able to make out who they were.

Joel walked over to the bed where Muna was still asleep. He leaned down and whispered her name. She awoke with a start, looking up at Joel in a haze of confusion.

"What is the matter, Joel?" she asked.

"We need to get out of here. I just saw two men drive up," Joel said. "I don't know who they are, but..."

Joel was interrupted by a knock on the bedroom door. He went to open it, and Ngozi was standing there with an agitated look on his face.

"What's going on?" Joel asked.

"I hear steps approaching. They may be the ones who followed us last night. Climb out the window and cross the street," Ngozi said quickly.

He turned as he heard a knock at the front door and then he ran to the window and pointed to an alley across the street lined with garbage cans.

"Hide behind those cans and I will be there as soon as I am able! I need to borrow my neighbor's car somehow. Go now!" he said, and helped Muna out the window. Joel grabbed their things and followed her quickly as Ngozi walked slowly to the front door. As he saw the two disappear from sight he opened the door.

"May I help you?" he asked as he rubbed his eyes.

"We are looking for two people who are in Libya illegally. We were informed that they were travelling with you from Egypt," the man said.

"I had two people with me, but I was not aware they were here illegally," Ngozi said.

"You realize that if you know where they are and we find you have been lying that you will go to prison?" the man asked.

"Yes sir, I realize that. I am sorry that I cannot help you. I dropped the two people off in An Nawfaliyah. I do not know where they are," Ngozi replied, and began to close the door.

The man pushed the door back open. "We will keep an eye on you. You have been reported as an accomplice in smuggling them out of Egypt and into Libya. One of them is the wife of Hamas leader Husaam Bishara, and he is very worried about her. The other is an American who has broken the law in several countries. There is a warrant out for his arrest. Do you have anything to say now?" the man asked.

"No, I am very sorry. I do not know where they are," Ngozi said simply.

"We will be in touch," the man said finally, and the two turned and walked away.

Ngozi shut the door and went to the kitchen where there was a small window facing the street. He shakily peered out from behind the curtains and saw the two men standing in front of the apartment by their car. The one who had done the talking was on his cell phone. Aman walked in as Ngozi was at the window and asked her husband of his plans.

"I tell you, my wife, we need a miracle. There is no way I will be able to leave this apartment with those two watching me. We need to get to Joel and Muna across the street, so I may have to ask you to do something very risky," Ngozi said.

"You know that I will do anything to help them. Just tell me what to do," Aman said.

The two prayed they would be able to get Joel and Muna out of the country and safely to embassies that would help them. He then told his wife his plan to have her go to the market. She would be a diversion for him to get across the street.

"I know this is a dangerous thing for me to ask you, Aman. I do not want to put you in a situation that you cannot handle," Ngozi said.

"Of course I can handle it! I will call my friends and we will walk to the market together. There is safety in numbers, and God will be with us. Do not worry, Ngozi, God will be with you too," Aman said.

Joel and Muna ran to the end of the alley across the street and waited behind a large mound of garbage piled on top of garbage cans. The air was still at this hour of the morning, and the streets were quiet, with the occasional car or truck passing by.

Joel heard the men's voices as they stood by their car, but he didn't dare venture out to see who they were. The two sat in silence as they waited for Ngozi's opportunity to find them and get them to safety.

"Nadeem!" Ngozi said suddenly.

"What about Nadeem?" Aman asked.

"Of course! Why did we not think about him before? He can help us!" He picked up the phone and dialed his friend. Nadeem was a commercial fisherman from Tunisia and a fellow believer. He explained the situation to his friend and asked for any ideas of how to get Joel and Muna to safety.

"I do not believe we will be able to get them to their embassies in Tripoli. They will be followed, and Muna will be sent back to Israel. Who knows what will become of her there, my brother?" Ngozi said pleadingly.

"You caught me just in time. I am in Tripoli, but my crew and I are leaving this morning to go back to Tunis. I will be happy to take your friends with us," Nadeem replied.

"What if there is no Palestinian embassy in Tunis? What then?" Ngozi asked.

361

Nadeem thought for a moment, and then replied, "It does not matter, brother. I have a friend who I have spoken to you about before. He is the President of Voies Aeriennes Tunisiennes. His name is Rashid Guerrero. He has been a very good friend to me. He has provided many contacts in Europe for my business," Nadeem said.

"He can fly your friends to safety. He is the best of men," Nadeem said. "I am sure he will be able to get them to their embassies with the contacts he has."

"I thank you, Nadeem. You are a true friend. These people have nowhere to go, and have been trying to get to America for several months. The American boy has been away from home for close to a year now. His family must have given up on ever finding him," Ngozi said.

"I promise you that with God's help we will get him and his companion home," Nadeem said. "My men are making repairs to the boat as we speak, and have told me it should be ready by eight a.m. I will wait for you there."

Ngozi thanked Nadeem and promised to have them at the dock on time. He paced back and forth, periodically walking to the window to peek out and check on whether the men had left. They seemed to be camped outside his home, so he and his wife were forced to stay inside, keeping watch.

The clock ticked by as Ngozi continued his pacing, stopping only to sit down for the morning meal. As soon as he was finished, he jumped up and walked back to the window to peer out, only to find the men still standing outside, looking up at his building and talking to each other.

"You will drive me out of my mind with your pacing. Sit down, you are making me nervous. Better yet, come and help wash these dishes," Aman said.

Ngozi walked over and picked up a towel, absent mindedly drying the dishes she had given him. Several minutes went by and he heard an engine start up. He ran to the window and saw the car disappearing from sight.

"This could be a trap. We need to wait a little longer, and then you can go to the market. When you join the women, tell Laila we need to borrow their car. Ask her to go back home as if she forgot something, and have her put the keys in the car. Watch to see if anyone is following you, and I will try to get across the street when you distract them," Ngozi said.

When Ngozi thought it was safe for her to leave, his wife picked up her basket for the market and walked out the door. She met with two of their neighbors and walked across the street, where three other women were waiting for them. As the women made their way to the market, Ngozi saw a man suddenly emerge and begin to follow them.

He waited a while longer and then left the apartment himself. He walked outside and strolled along slowly, looking around for anyone who appeared suspicious. He turned and began walking in the opposite direction of where Joel and Muna were hidden across the street. As he turned the corner to his apartment building he looked behind him—no one was there.

He continued on and made his way around the entire apartment building until he ended up where he'd started. When he saw the street was empty he jumped in his neighbor's car, and turned the key that had been left in the ignition for him. He drove down the street, passing the alley where his friends were hidden.

He went to the end of the next block and turned down the street where the alley was and jumped out, running to the stacks of garbage he'd told Joel and Muna to hide in. As he approached, Joel and Muna jumped up and ran with him to the car. Ngozi roared off toward the fishing docks where his friend Nadeem would be waiting. As he drove through the streets of Tripoli, he explained to Joel and Muna where he was taking them.

"You followed a woman? I cannot believe what I am hearing! The man is the one who was helping them, not the woman! You fools! Do I have to find them myself?" Bishara yelled, and slammed down the phone.

363

He was at the end of his rope. The group of his men who had gone to America had been arrested for attempting to kidnap his daughter against her will, and for stealing a taxi. Now Jabari had led him on a wild goose chase through Egypt and Libya, and the next group of men he sent to Tripoli had followed a worthless woman to a marketplace. For all he knew, Joel and Muna had also left *this* country by now.

"Why do they continue to elude me? Why have the cleverest of my men become a flock of idiots?" Bishara asked himself aloud. He realized he would have to go to Tripoli himself in order to track Joel and Muna down. He called the leader of his group in Tripoli to let him know he was on his way there, and to continue looking for his wife and the American.

⁂

Ngozi pulled up to the large boat where Nadeem and his men were furiously working to prepare the boat for departure. He led Joel and Muna onto the boat, and the three embraced as Joel and Muna thanked Ngozi profusely for his help.

"We'll never forget you or your wife, Ngozi. Thank you for stopping for us and risking your own life to get us to safety. I promise I'll repay you someday," Joel said, and hugged his friend.

"No need to repay me. It was a pleasure, Joel. Our journey together was a bit frightening, but very rewarding. You see? You and Muna are on your way home! Thanks be to God!" Ngozi exclaimed.

Muna thanked Ngozi once more, and the two waved as he walked off the boat. He got back into his car and drove off, disappearing from sight.

Nadeem welcomed Joel and Muna aboard the large fishing boat headed for Tunis, and each were given a pair of overalls to put on. Nadeem showed them around the boat and told them he was going to put them to work on the trip to Tunis. He then introduced them to the rest of the crew.

Joel was surprised at how Muna acclimated herself to the roughness of the sea. The boat dipped and tossed as it roared along at a

364

much higher speed than Joel would have thought possible for a boat its size. The men explained the many types of exotic fish they generally caught, and why their business was in such high demand.

Nadeem approached Joel and Muna as they helped the men sort through fish they had caught earlier that morning. "How do you like it so far?" he asked.

"I have never been on a boat this large—it is quite exhilarating!" Muna replied. "Why do you have a Tunisian flag flying on your boat?"

"My boat is registered in Tunisia, but I also have an agreement with Libya to fish off their coasts. Tunisia does not allow foreign vessels to fish off their coasts, so that is my home port," Nadeem explained.

When Nadeem was finally able to take a break from his duties he asked Joel and Muna to go below deck so he could speak with them. Nadeem motioned for his passengers to sit down at a table near the galley. He told them about his friend Rashid with whom he'd made contact earlier that day. Rashid was in Rome and wouldn't be back in Tunis until the next day.

"He told me he will make the contacts to get the paperwork started for your passports. When we arrive in Tunis he will get your signatures and fax the documents to the embassies in Rome. He will also make the flight arrangements to get you to Rome where you will be able to pick up your passports. I believe you and Miss Muna will be on your way to America in just a few days, Mr. Joel," Nadeem said.

"I can't believe it!" Joel exclaimed. "After all this time, I might finally be going home."

"Do not worry, my friend. I can assure you that you are as good as home with Rashid's help," Nadeem said.

Joel and Muna looked at each other, barely able to contain their excitement. Muna grabbed Joel's hands and jumped up and down like a child, squealing with delight. He hugged her tightly and twirled her around until they were both dizzy. They collapsed back into their seats, laughing and hugging one another as some of the crew looked on, confused but smiling.

365

The three made their way back to the deck of the boat where the crew had Joel and Muna pitch in and help with small tasks to keep them occupied for the remainder of the journey. By the time they stopped to make a delivery and refuel along the way, the trip ended up taking over ten hours.

When they pulled into port in Tunis the crew took an hour to clean the boat and gather their belongings. The night crew would arrive shortly to begin packing the fish and delivering them to markets and restaurants all over Tunis. Some of the more exotic fish would be flown to Rome the next day.

Nadeem, Joel, and Muna walked off the boat and to his car. They drove the short distance to his home through narrow streets lined with flowers and overgrown vines. They were very surprised when he pulled up to a large rectangular white-washed home with blue shuttered windows.

On the front of the house was an enormous façade, which had windows and rectangles painted on it in the same colors as the shutters. It had a spectacular view of the Mediterranean, and the house was surrounded by exotic flowers and trees.

Nadeem led his guests up the walk from the driveway to the back of the house. His wife, who was French, ran out to greet them.

"Bonsoir!" She cried. "I am so glad you are home! And now you must introduce me to your friends."

"Joel and Muna, this is my wife, Clotilde. Clotilde, this is Joel from America, and Muna, from Israel. They will be staying with us until tomorrow morning. My dear, it is late and we are famished. Would you have anything left from dinner for us to eat?" Nadeem asked.

"Of course! We roasted a beautiful lamb with vegetables and rice. The children did not eat much of the meat or vegetables—mostly rice, you know? Come in and I will show you to your room, Muna," she said.

They went into the house, which to their surprise was full of adults and children, all laughing and talking. The children were running around after one another and playing.

"My home is large for a reason, Joel and Muna. I have two children who still live with my wife and I, and they now have children of their own, as you can see. Clotilde and I have seven grandchildren!

"There is a small addition in the back where my oldest son lives with his wife and three children, and my daughter also lives here with her child. There is never a moment of peace, but we would not have it any other way!" Nadeem chuckled.

Clotilde led Muna upstairs to show her a small room in the back of the house. She explained that it had been a maid's quarters many years ago before they owned the home, but now she mostly used it as a sewing room.

"I am sorry I do not have anything larger for you, but it is clean, and the bed is comfortable," Clotilde said.

"Thank you for your kindness in having us," Muna said.

"You may wash in the bathroom down the hall, and then meet us downstairs in a few minutes for dinner," Clotilde said, and closed the door to the room.

Muna sat down on the bed, and her tense muscles instantly relaxed. She then lay back on the bed, thinking to rest for just a moment before washing for dinner, but she fell asleep instantly.

Clotilde prepared the dinner as Nadeem introduced his family to Joel. The children took an instant liking to him, and asked if he would play games with them.

"Why don't you all go upstairs and start getting ready for bed? Mr. Joel is very tired from travelling all day and needs to eat now. Joel, would you mind going upstairs to let Muna know that dinner is ready?" Clotilde asked.

Joel walked upstairs and found the door at the end of the house where Clotilde said Muna was staying. He saw the door was ajar, so he peeked around when he didn't hear anything. Muna was fast asleep, and he didn't have the heart to wake her. He shut the door and turned to go back downstairs.

As they were eating dinner, their friend Rashid knocked on the back door. Nadeem ushered him in and introduced him to Joel.

"You know, I have watched the stories about you on television. The news of you missing has reached us, even here in Tunis. But we need to keep your presence here quiet. You have come so far, it would be a shame to have someone find you," Rashid said, looking Joel up and down.

He continued, "The photo I saw of you is very different from how you now look, however. It is a good thing you have not shaved your beard. You fit right in with anyone in North Africa!" Rashid said.

"I feel a little scruffy, but I guess I can wait to shave until I get back to the States. Rashid Guerrero...that's an interesting name," Joel said.

"I am from Spain originally, but my mother is Egyptian. Now young Joel, I have the papers for you to sign. We will need to have your friend sign as well. Is she here?"

"I'll take them up to her," Joel said, and walked upstairs.

He went into Muna's room, feeling badly that he had to wake her. He walked over and whispered her name. She awoke with a start and apologized for falling asleep.

"Did I keep everyone waiting for dinner?" she asked.

"No, I didn't have the heart to wake you, so I just let you sleep. Rashid is downstairs waiting for us to sign the papers for our passports. I'm sorry Muna, but I need to have you sign them," Joel said, and held out the papers and a pen for her to sign. "Are you hungry?"

"I am more sleepy than hungry. I think I will just go back to sleep, and you can wake me in the morning when it is time to leave," she said.

Muna signed the papers and gave them back to Joel. He walked out of her room, closing the door behind him. When he entered the kitchen, he handed the papers to Rashid. He thanked the stranger for helping people he didn't even know, and would possibly never see again.

"So why should I not do a kindness for you? It is my honor," Rashid said. "I will come by first thing tomorrow morning to take you to the airport myself. I need to get these documents faxed this evening so they will be at the consulate tomorrow morning. I only hope this will work for us! I must go. I will see you tomorrow," he said as he turned and left.

As the door closed, Nadeem turned back to Joel and said, "I believe it is time for you to call your parents and let them know you are coming home."

He walked over and picked up his phone, handing it to Joel. Joel looked at Nadeem, and then back at the phone.

"I'm almost afraid to call my mother. I don't know how she'll react."

"She will be overjoyed, Joel. Make the call," Nadeem said.

Joel dialed the number to his parents' house, and his mother answered.

"Mom...it's Joel," he said simply, feeling choked up at hearing her voice.

"What...Joel? Joel, is that really you? I hope someone isn't playing a practical joke..." she trailed off.

"No Mom, it's really me. I'm in Tunisia. It's a long story, but we'll be flying to Rome tomorrow, and then I'll be home the following day," Joel said.

"Joel! Joel, I can't believe it's you! Oh honey...." She said, and became very quiet.

"Mom, are you still there?" Joel said.

The silence continued for several moments, and then Joel asked his mother once more if she was still on the line.

"I'm sorry..." his mother said, and then Joel heard soft muffled sobs in the background.

"Mom, are you okay?" he asked.

A few more moments went by, and finally, "I thought you were...oh Joel, I just can't believe it...." She said, trying to contain her tears so she could speak.

"Mom, I'm okay, and I have Hessa's mother, Muna Bishara, with me. I'll tell you all about it when I get home. I'm bringing Muna home to Boston—she can't go back to Israel. There's so much I need to tell you, but I can't stay on the phone for long," he said.

"But why are you in Tunisia? How on earth did you get there?" Anna asked.

"Believe me, it's been a long haul, and I have a lot to tell you. I just wanted you to know that I'm all right, and I'll be home soon. I'll call you tomorrow when we find out our arrival time," Joel said.

"I can't believe it…you're coming home! Oh Joel, I love you so much. I know I've rarely told you I love you, but things are going to change. You'll never stop hearing me say it from now on!" his mother said.

"I love you too, Mom, and I really missed you," Joel said. "I'll talk to you tomorrow, okay?"

"All right. Sleep well, and I'll look forward to hearing from you!" his mother said, and they hung up.

As Joel put the phone back in its cradle, he looked at Nadeem and Clotilde, who had been listening to his end of the conversation.

"She said she loved me. I don't think she's ever said that to me," Joel said, staring at the phone.

"Well, it sounds as though that will change now. I only wish I could be there to watch when you reunite with your family!" Clotilde said. "But now you need to go to bed, young man. Let me show you where I've made up a place for you."

Clotilde led Joel into the large living area where there were two sofas facing each other. She had brought blankets and a pillow for him and laid them out.

"I hope you do not mind sleeping out here tonight, Joel. As you can see, we have a full house, and the sofa is all I have left," Clotilde said.

"I'm really grateful for all you and your husband have done for Muna and me. The sofa's perfect," Joel said and hugged his hostess.

"Sleep well, Joel. You will see your family and friends very soon," she said and walked out of the room, turning off the overhead light.

Anna went to her phone book and got Ruth's number to dial. Ruth picked up the phone, and without exchanging pleasantries, Anna got right down to the reason for her call.

"Ruth, is Hessa at home?" Anna asked.

"She isn't home from school yet, but I can have her call you..." Ruth began, but Anna cut her off.

"No, I just wanted to make sure she doesn't hear what I have to say. You'll never believe who just called me! My Joel!" Anna exclaimed.

"What? Are you sure?" Ruth asked, confused by the abrupt news.

"Of course! I know my own son's voice! He's in Tunisia, and will be flying out of Rome tomorrow. He also said he has Hessa's mother with him! He's bringing her back here to Boston! I just can't believe it..." Anna said.

"Her mother? How..."

"I don't know. Joel couldn't stay on the phone long. He said he'd fill us in on all the details when they get home."

"I can't believe this either! What a miracle! Our prayers have been answered. Hessa's going to be out of her mind with happiness. I've been really concerned about her lately. She's been so quiet and withdrawn. She misses her mother so much, and has been so sad about Joel. Little does she know that her life is about to change radically!" Ruth said.

"It sure is. I'm still in shock...but I do have a request. Could you drive to our house with Hessa in a couple of days? Luckily it'll be Friday, so you won't have to make excuses to her about her skipping school." Anna said.

"Of course! We'll be there whenever you say. This is so exciting!" Ruth said.

"One more thing—would you keep this a secret until Hessa sees Muna and Joel? I'd like this to be a surprise for her. I guess I'm still so overwhelmed that they're alive. I won't believe it until I actually see them. I hope you understand," Anna said.

371

"Of course. My lips are sealed. We'll leave for your house as soon as Hessa gets out of school on Friday. See you then!" Ruth said, and the two hung up, each shouting aloud with excitement.

CHAPTER 50

$\mathbf{E}$arly the next morning as Joel awoke he opened his eyes to see a little girl about the age of four staring at him. She had riots of curly dark brown hair falling around her shoulders, and large brown eyes.

"Hello, what's your name?" Joel asked.

The little girl just looked at him.

"Do you speak English?" he asked.

She continued to look at him, putting a finger in her mouth.

"Parlez-vous Francais?" he asked, thinking her grandmother may have taught her French.

"Oui," she said simply.

"Quel est votre nom?" he asked.

"Amelie," she replied.

"Quel age avez-vous?" he asked.

"Quatre," she replied, holding up four fingers as she moved closer to Joel.

Joel chatted with the little girl for a few minutes, happy that he remembered some of his high school and college French. He looked over at a clock on the wall and jumped off the couch suddenly, frightening little Amelie, who ran out of the room.

"Eight o'clock! Where *is* everyone?" he asked aloud, and rushed into the kitchen.

Clotilde had just walked into the kitchen and was making coffee. She turned to Joel as he entered and greeted him.

"It's after eight o'clock? Where's Rashid? Did we miss our plane?" he asked anxiously.

"No, dear one, Rashid called first thing this morning. There is a bit more for him to do to get you to Rome. You will not be able to fly out until this afternoon. I am very sorry. Sit down and I will pour you some coffee when it's ready," she said.

Joel relaxed a little, but was disappointed they had to wait around for an afternoon flight. He was so excited to return to his family and friends he was like a child waiting to go to an amusement park.

One by one the rest of the family, followed by Muna, filed into the kitchen. The older children had left for school, and little Amelie had gathered up the courage to approach Joel once again. He put his hands out, and as she walked up to him he lifted her into his lap.

"I think you have made yourself a new friend," Clotilde laughed. "She has taken quite a liking to you, Joel. She is normally quite shy."

"I hope I can have a daughter someday. I haven't been around a lot of women. I have a brother, and most of my friends have brothers. I'd like a little girl who looks just like..." he trailed off, thinking of Hessa with a sinking pain inside, and then quickly changed the subject.

Joel looked over at Muna as she walked to the table with a cup of coffee and told her, "Rashid won't be here until this afternoon. Evidently there are a few more things he needs to do in order for us to get to Rome."

"As long as we get there safely, I can surely wait," Muna replied.

Clotilde poured coffee for everyone as she continued to prepare the morning meal. Nadeem took a sip of coffee and told Joel and Muna that he was going to stay around that day to help his guests prepare for their trip home.

"Joel, you cannot go to America looking like that! Your pants are too short for you—you look ridiculous!" Nadeem said. "We will go and buy something for you and Muna to wear for your trip to Rome."

"We can't take advantage of you like that," Joel said.

"What advantage? What I have is yours!" he said.

"My husband speaks for both of us. We are very happy to help you. From what Nadeem has told me, the two of you have been through quite a lot. Your tunic is dirty and torn, Joel, and Muna, you look a little

374

rumpled. After my daughter goes to work, we will all go shopping. How is that?" Clotilde said.

Joel and Muna looked at each other, and then back at Clotilde and Nadeem. Joel shrugged his shoulders and they both smiled, thanking them for their generosity.

"Rashid has also asked me if we can have passport photos taken of the two of you, so we will get that done while we are out today. The photos need to be sent off to Rome this morning. We have much to do my friends, so let us eat and be on our way," Nadeem said.

Clotilde set out a large platter filled with all sorts of pastries, fresh fruit, and boiled eggs. She also placed a large bowl of yogurt in the middle of the table for everyone to help themselves. Their daughter ran into the kitchen complaining that she'd overslept, and grabbed a pate filled with cheese and olives from the platter. She walked over to Amelie, kissed her on the cheek, and ran out the door.

"My daughter is a widow. She lost her husband a couple of years ago when Amelie was only two. She went back to work to help with the household expenses, but it is very difficult for her," Clotilde explained.

When they were finished eating and Clotilde had put the last of the dishes away, she and Nadeem walked with Joel and Muna to the car. Little Amelie was glued to Joel's side the whole way, and he helped her get strapped in to her seat.

They drove into the heart of the city where there were all sorts of shops, restaurants and exotic-looking hotels. Joel wished they would have been here under different circumstances. The place was beautiful. Nadeem told Joel they would go into a men's shop for him, and the women would be a short distance away to get something for Muna.

Clotilde had to practically pry little Amelie's hand from Joel's, but finally convinced her that it would be much more fun looking at girl's clothes than men's. The little girl's eyes brightened at the thought that she might be getting a new dress, so she happily skipped off holding her grandmother's hand.

Muna and Clotilde walked into a small shop where Clotilde immediately went to work looking for something that would be comfortable and stylish for Muna to wear to Rome. Muna had become very thin in the last few months, so the first thing she tried on in her old size almost swam on her.

"I forgot that I was…sick for a while. I must have lost weight," Muna said, not wanting to explain the chain of events that had led to her weight loss. She took the clothes off and handed them to Clotilde and waited in the dressing room for her to replace it with a smaller size.

Clotilde came back a couple of minutes later and handed Muna a pair of cream-colored silk pants and a lilac-colored blouse with a darker lavender sweater.

"Try this on!" Clotilde said excitedly.

"I have never worn anything like that before," Muna said of the Western style of dress. A feeling of obstinacy shot through her and she took the clothes, walking back into the dressing room. A short time later she walked back out without her hijab, wearing the beautiful clothes.

"Oh, Muna, you look like a girl in her twenties!" Clotilde exclaimed. "I will have the saleswoman cut the tags off. You will wear it home. Next we will need to get you a pair of shoes."

Clotilde paid for the clothes and the two walked out toward the men's shop where Joel and Nadeem were, but they had finished shopping and were almost to the front door of the women's shop. Joel had on a pair of khaki pants and a light blue dress shirt with soft leather slip-on shoes. In a bag he carried a sweater.

"Wow, don't we look dapper?" Joel said to Muna.

"We still have a few things to do, gentlemen. If you will excuse us, Muna and I still have to buy shoes. Why don't you go and get yourselves a cup of coffee, and we will meet you there in about an hour?" Clotilde said.

Amelie begged her grandmother to go with Joel and Nadeem, and she relented.

"We will buy Amelie juice and a pastrie," Nadeem said as the three walked off toward the café.

Clotilde and Muna made quick work out of buying a pair of taupe suede pumps for Muna, and then stopped at a little market selling trinkets, where Clotilde bought her a small handbag with a hairbrush and other accessories. The two finally walked to the café, and found the two men and little Amelie, who was sitting in Joel's lap.

The five of them made one last stop to have Joel and Muna's photos taken for their passports, dropping them off at Rashid's office before going home to eat the midday meal. After they finished eating, Clotilde brought out a little satchel she had filled with their old clothes which she had cleaned, and gave it to Joel.

Rashid arrived a short time later to pick up his passengers. Joel and Muna thanked their hosts, and Joel once again said he would repay them for their kindness. Nadeem waved away the offer and told Joel he was very happy to be able to help them.

"I hope you can come to America someday and visit. You're always welcome, and my parents have plenty of room. We have each other's addresses and phone numbers, so I hope we'll stay in touch," Joel said.

"You never know, Joel. We could very well show up in America someday. We have talked about travelling there before!" Clotilde said.

The four hugged each another, and little Amelie began to cry as she realized Joel was about to leave. Joel and Muna followed Rashid out to his car as Amelie ran to Joel for one last hug. He bent down and kissed her on the cheek, saying to her in French, "'til we meet again". He stood up and gave a quick wave to his hosts as he walked out the door.

Rashid parked at the airport and led his passengers through a side entrance next to the terminal. Joel and Muna, being suspicious of any unusual behavior, were a little hesitant to walk through the strange entrance, and said as much.

"I'm sorry Rashid, but Muna and I have been through so much, I'm a little skittish of anything that looks strange. I hope you understand," Joel said.

"After Nadeem told me your story, I would be surprised if you were *not* a little suspicious of any strange activity. I guess you will just need to trust me, my friend," Rashid said smiling warmly, and motioned for them to enter through the storm gate.

As Joel and Muna entered, they realized this was an area where private planes were located. Joel looked at Rashid questioningly as he led them to a small jet.

"I could not just leave the two of you to get on a plane by yourselves for Rome. I decided to take you there myself. I would never be able to live with myself if I knew something had happened to you that I could have prevented," Rashid said as he motioned for Joel and Muna to climb the steps into the jet.

"I cannot believe this," Muna said as she stared wide-eyed into the entrance of the jet.

"I'm sorry I didn't trust you, Rashid," Joel said. "Wow, I've never been on a private plane before!"

Joel and Muna sat down and buckled themselves in. Rashid offered drinks and an assortment of nuts, cheeses, olives, and Italian salami. He set them down in a secure spot for everyone. He then sat down to buckle himself into his seat. Within a few minutes they were headed down the runway and into the sky, on their way to Rome.

As they made their final descent into Rome, Rashid informed Joel and Muna that their plane for Boston would be departing the following morning at 11 a.m. He also told them they would be staying at a villa outside of Rome that belonged to old friends of his.

"The villa is now a small resort, and is located on the Mediterranean Sea. My only concern is that you will never want to leave!" Rashid laughed.

378

As the plane landed, Rashid made a phone call to his friends, telling them they would be arriving shortly. Joel grabbed their bag of meager belongings and the three walked outside as Rashid flagged a taxi.

On their way, Rashid made a couple of detours to the American and Palestinian embassies to pick up their passports. When they had finally finished their business, they continued on to the villa. Rashid told Muna and Joel that he had a passion for Rome, and spent a lot of time there. Along the way he pointed out several sights that Joel and Muna took in with fascination.

They finally reached their destination and turned onto the winding road that led to the villa. As they parked, Joel looked up at the colorful inlaid tiles on the steps leading up to the front door. There were enormous clay and terra cotta pots of colorful flowers lining the stairway, which were also scattered around the gardens that surrounded the place.

The afternoon was very warm, and the sun was still shining when they arrived. As they climbed the front steps the door opened, and a woman with salt and pepper-colored hair pulled up into a bun emerged, smiling with her arms wide in a welcoming gesture.

"Hallo, hallo! Nando, it is Rashid! Come and meet our guests!" the woman said.

A man came up behind the woman and smiled at Rashid, hurrying to hug his friend and shake his hand.

"Welcome to Villa Incantato! But Rashid, you must introduce us to your friends!" the man said.

"Of course. This is Joel from America and his friend Muna, from Israel," Rashid said.

"Welcome to our little villa. We are the Biaggio's. My name is Ferdinando, and this is my wife, Gisella. But you must call me 'Nando', as all my friends do," he said.

"Come in and make yourselves comfortable," Gisella said, and led the group into the house.

She showed Joel, Muna, and Rashid to their rooms, and then told them to meet under the loggia in the back patio after they got settled in.

Joel left the small sack of his belongings in the room, and was the first to walk out to the back of the house. Several of the other guests were milling about, sipping wine and happily chatting as they looked at the scenery.

The view was spectacular, with the broad expanse of a harbor filled with boats. The loggia looked to be made of thatching, and there were seats built into the landscape that looked like whitewashed stone and concrete, decorated with colorful cushions. There were also wooden chairs with oversized arms and puffy cushions.

Rashid and Nando wandered in moments later, having caught each other up on business. Muna was the last to join them, and Gisella handed everyone, including the other guests at the villa, a glass of Prosecco from bottles she had just opened.

"My friends, this is a time for celebration. Rashid has informed my wife and me of Joel and Muna's extraordinary adventure. We can only say that we are thankful you are safe, and are honored that you will be staying with us tonight," Nando said.

Everyone raised their glasses and followed suit in the toast as Gisella had the staff serve the antipasti. It was now dusk and the whole place lit up with colorful lamps and large candles.

Joel tried to pace himself as the next course arrived. Large bowls of pasta of every size and shape were placed on the table and passed around. Gisella told the group that in Italy this was called the 'Primo Piatto', or the warm starter. She explained that this course was typically made up of pasta dishes.

"I hope you have all made room for the 'Secondo Piatto', Gisella said as the servers laid out plates of Veal Saltimbocca and Abacchio alla Romana.

Joel and Muna had been separated on opposite ends of the table, and at one point during the evening he noticed the guest sitting next to her. The man was close to Muna's age, and had been giving her his attention almost exclusively. He noticed that Muna seemed very captivated by the man, who talked to her a little too closely in Joel's estimation. She seemed to be enjoying herself as she listened attentively to his stories.

380

Feeling protective, he decided it was time for the two of them to call it a day. He got up and thanked his host and hostess for the meal and asked to be excused, saying they needed to get their rest for their long trip the next day.

He walked over to Muna and hearing her name, she turned around. "Oh Joel, you must meet my new friend, Anders Lokken. He has had the most adventurous life, and has entertained me all evening with stories of the many things he has done and places he has visited," Muna said, introducing Joel to Christof.

Joel said hello to Anders and asked Muna if he could speak with her. She excused herself and walked with Joel over to the edge of the patio overlooking the harbor.

"Muna, we need to get to bed. We have to be at the airport early tomorrow, and it looked like you were going to stay up talking to that guy all night," Joel said.

"Why Joel, you seem unhappy with me for talking to Mr. Lokken."

"I'm sorry, I just feel protective of you. That man looked like he had more on his mind than just talking."

Muna laughed and said, "Oh Joel, I am forty years old! No one is interested in an old woman like me!"

"I think you and I are going to have to have a chat on the way back to Boston. You've been so sheltered all your life, I don't think you realize that you're still a very attractive woman, and there are a lot of men who don't have the best of intentions. Why don't you say goodnight to the Biaggio's and Rashid, and I'll walk you to your room," Joel said.

Muna thanked Gisella and Nando and said goodnight to everyone. Rashid told Joel and Muna the time they would leave for the airport the next morning, and Gisella said she would make sure to wake them in plenty of time for breakfast before they departed.

Joel walked Muna to her room. "Well, tomorrow's the big day. I can't believe it's finally here. I don't think I'll believe it until we're actually in Boston."

381

"I cannot believe it myself. Thank you for being so kind and taking care of me. You saved my life. I owe everything to you."

"I'm just glad that you and I were able to escape with our lives. God sure had a hand on us, didn't He?" Joel said.

"He certainly did, dear Joel. Sleep well. I will see you in the morning," Muna said, and went into her room.

The next morning after finishing breakfast, Rashid told Joel and Muna it was time to leave for the airport. They thanked the Biaggios, who walked them to the car, asking them to be sure and return someday.

Shortly before 8:30 Joel and Muna pulled up to the airline they would be flying on. Rashid got out of the car to walk them inside and gave them directions to where they needed to go. He shook Joel's hand, and hugged them both.

"If you ever need anything, here is my card. I am happy to have met you, and wish you the very best," Rashid said.

"We're really grateful for everything you've done for us, Rashid. I hope you'll come to America for a visit. I'd love to show you as wonderful a time as you've shown us here in Rome," Joel said.

Joel and Muna walked to their gate, and a short time later they boarded the plane. They were on their way to America. The flight to Boston was long, and Joel had no appetite for the food being served.

He couldn't concentrate on the movie being shown and flipped through the magazines absent-mindedly. Muna slept most of the way, seeming to have finally relaxed, knowing she was safe and on her way to her new home in America.

As they neared Boston, the pilot came over the loud speaker and let them know they would be at their destination several minutes early. The plane started its descent, and Joel could hardly contain himself. It was hard to believe that he was almost home. At last he would see his family and friends.

Looking over at Muna as she blinked the sleep out of her eyes, he thought of everything they had been through together, and realized she had become one of his closest friends. He was happy that Muna would be able to live here freely and finally have a life of her own, and have a chance for happiness.

As the plane came to a stop everyone began their short journey to the baggage claim. Joel had told his mother he would meet her there, even though they had no luggage. As they entered the area, he immediately heard his name shouted. He looked in the direction of the voices, and it was his mother and father running toward him.

"Joel!" his mother shouted as she ran to him, throwing her arms around her son. She buried her face in his shoulder, crying and hugging him tightly. His father was right behind, and put his arms around his son, wiping tears from his own eyes.

The three stood for several moments in the middle of baggage claim holding one another and weeping openly. Joel's parents were unable to say a word. The emotions at seeing their son alive rendered them speechless. Joel finally pulled back and put his arm around Muna's shoulder, pulling her to his side.

"Mom and Dad, this is Muna Bishara. She's Hessa's mother. Do you remember Hessa?" Joel asked.

"Of course we do, son. Hello Mrs. Bishara, welcome back to Boston," Joel's father said. "Let's go home." Joel's mother took Muna's arm and walked out with her to the car.

The drive to the Volkenburg's home in Wellesley took close to an hour, which gave Joel time to tell his parents about the incredible adventure they'd had, and the people they'd met along the way who were so willing to help them, at the expense of putting their own lives in danger. He also told them about his miraculous conversion experience while imprisoned in Gaza.

As Joel spoke about everything they'd been through, his parents exchanged glances, their mouths gaping at the frightening and extraordinary events that he and Muna had been through.

When he finally finished, Joel's mother was the first to speak. "It really is a miracle you two are alive. It's almost as though you were guided along providentially."

383

"I was, Mom. There's no other explanation. Wherever we went, there was someone there to help us. When we left one place, someone would show up to help us get to the next place.

We were followed by Bishara's men, yet somehow we always got away. How do you explain a college kid and a sheltered wife being able to outsmart all those men?" Joel asked.

"It's an amazing story, honey. I just can't believe you escaped alive...I can't believe you're here. I just can't believe it..."

"We're just glad you were able to get home, son. We all missed you, Joel. It really made your mother and I think about our priorities. We misplaced them long ago, but this experience has changed us. Whatever you want to do with your life is okay by us. If you want to run an ice cream store, that's okay. As long as it makes you happy," his father said.

"Wow Dad, I guess this *has* changed you. I wonder if Friendly's Ice Cream is hiring..." he said, and they laughed as Muna smiled, wondering what a 'Friendly's Ice Cream' was.

They finally pulled up into the driveway, where several other cars were parked in front of the house and along the driveway. Everyone got out and made their way to the house as Joel asked why so many cars were there.

"Joel, you've been gone for close to a year. I know you're tired, but everyone is anxious to see you, and they couldn't wait. You can sleep all day tomorrow if you want," Joel's father said. "Ladies, go on inside. I need to talk to Joel about something before we go in."

As his mother and Muna walked in the house, Joel asked, "What is it, Dad?"

"I have something to tell you, Joel," his father said, and looked down in thought as he struggled with how to break the news to his son.

"Your friend, Hessa...she was in England when you went to Israel. She was attending school there. Your friends found out, and went over there to see her. What I mean to say, Joel, is that Hessa is here in America. Henry and Petie brought her back with them, and she's living in New Haven with a friend."

384

"Wha…" Joel's heart leaped in his chest, and he felt his head start to spin. It took a moment for the reality to sink in. "Dad, are you serious?"

"Yes, I am. Not only that, but I need to tell you something else…son, she's inside," his father said, and grabbed Joel by the shoulder as he turned to run into the house.

"Wait for just a moment, Joel. Let her have this time with her mother. Hessa thought her mother was dead. I'm sure you understand. Everyone has been instructed to keep your being here a secret until Hessa has been reunited with her mother.

"You'll see her soon enough—we'll go inside shortly," his father said, and the pair stood talking as they stared up into the starlit sky, chatting like two old friends.

⚘⚘⚘

As Muna and Anna walked in the house everyone ran to them, hugging Muna and welcoming her. Just then Hessa came around the corner. Her eyes lit up and she gasped as she saw her mother standing in the kitchen. Her mother looked up and seeing her daughter, she covered her mouth, trying to muffle a scream.

"Hessa! Oh Hessa!!" she cried, as Hessa ran to her and they embraced. Hessa held her mother tightly as she wept, burying her face in her mother's hair.

"Mama, I thought you were dead!" She hugged her mother again and put her head on her shoulder. When she was able to speak again, she said, "I began to lose hope. I felt so lost without you. But you are safe, you are safe…" Hessa cried as she looked at Muna, and buried her face in her mother's hair once again, holding her tightly.

Mrs. Sully hurried over to Muna and hugged her, welcoming her back to America. The two chatted for a few moments, and then she told Muna to go in to the living room and sit down with her daughter.

Muna hugged Mrs. Sully and then took Hessa by the arm and went into the living room to be with her daughter, eager to exchange stories with her about what had happened in the last year.

After what seemed like an eternity to Joel, he couldn't contain his excitement another minute.

"Dad, can we go in now? I can't wait any longer."

"Sure son. I think we've given them enough time," his father said, and the two went into the house.

As Joel walked through the door, the whole house went into an uproar with everyone shouting and hugging Joel. Henry, Petie and Eddie yelled, "Burgermeister!" and grabbed their friend, pushing him back and forth between them, hugging him and slapping him on the back.

Mrs. Sully walked over and hugged her 'seventh son'. "Welcome home, honey! I prayed for you every day for your safe return!" She smiled at him and hugged him once more.

"I'm really sorry, Mrs. Sully. I know I was selfish and stupid going to your house before I left the country. I just needed to talk to someone, and you were the only one I could think of who would listen," Joel said as his mother looked on, her eyes cast down.

"Well, all is forgiven. You're home now, Joel, and that's all that matters."

Mr. Sully, along with the Worthings and the Callahans, hurried over to greet Joel, as well as Helen, the Volkenburgs' housekeeper.

As everyone was talking over each other to ask Joel questions, he looked up and she appeared in the doorway. Hessa had slowly walked around the corner, and stood there as if frozen. It was as if she couldn't believe she'd heard his voice.

Everything seemed to stop, including his heart. He stood with his mouth open as everyone turned to see what he was looking at. He tried to find the words to say, but they wouldn't come. He just stared at her, trying to shake himself into reality.

"Joel," she said finally as she walked to him with tears streaming down her face.

386

"Hessa," he breathed as his legs finally moved under him, and he ran to her, wrapping her in his arms and lifting her off the ground. He held her as she softly wept against his chest, and the tears began to flow down his own face.

Joel finally set Hessa back down and looked at her, trying to take in everything about her. It was as if he wanted to make sure she was real—that she was no longer a dream or a distant memory. The two turned wordlessly and walked out of the room without looking back, as if no one else was in the house. He took her into his mother's sitting room where they could be alone.

As the rest of the group gathered in the family room, they realized they would have to wait their turn to talk with Joel. Muna recounted their story while everyone listened in rapt attention as she recounted the unbelievable chain of events that led them back to America.

…"Oh yes, it was real…every bit of it. But God took care of us and ordered every one of our steps. I now know He is a God of miracles. He watched over everything that happened to us, and guided us to safety," she said as Mrs. Sully looked on with a smile.

As the evening wore on, Joel and Hessa filled each other in on the amazing adventures each had lived for close to a year. They sat the whole time holding each other's hands while they talked, as though the other would disappear if they let go.

Hessa suddenly realized they had spent close to an hour alone together, being apart from their family and friends. "I think we should go back out and spend some time with the people who came to see us, Joel. It is very late, and no one has gotten much of a chance to visit with us."

Joel nodded his head in agreement as they stood to go back out to the group that anxiously awaited them. Then he turned to Hessa and grabbed her hands once more.

"Could you sit down for just another minute?"

Puzzled, she looked at him, but sat down. He looked at Hessa, stroking her hair as he tried to find the right words to say.

387

"You know, during these months when your mother and I were constantly running for our lives, I never stopped thinking about you, or praying that you were safe somewhere. After what I saw your mother go through, I didn't know how you could even be alive."

Joel looked down, and then back into Hessa's eyes...he felt shy and self-conscious, not having seen her in almost a year. Then he blurted out, "Hessa...I love you. I'm never going to let you out of my sight again. I...just wanted you to know that I'll be here to protect you from now on."

"Joel, I missed you so, I thought my heart would break. I love you too—thank you for coming back to me. The hope of your being alive is the only thing that has kept me going."

He slid over next to her, and looking up into his eyes she added: "And Joel, thank you for taking care of my mother, and bringing her safely back to me. God *did* answer my prayers for a miracle!" Hessa said, as Joel pulled her into his lap and kissed her, wrapping his arms around her.

He looked at her and said, "He answered both our prayers."

"You and I found the Messiah in very different ways, Joel, but He still came after us, even though both of us are from entirely different backgrounds and religions. What are the chances, I ask you?"

"I don't think there was any 'chance' involved. It all happened in His plan and order," Joel replied. Hessa just smiled and nodded.

Joel and Hessa finally walked back into the family room where everyone was still gathered around Muna, who was happily answering questions about how she and Joel had miraculously made it from one country to another. When they entered the room, everyone stood up and surrounded the couple, hugging them and slapping Joel on the back.

"Oh Joel, it's so wonderful to have you home. I just want to sit and look at you. Tell me, now that you're home, what's the first thing you'd like to do?" his mother asked.

"I'd like to celebrate Christmas," Joel said with a smile.

Epilogue

On Christmas morning Joel awoke before dawn, too excited to sleep. He ran downstairs and into the living room to see the enormous Christmas tree decked with glittering balls and lights. Beautifully wrapped gifts were piled under the tree, waiting to be opened. He stood in the dark alone, staring at the symbol that had eluded him his whole life.

Christmas would finally be a day of celebration. This day that had always made him feel alone and different would now be a part of his life. He sat down in a chair by the front window and reflected on everything that had taken place that year—the good, the bad, the frightening, the painful. Everything that had led him to make the one decision that had changed his life, and his place in the world.

He happily anticipated the activities planned for the day. Ruth would be coming from Connecticut with Hessa and Muna, who were both living with her. Muna would continue to live with Ruth, and Hessa would be attending Harvard once again starting winter semester. Henry, Eddie, and their families would be joining the Volkenburgs for Christmas dinner this year.

His brother David couldn't quite make out what had happened to Joel in his experience across the ocean, but Joel was determined to break down his walls and get him to open up so he could have a real relationship with his older brother.

The whole Sullivan clan would be down the day after Christmas to celebrate with the Volkenburgs. Anna's sister, Klara, would be joining them as well. It would be her first time in the United States since she'd graduated college and moved to Israel.

So many things had happened in just one year. The biggest and most profound changes in Joel's life had taken place, and he wouldn't have had it any other way.

GLOSSARY

Abacchio alla Romana – Roast lamb.

Aqeeqah - When a child is born to a family, the father is strongly recommended to slaughter one or two sheep and to invite relatives and neighbors to a meal, so the community can share in the happy event. The aqeeqah is normally carried out shortly after the birth of a baby, preferably on the seventh day of his/her birth. One sheep is adequate for the aqeeqah for either a girl or a boy. The meat is distributed as follows: One third to charity and the remaining two thirds to be distributed amongst friends and relatives.

Baklawa – Sweet and crunchy phillo dough pastries filled with crushed walnuts and honey.

Halawa - Sugar, ground sesame seeds, citric acid, pistachios. Eaten for breakfast and dessert.

Hijab - commonly understood in the English-speaking world, is the type of head covering traditionally worn by Muslim women, but can also refer to modest Muslim styles of dress in general.

Hwerneh – Mustard green and yogurt salad

Incantato - Enchanted

Kanafeh - Kunafah is made by drizzling a row of thin streams of flour-and-water batter onto a turning hot plate, so they dry into long threads resembling shredded wheat. The threads are then collected into skeins.

Katif – Harvest

Keffiyeh – Headdress worn by Palestinian men.

Kunafah - The pastry is heated with butter or palm oil, then spread with soft cheese (see Nabulsi cheese) and more pastry; or the *khishnah kunafah* is rolled around the cheese. A thick syrup consisting of sugar, water and a couple of drops of rose water, is poured on the pastry when almost done. Often the top layer of *kadaif* pastry is colored using orange food coloring. Crushed pistachios are typically sprinkled on top as a garnish.

Leka'ek - A kind of shortbread, made of flour, baking powder, and olive oil. Once the dough is kneaded, a small piece is taken and rolled into long round strips (like sausage), then cut into short lengths and rolled each one into a ring. There are two varieties, one with sugar added to the mixture to make sweet, and the other is salty, which makes it more like bread sticks.

Musakhan - Palestinian national dish. It is composed of roasted chicken baked with onions, sumac, allspice, saffron, and fried pine nuts atop one or more taboon breads.

Panzanella – An Italian bread dish that derives from the *cucina povera*. This could best be called bread salad.

Pate - A flaky outside, filled with either tuna and cheese, chicken and cheese, turkey and cheese, or just cheese. Some add olives to this.

Shakshoukeh – Fried tomato dish with peppers.

Tahina – A thick paste made from ground sesame seeds. Used as a dip with bread or crackers.

Tartufo - The famed dessert created by Tre Scalini in the Piazza Navona of Rome. This Roman confection is a ball of luscious dark chocolate ice cream which has chunks of an even richer chocolate scattered throughout and offers a cherry in its heart.

Veal Saltimbocca – Veal escalopes with ham.

ACKNOWLEDGEMENTS

Before falling asleep one night in late January of 2010, I had a vision of this story from beginning almost to the end, but no details in between. I thought to myself, *That's a great idea for a book!* There was a drawback, however. I'm not a writer—my background is in investments. The next morning when I woke up, I sat down at the computer and said aloud, "Lord, if that was You who gave me that vision last night, what's the name of the book?' Immediately the thought popped into my head: 'The Order of Heaven'. I typed it on the top of the page and then said, "What's next?" The rest just flowed out, and by the end of May of 2010, the book was complete. It was put on the back burner for a while, but in 2015 I began an edit with the help of a professional writer friend, and finally completed the book.

Part of my inspiration was from several guest speakers at our church who had hated Jews and Christians--some of them even having had positions in Hamas and other organizations, including Tass Saada, a former sniper for Yasir Arafat. The transformation of their lives is nothing short of a miracle.

The Joel in my story is named after Joel C. Rosenberg, best-selling author and expert on eschatology and the Middle East. It is said that Joel's books read like they're being ripped right out of the headlines—tomorrow's headlines. Joel's writings and passion for the Middle East have had an impact on my life.

I need to thank my sister, Suzanne, for her support and encouragement as I wrote this book. She spent many hours poring over these pages, helping with the monotonous job of editing. I also want to thank my friend, Mindy Dreisewerd, for the beautiful artwork and painstaking attention to detail for the cover of this book. Thanks for your patience and incredible talent, Mindy.

I hope you enjoy reading this story as much as I enjoyed writing it. From one day to the next, I had no idea what was happening in this book, so as I wrote, it was like I was reading it for the first time!

ABOUT THE AUTHOR

Amanda Jarvis' fascination with the Middle East and surrounding areas inspired the story you are about to read. Her love of travel and various cultures brought this adventure to life. She lives in San Diego, California, and has been in the investment field since 1996. She is the mother of three children and grandmother to, as of this writing, four precious little grandchildren, with another on the way.

ajarvis1102@gmail.com

Visit me on Facebook! Also, the Order of Heaven has its own Facebook page...go in and "Like" it!

Made in the USA
San Bernardino, CA
06 April 2017